MAUROIS READER

MAUROIS READER

Novels, Novelettes and Short Stories

Introduction
by
Anne Fremantle

NEW YORK

DIDIER, Publishers

ACKNOWLEDGMENT

*is gratefully extended to: Apple-
ton-Century-Crofts, Inc., The At-
lantic Monthly, Esquire, Inc., Story
Digest and Viking Press, for their
kind permission.*

For information address:

DIDIER, Publishers
660 Madison Avenue
New York 21, N. Y.

CONTENTS

INTRODUCTION

ANDRE MAUROIS has described himself with too fine a discretion and too pleasant a wit, for anyone else to come scribbling hamhandedly after. As a Frenchman, he is the inheritor of centuries of aphorisms; as an Alsatian, of a patriotism, both devout and detached; and as himself, he has a capacity, unique among the French, of both understanding and loving the British. This last quality is, of course, most perfectly illustrated in his first, and perhaps still most popular book: *The Silence of Colonel Bramble,* given in its entirety in this *Maurois Reader,* and preceded by a new, and charming, preface, gracefully bringing the Colonel up-to-date. "I was shy, they were silent": surely no better explanation of the lifelong attachment between a man and a nation has ever been given so succinctly?

André Maurois was born in 1885; his grandfather had emigrated, with 400 workpeople, from Alsace after the French defeat of 1870, to the Pont-de-l'Eure of *Bernard Quesnay.* André Maurois' first book was published in 1918, and the next year, he published three books. In 1923 appeared *Ariel, or the Life of Shelley,* the first of his great biographies; followed by *Disraeli* in 1927; *Byron,* in 1930; *Lyautey,* in 1931, and in 1938, *Chateaubriand,* probably his best book, and, scarcely less probably, one of the best biographies ever published in any language. A year later, André Maurois was elected to the august Academie Francaise.

His own early life, the struggles in himself and in the cotton mills to which he was heir, are told here in *Bernard Quesnay;* elsewhere, in his moving autobiography, he has detailed the various challenges, to which he has responded so fully, so wisely, and so successfully.

Part, at least, of his success is due to the fact that he has always wished to be understood, and to make himself understandable. Of his generation of writers in France no one else has so completely "redeemed for the dull, the average way." André Maurois has demonstrated to all the many-layered, tierful quality of ordinary life, and has done so, neatly and simply, as a civilised adult might show children how to use microscope and telescope. Its easy, there's nothing to it, he seems to proclaim, no trick, no catch; you only need to look and to see. Somewhere, in his admirable *Art of Living,* he gives us Goethe's secret, which we can suspect he has found proven in, and by, his own experience: "Die ganze Arbeit ist ruhig sein"—to be still is the whole work. Silence, stillness; these are the refrains of this writer, this talker, this fighter in two wars. It may be that his awareness of his own need, helps us to see our own. His unerring certainty of the necessary, a wisdom as instinctive as that which leads beasts to lick salt, makes us able to see the two men in ourselves, by seeing them in him. The shadow of the dichotomy within us all, when thrown by the giants, by Paul or Racine, seems pedantic, or irrelevant. In ourselves, we are apt to overlook it, nearsightedly squinting. In André Maurois we can see it clearly, in excellent focus. For his sense of scale is palpably sure and just, and his truthfulness, for all that it is ironic, gentle, melancholy, is yet exigent and inviolable. The 'almost indecent clarity' so often observed in French thought, is tempered in him by a delicate perception of the degrees of shadow, as when he confides that man does not aspire to happiness, only Englishmen do that; or that almost all men improve on acquaintance; or that the world of appearance is, "I believe, the only one we will ever know", or that it is always easy to moderate sentiments that one does not feel.

In his story "The Weigher of Souls", he postulates, as an imagined, perhaps desired, immortality, existence as a luminous, volatile, essence. In some respects, that immortality already belongs to many of his works, his creations. In his *Preface* he himself recounts how Colonel Bramble, a composite character, now has his own, tangible, existence. Other characters from that book are already part of folk-lore, or of legend: the confessor who asked the murderer "How many times, my son?" is but one example. And his biographies also in their spendid sequence, will endure. After the era of Hollywoodian, torchlit romanticized, lives is burnt out, readers will return to André Maurois' biographies, finding gladly their green springing, and finding also in them, the solidity of good candles, the kind one is most thankful to have around, knowing they will light one safely, even if the brasher lights have fused. The effect of these biographies is already evident upon a whole generation of writers—Lytton Strachey, Emil Ludwig, and André Maurois in their different countries may be compared interestingly. Maurois' subjects, described without stodginess or bigotry (which before him had seemed almost necessary concomitants of any 'serious biography) are treated with courage and compassion, but also and above all, with humor. He sees his subjects as most real in their relationships, to their work, or their women; and he is at his best when both are subtle and complex, as in the cases of Shelley and Chateaubriand; he is less sure when the figuring is bold, in high relief, as in Disraeli and Lyautey.

To the American reader, however often he has read Maurois, the precision of his study of the subtleties of the feminine character will always come anew as a surprise. In no Anglo-Saxon country, and very rarely in the English language, does a man, and a very masculine man, devote so much care, perception, tenderness and concern to the woman's eye view as does André Maurois—with, for instance, Francoise, in *Bernard Quesnay,* or Delphine de Custine, in *Chateaubriand.* And the total pardon to which his total knowledge brings him, is without the slightest suspicion of contempt; he is so certain of the complete difference between men and women that he never makes the error of comparing them, their mistakes, or their triumphs.

André Maurois, some have complained, ignores the proletariat; his novels are void of social significance. But artists, Aristotle said, are either beasts or gods, and have no part in the city; Karl Marx said they were "kittle-cattle" and without social allegiance. Where these colossi are come together, let us not presume to sunder; let us not require of the artist what he has not the power to give. For some artists are *also* social philosophers, as some are *also* saints, as some are soldiers, or diplomats, or politicians. But what they render to Caesar is already Caesar's: upon the artist's art there can be no other image nor superscription, not even that of his earthly ruler, not even that of his Creator. André Maurois, in so far as he was divided, paid his dime in cotton goods; for the rest, he is wholly loyal, wholly a writer, a craftsman, a technician, and above all, a consummate artist.

ANNE FREMANTLE

NOVELS

THE SILENCE OF COLONEL
BRAMBLE

*(Translated by Thurfrida Wake; verses translated by
Wilfrid Jackson)*

In Memoriam
J. A. M.

PREFACE

I REMEMBER so well my first encounter with the British
Army. It was at the beginning of August, 1914. On the first
day of the mobilization I had joined my French regiment,
the 74th Infantry, at Rouen, and at once my captain had
said: "No, you don't belong to my company any more; you
don't leave Rouen with us tomorrow; you wait for the
British. . . ." I was astounded.

"For the British?" I said. "Why the British?"

"Because you are supposed to speak English. . . . But
perhaps they will never turn up; then you'll come back to
us."

They did turn up. One fine morning, I was sent to the
port of Rouen to meet my new regiment. It was a glorious
scene. The huge transports, overloaded with khaki soldiers,
looked like gigantic floating ant-hills. On the banks of the
Seine, thousands of women and children waved French and
British flags and shouted: *"Vive l'Angleterre!"* From the
ship came the loud and cheerful answer: "Hip! hip! hip!
Hurrah!"

As soon as they landed, I admired these first British regiments. They belonged, of course, to the regular army. They
were equipped with the wealth and magnificence that suited

3

an old and powerful Empire. Their well-groomed horses, their heraldic and painted drums, their regimental mascots, everything about them surprised and delighted me. At first I felt very shy. The language I had learned from Shelley and Keats was not exactly the army slang my new friends spoke. Even Kipling's soldiers seemed out of tune. But very soon I began to understand the vocabulary of my companions, and also many of their thoughts and ways.

I liked them very much. They were brave, quite unconsciously. To be frightened was bad form. They were tenacious, reliable, and, once they had adopted you, the most faithful of friends. Their sense of humor made regimental life amusing, easy, and pleasant. What were their faults? Perhaps a national pride so strong that they found it difficult to see the point of view of other nations, and an incurable optimism.

"The job may be long," they said, "it may be painful. But we'll muddle through somehow. We always did. Every British victory begins with a minor disaster."

It was reassuring, soothing, and sometimes dangerous.

After a few months I came to think that one could identify and classify among my Britishers a certain number of types, each of which was reproduced all through the Army. One of these types was Colonel Bramble, a silent, kindly Scotchman, admirable soldier, severe and beloved chief. No living colonel actually sat as a model for Colonel Bramble, but once I had conceived his character, I borrowed from a large number of field officers the essence of Bramble each of them contained. Little by little, this imaginary creature became to me more real than my real companions. I came to know exactly what, in such and such circumstances, Colonel Bramble would have said. Today I can hardly believe the colonel never existed. Indeed I feel certain that he did exist and that I knew him in the flesh.

When the War ended, I had become so accustomed to my life with a British staff that I could no more imagine a life without my friends. For a while we met, in London or Paris, once a year, and took pleasure in recalling old stories.

"And what has become of General Asser? Of Major Wake? Of Papa Westmacott? What has become of Colonel Bramble?"

"Colonel Bramble?" my friends said, half joking, half serious. "He has left the Army. He is now a retired Brigadier-General and lives in a small manor, somewhere in Wiltshire."

Later such meetings became less pleasant. Franco-British relations were not good. The politicians of both nations were doing, alas, all they could to prepare the recent European catastrophe. One year, about 1930, as things were going from bad to worse, I thought that time had come to resuscitate General Bramble, and I went to pay him a visit. I found him just the same as in 1918. His hair had become grey; his smile remained boyish and his silences impressive.

"What a pity, sir!" I said. "Our two nations fought together; together they won a fine victory. And now. . . ."

General Bramble, of course, said nothing, but he opened a drawer and produced an old gramophone record. Then he went to the gramophone which was on a table, by his armchair, like in the old days of Poperinghe; he verified the speed with great care, chose a needle and began to play the record. It was a waltz, *Destiny Waltz,* that he used to play "for me" every night, when we were on the Somme or on the Lys. Listening to the familiar tune, I could not help thinking of so many brave young men who had heard with me, time after time, that same waltz and who were now buried in the mud of Flanders. I remembered their laughter, their brave humor, their lovely frankness. 'Of course,' I thought, 'men of that type cannot have changed and those of them who are still alive remain as worthy as ever of our friendship. . . .' And all of a sudden, as the last notes of the waltz died out amongst the oaks and willows of the garden, I realized that the general, without a word, had said all there was to be said, much better than any orator.

When, in 1939, the second war broke out, and when I heard that a British Army once more was coming over to France, I felt very much like an old war-horse that hears the call of the trumpet. I became restless and discontented.

One morning a letter came from the British War Office. They asked if I would be willing to don my old uniform and to serve, as French Official Eye-Witness, at British General Headquarters. I accepted at once, and, having got permission from the French Army, joined my old friends at Arras where I had been with them in 1917.

What had become of General Bramble? He was now an old man, probably seventy-five, perhaps more. I discovered him, adorned with the red and golden tabs of a major-general, in the dining room of the Hôtel de l'Univers, which was at Arras our great social center. If his hair was now snow-white, his complexion remained that of a man who leads an active open-air life. I asked him what his job was.

"My boy," he said (and the "boy" was himself fifty-four), "I am now one of the King's Messengers, which means that I bring to the Commander-in-Chief, once or twice a week, the most secret despatches."

"It also means," I said, "sir, many a tiring journey."

He looked at me with honest surprise:

"Tiring?" he said. "Why tiring? It is just crossing the Channel and, when one has to dodge the mines, as we did yesterday, it can even be quite exciting."

By which I saw that General Bramble had not changed.

His sons and grandsons, who now formed the British Army, were not so very different from what he himself had been. Of course, they used different weapons; many of them were in the Air Force; they were a mechanized army and had lost their well-groomed horses. But the spirit was the same, and the courage, and the confidence in the destinies of the British Empire. The general liked to listen to them, every week, at Arras. He visited them in their regimental messes and was a little sad to find there, instead of a gramophone, a radio set.

"I do not like news," he said.

Then, one night, a German plane dropped a bomb on the Hôtel de l'Univers and General Bramble, asleep in his room, was killed. So direct was the hit that nothing was found of him, except his pipe. I feel certain it is the type of death he would have himself chosen.

But is he dead? A few months ago, I visited, somewhere in England, a school where young pilots of the Royal Air Force were learning the tricks of their trade. The wing commander asked me to address his boys and to talk to them of the British Army as I had known it. I accepted and he introduced me to the assembled school, mentioning in his brief speech Colonel Bramble. When I had finished, and as I was leaving, I overheard a conversation which took place, behind my back, between two very young Canadian pilots:

"And who was this guy?" said one of them.

"I have not the faintest idea," the second answered, "but didn't I understand the C.O. to say that he is a colonel named Bramble?"

I thus understood that the creature had outlived its creator, which greatly pleased the creator.

ANDRE MAUROIS

CHAPTER I

THE Highland Brigade was holding its regimental boxing match in a fine old Flemish barn in the neighborhood of Poperinghe. At the end of the evening the general got on to a chair and, in a clear, audible voice, said:

"Gentlemen, we have today seen some excellent fighting, from which I think we may learn some useful lessons for the more important contest that we shall shortly resume; we must keep our heads, we must keep our eyes open, we must hit seldom but hit hard, and we must fight to a finish."

Three cheers made the old barn shake. The motors purred at the door. Colonel Bramble, Major Parker and the French interpreter, Aurelle, went on foot to their billets among the hops and beetroot fields.

"We are a curious nation," said Major Parker. "To interest a Frenchman in a boxing match you must tell him that his national honor is at stake. To interest an Englishman in a war you need only suggest that it is a kind of a boxing match. Tell us that the Hun is a barbarian, we agree politely, but tell us that he is a bad sportsman and you rouse the British Empire."

"It is the Hun's fault," said the colonel sadly, "that war is no longer a gentleman's game."

"We never imagined," continued the major, "that such cads existed. Bombing open towns is nearly as unpardonable as fishing for trout with a worm, or shooting a fox."

"You must not exaggerate, Parker," said the colonel calmly. "They are not as bad as that yet."

Then he asked Aurelle politely if the boxing had amused him.

"I particularly admired, sir, the sporting discipline of your men. During the boxing, the Highlanders behaved as if they were in church."

"The true sporting spirit has always something religious about it," said the major. "A few years ago when the New Zealand football team visited England, and from the first match beat the English teams, the country was as upset as if we had lost this war. Every one in the streets and trains went about with long faces. Then the New Zealanders beat Scotland, then Ireland; the end of the world had come! However, there remained the Welsh. On the day of the match there were one hundred thousand persons on the ground. You know that the Welsh are deeply religious and that their national anthem, *Land of our Fathers,* is also a prayer. When the two teams arrived the whole crowd, men and women, exalted and confident, sang this hymn to God before the battle, and the New Zealanders were beaten. Ah, we are a great nation!"

"Indeed, yes," said Aurelle, quite overcome, "you are a great nation." He added, after a moment's silence, "But you were also quite right just now when you said you were a curious nation in some things, and your opinion of people astonishes us sometimes. You say, 'Brown looks an idiot, but he's not, he played cricket for Essex.' Or, 'At Eton we took him for a fool, but at Oxford he surprised us. Do you know he is plus four at golf, and won the high jump?'"

"Well?" said the colonel.

"Don't you think, sir, that cleverness—"

"I hate clever people— Oh, I beg your pardon, messiou."

"That's very kind of you, sir," said Aurelle.

"Glad you take it like that," growled the colonel into his mustache.

He spoke seldom and always in short sentences, but Aurelle had learnt to appreciate his dry and vigorous humor and the charming smile which often lit up his rugged countenance.

"But don't you find yourself, Aurelle," went on Major Parker, "that intelligence is over-estimated with you? It is certainly more useful to know how to box than how to write. You would like Eton to go in for nothing but learning? It is just like asking a trainer of racehorses to be interested in circus horses. We don't go to school to learn, but to be soaked in the prejudices of our class, without which we should be useless and unhappy. We are like the young Persians Herodotus talks about, who up to the age of twenty only learnt three sciences: to ride, to shoot and to tell the truth."

"That may be," said Aurelle, "but just see, major, how inconsistent you are. You despise learning and you quote Herodotus. Better still, I caught you the other day in the act of reading a translation of Xenophon in your dug-out. Very few Frenchmen, I assure you—"

"That's quite different," said the major. "The Greeks and Romans interest us, not as objects of study, but as ancestors and sportsmen. We are the direct heirs of the mode of life of the Greeks and of the Roman Empire. Xenophon amuses me because he is a perfect type of the English gentleman, with his hunting and fishing stories, and descriptions of battles. When I read in Cicero: 'Scandal in the Colonial Office. Grave accusations against Sir Marcus Varro, Governor-General of Sicily,' you can well understand that that sounds to me like old family history. And who was your Alcibiades, pray, but a Winston Churchill, without the hats?"

The scenery round them was very picturesque: the Mont des Cats, the Mont Rouge, and the Mont Noir made a framework for the heavy, motionless clouds of an old Dutch painting. The peasants' houses with their weather-beaten, thatched roofs faded into the surrounding fields; their dull walls had turned the color of yellow clay. The grey shutters bordered with green struck the only vivid and human note in this kingdom of the earth.

The colonel pointed with his cane to a new mine crater; but Major Parker, sticking to his point, went on with his favorite subject:

"The greatest service which sport has rendered us is that it has saved us from intellectual culture. Luckily, one hasn't time for everything, and golf and tennis cut out reading. We are stupid—"

"Nonsense, major!" said Aurelle.

"We are stupid," emphatically repeated Major Parker, who hated being contradicted, "and it is a great asset. When we are in danger we don't notice it, because we don't reflect; so we keep cool and come out of it nearly always with honor."

"Always," amended Colonel Bramble with his Scotch curtness.

And Aurelle, hopping agilely over the enormous ruts by the side of these two Goliaths, realized more clearly than ever that this war would end well.

CHAPTER II

"CLEAR the table," said Colonel Bramble to the orderlies. "Bring the rum, a lemon, some sugar and hot water, and keep some more boiling. Then tell my batman to give me the gramophone and the box of records."

This gramophone, a gift to the Highlanders from a very patriotic old lady, was the colonel's pride. He had it carried about after him everywhere and treated it with delicate care, feeding it every month with fresh records.

"Messiou," he said to Aurelle, "what would you like? 'The Bing Boys,' *Destiny Waltz,* or 'Caruso.'"

Major Parker and Dr. O'Grady solemnly consigned Edison and all his works to a hotter place; the padre raised his eyes to heaven.

"Anything you like, sir," said Aurelle, "except 'Caruso.'"

"Why?" said the colonel. "It's a very good record, it cost twenty-two shillings. But first of all you must hear my dear Mrs. Finzi-Magrini in *La Tosca.* Doctor, please regulate it, I can't see very well—Speed 61. Don't scratch the record, for God's sake!"

He sank down on his biscuit boxes, arranged his back comfortably against a heap of sacks, and shut his eyes. His rugged face relaxed. The padre and the doctor were playing chess, and Major Parker was filling in long returns for brigade headquarters. Over a little wood, torn to bits by shells, an airplane was sailing home among fleecy white clouds in a lovely pale-green sky. Aurelle began a letter.

"Padre," said the doctor, "if you are going to the division tomorrow, ask them to send me some blankets for our dead Boches. You saw the one we buried this morning? The rats had half eaten him. It's indecent. Check to the king."

"Yes," said the padre, "and it's curious how they always begin at the nose!"

Over their heads a heavy English battery began to bombard the German line. The padre smiled broadly.

"There'll be dirty work at the cross roads tonight," he remarked with satisfaction.

"Padre," said the doctor, "are you not the minister of a religion of peace and love?"

"The Master said, my boy, that one must love one's fellow-man. He never said that we must love Germans. I take your knight."

The Reverend John MacIvor, an old military chaplain, with a face bronzed by Eastern suns, took to this life of war and horrors with the enthusiasm of a child. When the men were in the trenches he visited them every morning with his pockets bulging with hymnbooks and packets of cigarettes. While resting behind the lines, he tried his hand at bombing and deplored the fact that his cloth forbade him human targets.

Major Parker suddenly stopped his work to curse Brass Hats and their absurd questions.

"When I was in the Himalayas at Chitral," he said, "some red-hats sent us a ridiculous scheme for maneuvers; among other details the artillery had to cross a rocky defile hardly wide enough for a very thin man.

"I wired, 'Scheme received; send immediately a hundred barrels of vinegar.' 'Report yourself to the P.M.O. for mental examination,' courteously remarked headquarters. 'Reread "Hannibal's Campaign,"' I replied."

"You really sent that telegram?" asked Aurelle. "In the French army you would have been court-martialed."

"That's because our two nations have not the same idea of liberty," said the major. "To us the inalienable rights of man are humor, sport, and primogeniture."

"At the headquarters of the brigade," said the padre, "there is a captain who must have had lessons from you in military correspondence. The other day, as I had no news of one of my young chaplains who had left us about a month, I sent a note to the brigade: 'The Reverend C. Carlisle was invalided on September 12th. I should like to know if he is better, and if he has been given a new appointment.' The reply from the hospital said simply: '1. Condition unchanged. 2. Ultimate destination unknown.' The officer in transmitting it to me had added, 'It is not clear whether the last paragraph refers to the unit to which the Rev. C. Carlisle will be eventually attached, or to his eternal welfare.' "

The Italian air came to an end with a triumphant roulade.

"What a voice!" said the colonel, opening his eyes regretfully.

He carefully stopped the record and put it affectionately in its case.

"Now, messiou, I am going to play *Destiny Waltz*."

One could just see outside the Verey lights gently rising and falling. The padre and the doctor went on describing their corpses while carefully maneuvering the ivory pieces of the little set of chessmen; the howitzers and machine-guns broke into the voluptuous rhythm of the waltz, creating a sort of fantastic symphony highly appreciated by Aurelle. He continued to write his letter in easy verses.

> "Death is a-foot; Fate calls the tune;
>   Lose not a minute—
> Forget! But wear your black till—June;
>   You're charming in it.

> I will not have you come with tears,
>   With roses vain;
> Young life will ask, in coming years,
>   Your rose again.

Don't be angry with me, dearest, if I descend to the lowest level of 'romantics'; a clergyman and a doctor, beside me, are intent on playing the rôle of the Grave-diggers in *Hamlet*.

> Pity me not, for I shall sleep
>   Like any child,
> And from my changing earth up leap
>   The grasses wild.

But if, when summer hours grow few,
  And dusk is long,
Your gaze, madonna-calm, should do
  Your beauty wrong,

Nor lend that sadness to your face
  I cherish yet,
Forget, then, for a little space,
  That you forget."

"Do you like my waltz, messiou?" said the colonel.

"Very much indeed, sir," said Aurelle sincerely.

The colonel gave him a grateful smile.

"I'll play it again for you, messiou. Doctor, regulate the gramophone slower, speed 59. Don't scratch the record. For *you*, this time, messiou."

CHAPTER III

BOSWELL: *"Why then, sir, did he talk so?"*
JOHNSON: *"Why, sir, to make you answer as you did."*

THE batteries were asleep; Major Parker was answering questions from the brigade; the orderlies brought the rum, sugar and boiling water; the colonel put the gramophone to speed 61 and Dr. O'Grady talked about the Russian Revolution.

"It is unprecedented," said he, "for the men who made a revolution to remain in power after it is over. Yet one still finds revolutionaries: that proves how badly history is taught."

"Parker," said the colonel, "pass the port."

"Ambition," said Aurelle, "is after all not the only motive that inspires men to action. One can be a revolutionary from hatred of a tyrant, from jealousy, or even from the love of humanity."

Major Parker abandoned his papers.

"I admire France very much, Aurelle, especially since this war; but one thing shocks me in your country, if you will allow me to speak plainly, and that is your jealousy of equality. When I read the history of your Revolution I am sorry I was not there to kick Robespierre and that horrible fellow Hébert. And your *sans-culottes*. Well, that makes me long to dress up in purple satin and gold lace and walk about the Place de la Concorde."

The doctor allowed a particularly acute attack of hysteria on the part of Madame Finzi-Magrini to pass, and went on:

"The love of humanity is a pathological state of a sexual origin which often appears at the age of puberty in nervous and clever people. The excess of phosphorus in the system must get out somewhere. As for hatred of a tyrant, that is a more human sentiment which has full play in time of war, when force and the mob are one. Emperors must be mad fools to decide on declaring wars which substitute an armed nation for their Praetorian Guards. That idiocy accomplished, despotism of course produces revolution until terrorism leads to the inevitable reaction."

"You condemn us then, doctor, to oscillate between rebellion and a *coup d'état?*"

"No," said the doctor, "because the English people, who have already given the world Stilton cheese and comfortable chairs, have invented for our benefit the Parliamentary system. Our M.P.'s arrange rebellions and *coups d'état* for us, which leaves the rest of the nation time to play cricket. The Press completes the system by enabling us to take our share in these tumults by proxy. All these things form a part of modern comfort and in a hundred years' time every man, white, yellow, red or black, will refuse to inhabit a room without hot water laid on, or a country without a Parliament."

"I hope you are wrong," said Major Parker. "I hate politicians, and I want, after the War, to go and live in the East, because nobody out there pays any attention to a government of babblers."

"My dear major, why the devil do you mix your personal feelings with these questions? Politics are controlled by laws as necessary as the movements of the stars. Are you annoyed that there are dark nights because you happen to prefer moonlight? Humanity lies on an uncomfortable bed. When the sleeper aches too much he turns over, that is a war or an insurrection. Then he goes to sleep again for a few centuries. All that is quite natural and happens without much suffering, if one does not mix up any moral ideas with it. Attacks of cramp are not virtues. But each change finds, alas, its prophets who, from love of humanity, as Aurelle says, put this miserable globe to fire and sword."

"That's very well said, doctor," said Aurelle, "but I return the compliment; if those are your sentiments, why do you take the trouble to belong to a party? Because you are a damned socialist."

"Doctor," said the colonel, "pass the port."

"Ah," said the doctor, "that's because I would rather be persecutor than persecuted. You must know how to recognize the arrival of these periodical upheavals and prepare. This war will bring socialism, that is to say, the total sacrifice of the aristocrat to the Leviathan. This in itself is neither a blessing nor a misfortune: it is a cramp. Let us then turn over with a good grace, as long as we feel we shall be more comfortable on the other side."

"That's a perfectly absurd theory," said Major Parker, angrily sticking out his square chin, "and if you adopt it, doctor, you must give up medicine! Why try and stop the course of diseases? They are also, according to you, periodic and necessary upheavals. But if you pretend to fight against tuberculosis do not deny me the right to attack universal suffrage."

At this moment a R.A.M.C. sergeant entered and asked Dr. O'Grady to come and see a wounded man: Major Parker remained master of the situation. The colonel, who had a horror of arguments, seized the opportunity to talk about something else.

"Messiou," he said, "what is the displacement of one of your largest cruisers?"

"Sixty thousand tons, sir," hazarded Aurelle wildly.

This knock-out blow put the colonel out of action, and

Aurelle asked Major Parker why he objected to universal suffrage.

"But don't you see, my dear Aurelle, that it is the most extravagant idea that humanity has ever conceived? Our political system will be considered more monstrous than slavery in a thousand years. One man, one vote, whatever the man is! Do you pay the same price for a good horse as for a crock?"

"Have you ever heard the immortal reasoning of our Courteline? 'Why should I pay twelve francs for an umbrella when I can get a glass of beer for six sous?' "

"Equal rights for men!" continued the major vehemently. "Why not equal courage and equal intelligence while you are about it?"

Aurelle loved the major's impassioned and pleasant harangues and, to keep the discussion going, said that he did not see how one could refuse a people the right to choose their leaders.

"To control them, Aurelle, yes; but to choose them, never! An aristocracy cannot be elected. It is or it isn't. Why, if I were to attempt to choose the Commander-in-Chief or the Superintendent of Guy's Hospital, I should be shut up; but, if I wish to have a voice in the election of the Chancellor of the Exchequer or the First Lord of the Admiralty, I'm a good citizen!"

"That is not quite correct, major. Ministers are not elected. Mind, I agree with you that our political system is imperfect; but so are all human affairs. And then, *'La pire des Chambres vaut mieux que la meilleure des antichambres.'* "

"I piloted round London lately," replied the major, "an Arab chief who honored me with his friendship, and when I had shown him the House of Commons and explained what went on there, he remarked, 'It must give you a lot of trouble cutting off those six hundred heads when you are not pleased with the Government.' "

"Messiou," said the colonel, exasperated, "I am going to play *Destiny Waltz,* for you."

.   .   .   .

Major Parker remained silent while the waltz unrolled its rhythmic phrases, but he ruminated over his old resentment against that "horrible fellow Hébert" and, as soon as the record had ground out its final notes, he started a new attack on Aurelle.

"What advantage," he said, "could the French have found in changing their government eight times in a century? Revolutions have become a national institution with you. In England, it would be impossible. If a crowd collected at Westminster and made a disturbance, the policeman would tell them to go away and they would do so."

"What an idea!" said Aurelle, who did not like revolutions, but who thought he ought to defend an old French lady against this hot-headed Saxon. "You must not forget, major, that you also cut off your king's head. No policeman intervened to save Charles Stuart, as far as I know."

"The assassination of Charles I," said the major, "was the sole work of Oliver Cromwell; now Oliver was a very good cavalry colonel, but he knew nothing of the real feelings of the English people, which they showed pretty plainly at the time of the Restoration. "Cromwell's head, which had been embalmed, was stuck on a pike on the top of Westminster Hall. One stormy night the wind broke the shaft of the pike and the head rolled to the feet of the sentry. He took it home and hid it in the chimney of his house, where it remained until his death. It passed through various hands till it came into the possession of a friend of mine, and I have often sat at tea opposite the head of the Protector still on its broken pike. One could easily recognize the wart which he had on his forehead and there still remains a lock of chestnut hair."

"Humph," grunted the colonel, at last interested in the conversation.

"Besides," continued the major, "the English Revolution does not compare in any way with the French one: it did not weaken the ruling classes. As a matter of fact, all the bad business of 1789 was caused by Louis XIV. Instead of leaving your country the strong armor of a landed gentry he made his nobles into the ridiculous puppets of Versailles, whose sole business was to hand him his coat and his waistcoat. In destroying the prestige of a class which should be the natural supporters of the monarchy, he ruined it beyond repair, and more's the pity."

"It is very easy for you to criticize us," said Aurelle. "We made our Revolution for you: the most important event in English history is the taking of the Bastille, and well you know it."

"Bravo, messiou," said the colonel, "stick up for your country. One ought always to stick up for one's country. Now please pass the port. I am going to play you *The Mikado*."

CHAPTER IV

AURELLE'S LETTER

Somewhere in France.

Singing, the soldiers go their way:
   "Stow your troubles inside your kit."
Such rain and wind, that you'd rather stay
   Indoors, than walk out with your girl in it.
Singing, the soldiers go their way:
   I'm making you verses so here I sit;
Singing, the soldiers go their way:
   "Stow your troubles inside your kit."

Here is the orderly bringing, let's say,
   Last week's papers, perhaps a chit;
Stale chatter of old political play,
   "Stow your troubles inside your kit."
All we can do, though the year is at May,
   Best we can furnish by way of wit;
Singing, the soldiers go their way:
   "Stow your troubles inside your kit."

Rain on the window, beating like spray,
   Storms an accompaniment, noisily fit,
To some prelude of Wagner's forgotten day.

"Stow your troubles inside your kit."
Who knows but tomorrow a howitzer may
Give me uncivil notice to quit.
But Satan may ask me to wet my clay—
So "stow your troubles inside your kit":
Singing, the soldiers go their way.

GREY dawn is breaking over the spongy plain. Today will
be the same as yesterday, tomorrow like today. The doctor
will wave his arms and say, "Très triste, messiou," and he
will not know what is sad, no more shall I. Then he will
give me a humorous lecture in a style between Bernard
Shaw and the Bible.

The padre will write letters, play patience and go out
riding. The guns will thunder, Boches will be killed, some
of our men too. We shall lunch off bully beef and boiled
potatoes, the beer will be horrible, and the colonel will say
to me, "Bière française no bonne, messiou."

In the evening, after a dinner of badly cooked mutton,
with mint sauce, and boiled potatoes, the inevitable gramophone will appear. We shall have *The Arcadians, The
Mikado*, then *Destiny Waltz*—"pour vous, messiou"—and
"Mrs. Finzi-Magrini" for the colonel, and finally *The Lanca-
shire Ramble*. Unfortunately for me, the first time that I
heard this circus tune I imitated a juggler catching balls
in time to the music. This little comedy henceforth took its
place in the traditions of the Mess, and if this evening at
the first notes of the *Ramble* I should forget to play my part
the colonel will say, "Allons, messiou, allons," pretending to
juggle, but I know my duty and I shall not forget; for
Colonel Bramble only cares for familiar scenes and fine old
crusted jokes.

His favorite number is a recitation by O'Grady of "Going
on leave." When he is in a bad temper, when one of his old
friends has been made a brigadier-general, or been given a
C.B., this recitation is the only thing that can make him
smile. He knows it by heart and, like the children, stops the
doctor if he misses a sentence or alters a reply.

"No, doctor, no; the Naval officer said to you, 'When you
hear four loud short whistles, it means that the ship has

been torpedoed,' and you replied, 'And what if the torpedo carries away the whistle?' "

The doctor, having found his place, goes on.

Parker, too, one day found a remark which ever afterwards had a brilliant success. He got it out of a letter that a chaplain had written to the *Times*. "The life of the soldier," wrote this excellent man, "is one of great hardship; not infrequently mingled with moments of real danger."

The colonel thoroughly enjoys the unconscious humor of this remark, and would quote it whenever a shell scattered gravel over him. But his great resource, if the conversation bores him, is to attack the padre on his two weak points: bishops and Scotchmen.

The padre, who comes from the Highlands, is madly patriotic. He is convinced that it is only Scotchmen who play the game and who are really killed.

"If history told the truth," he says, "this war would not be called the European War, but the war between Scotland and Germany."

The colonel is Scotch himself, but he is fair, and every time he finds in the papers the casualty lists of the Irish Guards or the Welsh Fusiliers he reads them out in a loud voice to the padre, who, to keep his end up, maintains that the Welsh Fusiliers and Irish Guards are recruited in Aberdeen. This is his invariable retort.

All this may appear rather puerile to you, my friend, but these childish things are the only bright spots in our boring, bombarded existence. Yes, these wonderful men have remained children in many ways; they have the fresh outlook, and the inordinate love of games, and our rustic shelter often seems to me like a nursery of heroes.

But I have profound faith in them; their profession of empire-builders has inspired them with high ideals of the duty of the white man. The colonel and Parker are "Sahibs" whom nothing on earth would turn from the path they have chosen. To despise danger, to stand firm under fire, is not an act of courage in their eyes—it is simply part of their education. If a small dog stands up to a big one they say gravely, "He is a gentleman."

A true gentleman, you see, is very nearly the most sympathetic type which evolution has produced among the pitiful group of creatures who are at this moment making such a noise in the world. Amid the horrible wickedness of the species, the English have established an oasis of courtesy and phlegm. I love them.

I must add that it is a very foolish error to imagine that they are less intelligent than ourselves, in spite of the delight my friend Major Parker pretends to take in affirming the contrary. The truth is that their intelligence follows a different method from ours. Far removed from our standard of rationalism and the pedantic sentiment of the Germans, they delight in a vigorous common sense and all absence of system. Hence a natural and simple manner which makes their sense of humor still more delightful.

But I see, from the window, my horse waiting for me; and I must go round to the surly farmers and get some straw for the quartermaster, who is trying to build stables. But *you* are furnishing boudoirs, and mind you choose, O Amazon, soft, oriental silks.

> In your salon, style "Directory"
> (Lavender-blue and lemon-yellow)
> Ancient armchairs sit, hail-fellow,
> In a fashion contradictory,
> With a sofa lacking history
> (Lavender-blue and lemon-yellow).

> To our Merveilleuses notorious
> (Lavender-blue and lemon-yellow)
> Dandies striped with chevrons mellow
> Shall proclaim a day victorious,
> Decked in dolmans all-vainglorious
> (Lavender-blue and lemon-yellow).

> Walls severe, as bare as a church
> (Lavender-blue and lemon-yellow),
> May wait awhile the brutal bellow
> Of some First-Consul, who may lurch

Upon their calm of days memorial
With his visage dictatorial
(Lavender eyed and skin of yellow).

"Are you a poet?" the colonel asked me doubtfully, when he saw me writing lines of equal length.

I denied the soft impeachment.

CHAPTER V

IT HAD been raining for four days. The heavy raindrops played a monotonous tattoo on the curved roof of the tent. Outside in the field the grass had disappeared under yellow mud, in which the men's footsteps sounded like the smacking of a giant's lips.

" 'And God looked upon the earth, and behold, it was corrupt,' " recited the padre; " 'and God said to Noah, Make thee an ark of gopher wood; rooms shalt thou make in the ark, and shalt pitch it within and without with pitch.' "

" 'The same day were all the fountains of the great deep broken up, and the windows of heaven were opened,' " continued the doctor.

"The Flood," he added, "was a real event, for its description is common to all oriental mythology. No doubt the Euphrates had burst its banks; that's why the Ark was driven into the interior and came to rest on a hill. Similar catastrophes often occur in Mesopotamia and in India, but are rare in Belgium."

"The cyclone of 1876 killed 215,000 people in Bengal," said the colonel. "Messiou, send round the port, please."

The colonel loved statistics, to the great misfortune of Aurelle, who, quite incapable of remembering figures, was interrogated every day on the number of inhabitants in a village, the strength of the Serbian army, or the initial velocity of the French bullet. He foresaw with terror that the colonel was going to ask him the average depth of rain in feet and inches in Flanders, and he hastened to create a diversion.

"I found in Poperinghe," he said, showing the book he was reading, "this very curious old volume. It is a description of England and Scotland by the Frenchman, Etienne Perlin, Paris, 1558."

"Humph! What does this Mr. Perlin say?" asked the colonel, who had the same respect for ancient things as he had for old soldiers.

Aurelle opened the book at hazard and translated:

"'After dinner, the cloth is withdrawn and the ladies retire. The table is of beautiful glossy Indian wood, and stands of the same wood hold the bottles. The name of each wine is engraved on a silver plate which hangs by a little chain round the neck of the bottle. The guests each choose the wine they like and drink it as seriously as if they were doing penance, while proposing the health of eminent personages or the fashionable beauties; this is what is known as a toast.'"

"I like 'fashionable beauties,'" said the doctor. "Perhaps Aurelle will take to drinking port, now he can pour libations to Gaby Deslys or Gladys Cooper."

"There are toasts for each day in the week," said the colonel, "Monday, our men; Tuesday, ourselves; Wednesday, our swords; Thursday, sport; Friday, our religion; Saturday, sweethearts and wives; Sunday, absent friends and ships at sea."

Aurelle went on reading aloud:

"'The toasts are of barbaric origin, and I have been told that the Highlanders of Scotland, a semi-savage folk who live in a state of perpetual feud—'"

"Listen to that, padre," said the colonel. "Read it again, messiou, for the padre. 'I have been told that the Highlanders of Scotland—'"

"'A semi-savage folk who live in a state of perpetual feud, have kept to the original character of this custom. To drink the health of anyone is to ask him to guard you while you drink and cannot defend yourself; and the person to whom you drink replies, "I pledge you," which means in their language, "I guarantee your safety." Then he draws his dagger, places the point on the table and protects you until your glass is empty.'"

"That's why," said Major Parker, "the pewter pots that they give for golf prizes have always got glass bottoms through which one can see the dagger of the assassin."

"Send round the port, messiou, I want to drink the padre's health in a second glass to hear him reply, 'I pledge you,' and to see him put the point of his dagger on the table."

"I've only got a Swiss knife," said the padre.

"That's good enough," said the colonel.

"This theory of the origin of toasts is very probable," said the doctor. "We are always repeating ancestral signs which are quite useless now. When a great actress wants to express hate she draws back her charming lips and shows her canine teeth, an unconscious sign of cannibalism. We shake hands with a friend to prevent him using it to strike us, and we take off our hats because our ancestors used to humbly offer their heads, to the bigwigs of those days, to be cut off."

At that moment there was a loud crack, and Colonel Bramble fell backwards with a crash. One of the legs of his chair had broken. The doctor and Parker helped him up, while Aurelle and the padre looked on in fits of laughter.

"There's a good example of an ancestral survival," said the major, kindly intervening to save Aurelle, who was trying in vain to stop laughing. "I imagine that one laughs at a fall because the death of a man was one of the most amusing sights for our ancestors. It delivered them from an adversary and diminished the number of those who shared the food and the females."

"Now we know you, messiou," said the padre.

"A French philosopher," said Aurelle, who had by this time recovered, "has constructed quite a different theory of laughter: he is called Bergson and—"

"I have heard of him," said the padre; "he's a clergyman, isn't he?"

"I have a theory about laughter," said the doctor, "which is much more edifying than yours, major. I think it is simply produced by a feeling of horror, immediately succeeded by a feeling of relief. A young monkey who is devoted to the old father of the tribe sees him slip on a banana skin, he fears an accident and his chest swells with fright, then he discovers that it's nothing and all his muscles pleasantly relax. That was the first joke, and it explains the convulsive motions in laughing. Aurelle is shaken physically because he is shaken morally by two strong motives: his anxious affection and respect for the colonel—"

"Ugh," grunted the colonel.

"And the consoling certainty that he is not hurt."

"I wish you would talk about something else," said the colonel. "Read a little more of the book, messiou."

Aurelle turned over some pages.

" 'Other nations,' " he read, " 'accuse the English of incivility because they arrive and depart without touching their hats, and without that flow of compliments which are common to the French and Italians. But those who judge thus see things in a false light. The English idea is that politeness does not consist in gestures or words which are often hypocritical and deceptive, but in being courteously disposed to other people. They have their faults like every nation, but, considering everything, I am sure that the more one knows them the more one esteems and likes them.' "

"I like old Mr. Perlin," said the colonel. "Do you agree with him, messiou?"

"The whole of France now agrees with him, sir," said Aurelle warmly.

"You are biased, Aurelle," said Major Parker, "because you are getting quite English yourself. You whistle in your bath, you drink whisky and are beginning to like arguments; if you could only manage to eat tomatoes and underdone cutlets for breakfast you would be perfect."

"If you don't mind, major, I would rather remain French," said Aurelle. "Besides, I never knew that whistling in one's bath was an English rite."

"So much so," said the doctor, "that I have arranged to have carved on my tombstone: 'Here lies a British subject who never whistled in his bath or tried to be an amateur detective.' "

CHAPTER VI

BRITISH conversation is like a game of cricket or a boxing match; personal allusions are forbidden like hitting below the belt, and anyone who loses his temper is disqualified.

Aurelle met at the Lennox Mess veterinaries and generals, tradesmen and dukes. Excellent whisky was provided and the guests entertained in a friendly way without boring them with too much attention.

"It rains a lot in your country," said a major in the Engineers who sat next him one evening.

"So it does in England," said Aurelle.

"I intend," said the major, "when this damned war is over, to leave the army and go and live in New Zealand."

"You have friends there?"

"Oh, no, but the salmon fishing is very good."

"Bring your rod over here while we are resting, major, the pond is full of enormous pike."

"I never fish for pike," said the major, "he is not a gentleman. When he sees he is caught he gives up; the salmon fights to the end, even without hope. A thirty-pound fellow will sometimes fight two hours; that's something like, isn't it?"

"Admirable!" said Aurelle. "And what about trout?"

"The trout is a lady," said the major; "you must deceive her; but it is not easy, because she is a judge of flies. And you," he added politely, after a short silence, "what do you do in peacetime?"

"I write a little," said Aurelle, "and I am trying for a degree."

"No, no; I mean what is your sport—fishing, hunting, golf, polo?"

"To tell the truth," acknowledged Aurelle, "I am not much good at sport. I am not very strong and—"

"I'm sorry to hear that," said the major, but he turned to his other neighbor and bothered no more about the Frenchman.

Aurelle was thrown back to the Veterinary Captain Clarke sitting on his left, who had up to then been eating and drinking without saying a word.

"It rains a lot in your country," said Captain Clarke.

"So it does in England," said Aurelle.

"I intend," said Clarke, "when this damned war is over to go back to Santa Lucia.".

Aurelle asked if the captain's family lived in the Antilles. He was horrified.

"Oh, no! I belong to a Staffordshire family. I went out there quite by chance; I was traveling for pleasure and my boat touched at Santa Lucia; I found the heat very agreeable and I stayed there. I bought some land very cheap and I grow cocoa."

"And it does not bore you?"

"No, the nearest white man is six miles off, and the coast of the island is excellent for sailing. What more could I do at home? When I go to England for three months' holiday, I spend a week at my old home, then I go off in a yacht alone. I have been all round your Brittany coast; it is delightful because the currents are so difficult and your charts are so good; but it is not warm enough. At Santa Lucia I can smoke cigarettes in my pajamas on my veranda."

He slowly swallowed his port and concluded:

"No, I don't like Europe—too much work. But, out there, there is enough food for everybody."

The colonel at the other end of the table was holding forth about India, the white ponies of his regiment, the native servants with their complicated names and varied duties, and the lax life in the Hills. Parker described hunting on an elephant.

"You stand up on your animal firmly tied on by one leg, and when the elephant gallops you fly into space: it's really most exciting."

"I'll take your word for it," said Aurelle.

"Yes, but if you try it," said the colonel solicitously to Aurelle, "don't forget to slide off by the tail as quickly as you can if the elephant comes to marshy ground. His instinct, when the ground gives way beneath him, is to seize

you in his trunk and put you down in front of him to have
something solid to kneel on."

"I'll remember, sir," said Aurelle.

"In the Malay States," said the major of Engineers, "the
wild elephants wander about the main roads. I often met
them when I was on my motor-bike; if your face or your
clothes annoy them they pick you off and smash your head
by treading on it. But except for that they are quite
inoffensive."

A long discussion on the most vulnerable part of an
elephant followed. The padre showed his knowledge by explaining how the anatomy of the Indian elephant differed
from that of the African species.

"Padre," said Aurelle, "I always knew you were a sportsman; but have you ever really done any big-game shooting?"

"What! my dear fellow? Big game? I've killed pretty
nearly everything a hunter *can* kill, from the elephant and
rhinoceros to the lion and tiger. I've never told you the
story of my first lion?"

"Never, padre," said the doctor, "but you are going to
now."

"Padre," said the colonel, "I should like to hear your
stories, but I make one condition: someone must start the
gramophone for me. I want my dear 'Mrs. Finzi-Magrini'
tonight."

"Oh, no, sir, for pity's sake! I'll let you have a rag-time
if you absolutely must grind that damned machine."

"Not at all, doctor, you aren't going to get off so easily. I
insist on 'Finzi-Magrini.' Come, Aurelle, like a good chap,
and remember, speed 65, and don't scratch my record.
Padre, you may now begin the story of your first lion."

"I was at Johannesburg and very much wanted to join a
sporting club, as a number of the members were friends of
mine. But the rules did not admit any candidate who had
not at least killed a lion. So I set out with a nigger loaded
with several rifles, and that evening lay in wait with him
near a water-hole where a lion was accustomed to come
and drink.

"Half an hour before midnight I heard the crashing of

branches and over the top of a bush appeared the head of a lion. He had winded us and looked our way. I aimed and fired. The head disappeared behind the bush, but appeared again after a minute. A second shot, the same result. The brute got frightened, hid his head and then put it up again. I remained quite cool, I had sixteen shots to fire in my various rifles. Third shot, same old game; fourth shot, ditto.

"I got unnerved and shot badly, so that after the fifteenth shot the beast put up his head again. 'Miss that one, him eat us,' said the nigger. I took a long breath, aimed carefully and fired. The animal fell. One second—two—ten—he did not reappear. I waited a little longer, then I rushed out followed by my nigger, and guess, messiou, what I found behind."

"The lion, padre."

"*Sixteen* lions, my boy, and very one had a bullet in its eye! That's how I made my début."

"By Jove, padre! Who says the Scotch have no imagination?"

"Now listen to a true story. It was in India that I first killed a woman. Yes, yes, a woman! I had set out tiger-shooting when in passing through a village, buried in the jungle, an old native stopped me. 'Sahib, sahib, a bear!' And he pointed out a moving black shape up a tree. I took aim quickly and fired. The mass fell heavily with a crashing of branches, and I discovered an old woman, whom I had demolished while she was picking fruit. Another old nigger, the husband, overwhelmed me with abuse. They went and fetched the native policeman. I had to buy off the family; it cost a terrible lot, at least two pounds.

"The story soon got about for twenty miles around, and for several weeks I could not go through a village without two or three old men rushing at me and crying, 'Sahib, sahib, a bear up the tree!' I need hardly tell you that they had just made their wives climb up."

Then Parker described a crocodile hunt, and Captain Clarke gave some details about sharks in Bermuda, which are not dangerous as long as people take the precaution of jumping into the water in company. The colonel, meanwhile, played *The March of the Lost Brigade* in slow time. The

New Zealand major put some eucalyptus leaves in the fire so that the smell might remind him of the Bush. Aurelle, rather dazed, fuddled with the Indian sun and the scent of wild animals, at last realized that this world is a great park laid out by a gardener-god for the gentlemen of the United Kingdoms.

CHAPTER VII

Since you are kept indoors beside the ember,
Since you despise the novels on your lists,
Since, happily, no happy man exists,
And since this August wickedly persists
     To play December,

I scribble you these lines sans form or feet,
Sans rhyme—and reason, which one more deplores,
Which I shall call, when stand my works complete,
"Talk with a lady who was kept indoors
     By rain and sleet."

I know not if your sentiment's the same,
But when I idly sit, in idle dreams,
And the rain falls upon my heart, it seems . . .

"AURELLE," said the doctor, "this time you *are* writing verses; deny it if you can. You are taken red-handed."

"M-ph!" grunted the colonel scornfully, but with indulgence.

"I own to it, doctor, but what then? Is it contrary to King's Regulations?"

"No," said the doctor, "but I'm surprised. I have always been convinced that the French cannot be a nation of poets. Poetry is rhymed foolishness. Now you are not a fool, and you have no sense of rhythm."

"You do not know our poets," said Aurelle, annoyed. "Have you read Musset, Hugo, Baudelaire?"

"I know Hugo," said the colonel. "When I commanded the troops in Guernsey I was shown his house. I also tried to read his book, *The Toilers of the Sea,* but it was too boring."

The arrival of Major Parker, pushing in front of him two boyish-looking captains, put an end to this conference.

"Here are young Gibbons and Warburton. You must give them a cup of tea before sending them back to their companies. I found them sitting on the side of the Zillebeke Road, no doubt waiting for a taxi. These London people will expect anything."

Gibbons was returning from leave, and Warburton, a dark Welshman very like a Frenchman, who had been wounded two months before in Artois, was rejoining the Lennox after sick leave.

"Aurelle, give me a cup of tea like a good fellow," said Major Parker. "Oh, the milk first, I beseech you! And ask for a whisky and soda to wake up Captain Gibbons, will you? He looks as if he had just come out of his wigwam and had not dug up his war hatchet yet."

"It's such a horrible change," said Gibbons. "Yesterday morning I was still in my garden in a real English valley, with hedges and trees. Everything was clean and fresh and cared-for and happy. My pretty sisters-in-law were playing tennis. We were all dressed in white, and here I am suddenly transported into this dreadful mangled wood among you band of assassins. When *do* you think this damned war will be over? I am such a peaceable man! I prefer church bells to guns and the piano to a Hotchkiss. My one ambition is to live in the country with my plump little wife and a lot of plump little children." And, raising his glass, he concluded, "I drink to the end of these follies, and to hell with the Boches who brought us here!"

But keen Warburton cut in immediately.

"I like the War. It is only War that gives us a normal existence. What do you do in peacetime? You stay at home; you don't know what to do with your time; you argue with your parents, and your wife—if you have one. Everyone thinks you are an insufferable egotist—and so you are. The War comes; you only go home every five or six months. You are a hero, and, what women appreciate much more, you are a change. You know stories that have never been published. You've seen strange men and terrible things. Your father, instead of telling his friends that you are embittering the end of his life, introduces you to them as an oracle. These old men consult you on foreign politics. If you are married, your wife is prettier than ever; if you are not, all the girls lay siege to you.

"You like the country? Well, you live in a wood here. You love your wife? But who was it said that it is easier to die for the woman one loves than to live with her? For myself I prefer a Hotchkiss to the piano, and the chatter of my men to that of the old ladies who come to tea at my home. No, Gibbons, War is a wonderful epoch," and, holding up his glass, he said, "I drink to the gentle Hun who procures these pleasures for us."

Then he described his time at the Duchess' Hospital.

"I thought I was with the Queen of the Fairies. We got everything we wanted without asking for it. When our fiancées were coming to see us, we were propped up with cushions to match the color of our eyes. A fortnight before I could get up they brought twelve brightly colored dressing-gowns for me to choose which one I would wear the first time I was allowed out of bed. I chose a red and green one, which was hung up near me, and I was in such a hurry to put it on that I got well three days quicker. There was a Scotch captain with such a beautiful wife that all the patients' temperatures went up when she came to see him. They ended by making a special door for her near her husband's bed, so that she need not walk down the whole ward. Oh, I hope I shall be wounded soon! Doctor, promise to send me to the Duchess' Hospital!"

But Gibbons, with eyes still full of tender memories of home, would not be consoled. The padre, who was wise and kind, made him describe the last revue at the Palace, and complacently discussed the legs and shoulders of a "sweet little thing." The colonel got out his best records and played "Mrs. Finzi-Magrini" and *Destiny Waltz* to his guests. Gibbons sat with his head in his hands during the waltz. The colonel was going to chaff him mildly about his melancholy thoughts, but the little captain got up at the end of the tune and said:

"I had better be off before dark." And off he went.

"Silly ass," said Parker, after a pause.

The colonel and the padre agreed. Aurelle alone protested.

"Aurelle, my friend," said Dr. O'Grady, "if you want to be thought anything of amongst Englishmen, you must make yourself see their point of view. They don't care for melancholy people, and have a contempt for sentiment. This applies to love as well as to patriotism and religion. If you want the colonel to despise you, stick a flag in your tunic. If you want the padre to treat you with contempt, give him a letter to censor full of pious rubbish; if you want to make Parker sick, weep over a photograph. They spend their youth hardening their skins and their hearts. They fear neither physical blows nor the blows of fate. They look upon exaggeration as the worst of vices, and coldness as a sign of aristocracy. When they are very miserable, they smile. When they are very happy, they say nothing at all. And *au fond* John Bull is terribly sentimental, which explains everything."

"All that is perfectly true, Aurelle," said Parker, "but you must not say it. The doctor is a confounded Irishman who cannot hold his tongue."

Upon which, the doctor and Major Parker began a discussion on the Irish question in their usual amusingly sarcastic manner. The colonel looked in his box of records for *When Irish Eyes Are Smiling*, then wisely and courteously interrupted them.

"And so, Aurelle," concluded Major Parker, "you see us poor Englishmen searching hard for the solution of a problem when there isn't one. You may think that the Irish want certain definite reforms, and that they will be happy and contented the day they get them; but not at all. What amuses them is discussion itself, plotting in theory. They play with the idea of Home Rule; if we gave it them, the game would be finished and they would invent another, probably a more dangerous one."

"Go to Ireland after the War, messiou," said the colonel,

"it's an extraordinary country. Everyone is mad. You can commit the worst crimes—it doesn't matter. Nothing matters."

"The worst crimes?" said Aurelle. "Oh, I say, sir!"

"Oh, yes, anything you like—the most unheard-of things. You can go out hunting in brown breeches, fish in your neighbor's salmon river—nothing will happen; no one will take the smallest notice of you."

"I do believe," said Aurelle, "that I am beginning to understand the Irish question."

"I will finish your education," said the doctor. "A year before the War a Liberal M.P. who was visiting Ireland said to an old peasant, 'Well, my friend, we are soon going to give you Home Rule!' 'God save us, your honor,' said the man, 'do not do that.' 'What?' said the astonished Member. 'You don't want Home Rule now?' 'Your honor,' said the man, 'I'll tell you. You are a good Christian, your honor? It's to heaven you want to go? So do I, but we do not want to go there tonight.' "

CHAPTER VIII

CHORUS: *"What, Jupiter not so strong as these goddesses?"*
PROMETHEUS: *"Yes, even he cannot escape destiny."*

WHEN young Lieutenant Warburton, temporarily commanding B Company of the Lennox Highlanders, took over his trench, the captain he came to relieve said to him:

"This part is not too unhealthy; they are only thirty yards off, but they are tame Boches. All they ask is to be left alone."

"We will wake things up a bit," said Warburton to his men, when the peaceable warrior had departed.

When wild beasts are too well fed, they become domesticated; but a few well-directed rockets will make them savage again. In virtue of this principle, Warburton, having provided himself with a star shell, instead of sending it straight up, fired it horizontally towards the German trenches.

A distracted Saxon sentry cried, "Liquid-fire attack!" The Boche machine-guns began to bark. Warburton, delighted, replied with grenades. The enemy called the artillery to its assistance. A telephone call, a hail of shrapnel, and immediate reprisals by the British big guns.

The next day the German communiqué said: "An attack by the British under cover of liquid-fire at H—— was completely checked by the combined fire of our infantry and artillery."

0275 Private Scott, H. J., who served his King and country under the strenuous Warburton, disapproved heartily of his officer's heroic methods. Not that he was a coward, but the War had taken him by surprise when he had just married a charming girl, and, as Captain Gadsby of the Pink Hussars says, "a married man is only half a man." Scott counted the days he spent in the trenches, and this one was the first of ten, and his chief was reckless.

The god who guards lovers intervened the next day by the simple means of a scrap of paper asking for a man from the regiment, mechanic by trade, to look after a machine at P—— for disinfecting clothes. P—— was a pretty little town at least eight miles from the front line, rather deserted by the inhabitants on account of *marmites,* but all the same a safe and comfortable retreat for a troglodyte of the trenches.

0275 Private Scott, mechanic by trade, put his name down. His lieutenant abused him; his colonel recommended him; and his general nominated him. An old London omnibus painted a military grey took him away to his new life, far from Warburton and his perils.

The machine which Scott had to look after was in the yard of a college, an old building covered with ivy; and Abbé Hoboken, the principal, received him, when he arrived, as if he were a general.

"Are you a Catholic, my son?" he asked him in the English of the college.

Luckily for Scott, he did not understand, and answered vaguely:

"Yes, sir."

This involuntary renunciation of the Scotch Presbyterian Church procured him a room belonging to a mobilized Belgian professor and a bed with sheets.

Now, at that very moment, Hauptmann Reineker, who commanded a German battery of heavy artillery at Paschendaele, was in a very bad temper.

The evening post had brought him an ambiguous letter from his wife in which she mentioned too often, and with an affectation of indifference, a wounded officer of the Guards, whom she had been nursing for several days.

During the night, he surveyed his gun-emplacements on the outskirts of a wood, then he said suddenly:

"Wolfgang, have you any shells available?"

"Yes, sir."

"How many?"

"Three."

"Good! Wake up Theresa's crew."

He then verified his calculations by his map.

The men, half awake, loaded the enormous gun. Reineker gave the order, and, shaking up everyone and everything, the shell started forth, hurtling through the night.

0275 Private Scott, then, who adored his wife and had accepted a post without honor for her sake, was sleeping peacefully in the bedroom of a mobilized Belgian professor: and Captain Reineker, whose wife no longer loved him, and whom he mistrusted, was striding furiously up and down amongst the frozen woods, and these two circumstances, widely apart from one another, were developed independently in an indifferent world.

Now the calculations of Reineker, like most calculations, went wrong. He was 400 yards out. His landmark was the church. From the church to the college was 400 yards. A light wind increased the deviation by 20 yards, and from that moment the Reineker and the Scott situation began to have points in common. At this particular point the chest of 0275 Private Scott received the full force of the 305 shell, and he was blown into a thousand bits, which, amongst other things, put an end to the Scott situation.

CHAPTER IX

"The ideal of the English Church has been to provide a resident gentleman for every parish in the Kingdom, and there have been worse ideals."

SHANE LESLIE.

AURELLE, arriving for tea at the Mess, found only the padre repairing a magic lantern.

"Hullo, messiou," he said, "very glad to see you. I am getting my lantern ready for a sporting sermon to the men of B Company when they come out of the trenches."

"What, padre, you preach sermons now with a magic lantern?"

"My boy, I am trying to make the men come; there are too many who keep away. I know very well that the regiment has a good many Presbyterians, but if you could see the Irish regiments—not a man misses going to Mass. Ah, messiou, the Catholic padres have more influence than we have. I ask myself, why? I go every day to the trenches, and even if the men think me an old fool they might at least recognize that I am a sportsman."

"The regiment is very fond of you, padre. But, if you don't mind my saying so, I think that Catholic priests have a special influence. Confession has something to do with it, but their vow of celibacy more, because, in a sort of way, it makes them different from other people. Even the doctor tones down his best stories when Father Murphy dines with us."

"But, my boy, I love O'Grady's stories; I am an old soldier and a man of the world. When I was shooting in Africa a Negro queen made me a present of three young Negresses."

"Padre!"

"Oh, I let them go the same day, which annoyed them somewhat. But I don't see why, after that, I need play Mrs. Grundy in the Mess."

One of the orderlies brought some boiling water, and the padre asked Aurelle to make the tea.

"When I was married—*not* that way, messiou; it's curious that no Frenchman can make tea. Always warm the teapot first, my boy; you cannot make good tea with a cold teapot."

"You were talking about your wedding, padre."

"Yes, I wanted to tell you how indignant all these Pharisees were, who want me to behave like a prude with young people, when I merely wanted to be reasonable. When I was going to be married, I naturally had to ask one of my colleagues to perform the ceremony. After having settled the important points, I said to him, 'In the Marriage Service of the Church of England there is one passage which I consider absolutely indecent. Yes, yes, I know quite well that it is what St. Paul said. Well, probably in his time he had a perfect right to say such things, and they were adapted to the manners and customs of the Corinthians, but they are not meant for the ears of a young girl from Aberdeen in 1906. My fiancée is innocent, and I will not have her shocked.' The young man, a worldly minded little curate, went and complained to the bishop, who sent for me and said haughtily. 'So it is *you* who are taking upon yourself to forbid the reading of the Epistle to the Corinthians? I would have you know that I am not the man to put up with nonsense of this sort.' 'All right,' I replied, 'I would have you know that I am not the man to put up with an insult to my wife. If this fellow insists on reading the passage, I shall say nothing in the church, out of respect for the sacred edifice, but I promise you that after the ceremony I shall box his ears.'

"Well, messiou, the bishop looked at me carefully to see if I was in earnest. Then he remembered my campaign in the Transvaal, the Negro queen, and the dangers of a scandal, and he answered me with unction, 'I do not see after all that the passage that shocks you is absolutely essential to the marriage ceremony.'"

Dr. O'Grady here came in and asked for a cup of tea.

"Who made this tea?" he demanded. "You, Aurelle? How much tea did you put in?"

"One spoonful for each cup."

"Now listen to an axiom—one spoonful for each cup and

then one for the pot. It is curious that no Frenchman knows how to make tea."

Aurelle changed the subject.

"The padre was telling me about his wedding."

"A padre ought not to be married," said the doctor. "You know what St. Paul said, 'A married man seeks to please his wife and not God.' "

"You have put your foot in it now," said Aurelle. "Don't talk to him about St. Paul; he has just been strafing him badly."

"Excuse me," said the padre, "I only strafed a bishop."

"Padre," said the doctor, "judge not—"

"Oh, I know," said the padre, "the Master said that, but He did not know any bishops." Then he returned to his old subject. "Tell me, O'Grady, you are Irish; why have the Catholic chaplains more influence than we?"

"Padre," said the doctor, "listen to a parable. It is your turn. A man had committed a murder. He was not suspected, but remorse made him restless and miserable. One day, as he was passing an Anglican church, it seemed to him that the secret would be easier to bear if he could share it with some one else, so he entered and asked the vicar to hear his confession.

"The vicar was a very well brought up young man, and had been at Eton and Oxford. Enchanted with this rare piece of luck, he said eagerly, 'Most certainly, open your heart to me; you can talk to me as if I were your father!' The other began: 'I have killed a man.' The vicar sprang to his feet. 'And you come here to tell *me* that? Horrible murderer! I am not sure that it is not my duty as a citizen to take you to the nearest police station. In any case it is my duty as a gentleman not to keep you a moment longer under my roof.'

"And the man went away. A few miles farther on he saw a Roman Catholic church. A last hope made him enter, and he knelt down behind some old women who were waiting by the confessional. When his turn came he could just distinguish the priest praying in the shadows, his head in his hands. 'Father,' he said, 'I am not a Catholic, but I should like to confess to you.' 'I am listening, my son.' 'Father, I have committed murder.'

"He awaited the effect of this terrible revelation. In the austere silence of the church the voice of the priest said simply, 'How many times, my son?' "

"Doctor," said the padre, "you know that I am Scotch. I can only take in a story a week after I hear it."

"That one will take you longer, padre," said the doctor.

CHAPTER X

S. W. TARKINGTON, an officer of fifty-three, honorary lieutenant and quartermaster, was possessed of a vain but keen desire to win one more ribbon before retiring. The laws of nature and eighteen years of good conduct had given him the South African medal and the long service ribbon. But with a little luck even an honorary lieutenant may pick up a Military Cross if the bullets fall in the right place. That is why Tarkington was always to be found in dangerous corners where he had no business, and that is why, on the day Loos was taken, he wandered with his rheumatic old joints over the soaking battlefield and carried in eighteen wounded men on his back. But he met no general and no one knew anything about it, except the wounded, who have no influence.

From there the regiment was sent to the north and went into the line in the Ypres salient. There existed, no doubt, excellent sentimental and military reasons for defending this piece of ground, but as a winter residence it left much to be desired. Tarkington did not fear the danger—shells were part of the day's work—but his rheumatism feared the water, and the rain falling incessantly on the greasy clay made a damp and icy paste which no doctor would recommend for the oiling of old joints. Tarkington, whose painfully swollen feet now made the shortest march a Chinese torture, finally realized that he must apply to be sent to hospital.

"It's just my luck," he said to his confidant, the sergeant-major. "I have the pain without the wound."

So he went off limping and swearing to find the colonel in his dug-out, and told him of the state of his legs.

The colonel was in a bad temper that morning. A communication from the headquarters of the division had pointed out to him that the proportion of trench feet in his regiment had reached 3.6 per cent., whereas the average of the corps was only 2.7. And would he take the necessary precautions to reduce his percentage in the future?

The necessary precautions had been taken; he had sent for the doctor and given him the communication.

"And see here, O'Grady. You may have bronchitis, sore throats and gastric enteritis, but I do not want any more trench feet for three days."

You may imagine how Tarkington was received when he came to exhibit his paralyzed feet.

"Now that's the limit. *I* send down an officer for trench feet? Read, Tarkington, read, and do you imagine I am going to transform 3.5 into 3.6 to please *you?* Look up, my friend, General Routine Orders No. 324—'Trench Feet result from a contraction of the superficial arteries with the consequence that the skin no longer being nourished dies and mortifies.' Therefore, all you have to do is to watch your arteries. Tarkington, I am extremely sorry, old man, but that is all I can do for you."

"Just my luck," said the old man to his friend the sergeant-major. "I have thirty-seven years' service; I have never been ill; and when, for the first time in my life, I ask for sick leave, it happens on the very same day that headquarters have strafed the colonel over that very subject."

His feet became red, then blue, and had begun to turn black when the colonel went away on leave. The command in his absence was taken over by Major Parker, who, being the second son of a peer, paid small attention to remarks from the brigade. He saw the distress of the unfortunate Tarkington, and sent him to the field hospital, where they decided to send him to England. It seemed that Tarkington was not the kind to be acclimatized in the Flemish marshes.

He was taken to B—— and put on board the hospital ship *Saxonia,* with the wounded, doctors and nurses. The port officials had ascertained to their annoyance the day before that a number of floating mines were in the Channel.

The authorities argued over the origin of these mines, which the N.T.O. said were those of the Allies, while the M.L.O. thought they were the enemy's. But there was no argument about one detail: every boat that had come into contact with one had been cut in two and sunk immediately.

The captain of the *Saxonia* was convinced that the Channel was free from mines. He risked it—and was blown up.

So Tarkington jumped into the sea. As a good soldier, his instinct was to devote his last minutes to keeping calm, and he swam about quietly with the gas mask that he had been advised never to lose hanging round his neck.

A salvage boat picked him up, unconscious, and he was taken to a hospital on the English coast. He recovered consciousness, but felt very ill from his immersion in the water.

"Just like my cursed luck!" he groaned. "They stop me starting for a month, and when at last I do get off, it is in the only ship that has gone down for a year."

"They are all alike," said the colonel, on his return from leave. "Here's a blighter who grumbles at having his feet in water, and then takes advantage of my absence to go and have a salt-water bath!"

Now, a few months before, King George, after his accident in France, had crossed the Channel on board the *Saxonia.* The fate of the ship naturally interested His Majesty, who came to see the survivors, and, as Tarkington was the only officer, he had the inestimable privilege of quite a long conversation with the King. The result of this was that a few days afterwards a regiment "somewhere in France" received a memorandum from general headquarters asking for a statement of the services of Tarkington, S. W.

The memorandum being accompanied by certain verbal comments on the subject of "a very distinguished personage" by an officer in a red-banded gold-peaked cap, the colonel wrote nice things—which he had never said to him— of Tarkington, S. W., and the sergeant-major gave details of the brilliant conduct of the quartermaster at Loos.

The *London Gazette* a fortnight later recapitulated these
exploits in a supplement to the list of awards and honors,
and Tarkington, honorary captain, M.C., meditating on his
fate, found the world not such a bad place after all.

CHAPTER XI

THE first encounter that the brigade had with the village
was not very happy.

The village looked distrustfully on the brigade, with its
bare knees and its language like the rolling of a drum. The
brigade found the village short of *estaminets* and pretty
girls. The people of Hondezeele bewailed the departure of a
division of London Territorials, with their soft voices and
full pockets, and wherever Aurelle went they did nothing
but sing the praises of these sons of their adoption.

"Your Scotchmen, we know them. We cannot understand
what they say—and my little girls can speak English."

"Scotch—Promenade—no bon!" said the little girls.

"I had the general's chauffeur here," went on the old
woman, "a nice boy, sir. Billy, they called him. He washed up
for me, and pleasant spoken, too, and good manners. An
officers' Mess? Certainly not. I can make more selling fried
potatoes and beer to the boys, and even eggs, although they
cost me threepence each."

"Fried potatoes, two painnies a plate, aigs and bacon, one
franc," chorused the little girls.

Aurelle went on to the next house, where other old women
mourned other Billys, Harrys, Gingers, and Darkies.

One stout lady explained that noise gave her palpitations;
another, quite seventy-five, that it was not proper for a
girl living alone.

At last he found a corpulent lady whom he overwhelmed
with such eloquent protestations that she could not get in a
word. The next morning, he sent her the orderlies with the
plate and crockery, and at lunch-time brought along Parker
and O'Grady. The servants were waiting for them at the
door.

"Madame is a regular witch, sir. She's a proper fury, that's what she is, sir."

"Madame" welcomed them with confused complaints.

"Ah! bien merci! Ah! bien merci! How I have regretted having agreed to have you. I have not had a wink of sleep with my husband abusing me. He nearly beat me, monsieur. Oh, don't touch that! I forbid you to enter my clean kitchen. Wipe your feet, and take those boxes off there!"

"Put the boxes in the dining room," ordered Aurelle, to conciliate her.

"Thank you! Put your dirty boxes in my dining room, with my beautiful table and my fine dresser! I should think so, indeed!"

"But, in heaven's name, madame," said Aurelle, quietly, "where shall I put them?"

He half opened a door at the end of the dining room.

"Will you kindly leave that door alone! My lovely *salon*, where I do not even go myself for fear of making it dirty! And, besides, I have had enough of your Mess, I'm about tired of it."

A little later, Aurelle went into Madame Lemaire's, the draper's, to buy some chocolate. She had relegated all her pre-war trade to a corner of the shop, and now sold, like the rest of the village, Quaker Oats, Woodbine cigarettes, and post-cards with the words: "From Your Soldier Boy."

While she was serving him, Aurelle espied behind the shop a charming, bright little apartment, decorated with plates on the wall, and a clean cloth, with green and white squares, on the table. He strolled carelessly towards the door. Madame Lemaire looked suspiciously at him and folded her arms across her enormous bust.

"Would you believe, madame, that there are in this village people so unpatriotic as to refuse to take in officers, who do not know where to eat their meals?"

"Is it possible?" said Madame Lemaire, blushing.

He told her who they were.

"Ah, the carpenter's wife!" said Madame Lemaire, turning up her nose in disgust. "I am not surprised. They come from Moevekerke, and the people of Moevekerke are all bad."

"But it seems to me," insinuated Aurelle gently, "that you have a room here that would just do."

.   .   .   .

A week later the village and the brigade were tasting the pure joys of the honeymoon. In each house a Jack, a Ginger or a Darkey helped to wash up, called the old lady "Granny," and joked with the girls. The London Territorials were quite forgotten. At night, in the barns, beribboned bagpipes accompanied the monotonous dances.

Aurelle had lodged the padre at Madame Potiphar's, a lively young widow to whom the divisions, billeted in turn in the village, had handed on this nickname, like a local password.

The virtue of the padre, which had protected him against the solid charms of three young Negresses, feared nothing from the maneuvers of a village Potiphar.

Parker and O'Grady shared a large room in the inn. They called the publican and his wife "Papa" and "Mamma." Lucie and Berthe, the daughters of the house, taught them French. Lucie was six feet high; she was pretty, slender, and fair. Gerthe was more substantial and remarkably good-natured. These two fine Flemish girls, honest without prudishness, greedy of gain, lacking in culture but not in shrewdness, were the admiration of Major Parker.

Although their father was in a fair way to making a fortune by selling the Tommies English beer made in France, they never thought of asking him for money for their clothes or of making a servant work in their stead.

"One ought to be able to fight when one leaves such women at home," said the major admiringly.

The father was the same sort. He described to Aurelle the death of his son, a splendid boy, three times mentioned in despatches. He talked of him with a pride and resignation truly admirable.

Aurelle advised the publican, if he had a few hundred francs to spare, to put them in the War Loan.

"I have already put in fifty thousand francs," said the old man. "I shall wait a little now."

The whole village was rich.

Colonel Bramble gave two sous one day to Madame Lemaire's son, an urchin of five or six.

"To buy some sweets with," Aurelle told him.

"Oh, no, I don't care for them."

"What will you do with your sous, then?"

"Put them in my money-box till I have got enough to get
a deposit book in the Savings Bank; then, when I am grown
up, I shall buy some land."

That evening Aurelle repeated this to Lucie and Berthe,
thinking it would amuse them. He soon found out that no
one was amused: jokes about money were sacrilege. The
publican related a little moral story to make this clear.

"When I was small," he said, "I often used to go on messages into the town for Monsieur le curé, and each time he
gave me two sous, which I took to my father. But after a
time, Monsieur le curé made old Sophie, his servant, send
me on his commissions and she never gave me my two sous.
My father, who asked me for them, was very indignant. He
consulted my grandfather, and the whole family were called
in one evening to discuss the matter.

"My father said, 'The child cannot go and complain to
Monsieur le curé, because if it is he who has stopped the
two sous he might be offended.' 'And if it is old Sophie
who has diddled the child out of it she would box his ears,'
said my mother. My grandfather, who was no fool, hit upon
the best way. He said to me, 'You will go and make your
confession to Monsieur le curé. You will tell him that you
have sinned by getting angry with old Sophie because she
sent you to the town without giving you anything.'

"It was a great success. 'What,' said the curé. 'The old
wretch! She charged me for them every time. Release me
from the secret of the confessional and I will give her a good
talking-to!' I remembered that her hand was heavy and I
did not release him; but in future he always sent me himself."

The schoolmistress from Lille, who possessed the only
piano in the village, explained to Aurelle that she had had
to cut out of her lesson the whole chapter on economy and
thrift, substituting a lesson on generosity. A little girl of

eight then said to her, "I can never do that, mademoiselle. My mother is mean, and I am sure I shall be meaner than she."

Meanwhile the Highlanders were turning the King's shillings into glasses of beer, and were showering on these economical little girls embroidered aprons, sugar-plums and post-cards, with "From Your Soldier Boy" on them, price ninepence.

The plump and active mothers of these nice little Flemish girls sold the aprons and post-cards.

"Ah, messiou," said Colonel Bramble, "before the War we used to talk about frivolous France; now it is stern and prudent France."

"Yes," added the doctor, "the French are hard and severe on themselves. I begin to understand the Boche who said, 'Man does not aspire to happiness, only Englishmen.' There is, among your peasants of the north, an admirable voluntary asceticism."

"Did you ever see, messiou," said the padre, "in our country, before the War, the Frenchman of the music-hall? The little fellow with the black beard, who gesticulates and harangues? I believed it, messiou, and never pictured these devout and industrious villagers."

"I like to see them on Sunday morning," said the major, "when the bell for Mass starts ringing, and they all come out of their houses together, old men, women and children, as if they were going to a theater. Ah, messiou, why didn't you tell us all about this before the War?"

"The reason is," said Aurelle, "that we didn't know it ourselves."

CHAPTER XII

ORION'S belt rose higher in the wintry sky; the roads were frozen hard. The mail vans overflowed more and more every day with enormous quantities of puddings and Christmas cards, and the festive season recalled the joys of life to the division and the village.

The preparations for the Christmas dinner occupied Aurelle and the padre for some time. The latter found a turkey worthy of the royal table at a farm; Aurelle hunted from house to house for chestnuts; Parker attended himself to the cooking, and mixed a salad of which he was very proud, but the colonel examined it long and doubtfully. As for the doctor, he was sent off with Aurelle to Bailleul to buy some champagne, and insisted on sampling several different brands, which inspired him to give vent to some strange doctrines on things in general on the way home.

He obtained permission to invite his friends Berthe and Lucie to come in at the end of dinner to drink a bumper of champagne in the Mess, and when they entered in their Sunday dresses, the colonel played *Destiny Waltz*, speed 61. The orderlies had hung a great bunch of mistletoe over the door, and the girls asked ingenuously if it was not the custom in England to kiss under the mistletoe.

"Oh, certainly," said the doctor, and with his hands behind his back, he pecked Berthe on the cheek which she turned towards him. Parker, equally nervous, did the same to pretty Lucie, and Aurelle gave them both a good hug in the French way.

"That's fine, mademoiselle?" said the little doctor.

"Yes," said Lucie with a sigh. "We wish it was always Christmas."

"Oh, but why?" said the doctor.

"Think how dull it will be for us after the War," replied Berthe, "when you are all gone! Before, one did not think of it—one saw no one—one worked, one knew no better, but now, without the boys, the village will be empty indeed. My sister and I will not stay here. We will go to Paris or London."

"Oh, but that's a pity," said the doctor.

"No, no," said Aurelle, "you will just get married. You will marry rich farmers, you will be very busy with your beasts and your chickens and you will forget all about us."

"It's easy to say 'get married,' " observed Berthe, "but it takes two for that. And if there are not enough men for all the girls we shall probably get left in the lurch."

"Every man will have several wives," said Aurelle. "You

will be much happier; with one husband between you two, you will only have half the housework to do."

"I do not think I should like it," said Lucie, who was very refined.

But the padre, to whom the doctor had just treacherously translated Aurelle's cynical proposals, indignantly protested.

"*You* ought not to criticize polygamy, padre," said the doctor. "Reread your Bible. What have you to say about old Laban, who, having sold his two daughters to the same man, payable monthly for fourteen years, gave the purchaser in addition two waiting-maids as a bonus?"

"But," said the padre, "I am not responsible for the actions of a doubtful patriarch. I have no sympathy with Laban."

"No more have I," said Aurelle. "This Dufayel of marriage has always profoundly disgusted me, but more on account of his matrimonial methods than for having gone in for the polygamy natural to his tribe. Moreover, is the number of women to be apportioned to one man a question of morals? It appears to me to be a question of arithmetic. If there are nearly as many women as men, monogamy is the rule; if for some reason the number of women is increased, polygamy is perhaps better for the general welfare."

The two girls, who understood this conversation much less than the "promenade" and the "na poo" of the Tommies, went up to the colonel, who talked to them paternally in his gruff way and got the "Caruso" record for them out of its pink cover.

"You have some weird ideas about animal psychology, Aurelle," said the doctor. "If you have observed nature, you would have proved, on the contrary, that the question of the numbers of mates is certainly not a question of arithmetic. With gnats, ten females are born to one male. Now gnats are not polygamous. Nine out of those females die spinsters. It is only the old maids who bite us, from which one sees that celibacy engenders ferocity among insects as well as among women."

"I have known some charming old maids," said Aurelle.

"Indeed!" said the doctor. "But, however that may be, the number of married pairs varies simply according to the way the species feed. Rabbits, Turks, sheep, artists, and, generally speaking, all herbivorous creatures are polygamous; while foxes, Englishmen, wolves, bankers, and, generally speaking, all carnivorous animals are monogamists. That is because of the difficulty which carnivorous animals find in rearing their young until they are strong enough to kill for themselves. As for polyandry, it occurs in wretched countries like Thibet, where several men must unite forces to keep one wife and her progeny."

The howls of Caruso rendered all conversation impossible for a minute, then Aurelle said to Lucie: "The other girls in the village will perhaps find it difficult to get husbands, it is true, but you and your sister need not worry; you are the prettiest, and you will soon have the richest father. You will have fine marriage portions."

"Yes, that's true. Perhaps they will marry us for our money," said Berthe, who was modest.

"I should not care to be married for my money," said Lucie.

"Oh, strange creature!" said the doctor, "you would like to be loved for your face alone, that is to say, for the position in space of the albuminoids and fatty molecules placed there by the working of some Mendelian heredity, but you would dislike to be loved for your fortune, to which you have contributed by your labor and your domestic virtues."

Berthe regarded the doctor nervously and reminded her sister that they had some glasses to wash before going to bed; so they emptied their bumpers and departed.

After a restful silence, Major Parker asked Aurelle to explain the institution of the marriage *dot,* and, when he had grasped it, indignantly replied:

"What? A man receives this splendid gift, a pretty woman, and he exacts money before accepting her? But what you tell me is monstrous, Aurelle, and dangerous. Instead of marrying beautiful and good women who would have beautiful and good children, you marry ugly, quarrelsome creatures provided with a checkbook."

" 'He who has found a good wife has found great happiness,' " quoted the padre, " 'but a quarrelsome woman is like a roof that lets in the rain.' "

"It is wrong to suppose the children of love-matches better made than others," interrupted the doctor, becoming rather warlike, obviously owing to champagne. "Oh, I know the old theory: every man chooses his natural complement, and thus rears children which revert to the average type of the race. Big men like little women, large noses like little snub-noses, and very feminine men fall in love with Amazons.

"As a matter of fact, a nervous, short-sighted, intellectual man marries a pedantic, nervous, short-sighted woman because their tastes are similar. Good riders make acquaintance with girls who hunt, and marry them for their sporting tastes.

"So, far from reverting to the average type, love-matches tend to exaggerate the differences. And then is it desirable for selection to operate? There are very few really brilliant men who have not had at least one madman among their ancestors. The modern world has been founded by three epileptics—Alexander, Julius Caesar and Luther, without mentioning Napoleon, who was not altogether well balanced."

"In a thousand men of genius, how many mad relations?" asked the colonel.

"I can't tell you, sir," said the doctor.

"You can talk nonsense to your heart's content, doctor," said Major Parker. "But as far as I am concerned, if I ever marry, I shall only marry a very pretty woman. What's the name of that charming cinema actress we saw together at Hazebrouck, Aurelle?"

"Napierkowska, sir."

"Oh, yes. Well, if I knew her I would marry her at once. And I am sure that she is if anything better and more intelligent than the average woman."

"My friend Shaw," said the doctor, "says that to desire to be perpetually in the society of a pretty woman, until the end of one's days, is as if, because one likes good wine, one wished always to have one's mouth full of it."

"Rather a flimsy argument," observed the major. "For surely that is better than having it always full of bad wine."

"Anyhow," the doctor replied, "women who exhibit more surely than us the underlying instincts of mankind are far from bearing out your theory; I know very few who make a point of marrying a good-looking man."

"Well, do you know the story about Frazer?" said the major.

"Which Frazer?" said the colonel. "G.R. of the 60th?"

"No, no. A.K. of the 5th Gurkhas—the one who played polo for the regiment in 1900, an awfully good-looking fellow, the finest chin in the army."

"Oh, I know him," said the colonel, "the son of old Sir Thomas. His father sold me a damned good pony, when I was a subaltern, and I only paid 200 rupees for it. Well, what is his story?"

"At the beginning of 1915," said the major, "Frazer, who was crossing London on his way home on leave, went to the theater one evening alone. Towards the end of the first act, he felt vaguely that someone was staring at him. He looked up and saw a woman in a box looking at him. But, owing to the darkness of the theater, he could not distinguish her features.

"In the interval, he tried to see her, but she had withdrawn to the back of her box. During the next two acts she looked at him fixedly. Frazer, decidedly intrigued, was waiting at the exit of the theater, when a magnificent footman approached him, saying, 'A lady wishes to speak to you, sir,' and led him to the door of a carriage which had stopped in a side street.

"'You do not know me, Captain Frazer,' said a very pretty voice, 'but I know you; have you anything to do this evening or will you come to supper with me?' Frazer did what we should all have done."

"He ran away?" said the padre.

"He got into the carriage," said Parker. "He was asked to allow himself to be blindfolded. When the bandage was taken off he found himself in a charming room, alone with the fair unknown, who was *décolletée* and wearing a mask, and who had the most beautiful shoulders in the world!"

"Is this by Dumas *père* or R. L. Stevenson?" asked Aurelle.

"It is a story of what actually happened in January, 1915, and was told me by a man who never lies," said Major Parker. "The house was in silence. No servant appeared, but Frazer, delighted, was offered by the unknown herself what you French call, I believe, *bon souper, bon gîte et le reste.*

"At break of day, she bandaged his eyes again. He told her how much he had enjoyed himself and asked her when he could see her again. 'Never,' she replied, 'and I take it that I have your word of honor as a gentleman and a soldier that you will never try to find me again. But in one year from now, to the day, go back to the same theater where we met, and there will, perhaps, be a letter for you.' Then she saw him into the carriage again, and asked him to keep his eyes blindfolded for ten minutes: when he took off the bandage, he was in Trafalgar Square.

"Frazer naturally moved heaven and earth to get leave in January, 1916, and on the evening of the anniversary of his adventure appeared at the box office of the theater and asked for a stall. 'Have you by any chance a letter for me?' he said, giving his name. The clerk handed him an envelope, and Frazer, eagerly opening it, read this short line: 'It is a fine boy. Thank you.' "

"What is still more strange," said the doctor with sarcasm, "is that another good-looking lad told me the same story some time before the War, and that that time he was the hero of it."

"Then this lady must have several children," said the colonel.

CHAPTER XIII

YOU, pretty shopgirl, whose fresh charm
　　Was once engrossing,
And you, who kept, with strong bare arm,
　　The level-crossing,

And you, the Teacher, you who went
　　In dress less candid,
Or, soft-eyed, o'er your keyboard leant,
　　And slender-handed;

Fair Baker's wife, who had our love,
　　Yet counted pence
As one who had a soul above
　　Their vulgar sense;

All you whose wayside smile could then
　　So quickly chase
The black despond of us poor men
　　Those hateful days!

Who sprawled across your open door
　　And loosed their speech
To tell of hopes and plans in store,
　　Beyond their reach. . . .

You did not always understand,
　　But never mind,
No wiser they, the glitt'ring band
　　We left behind.

No man but thinks his worth impressed
　　Where he desires;
And there, as in a mirror drest,
　　Himself admires.

And Margot, to his talk resigned,
　　One ear in guile lent,
A very Sévigné he'll find
　　So she be silent.

CHAPTER XIV

EXTRACTS FROM AURELLE'S DIARY

Hondezeele, *January 19—*.

MADAME LEMAIRE has presented the Mess with a bottle of old brandy, and the doctor is in very good form this evening. He is the true Irish type; a lover of surprising epigrams.

He says, "We owe to the Middle Ages the two worst inventions of humanity—romantic love and gunpowder." Again, "The whole reason of this War is because the Germans have no sense of humor."

But, above all, you must hear his scientific and precise demonstration of his favorite theory: "Two telegrams contrary in sense, and from officers equal in rank, cancel one another."

January 4th.

Rode with the colonel and Parker. How delicate and clear the atmosphere is in this northern part of France! The colonel was highly indignant to hear that I have never been out hunting.

"You *must*, messiou, it is the only sport. You jump banks as high as your horse. At eighteen I had nearly broken my neck twice. It is most exciting."

"Yes," said Parker, "one day I was galloping in a wood and a branch went into my right eye. It is a miracle I wasn't killed. Another time—"

He described how his horse fell on top of him and broke two of his ribs. Then both of them together, certain of having convinced me:

"You must hunt after the War, messiou."

January 7th.

This morning, I do not know why, some French troops

came through Hondezeele. The village and I were delighted. We like the shrill bagpipes, but no music in the world is like "Sidi-Brahim" and "Sambre-et-Meuse."

I was pleased, too, to be able to show Parker these *Chasseurs à pied,* as all he had seen of our army were old Territorials. He was much impressed.

"They are as fine as the Highlanders," he told me.

And then he described the Lennox as they were when he joined as second lieutenant in Egypt.

"I was forbidden to speak at Mess for six months. An excellent practice! It taught us to realize how humble we were, and the respect due to our elders.

"If some 'swelled head' did not conform to these rules, he soon found his things all packed up in his room, labeled for England. If he still refused to understand, he was called up before a subaltern's court-martial, and heard some home truths about himself.

"It was hard, but what *esprit de corps* and what discipline those rough ways taught us. We shall never see a regiment again like the Lennox of 1914. The officer of today has seen active service, it's true, but as a matter of fact it is quite sufficient in war to have good health and no more imagination than a fish. It is in peacetime that one ought to judge a soldier."

"You remind me," said the doctor, "of the sergeant-major in the Guards who said: 'How I wish the war would finish so that we could have real maneuvers once more!' "

This evening, while the gramophone was raging, I forced myself to translate into French Rudyard Kipling's admirable poem: "If."

I showed it in English to Parker whom it describes so well, and we talked about books. I made the mistake of mentioning Dickens.

"I detest Dickens," said the major. "I never could understand how anyone could find him interesting. His books are all stories of the lower classes and Bohemians. I do not want to know how they live. In the whole of Dickens' works there is not one gentleman. No, if you wish to know the *chef-d'oeuvre* of English novels read *Jorrocks.*"

January 13th.

A little English telephonist who came to mend our apparatus said to me, "Telephones are like women, sir. No one really knows anything about them. One fine day, something goes wrong; you try to find out why, no good, you swear, you shake them up a bit and all is well."

January 14th.

At dinner an Irish colonel remarked:

"I am very annoyed; during my last leave I rented a house for my family, and now my wife writes that it is haunted. The owners really ought to tell one these things."

"Perhaps they did not know it," said our indulgent colonel.

"They knew it very well. When my wife went to complain, they got very confused, and ended by owning up. One of their great-grandmothers has walked from the drawing room to her old bedroom for the last hundred and fifty years. They tried to excuse themselves by saying she was perfectly harmless. That is possible, and I am quite willing to believe it, but it is none the less annoying for my wife. Do you think I can cancel my lease?"

I here risked a sceptical remark, but the whole Mess jumped on me. Irish ghosts are scientific facts.

"But why do phantoms love Irish houses more than others?"

"Because," said the Irish colonel, "we are a very sensitive race and we enter into communication with them more easily."

And he crushed me with technical arguments on wireless telegraphy.

January 15th.

The colonel, having found out this morning that a motor-ambulance was going into Ypres, took me with him. In front of the hospital we found ourselves wedged in by a terrible block of wagons, under a fierce bombardment.

A horse with its carotid artery cut by a bit of shell, and

only held up by the shafts, was writhing in agony close by us. The drivers were swearing. Nothing to do but wait patiently in our car, shaken by explosions.

"Dr. Johnson was right," said the colonel to me. "Whoever wants to be a hero ought to drink brandy."

Then, as a fresh explosion made the débris of the ruined town in front of us tremble, he said:

"Messiou, how many inhabitants were there in Ypres before the War?"

January 20th.

We are going to leave Hondezeele. The red-hats are getting agitated and already one sees the cyclists passing, the natural advance-guard of our migrations.

We were beginning to love this country: the village and the brigade, so distrustful of one another a month ago, had become really quite affectionate. But the gods are jealous.

> *Brigade to march*—tomorrow's sky
>   Will see us on the move,
> The drums and pipes will sing good-bye
>   To every light-o'-love.
>
> The Highlanders, their kilts a-swirl,
>   Like eddies on the sand,
> With steadfast hymn and fiery skirl,
>   Must join the devil's band.
>
> When Victory unveils the sun,
>   Cold earth shall shrine their faith,
> But every field and farm they won
>   Shall know their constant wraith.
>
> And in our Flemish villages . . . .

Interrupted by the arrival of our successors, the Canadians, regarded by Madame Lemaire and her little boy with great suspicion. *That* won't last long.

CHAPTER XV

A GREAT attack was in preparation; it was a terrible secret jealously guarded by headquarters; but Aurelle was informed of it several days beforehand by the German communiqué published in the *Times,* and by Madame Lemaire's little boy, who advised him not to repeat it.

However, the division was soon ordered to occupy one of the sectors in the attack. The padre, optimistic as ever, already foresaw triumphant marches, but the colonel gently reminded him that the objectives were simply a ridge, which in peacetime would be called "a slight undulation in the ground," and two villages already destroyed. The real object was to engage the forces of the enemy, who were at that moment advancing in Russia. But this information only redoubled the enthusiasm of the padre.

"You can say what you like, sir; if we hold this ridge they cannot hold out in the valley, and we shall break through their line. As for the retreat of the Russians, that's capital. The Boche gets farther from his base, lengthens his lines of communications, and he's done."

"He is not," said the colonel, "but he will be one day, and that's all that matters."

The evening of the offensive, Aurelle received orders from the colonel to go and act as liaison officer between the headquarters of the division and some French batteries, which were reinforcing the British artillery in this sector. He wished the Lennox good luck and left them for a day.

He spent the night in the garden of the little château where the general was living. The bombardment thundered on without ceasing. Aurelle walked up and down the paths of this garden, which had been pretty, but was now honeycombed with trenches and dug-outs, while camouflaged huts covered the lawns.

Towards midnight, the rain, the classic rain of an offensive, began to fall in large drops. The interpreter took shelter in a shed with some chauffeurs and motor-cyclists. He always liked to find himself among this class of Englishmen with their strong language and simple minds. These, like the rest, were good fellows, careless, courageous and light-hearted. They hummed the latest music-hall airs from London, showed him photographs of their wives, sweethearts and babies, and asked him when the damned war would be over. They shared on this subject the perfect optimism of the padre.

One of them, a little, quick-witted electrician, asked Aurelle to explain the Alsatian question. And so he told them about Saverne, the march past of the Strasburg students before Kléber's statue, the pilgrimages of the Alsatians to Belfore for the 14th of July Review, and about the young men who at the age of twenty left family and fortune to go to France and become soldiers.

They told him that they could understand anyone loving France: it was a fine country. All the same there were not enough hedges in the landscape. But they appreciated the thrifty qualities of the women, the trees along the road, and the out-of-door cafés. They talked with enthusiasm about Verdun, but many of them had only grasped the idea of the Entente through Carpentier's victory in London.

The day dawned; the rain was now falling in torrents; on the lawn, the grass and soil were trodden into a sticky mass. Aurelle went up to the château; he met an aide-de-camp whom he knew and explained his orders.

"Oh, yes," he was told. "I arranged that myself with the French liaison officer. If the telephone from the batteries happens to get cut, we shall have recourse to you. Go into the signaling room and sit down. In ten minutes from now," he added, "our men go over the top."

The signaling room was the old winter garden. On the wall, a large-scale map of the trenches showed the British lines in black, and those of the enemy in red. At two long tables six telephone operators were installed. Silent officers with red tabs paced calmly up and down the room, and Aurelle thought of one of Major Parker's favorite remarks: "A gentleman is never in a hurry."

As five o'clock struck, the general came in and the officers stood still and said all together:

"Good-morning, sir."

"Good-morning," said the general politely.

He was very tall; his carefully brushed grey hair, neatly

parted, framed his fine features. Gold lace shone on the red facings of his well-cut tunic.

Discovering Aurelle in his corner, he very kindly gave him a little "Good-morning" all to himself, and then he walked slowly, with his hands behind his back, between the two long tables of the telephonists. The noise of the guns had suddenly ceased, and nothing was heard in the room but the authoritative and measured step of the general.

A muffled bell tingled; an operator quietly made a note of the message on a pink form.

"5.5 a.m.," read the general softly, "10th Brigade. Attack begun, enemy barrage not very effective, violent machine-gun fire."

Then he passed the telegram to an officer, who stuck it on a long pin.

"Transmit it to the corps," said the general.

And the officer wrote on a white paper: "5.10 a.m. 10th Brigade reports as follows: Attack begun. Enemy barrage not very effective. Violent machine-gun fire."

He filed a carbon copy on another pin, and handed the original to an operator, who, in his turn, read it into the machine.

Inflexibly and monotonously the white and pink messages slowly accumulated. One brigade was in the enemy's first line trenches, the other had stopped before a concreted nest of machine-guns. The general reinforced them with details from the 3rd Brigade, then rang up the artillery several times to tell them to destroy the pill box. And these orders were transcribed on to the pink and white forms. An officer, standing before the huge map, carefully maneuvered small colored flags, and all this methodical agitation reminded Aurelle of a large banking house on the Stock Exchange.

Towards six o'clock in the morning, a Staff officer beckoned to him, and, leading him up to the map, showed him the emplacement of a French .155 and asked him to go and see the officer, and tell him to destroy at all costs a certain railway cutting in which one or two enemy machine-guns were still firing. The telephone was no longer working.

Outside everything was calm; it was raining and the road was a river of yellow mud. The noise of the guns seemed farther off, but it was only an illusion, because one could see the wicked red light of the shells as they burst over the village in front of the house.

A few wounded, in hasty field-dressings, bleeding and muddy, were coming slowly up to the ambulance in small groups. Aurelle entered a little fir wood; the wet pine-needles seemed delightful walking after the mud. He heard the guns of the French battery quite close, but could not find it. He had been told: "Northeast corner of the wood." But where the devil was the northeast? All at once a blue uniform moved among the trees. At the same moment a gun went off quite close to him, and, turning to the right, he saw the gunners on the edge of the wood well hidden by some thick bushes. A sergeant-major, astride a chair, tunic undone, *képi* pushed back, was in command. The men served the gun cleverly and without hurrying, like skilled workmen. One might have thought it a peaceful, open-air factory.

"Sir," said one of the men, "here is an interpreter."

"Ah, now, perhaps, we shall find out why we can't get an answer from the English," said the sergeant-major.

Aurelle gave him the orders, as the captain was at the observation post, and the lieutenant trying to repair the telephone.

"Right," said the sergeant-major, a native of Lorraine with a quiet, sing-song voice. "We will demolish it for you, young man."

He telephoned to the captain; then, having found the cutting on the map, began his calculations. Aurelle stayed a few moments, glad to find this corner of the battlefield with no false romance, and also to hear French spoken again at last.

Then he took the path back to the château. Cutting across a meadow to find the high road, he approached the battle-field. A brigade of reinforcements was going up in line; he passed it in a contrary direction, with a few wounded to whom he offered a little brandy. The men who were going up to fight looked at the wounded in silence.

A shell whistled above the column; the heads bent like poplars in a wind. The shell burst in a deserted field. Then Aurelle, having passed the brigade, found himself on the road with the informal procession of wounded men. They had fever, they were dirty, they were bloody; but, thankful to be out of it, they hurried at the best pace they could muster towards the haven of white beds.

A company of German prisoners passed, guarded by a few Highlanders. Their terrified eyes, like those of trained animals, seemed to be looking for officers to salute.

As Aurelle arrived at the house, he saw two men in front of him carrying an officer on a stretcher. The officer evidently had some terrible wound, for his body was covered with dressings through which the blood had soaked, and was dripping slowly on to the muddy road.

"Yes, Aurelle, it's I," said the dying man in a strange voice, and Aurelle recognized Captain Warburton. His good-looking, merry face had become grave. "O'Grady will not send me to the Duchess' Hospital this time, messiou," he gasped painfully. "Will you say good-bye to the colonel for me—and let him write home that I did not suffer much. Hope that won't bother you. Thanks very much indeed."

Aurelle, without being able to get out a word, pressed the hand of this maimed boy who had been so fond of War, and the stretcher-bearers carried him gently away.

On arriving at the château he found every one as calm as ever, but very serious. He gave in a report of his mission to the Staff officer, who thanked him absently.

"How is it going?" he asked an operator in a low voice.

"All right," growled the man. "All objectives attained, but the general killed. Would go himself to see why the Second Brigade did not come up—a shell buried him with Major Hall."

Aurelle thought of the grey, smooth hair and fine features of the general, the gold and scarlet of his facings all soiled by the ignoble mud of battles. So much easy dignity, he thought, so much courteous authority, and tomorrow carrion, which the soldiers will trample under foot without knowing. But already, all round him, they were anxiously discussing who would be his successor.

In the evening, he went over to the Lennox with the regiment that was going to relieve them. The first person he saw was the doctor, who was working in a dug-out.

"I don't think the regiment did badly," he said. "I have not seen the colonel yet, but all the men tell me he was a marvel of courage and presence of mind. It appears, messiou, that we have the record number of Germans killed by one man. Private Kemble bayoneted twenty-four. Not bad, is it?"

"No," said Aurelle, "but it's horrible. Have you looked at Warburton, doctor? I met him on the road and he seemed very bad."

"Done for," said the doctor. "And his friend Gibbons died here this afternoon, both legs blown off."

"Oh, Gibbons too. Poor Gibbons! Do you remember, doctor, his talking about his plump little wife? No doubt at this very moment she is playing tennis with her sisters in some lovely English garden. And the bleeding limbs of her husband are there, in that blanket. It's terrible, doctor, all this."

"Pooh!" answered the doctor, going to wash his hands, which were covered with blood. "In three months you will see her portrait in the *Tatler*: 'The beautiful widow of Captain Gibbons, M.C., who is shortly to be married to——' "

CHAPTER XVI

CHANSON DU COMTE DE DORSET.   (1665)

CERTES, just now, dear ladies, some
  Curled juvenile, your deary,
Is but too apt that song to hum
  Of which ye never weary—

                    Fa, do, sol, re.

The while he smooths each glist'ning tress,
  With studied grace and air he,
With amorous glance and soft address,
  Is seeking to ensnare ye.

                    Fa, do, sol, re.

Meanwhile our battered vessel rocks
  To wild wave-music eerie,
And whistling wind our sort bemocks
  With doleful *Miserere.*

                              Fa, do, sol, re.

Vainly, to chase the vision pale
  Of Fate that needs no query,
We crouch behind our bulwarks frail
  And croon in chorus dreary

                              Fa, do, sol, re.

Devoted to th' infernal shades
  By ladies' light vagary,
The dismalest refrain invades
  Our hearts in sad quandary.

                              Fa, do, sol, re.

How now! Are ye so slight of soul,
  Of love are ye so chary,
Already you forget the rôle,
  The text we never vary?

                              Fa, do, sol, re.

Bethink you of those Roman dames
  In household virtue wary,
And, spinning wool, invoke the names
  Of Powers tutelary.

                              Fa, do, sol, re.

Can ye not, then, be such as they?
  O hearken to the prayer he
Intones, your lover far away,
  And ill-content to share ye!

                              Fa, do, sol, re.

For if inconstant you should prove,
  With wave and weather veer ye,
Beware lest this soft song of love
  Should turn to *Dies Irae.*

                              Fa, do, sol, re.

CHAPTER XVII

THE Lennox Highlanders, when the brigade was relieved, were sent for six days to a muddy field near Dickebusch. Dr. O'Grady and Aurelle shared a tent, and dined together, the first evening, at the inn of the *Trois Amis*.

On their return, the stars shone brightly in a dark-blue velvet sky. The soft moonlight lay on the grass of the meadows. A few tents in which a light was burning resembled great white lanterns ; round the bivouac fires, blown about by the wind, the men sat swearing and singing.

"War makes light of time," said the doctor, "it is eternal and unalterable. This camp might be Caesar's, the Tommies round their fires, talking of their wives and their dangers, their boots and their horses, like the legionaries of Fabius or the veterans of the Grand Army. And, as in those days, on the other side of the hill, repose the barbarous Germans by their unyoked chariots."

The burgundy of the *Trois Amis* inspired the doctor to hold forth like this.

"This tent is six thousand years old," he said, "it belongs to the warlike Bedouins who founded the empires of Babylon and Carthage. The restlessness of the ancient migrating people inspired them with a longing for the desert every year, and sent them forth from the city walls on profitable raids. It is this same force, Aurelle, which each summer, before the war, covered the deserted shores of Europe with nomadic tents, and it is the dim recollection of ancestral raids which, on August 1, 1914—holiday time, Aurelle, the time of migrations—incited the youngest of the barbarians to let loose their Emperor on the world. It is an old comedy which has been played for two thousand years, but the public still seem to take an interest in it. It is because there is always a fresh audience."

"You are pessimistic this evening," said Aurelle.

"What do you call pessimism?" said the doctor, painfully pulling off his stiff boots. "I think that men will always have passions, and that they will never cease to go for one another at regular intervals with the most energetic means which the science of their time can procure for them, and the best chosen weapons with which to break each other's bones. I think that one sex will always try to please the other, and that from this elementary desire will eternally be born the need to vanquish rivals. With this object, nightingales, grasshoppers, prima donnas and statesmen will make use of their voices; peacocks, niggers and soldiers, of bright colors; rats, deer, tortoises and kings will go on fighting. All that is not pessimism, it is natural history!"

While talking the doctor had got into his sleeping-bag, and had seized a little book from a shelf made out of a biscuit box.

"Listen to this, Aurelle," said he, "and guess who wrote it.

" 'My regrets about the War are unceasing, and I shall consent to admire your invincible general when I see the fight ended under honorable conditions. It is true that the brilliant successes which are your delight are also mine, because these victories, if we would use fortune wisely, will procure for us an advantageous peace. But if we let the moment pass when we might appear to give peace rather than receive it, I much fear that this splendid achievement will vanish in smoke. And if fate sends us reverses I tremble to think of the peace which will be imposed on the conquered by an enemy who has the courage to refuse it to the conquerors.' "

"I don't know," said Aurelle, yawning. "Maximilian Harden?"

"Senator Hanno at the Senate of Carthage," said the doctor triumphantly. "And in two thousand three hundred years some Negro doctor, finding after the Great African War a speech by Lloyd George, will say, 'These old sayings are sometimes very true.' Your formidable European War is about as important, Aurelle, as the fights between two ant-heaps in the corner of my garden in Ireland."

"It is much more than that to us," said Aurelle, "and it appears to me that the sort of sentiments it gives rise to are not animal. Do you think that ants are patriotic?"

"Most certainly," replied the doctor, "the ants must be

extremely patriotic. With them the warriors are highly fed by a race of servitors. Every season their armies set out to steal the eggs of the weaker species. Workers are hatched from them, born slaves in a foreign country. The military citizens are thus delivered from the slavery of work and these soldiers cannot even feed themselves. Shut up without honey, and without their nurse-slaves, they die of hunger. That is what is called civil mobilization. And if this war lasts long enough, one day, Aurelle, you will see a new human species appear: soldiermen. They will be born with helmets and armor, impervious to bullets and provided with natural weapons; the Suffragettes will be the sexless slaves who will feed these warriors, while a few queens will, in special institutions, bring national infants into the world."

Thus discoursed the doctor, in the friendly silence of the camp by the soft light of the moon; and Aurelle, who had gone to sleep, saw visions of enormous ants in khaki marching by, commanded by the little doctor.

CHAPTER XVIII

THE orderlies brought the rum, sugar, and boiling water. The padre began patience, the colonel played *Destiny Waltz,* and Dr. O'Grady, who in times of peace was doctor at an asylum, talked about lunatics.

"I had the care of a rich American who thought he was surrounded by a belt of poisoned gas," he said. "In order to save his life, he had a special bed made for himself surrounded by a cage of white wood. He passed his days in this safe shelter, dressed in nothing but a red bathing suit, writing a book in twenty thousand chapters on the life and works of Adam. His room had a triple door on which he had carved, 'Gas carriers are warned that there are wolf-traps inside.' He sent for me every day, and when I went in he always said, 'I have never seen any creatures so stupid, so wicked, so rotten, or so dense as English doctors.' "

" 'I have never seen,' " repeated the padre with great

satisfaction, " 'any creatures so stupid, so wicked, or so dense as English doctors.' "

"Upon which," continued the doctor, "he turned his back on me, and, clothed in his red bathing suit, set to work again at the twenty-thousandth chapter on the works of Adam."

"Here, messiou," interrupted the colonel, who was examining some official papers, "is some work for you," and he passed over to Aurelle a thick bundle of papers covered with multi-colored seals.

It commenced thus:

"From the Stationmaster at B—— to the Military Superintendent of the Station at B——

"I have the honor to inform you that Mademoiselle Héninghem, gate-keeper at Hondezeele, complains of the following facts: the English soldiers camped along the railway line are in the habit of performing their ablutions in the open air, which is a shocking sight for the lady in question, who, from the nature of her work, cannot avoid seeing them. I shall be obliged if you will give orders that this regrettable state of affairs shall be put a stop to as soon as possible."

(Signature.)

(Seal.)

"From the Military Superintendent of the Station at B—— to the Superintendent at W——

"Transmitted to the proper quarter."

(Signed.)

(Seal.)

"The Superintendent W—— to the D.A.D.R.T.

"I shall be obliged if you will give orders that the camp in question be surrounded with a fence of sufficient thickness to render the visibility at fifty yards' distance practically nil."

"That last man," said Aurelle, "is a polytechnician."

The padre asked what that was.

"A polytechnician is a man who believes that all beings, alive or dead, can be precisely defined and submitted to an algebraic calculation. A polytechnician puts, on the same plane, victory, a tempest, and love. I knew one who, commanding a fortress and having to draw up some orders in case of aerial attack, began thus: 'The Fortress of X—— will be attacked by an aerial engine when a vertical line from the engine to the earth finds the center of the fortification,' and so on."

"Do not abuse the Polytechnic, Aurelle," said the doctor. "It is the most original of your institutions and the best. The personal cult of Napoleon is so well preserved that each year France presents two hundred Lieutenant Buonapartes to the astonished Government."

"Go on translating, messiou," said the colonel.

"D.A.D.R.T. to the Superintendent.

"This does not concern me but a division that is resting. You must address your claim to the A.G. by the intermediary of the French Mission."

(Signed.)

(Seal.)

"Superintendent —— to the Base Commandant G.H.Q.

"I have the honor to forward herewith, for any action you consider necessary, a Memorandum concerning a complaint from Mademoiselle Héninghem of Hondezeele."

(Signed.)

(Seal.)

And so it went on: Base Commandant to the French Mission; French Mission to the Adjutant-General; A.G. to the Army; Army to the Corps; Division to the Brigade; Brigade to the Colonel of the Lennox Highlanders. And it was signed with illustrious names, Colonel, Chief Staff Officer for the General, Brigadier, Major-General; thus the modest scruples of Mademoiselle Héninghem of Hondezeele were clothed, in the course of a long journey, with purple, gold and glory.

"This is a tiresome business," said Colonel Bramble solemnly. "Parker, answer it, will you, like a good chap."

The major wrote for several minutes, then read out:

"This regiment having left the Camp at Hondezeele two

months and a half ago, it is unfortunately impossible to take
the measures desired in the matter. Moreover, having ascertained the great cost of a fence of sufficient height, I beg
to suggest that it would be more advantageous to the allied
Governments to replace the gate-keeper at Hondezeele by
a person of mature age and proved experience, to whom the
spectacle described herewith would be inoffensive and even
agreeable."

"No, Parker, no," said the colonel firmly, "I shall not sign
that. Give me a piece of paper. I will answer myself."

He wrote simply:

"Noted and returned.
"BRAMBLE,
"Colonel."

"You are a wise man, sir," said Parker.

"I know the game," said the colonel. "I have played it
for thirty years."

"Once upon a time," said the doctor, "there were two
officers who, on the same day, each lost something belonging to His Majesty's Government. The first one mislaid a
coal-bucket; the second a motor-lorry. Now you must know,
Aurelle, that in our army an officer has to pay for anything
which he may lose by negligence out of his own pocket. The
two officers, therefore, received notices from the War Office
advising one that he would have to pay three shillings, and
the other that a thousand pounds would be stopped from his
pay. The first one wished to defend himself; he had never
had any coal-buckets, and tried to prove it. He stopped his
promotion, and in the end had to pay the three bob. The second, who knew a thing or two, just wrote at the bottom of
the paper, 'Noted and returned,' and sent it back to the
War Office. There, following an old and wise rule, a clerk
lost the correspondence and the officer never heard anything more of *that* little matter."

"That isn't a bad story, doctor," said Major Parker; "but
in the case of the loss of property belonging to the Government there is a much better method than yours—Colonel
Boulton's method.

"Colonel Boulton commanded an ammunition depot. He was responsible, among other things, for fifty machine-guns. One day he noticed that there were only forty-nine in the depot. All the inquiries, and punishment of the sentries, failed to restore the missing machine-gun.

"Colonel Boulton was an old fox and had never acknowledged himself in the wrong. He simply mentioned in his monthly return that the tripod of a machine-gun had been broken. They sent him a tripod to replace the other without any comment.

"A month later, on some pretext or other, he reported the sighting apparatus of a machine-gun as out of order; the following month he asked for three screw-nuts; then a recoil plate, and bit by bit in two years he entirely destroyed his machine-gun. And correspondingly, bit by bit, the Army Ordnance Department reconstructed it for him without attaching any importance to the requisitions for the separate pieces.

"Then Colonel Boulton, satisfied at last, inspected his machine-guns, and found fifty-one.

"While he had been patiently reconstructing the lost gun, some damned idiot had found it in a corner. And Boulton had to spend two years of clever manipulation of his books to account for the new gun which had been evolved out of nothing."

"Messiou," said the colonel, "do you remember the gatekeeper at Hondezeele? I should not have thought it of her."

"No more should I," said Aurelle. "She was very pretty."

"Messiou!" said the padre.

CHAPTER XIX

"DOCTOR," said the padre, "give me a cigar."

"Are you aware, padre, that my cigars were rolled on the bare thighs of the young girls of Havana?"

"O'Grady," said the colonel severely, "I consider that remark out of place."

"Give me one all the same," said the padre. "I must

smoke a cigar to help me find a text for my sermon. The quartermaster made me promise to go and see the motor-drivers who are at the back, and I don't know what to talk to them about."

"Look here, padre, I will give you an appropriate text; lend me your Bible a moment. Ah, here it is. Listen! 'But David said, Ye shall not do so, my brethren, with that which the Lord hath given us. . . . but as his part is that goeth down to the battle, so shall his part be that tarrieth by the stuff; they shall part alike.' "

"Admirable," said the padre, "admirable! But tell me, O'Grady, how is it that an old sinner like you knows the Holy Scriptures so well?"

"I studied the Book of Samuel a good deal from an asylum doctor's point of view," said the doctor. "Saul's neurasthenia interested me. His attacks are very well described. I have also diagnosed the madness of Nebuchadnezzar. They were two very different types. Saul was apathetic and Nebuchadnezzar violent."

"I wish you would leave Nebuchadnezzar alone," said the colonel.

"I am very much afraid of asylum doctors," said Major Parker. "Violent, depressed, or apathetic, we are all mad, according to them."

"What do you call mad?" said the doctor. "I certainly can see in you, and in the colonel, and Aurelle, all the phenomena which I observed in the asylum."

"Ugh!" said the colonel, horrified.

"But I do, sir. Between Aurelle, who forgets the war by reading Tolstoi, and some of my old friends who thought they were Napoleon or Mahomet, there is a difference in degree but not in nature. Aurelle browses on novels from a morbid desire to live the life of someone else; my patients substitute for their miserable life that of some great personage whose history they have read and whose lot they envy.

"Oh, I know your objections, Aurelle. You know, all the time you are dreaming of the loves of Prince Bolkonsky, that you are the Interpreter Aurelle, attached to the Lennox

Highlanders, but when Queen Elizabeth is scrubbing the floor in my office, she does not know that she is Mrs. Jones, charwoman, of Hammersmith. But incoherence is not the monopoly of madness: all the main ideas of a sane man are irrational erections built up, for better or worse, to express his deepest feelings."

"Parker," said the colonel, "can you think of anything to stop him?"

"A No. 5 grenade, sir," said the major.

But the doctor went on imperturbably:

"One of my patients was a country gentleman, who after being a model of piety for the first part of his life suddenly became an atheist. He gave carefully thought-out reasons for it, and discoursed with a good deal of erudition on questions of doctrine, but the only true cause of his conversion to the wrong side was because his wife ran away with the clergyman of his village. Oh, I beg your pardon, padre, you don't mind, do you?"

"I? I have not been listening to you for ages," said the padre, who was dealing out patience.

"It is just the same thing," continued the doctor, turning to the docile Aurelle, "with a man who is too refined for the class in which chance has placed him. At first he is simply jealous and unhappy. Influenced by these feelings, he becomes violently critical of society in order to account for his hate and disappointment.

"Nietzsche was a genius because he delighted in persecution. Karl Marx was a dangerous maniac. It is only when the feelings of discontent which he tries to explain coincide with those of a whole class, or a whole nation, that the impassioned theorist becomes a prophet, or a hero; while, if he confines himself to explaining that he would rather have been born an Emperor, they shut him up."

"Moral," said the major, "shut up all theorists."

"And the doctor," said the colonel.

"No, not all," said the doctor. "We treat the subject just as the ancients did. All primitive people thought that a lunatic was possessed by a spirit. When his incoherent words more or less accord with the moral prejudices of the time, the spirit is a good one, and the man is a saint. In the opposite case, the spirit is evil and the man must be suppressed. It is just according to the time and place and the doctors, whether a prophetess would be worshipped as a priestess or ducked as a witch. Innumerable violent lunatics have escaped the cells, thanks to the War, and their very violence has made heroes of them. And in every Parliament there are at least five or six undisputed idiots who got elected for their madness, through the admiration of their constituents."

"Say five or six hundred," said Major Parker, "and it will be the first sensible thing you have said tonight."

"That's because my madness agrees with yours on that subject," said the doctor.

"Doctor," said the colonel, "you understand treatment by suggestion, don't you? I wish you would calm down your hospital sergeant a bit. He is so nervous that he begins to tremble and becomes perfectly speechless if I speak to him. I really believe I terrify him. See what you can do, like a good fellow."

Next morning, Dr. O'Grady sent for Sergeant Freshwater to his tent and talked kindly to him.

Freshwater, a lean albino with heavy, stupid eyes owned that he lost his head whenever the colonel came near him.

"Well, my friend," said the doctor, "we will cure you of that in five minutes. Sit down there."

He made some passes to create an atmosphere favorable to suggestion, then began:

"You are not afraid of the colonel, you know he is a man just like you and me—you rather like talking to him. Look closely at his face when he speaks to you. His mustache is always cut a little too short on the left side."

The doctor went on like this for a quarter of an hour describing the rugged features and funny ways of the colonel, then sent away the sergeant, telling him that he was cured, and not to forget it the first time he met his commanding officer.

A few hours later, Colonel Bramble, going out for his lunch, met the hospital sergeant on one of the duck-boards used for going through the camp. Freshwater stepped on one side, saluted, and began to laugh silently.

"Whatever is the matter, sergeant?" said the astonished colonel.

"Oh, sir," replied Freshwater in fits of laughter, "I cannot help laughing when I look at you, you have such a funny face!"

The colonel, in a few well-chosen words, destroyed the doctor's learned suggestions forever; then, establishing himself in front of the tinned lobster, he complimented O'Grady on his miraculous cure.

"I have never seen," said the padre, "any creatures so stupid, so wicked, so rotten, or so dense as English doctors."

"Medicine is a very old joke," said Major Parker, "but it still goes on. Now, doctor, tell the truth for once: what do you know more than we do about illnesses and their remedies?"

"That's right," said the padre, "attack his religion; he often attacks mine."

"When I was in India," said the colonel, "an old army doctor gave me for every malady the remedy which just suited me. For palpitations of the heart, a large glass of brandy; for insomnia, three or four glasses of port after dinner; for stomachic disorders, a bottle of dry champagne at each meal. And, as long as one was feeling well, whisky and soda."

"Excellent, sir," said Aurelle. "Before the War I drank nothing but water and I was always ill; since I have been with you I have adopted whisky and I feel much better."

"Yes, you look it," said the colonel. "I had a friend, Major Fetherstonhaugh, who began to have fits of dizziness when he was about forty; he went to see a doctor who thought it was the whisky and advised him to drink milk for a time; well, in ten days he was dead."

"And a good thing too," said the padre.

"But I expect—" began the doctor.

"Happy are those who expect nothing," said the padre, "for they shall not be disappointed."

"What, you too, padre!" said the doctor. "Take care; if

you ruin doctors by your malevolent remarks, I shall found a society for the exportation to the Colonies of mechanical idols and ovens for cooking missionaries."

"That is an excellent idea," said the padre. "I must see about it."

CHAPTER XX

THE brigade, kept in reserve for the division, was ordered to go and camp at H——. As a dentist measures the extent of a cavity at a glance, the men of the Lennox, expert in bombardments, cast a professional eye over the village. Round the château and the church it was done for: houses in ruins, pavements torn up, trees smashed. The weaving factory had been badly damaged. The rest was not so unhealthy, a little knocked about, perhaps, but habitable.

The house where Colonel Bramble had established his Mess had already been hit by a shell. It had burst in the garden, breaking the window-panes and marking the walls. Madame, a dear little old lady, made light of these blemishes, which had depreciated her house in value.

"Oh, just a shell, monsieu l'officier!" she said. "Quite a small shell; I put the base of it there on my mantelpiece. It's nothing, as you can see. True, they make a mess of everything, but I am not afraid of them!"

The colonel asked her how many windows had been broken.

"I don't like this house," said the padre, as they sat down to dinner.

"The life of a soldier," replied the colonel, "is one of great hardship, not infrequently mingled with moments of real danger."

"Be not dismayed, padre," said the doctor. "Shells fall like drops of water: if it rains much the whole pavement gets wet."

"The Lennox Mess has always been lucky," said Major Parker.

"Luck is nothing," said the doctor.

"One can see you are not a gambler," remarked Aurelle.

"One can see that you are not a mathematician," said the doctor.

The padre expostulated:

"What? Luck nothing? How about little Taylor, killed by a shell in Poperinghe Station at the very moment that he was arriving at the front for the first time! You don't call that bad luck?"

"Not more than if an old habitué like me was wiped out by a whizz-bang, padre. You are astonished at Taylor being killed the first minute, just as you would be surprised if, in a lottery of a million tickets, Number One should win, although that number had obviously as much chance as, say, 327,645. Someone must be the last man killed in this war, but you will see that his family will not think it ordinary."

"You are a fanatic, O'Grady," said Parker, "you must have an explanation for everything; there are more things in heaven and earth than are dreamed of in your philosophy. I believe, myself, in good luck and bad luck because I have noticed it: I believe in presentiments because I have had them, and events have confirmed them. When I was being sent home, after the Transvaal War, I got an order to embark on a certain ship. Well, two days before it started I suddenly had a presentiment that I must avoid sailing in that ship at all costs. I went sick and waited a fortnight longer. The transport I missed was completely lost and no one ever knew how. Then again, why are you so certain, doctor, that aspirin will cure your headache? Because aspirin has cured it before. Where's the difference?"

"The major is right," said Aurelle. "To say that you do not believe in a man's bad luck because you cannot find it at his autopsy, is like saying that the tuner has taken the piano to pieces, and therefore Mozart had no soul."

The quartermaster, who was dining with them that evening, threw his weight into discussion:

"There *are* things that cannot be explained, doctor. For instance, I hit you in the face: you shut your eye—why?"

There was an astounded silence.

"Another instance," remarked the padre at last. "Why is it that if there is a pause in the conversation, it is always twenty minutes to, or twenty minutes past, the hour?"

"But that's not true," said the doctor.

"It was true this time, anyhow," said Aurelle, looking at his watch.

"It may be once or twice," said the doctor irritably, "but it cannot always happen."

"All right, doctor, all right," said the padre. "You notice it for several days and I think you will change your mind."

The colonel said:

"My men tell me that if a shell falls on a dug-out where there are gunners and infantry, the latter are killed and the gunners are spared. Why?"

"But it is not true, sir."

"And why must one never light three cigarettes with the same match?"

"But you may, sir, it does not matter a bit."

"Ah, there I disagree with you, doctor," said the colonel. "I am not superstitious, but I would not do that for anything in the world."

"Why do people dressed in green always lose at Monte Carlo?" said Aurelle.

"But it is not true!" roared the doctor, exasperated.

"It is easy to argue like you," said Parker. "Everything you do not agree with is not true."

"There are," said the padre, "no creatures so wicked and so dense as English doctors."

"Messiou," said the colonel, "are the gunners equally lucky in the French Army?"

"I have often remarked it," said Aurelle, who liked Colonel Bramble very much.

The colonel therefore triumphed, and tried to put an end to the discussion, which bored him.

"I am so very sorry," he said, "I cannot give you the gramophone tonight. I have no more needles."

"That *is* a pity," said the padre.

The window-panes shook; a big gun went off close to the house. Aurelle went to the window and saw behind a farm, silhouetted in black against the orange twilight of the sky, a yellowish smoke, slowly dispersing.

"There's the old man beginning to strafe again," said the padre. "I don't like this house."

"You will have to put up with it, padre; the Staff captain won't give us another; he's a boy who knows his own mind."

"Yes," said the colonel, "he is a very nice boy too; he is one of Lord Bamford's sons."

"His father, the old Lord, was a fine rider," said Parker.

"His sister," replied the colonel, "married a cousin of Graham, who was a major in our first battalion at the beginning of the War, and is now a brigadier-general."

Aurelle, foreseeing that such an interesting subject, so rich in the possibility of unexpected developments, would occupy the entire evening, tried to scribble some verses, still meditating on luck and chance.

> Pascal, thou said'st if Cleopatra's nose
> Had shorter been, we were not—where we are . . . .

A new and formidable detonation put a subtle rhyme out of his head; discouraged, he tried another:

> I trust you will not look askance
>   For once I deal in platitude;
> Tonight, to laws of luck and chance
>   The Mess defines its attitude.

Another shell fell so close that the colonel got up suddenly.

"They are beginning to bombard the château again," he said. "I am going to see where that one fell."

Major Parker and the doctor followed him into the street, but Aurelle, who was again rhyming, stayed with the padre, who had just begun the same patience for the fourteenth time that evening. The three officers had gone about a hundred yards when another explosion took place behind them.

"That one was not far from the Mess," said the doctor. "I am going to tell Madame to go down into the cellar."

He retraced his steps and found a new shell-hole in front of the house. The house seemed all right; through the broken window the doctor saw the padre and called out to him:

"A near thing that time, padre. Are you all right? Where is Aurelle?"

But the padre did not move: with his head leaning on his arms crossed over the scattered cards, he appeared to be gazing vaguely at the doctor, who entered at a bound and touched the padre on the shoulder.

He was dead. A piece of shell had entered his temple, which was bleeding slowly. Aurelle had fallen on the floor. He was unconscious and covered with blood, but the doctor, bending over him, found that he still breathed. As he was unfastening his tunic and shirt, the colonel and Parker arrived with their measured tread and stopped abruptly at the door.

"The padre has been killed, sir," said the doctor simply. "Aurelle is hit, too, but I don't think it is serious. No, it's his shoulder—nothing much."

The colonel groaned sympathetically.

Parker helped O'Grady to lay the Frenchman on a table; a crumpled piece of paper attracted the colonel's attention; he picked it up and read with difficulty:

> Why must you ever close my eyes
> Before you kiss my lips?

"What is it all about?" he said.

"It belongs to Aurelle," said the doctor.

The colonel carefully folded the little sheet of paper and slid it respectfully into the young Frenchman's pocket. Then, after the doctor had finished dressing the wound and had sent for an ambulance, they laid the padre on Madame's humble bed. They all took their hats off and stood silent for some time contemplating the strangely softened features of the childlike old man.

The doctor looked at his watch; it was twenty minutes past nine.

CHAPTER XXI

AURELLE, on leaving hospital, was attached, while convalescent, to the English colonel, Musgrave, who commanded
a supply depot at Estrées, a little village well behind the line.
He missed the evenings with the Lennox Mess, but buying
fodder and wood took him some way out into the pretty
undulating country with its clear streams, and he loved
Estrées, hiding its innumerable belfries among the flowery
hills.

It was a very antique city, and in its youth, in the time of
the *seigneurs* of Estrées, had played an important part in
the affairs of France. For several hundred years she had
defended her ramparts against the troops of the Kings of
England, and from her walls she could see those same
soldiers today camped about her, this time as familiar and
courteous guests. Her tenacious burghers had repulsed both
Leaguers and Spaniards with equal success. She now slept
in smiling old age, having seen too many things to be surprised any more, while still retaining from the times of her
glory her casket of beautiful mansions, built among courts
and gardens with the noble simplicity of line dating from
the best periods.

Colonel Musgrave and his officers inhabited the large and
handsome house of the Dutch merchant, Van Mopez, whom
Colbert had established at Estrées to introduce the art of
weaving and dyeing cloth. Aurelle liked to go and sit in the
garden and read a History of Estrées written by Monsieur
Jean Valines, correspondence member of the Amiens Acad-
emy, and author of *Nouvelles observations sur les miracles
de la chapelle d'Estrées.*

This excellent work contained accounts of the great rejoicings and high festivals with which Estrées the Faithful
had received the Kings, when they came to kneel and worship at the feet of the miraculous image in the Chapel of St.
Ferréol.

The municipal worthies, between the royal visits, prudently and carefully preserved the white and blue draperies

embroidered with fleurs-de-lis, and the decorations of painted scenery.

The Revolution had rather upset these domestic arrangements; the fleurs-de-lis had to be removed and a red fringe sewn along the blue and white draperies, so that the square of Saint-Ferréol could be decorated at a small cost for the fête of the Supreme Being. Aurelle loved the description:

"The cortège, preceded by music and drums, consisted first of a half-company of the National Guard carrying a banner on which was inscribed: 'Up with the People, down with Tyrants.'

"Then came the mothers of families carrying their infants in their arms; children of both sexes clothed in the most beautiful ornaments of their age—innocence and candor; young girls adorned with their charms and virtues; and the members of that Society so dreaded by traitors, in which were united the defenders of the truth, the upholders of public opinion, and the indefatigable guardians of the people.

"The whole cortège gathered at the foot of a mound erected in the square of Saint-Ferréol. There, the people of Estrées swore fidelity to the laws of nature and humanity, and subsequently a group of figures representing Despotism and Imposture were consumed by flames; Wisdom arose out of the ashes and on his shield was written: 'I guard the Republic.' "

Aurelle turned over some pages, very few, for, as Monsieur Jean Valines said, the happy sterility of the archives of Estrées during the Revolution recorded no other facts worthy of notice than two fêtes, a fire, and a flood. Next came the visit of the First Consul. He came to Estrées accompanied by his wife and several general officers, and was received by the authorities under a triumphal arch, erected at the Saint-Ferréol Gate, adorned with this inscription: "The Grateful Inhabitants of this City swear Allegiance and Fidelity to the Conqueror of Marengo."

The Major presented the keys of the town on a silver dish covered with bay leaves. "I take them, *citoyen maire,* and I return them to you," replied Buonaparte.

"The National Guard lined the route and cries of 'Long

live Buonaparte! Long live the First Consul!' were repeated
enthusiastically a thousand times. The First Consul visited
the Van Mopez factory and distributed a day's pay among
the workmen. The day ended with illuminations and a
brilliant ball.

"A short time after his marriage with Marie-Louise,
Napoleon came back, accompanied by the Empress. The
square of Saint-Ferréol was a magnificent spectacle, decorated with red and white draperies and garlands of green
leaves. A triumphal arch had been erected with the inscription: *'Augusto Napoleoni Augustoeque Mariae Ludovicae
Strataville semper fidelis.'* "

A few more pages farther on and it was March, 1814; for
six days no couriers got through to Estrées from Paris, and
then she heard of the fall of the Emperor.

"At three o'clock in the afternoon, the magistrates, assembled in the Town Hall, summoned the inhabitants with
the ringing of bells. The Mayor appeared on the balcony
of the large hall and proclaimed the allegiance of the town
to the restored Bourbons. The spectators received this speech
with oft-repeated cries of 'Long live the King!' 'Long live
Louis XVIII!' and all put on the white cockade.

"The news soon came that Louis XVIII had landed at
Calais and that he would pass through Estrées. A guard of
honor was formed and a triumphal arch was erected at the
Saint-Ferréol Gate. It bore this inscription: *'Regibus usque
suis urbs Stratavilla fidelis.'*

"The clergy from every parish approached to compliment
the King, and the Mayor presented the keys of the town on
a silver dish adorned with fleurs-de-lis. The King replied,
'Monsieur le maire, I take the flowers, and give you back the
keys.' Then the sailors and footmen unharnessed the horses
from the carriage, and drew him themselves into the town.
The excitement of the crowd was impossible to describe;
every house was decorated with blue and white draperies
and green garlands, mottoes and white flags, covered with
fleurs-de-lis.

"The King was present at a *Te Deum* sung in Saint-
Ferréol, and repaired, still drawn by sailors, to the Abbey of
Saint-Pierre, where he was to lodge the night."

The evening drew slowly on; the quaint, thick lettering of the old book was becoming indistinct, but Aurelle wanted to finish the melancholy history of these inconstant people. Skipping the triumphal entry of Charles X, he came to the July insurrection.

"On the 29th of July, 1830, there were no newspapers; but letters and a few travelers arriving from Paris announced that the tricolor flag had been hoisted on the towers of Notre-Dame. A few days later they learnt that the fighting had stopped, and that the heroic population of the capital remained in possession of all their outposts.

"Louis-Philippe, accompanied by the Dukes of Orleans and Nemours, soon after passed Estrées on his way to Lille. He was received under a triumphal arch by the Mayor and Corporation. Every house was hung with draperies in the three colors. An immense crowd filled the air with their acclamations. The King arrived at the square of Saint-Ferréol, where the National Guard and several companies of *douaniers* awaited him.

"The various corps of the urban guards in their best clothes; the strangeness of the rural guards, with a large number of Napoleon's old soldiers in their ranks with their original uniforms; the intrepid seamen of Cayeux carrying in triumph their fishing prizes, ten old tricolor banners; the sailors, with their carbines, bandoliers and cutlasses in their hands, all made the gayest of spectacles, and the picturesque fête delighted the King and the officers of his staff."

There Jean Valines' book concluded, but Aurelle, while watching the garden fading slowly in the twilight, amused himself by imagining what followed. A visit from Lamartine, no doubt; then one from Napoleon III, the triumphal arches and inscriptions, and quite lately, perhaps, Carnot or Fallières receiving from the mayor, in the square of Saint-Ferréol, the assurance of the unalterable devotion of the faithful people of Estrées to the Republic. Then in the future: unknown governors, the decorations, perhaps red, perhaps blue, until the day when some blind god would come and crush with his heel this venerable human ant-hill.

'And each time,' he mused, 'the enthusiasm is sincere and the vows loyal, and these honest tradesmen rejoice to see passing through their ancient portals the new rulers, in the choice of whom they have had no part.

'Happy province! You quitely accept the Empires which Paris brings forth with pain, and the downfall of a government means no more to you than changing the words of a speech or the flowers on a silver dish. If Dr. O'Grady were here he would quote Ecclesiastes to me.'

He tried to remember it:

"What profit hath a man of all his labor which he taketh under the sun?

"One generation passeth away, and another generation cometh; but the earth abideth for ever.

"The thing that hath been, it is that which shall be; and that which is done is that which shall be done; and there is no new thing under the sun."

"Aurelle," said Colonel Musgrave, who had quietly approached, "if you want to see the bombardment after dinner, go up to the top of the hill. The sky is all lit up. We attack tomorrow morning."

And a distant muffled thundering floated on the calm evening air. A melancholy and ancient peal of bells rang out from the Spanish belfry in the market-place. The first stars twinkled above the two ironical towers of the church of Saint-Ferréol, and the proud old town fell asleep to the familiar sound of battle.

CHAPTER XXII

IN the soft evening air the garden drowses;
J'ai du bon tabac thinly sounds afar;
The bells are chiming slow, and, farther, rouses
The distant, instant, deep-felt voice of war.

One star stands out upon the darkling sky;
Against the west the tree-tops draw, outlined,
A woodcut, Japanese, the moon behind;
A voice, singing; dogs bark; the day is by.

Life seems so sweet, so calm the valley's mood,
That, did not bitter memories undeceive,
On such a night almost could one believe
This false world was of God—that God was good.

But even now, where the faint hills decline,
Under this very sky, now calm as when
Its peace was real—past that near confine,
The gates of hell yawn wide for living men.

CHAPTER XXIII

COLONEL MUSGRAVE was drinking his coffee in the handsome *salon* of the merchant, Van Mopez; he opened a pink official telegram and read:

"Director of Commissariat to Colonel Musgrave. Marseilles Indian Depot overcrowded meet special train 1000 goats with native goatherds find suitable quarters and organize temporary farm."

"Damn the goats!" he said.

His job being to feed Australians, he thought it hard that he had to bear in addition the consequences of the religious laws of the Hindus. But nothing troubled Colonel Musgrave long; he sent for his interpreter.

"Aurelle," he said, "I am expecting a thousand goats this evening; you will take my motor and scour the country. I must have a suitable piece of ground in five hours and a small building for the shepherds. If the owner refuses to let you hire them, you will commandeer them. Have a cigar? Good-bye."

Having thus disposed of this first anxiety, he turned to his adjutant.

"We now want an O. C. Goats!" he said. "It will be an excellent reason for getting rid of Captain Cassell, who arrived yesterday. *Captain!* I asked him what he did in peacetime—musical critic of the *Morning Leader!*"

So that is how Captain Cassell, musical critic, was promoted goatherd-in-chief. Aurelle found a farmer's wife whose husband had been called up, and he persuaded her, at the cost of much eloquence, that the presence of a thousand goats in her orchards would be the beginning of all sorts of prosperity. He went in the evening to the station with Cassell to fetch the goats, and they both passed through the town at the head of the picturesque flock, herded by ancient Indians, who looked exactly like the shepherds in the Bible.

Colonel Musgrave ordered Cassell to send him a hundred goats per day for the front. After the fourth day Cassell sent over a short note by one of the children from the farm, announcing, as if it were quite a natural thing, that his flock would be exhausted the next day and asking for another contingent of goats.

On opening this extraordinary missive, the colonel was so choked with rage that he forgot to proclaim, according to custom, that Cassell was a damned fool. The numbers were too simple for an error to be possible. Cassell had received one thousand goats; he had sent off four hundred, he ought to have six hundred left.

The colonel ordered his car and commanded Aurelle to take him to the farm. A pretty, deeply cut road led them there. The buildings were in the rustic, solid style of the end of the eighteenth century.

"It is a charming spot," said the interpreter, proud of his find.

"Where is that damned fellow Cassell?" said the colonel.

They found him in the kitchen having a French lesson from the farmer's daughter. He got up with the easy grace of a rural gentleman whom friends from town had surprised in his hermitage.

"Hullo, colonel," he said, "I am very glad to see you."

The colonel went straight to the point:

"What's this damned letter that you sent me this morning? You received a thousand goats; you sent me four hundred of them. Show me the others."

The ground behind the farm sloped gently down to a wooded valley; it was planted with apple-trees. Near a stable, sitting in the mud, the Hindu shepherds tasted prematurely the joys of Nirvana.

A horrible smell arose from the valley, and, coming nearer, the colonel saw about a hundred swollen and rotting carcases of goats scattered about the enclosure. A few thin kids dismally gnawed the bark of the apple-trees. In the distance, among the copses which covered the other side of the valley, one could see goats which had escaped browsing on the young trees. At this lamentable sight, Aurelle pitied the unfortunate Cassell.

The colonel maintained a hostile and dangerous silence.

"Isn't it beautiful, colonel," said the musical critic with soft and stilted speech, "to see all those little white spots among the green?"

.   .   .   .

"Could not one," suggested Aurelle on the return journey, "ask the advice of a competent man? Perhaps goats cannot stand sleeping out of doors in this damp climate, and perhaps also they are not being fed properly."

The colonel frowned.

"In the South African war," he said after a silence, "we used a large number of oxen for our transport. One day these damned oxen started dying by hundreds, and no one knew why. Great excitement at headquarters. Some general found an expert, who, after boring the whole army with his questions, ended by declaring that the oxen were cold. He had noticed the same sickness in the north of India. There they protected the beasts by making them wear special clothing. Any normal individual with common sense could see that the oxen were simply overworked. But the report followed its course, and arrived at general headquarters, and from there they wired to India for a few thousand rugs for cattle.

"So far all went well, the oxen died as fast as ever, the well-paid expert had a damned good time—up to the arrival of the rugs. It is very easy to put clothing on an Indian cow who waits patiently with lowered head. But an African bullock—you try, and see what it's like. After several trials, our drivers refused to do it. They sent for the expert and said to him, 'You asked for rugs for the beasts: here they are. Show us how to put them on.' He was damned lucky to get out of hospital in six months."

That same evening another pink telegram arrived from the Director of Commissariat:

"Goats arrive at the front half dead pray take steps that these animals may have some wish to live."

Colonel Musgrave then decided to telegraph to Marseilles and ask for an expert on goats.

The expert arrived two days later, a fat farmer from the South, sergeant of Territorials. With the help of Aurelle, he had a long conversation with the colonel.

"There is one thing," he said, "that goats cannot get on without, and that is heat. You must make very low wooden sheds for them; without any openings; let them stew in their own juice, and they will be happy!"

He remarked to the interpreter when the colonel had gone, "Didn't I tell them a good tale about their goats, *hé?* In the South they live out in the open and are as well as you or I. But let's talk seriously. Couldn't you get your English to manage an extension of leave for me, to look after their beasts, *hé?*"

They had begun to build the huts described by the man from the South, when the Indian Corps wrote to Colonel Musgrave that they had discovered a British expert whom they were sending him.

The new seer was an artillery officer, but goats filled his life. Aurelle, who looked after him a good deal, found out that he regarded everything in nature from the point of view of a goat. A Gothic cathedral, according to him, was a poor shelter for goats; not enough air, but that could be remedied by breaking the windows.

His first advice was to mix molasses with the fodder which was given to the animals. It was supposed to fatten them and cure them of that distinguished melancholy which the Indian troops complained of. Large bowls of molasses were therefore distributed to the Hindu shepherds. The goats remained thin and sad, but the shepherds grew fat. These results surprised the expert.

Then he was shown the plans of the huts. He was astounded.

"If there is one thing in the world that goats cannot do without," he said, "it is air. They must have very lofty stables with large windows."

Colonel Musgrave asked him no more. He thanked him with extreme politeness, then sent for Aurelle.

"Now listen to me," he said: "you know Lieutenant Honeysuckle, the goat expert? Well, I never wish to see him again. I order you to go and find a new farm with him. I forbid you to find it. If you can manage to drown him, to run over him with my car, or to get him eaten by the goats, I will recommend you for the Military Cross. If he reappears here before my huts are finished, I will have you shot. Be off!"

A week later Lieutenant Honeysuckle broke his leg by falling off his horse in a farm-yard. The Territorial from Marseilles was sent back to his corps. As for the goats, one fine day they stopped dying, and no one ever found out why.

CHAPTER XXIV

ONE morning, Aurelle, seeing an English Staff officer come into his office in a gold-peaked hat with a red band, was surprised and delighted to recognize Major Parker.

"Hullo, sir! I *am* glad to see you again! But you never told me about that"—and he pointed to the signs of authority.

"Well," said the major, "I wrote and told you that Colonel Bramble had been made a general. He now commands our old brigade and I am his brigade major. I have just been down to the Base to inspect our reinforcements, and the general ordered me to pick you up on the way back and bring you in to lunch. He will send you back this evening. Your colonel is quite agreeable. We are camped for the moment next to the village where the padre was killed; the general thought you would like to see his grave."

Two hours later they drew near the front and Aurelle recognized the familiar landmarks: the little English military village with a policeman holding up his hand at every corner; the large market town, scarcely bombarded, but having here and there a roof with its beams exposed; the road, where one occasionally met a man in a flat steel helmet loaded like a mule; the village, the notice boards, "This road is under observation," and suddenly, a carefully camouflaged battery barking out of a thicket.

But Major Parker, who had seen these things every day for three years, discoursed on one of his favorite themes:

"The soldier, Aurelle, is always done in by the tradesman and the politician. England will pay ten thousand a year to a lawyer or a banker, but when she has splendid fellows like me who conquer empires and keep them for her, she only gives them just enough to keep their polo ponies. And again—"

"It is just the same in France—" began Aurelle; but the car stopped suddenly opposite the church of a nightmare village, and he recognized H——. "Poor old village, how it has changed!" he said.

The church, ashamed, now showed its profaned nave; the few houses still standing were merely two triangles of stone sadly facing one another; and the high building of the weaving factory, hit by a shell in the third story, was bent over like a poplar in a storm.

"Will you follow me?" said the major. "We have had to put the H.Q. of the brigade outside the village, which was becoming unhealthy. Walk twenty paces behind me; the sausage balloon is up and it's no good showing them the road."

Aurelle followed for a quarter of an hour through the bushes, and suddenly found himself face to face with General Bramble who, standing at the entrance to a dug-out, was watching a suspicious airplane.

"Ah, messiou!" he said. "That's good!" And the whole of his rugged red face lit up with a kindly smile.

"It will be like a lunch in the old days," he continued, after Aurelle had congratulated him. "I sent the Staff captain out with the interpreter—for we have another interpreter now, messiou—I thought you would not like to see him in your place. But he has not really replaced you, messiou; and I telephoned to the Lennox to send the doctor to lunch with us."

He showed them into the Mess and gave Major Parker a few details of what had been happening.

"Nothing important; they have spoilt the first line a bit at E 17 A. We had a little strafe last night. The division wanted a prisoner, so as to identify the Boche reliefs—yes, yes, that was all right—the Lennox went to fetch him. I have seen the man, but I haven't had their written report yet."

"What, not since last night?" said Parker. "What else have they got to do?"

"You see, messiou," said the general, "the good old times are over. Parker no longer abuses red hats. No doubt they are abusing him in that little wood you see down there."

"It is true," said Parker, "that one must be on the Staff to realize the importance of work done there. The Staff is really a brain without which no movement of the regiment is possible."

"You hear, messiou?" said the general. "It is no longer the same; it will never be the same again. The padre will not be there to talk to us about Scotland and to abuse bishops. And I have no longer got my gramophone, messiou. I left it to the regiment with all my records. The life of the soldier is one of great hardship, messiou, but we had a jolly little Mess with the Lennox, hadn't we?"

The doctor appeared at the entrance to the tent.

"Come in, O'Grady, come in. Late as usual; there is no creature so wicked and so dense as you."

The lunch was very like those of the good old times—for there were already good old times in this War, which was no longer in the flower of its youth—the orderlies handed boiled potatoes and mutton with mint sauce, and Aurelle had a friendly little discussion with the doctor.

"When do you think war will be finished, Aurelle?" said the doctor.

"When we win," cut in the general.

But the doctor meant the League of Nations: he did not believe in a final war.

"It is a fairly consistent law of humanity," he said, "that

men spend about half their lives at war. A Frenchman, called Lapouge, calculated that from the year 1100 to the year 1500, England had been 207 years at war, and 212 years from 1500 to 1900. In France the corresponding figures would be 192 and 181 years."

"That is very interesting," said the general.

"According to that same man Lapouge, nineteen million men are killed in war every century. Their blood would fill three million barrels of 180 litres each, and would feed a fountain of blood running 700 litres an hour from the beginning of history."

"Ugh!" said the general.

"All that does not prove, doctor," said Aurelle, "that your fountain will go on running. For many centuries murder has been an institution, and nevertheless courts of justice have been established."

"Murder," said the doctor, "never appears to have been an honored institution among primitive peoples. Cain had no reason to care for the justice of his country, if I mistake not. Besides, law courts have not suppressed murderers. They punish them, which is not the same thing. A certain number of international conflicts might be settled by civil tribunals, but there will always be wars of passion."

"Have you read *The Great Illusion?*" said Aurelle.

"Yes," said the major, "it's a misleading book. It pretends to show that war is useless, because it is not profitable. We know that very well, but who fights for profit? England did not take part in this war to conquer, but to defend her honor. As for believing that Democracies would be pacific, that's nonsense. A nation worthy of the name is even more susceptible than a monarch. The Royal Era was the age of gold, preceding the Iron Age of the people."

"There's an argument just like the old days," said the general. "Both are right, both are wrong. That's capital! Now, doctor, tell me the story about your going on leave and I shall be perfectly happy."

After lunch, they all four went to see the padre's grave. It was in a little cemetery surrounded by weeds; the ground broken up here and there by recent shell-holes. The padre lay between two lieutenants of twenty. Cornflowers and other wild plants had spread a living mantle over all three graves.

"After the war," said General Bramble, "if I am still alive, I shall have a stone carved with 'Here lies a soldier and a sportsman.' That will please him."

The other three remained silent, restraining their emotion with difficulty. Aurelle seemed to hear, in the murmuring summer air, the undying strains of *Destiny Waltz* and saw the padre setting out once more on horseback, his pockets bulging with hymn-books and cigarettes for the men. The doctor meditated: " 'Where two or three are gathered together, there I will be in the midst of them.' What a profound and true saying! And how the religion of the dead still lives."

"Come," said the general, "we must go, the Boche sausage is up in the air, and we are four; it is too many. They tolerate two, but we must not abuse their courtesy. I am going on up to the trenches. You, Parker, will take Aurelle back, and if you want to go with them, doctor, I will tell your colonel that I have given you leave for the afternoon."

The three friends passed slowly across the silent plains, which only a few months before had been the formidable battlefield of the Somme. As far as the eye could see, there were low, undulating hillocks covered with thick, coarse grass, groups of mutilated tree-trunks marking the place of the famous wood, and millions of poppies made these dead fields glow with a warm and coppery light. A few tenacious rose-trees, with lovely fading roses, had remained alive in this wilderness, beneath which slept the dead. Here and there posts, bearing painted notices, like those on a station platform, recalled villages unknown yesterday, but now ranking with those of Marathon or Rivoli: Contalmaison, Martinpuich, Thiepval.

"I hope," said Aurelle, looking at the innumerable little crosses, here grouped together as in cemeteries, there isolated, "that this ground will be consecrated to the dead who won it, and that this country will be kept as an immense rustic cemetery, where children may come to learn the story of heroes."

"What an idea!" said the doctor. "No doubt the graves

will be respected; but they will have good crops all round them in two years' time. The land is too rich to remain widowed; look at that superb lot of cornflowers on those half-healed scars."

And truly, a little farther on, some of the villages seemed, like convalescents, to be tasting the joy of life once more. Shop windows crowded with English goods in many-colored packets brightened up the ruined houses. As they passed through a straggling village of Spanish aspect the doctor resumed:

"Yes, this is a marvelous land. Every nation in Europe has conquered it in turn; it has defeated its conqueror every time."

"If we go a little out of the way," said Parker, "we could visit the battlefield of Crécy; it would interest me. I hope you are not annoyed with us, Aurelle, for having beaten Philippe de Valois? Your military history is too glorious for you to have any resentment for events which took place so long ago."

"My oldest resentments do not last six hundred years," said Aurelle. "Crécy was an honorably contested match; we can shake hands over it."

The chauffeur was told to turn to the west, and they arrived on the site of Crécy by the same lower road taken by Philippe's army.

"The English," said Parker, "were drawn up on the hill facing us, their right towards Crécy, their left at Vadicourt, that little village you see down there. They were about thirty thousand; there were a hundred thousand French. The latter appeared about three o'clock in the afternoon, and immediately there was a violent thunderstorm."

"I observe," said the doctor, "that the heavens thought it funny to water an offensive even in those days."

Parker explained the disposition of the two armies, and the varying fortunes of the battle. Aurelle, who was not listening, admired the woods, the quiet villages, the yellowing grass of the fields, and saw in imagination swarms of men and horses riding up to the assault of this peaceful hill.

"Finally," concluded the major, "when the King of France

and his army had left the field of battle, Edward invited the principal corps commanders to dinner, and they all ate and drank with great rejoicings because of the good luck which had befallen them."

"How very English, that invitation to dine at the King's Mess," said Aurelle.

"Then," continued Parker, "he ordered one Renaud de Ghehoben to take all the knights and clerks who knew heraldry—"

"The units," said the doctor, "will render to His Majesty's H.Q., not later than this evening, a nominal roll of all barons who have passed their heraldry test."

"And commanded them to count the dead, and to write down the names of all the knights whom they could recognize."

"The adjutant-general will compile a return of noble persons stating who have been killed, including their rank," said the doctor.

"Renaud found eleven princes, thirteen hundred knights and sixteen thousand foot soldiers."

Heavy black clouds were showing up against the brilliant sunshine: a storm was coming over the hill. By the valley of Renaud's clerks, they climbed up on to the summit and Parker looked for the tower from which Edward had watched the battle.

"I thought," he said, "that it had been made into a mill, but I don't see one on the horizon."

Aurelle, noticing a few old peasants, helped by children, cutting corn in the next field, went up to them and asked them where the tower was.

"The tower? There is no tower in these parts," one of them said, "nor mill either."

"Perhaps we are wrong," said the major. "Ask him if this is really where the battle was."

"The battle?" replied the old man. "What battle?"

And the people of Crécy turned back to their work, binding into neat sheaves the corn of this invincible land.

THE WEIGHER OF SOULS

(Translated by Hamish Miles)

I

I HAVE hesitated a long time before setting down this story. I am aware that it will astonish those who have been dearest to me, and be distasteful to more than one of them. Some will doubt my good faith, others my good sense. My own thoughts would have been the same had I not been the accidental, and protesting, eyewitness of the facts I am about to relate. So conscious am I of their apparent absurdity that I have never mentioned them even to my closest intimates. And if my mind is now made up to break this silence, it is because I do not feel that I have the right to leave to destruction after my own death the sole object remaining as evidence of this strange dream.

Before my readers reject Dr. James's theories as altogether improbable, I would ask them to recall what I believe to have been the extreme cautiousness of my mind. Like all men I have had my passions and weaknesses; I have tried to safeguard my judgment. In science, in metaphysics, in politics, and even in my sentimental life, I have made a point of never mistaking my wishes for proofs. I am far from having always succeeded, but perhaps that constant circumspection will be counted in my favor at a moment when I shall stand in every need of credence.

There is a second argument in my favor: the facts I have to narrate are surprising, but their nature is not impossible to verify. A few simple experiments, which can be easily repeated by any physicist, biologist or doctor, will show that James's theories, even if they are regarded as absurd, were based upon actual observations. Why did I not continue these experiments myself? Why have I not made them known until after my death? It is not very easy for me to explain. The main factor, I think, was shyness, together with a natural distaste for occupying myself with certain problems. Circumstances had made me a writer, not a scientist. I had access to neither a hospital nor a laboratory. I was reluctant to get into touch with men to whom I was one of the profane, in order that I might draw their attention to phenomena which, as I knew, would contradict their ideas. I regret my weakness, and I should be happy if the publication of this memoir were to inspire in some adventurous minds a desire to follow my hapless friend in the exploration of a new world, the knowledge of which might well lead to results of great significance.

.   .   .   .

I knew Dr. James during the War. We first met in a muddy Flanders field, and amidst a group of cheerful and healthy Englishmen his gaunt, prominent cheek bones and the look of torment on his face at once impressed me. He had been attached to the medical services of the division with which I served as French liaison officer. We immediately became friendly, and notwithstanding the horror of those days and scenes, the months which I spent in the Ypres Salient in his company left me with memories that might almost be termed enjoyable. Between our two camp beds a biscuit case served as table and library. At night, when sleep was denied us by the shells screaming their way overhead toward Poperinghe and the clacking of the soaked canvas in the wind, we held muttered converse about madmen and poets. I liked my companion. Beneath his casing of cynicism I caught glimpses of the bold and tender spirit within. So reticent was he that I shared his daily life for months on end without knowing whether he had either wife or children.

The armistice cut short this friendship, as it did so many others. For a year we exchanged letters, and I thus learned that James was on the staff of one of the London hospitals. Then one of us (which, I couldn't now say) failed to answer a letter. James became an image still entangled with my

memories, but an unreal image, like that of a character in
a novel. And in the end I ceased to think about him, even
in dream, until the spring of 1925.

During that year I had occasion to make a long stay in
London for some researches at the British Museum. I was
there alone, rather tired and depressed by too much continuous work. One morning the sunshine was so bright that
I had not the courage to immure myself in the reading
room. For a moment or two I stood watching the pigeons
under the Greek colonnade of the museum, as friendly and
as distant as those of Saint Mark's. I stood in a brown study.
The realization was forced on me that solitude, healthy
enough for a short time, was becoming intolerable. Yet I
did not lack English friends—why hadn't I tried to look
them up? Wouldn't it be pleasant to spend the evenings
with such an intelligent fellow as Dr. James? I had forgotten his address, but it is never hard to trace a doctor; and
entering the reading room, I discovered from a medical
directory that H. B. James, M.D., was on the resident staff
of Saint Barnaby's Hospital. I decided to drop my work for
that morning, and to go and hunt up my friend.

Saint Barnaby's Hospital lies south of the Thames, in the
crowded region that stretches beyond Blackfriars Bridge.
To cross the river thereabouts always impresses me in a
strange and compelling way. The Thames there is the
frontier of two worlds. One leaves the Gothic and Renaissance London, the London of chessboard squares, of the tree-
lined embankments beneath the great hotels, of the red
stream of busses, for a city of factories and warehouses,
bare walls, and blunt chimney stacks. And the contrast that
morning struck me the more forcibly as, just when I was
crossing the bridge, a great cloud suddenly obscured the
sun. In a gloomy, stormy light I reached the slime-covered
bankside where men were loading stranded barges with
sacks of cement. Along the thoroughfare roared the metallic
din of tramcars and steam tractors. Alongside the pavement seethed a wretched street market. I was entering the
territory of a different people.

A policeman told me how to reach Saint Barnaby's.
Situated on the river's edge, the hospital seemed to me like

a refuge amidst all the sordid houses and the blind walls of warehouses. Like so many London buildings, it resembled one of those edifices in romantic engravings, with long white streaks emphasizing the black violence of the shadows, but it was enlivened here and there by little splashes of vivid color—the green of turf, the lavender-blue uniform of a nurse, the bright red dressing gowns of three convalescents taking their first stroll. Above the iron gates a large streamer displayed an inscription to the effect that Saint Barnaby's was supported by voluntary contributions and that at the present moment there was a deficit of thirty thousand pounds. I entered and asked the porter whether Dr. H. B. James was attached to the hospital.

"Dr. James?" he said. "Certainly, sir. . . . At this time you'll probably find him in the residents' lodge. . . . Straight under the memorial arch, and first on your left."

I obeyed, and found a small detached block, likewise of smoke-blackened white stone, but covered with ivy and Virginia creeper. A board at the foot of the stairs showed the names of the doctors, each of them followed by the indication "IN" or "OUT." At the top of the list I read: "DR. H. B. JAMES, 1ST FLOOR, ROOM 21. IN." I went up, and found my friend's name inscribed on the wooden plate of one of the doors. Then suddenly I felt anxious—in fact, almost shy. Would he be pleased at seeing me after such long oblivion? Should I merely find myself alone again, after a few polite remarks, in that dismal cluster of chimneys and slums? I knocked, and with an unconscious movement took hold of the door knob. It did not turn. It seemed to be held fast from within. A voice, that once-familiar grating voice that seemed torn by the wind from rusted scrap iron, came in what struck me as a dry tone:

"Just one moment, please."

In the ensuing silence I heard hasty footsteps, the noise of sliding rings from a hurriedly pulled curtain, a squeal rather like that of a small animal pinched or hit by mistake, and then a clinking of glasses being thrown against each other. Water flowed into a basin, gentle and irritating. Standing in front of the door I waited, vaguely uneasy. What was James doing? Had I interrupted some operation, a dressing, an examination? It seemed unlikely. James was not a surgeon, and in any case he would not have brought a patient to his own room. Was he rising late after being on night duty? Had I wakened him? At last the water ceased, steps came towards me, the door knob turned beneath my hand, and through the half-opened door I saw the doctor's head. He was even more gaunt than during the War. His eyes, with deep hollows beneath the orbits, shone with a troubled and as it were veiled gleam; in the expression there was something haggard which I found extremely painful. For a moment he hesitated before picking on the exact memory that fitted his unexpected caller, then smiled and opened the door wide. I saw that he was wearing a white overall.

"Hullo, my boy! What the deuce are *you* doing in England? You're the last person I'd have expected to see this morning!"

The room was simply furnished: a camp bed, two chairs, a big leather armchair, and a few shelves, some laden with books, the rest hidden by a green canvas curtain, the same one, no doubt, that I had heard sliding on its rod. In one corner stood a hand basin full of soapy water. On the mantelpiece, several photographs of a young woman. James offered me the armchair and handed me a cigarette box, but he kept looking round with an air of such anxiety that I wondered if there could be a third person hidden in the room. Then he made an effort to talk, with just the air of feigned interest that might be assumed by one interrupted in some dubious occupation and trying to assume ease of manner.

"Well, well!" he said. "You certainly seem to have dropped me since you became an historian. . . . I read that last book of yours, although you didn't send me it. . . . Not bad. I shouldn't have thought you had it in you. . . . But books apart, what's been happening to you?"

I had arrived full of pleasure at seeing again a man of whom I had been fond, a man, too, who had given me some of my keenest intellectual enjoyment. But I felt vexed and so ill at ease that my pleasure was completely spoiled. I saw that James and I had almost nothing to say to each other. We had known each other as members of a group which had long ceased to exist. Of our 1918 soul, nothing survived. Our common anguish regarding the outcome of the War, our common affection for wounded friends, were sentiments as dead as the superficial cells which had then formed our earthly framework. To the self who had just entered this room, the James who dwelt there was a being almost as completely a stranger as any random passer-by I might have stopped in Piccadilly. I felt that the only way of again reaching the deeper and more stable layers in him was to confess my disappointment.

"It's an odd thing, James," I said, "but do you remember an evening of ours at Ypres when you told me about the dissociation of personality in madness? I feel something very like that at this moment! I came to your room to find a Self which no longer exists, and I am vainly longing for the moment of madness that might allow me to be pleased at seeing you. . . ."

Such a remark would have sufficed to rouse the James I had once known to a discourse at once learned and humorous. But he shrugged his shoulders wearily, lit a cigarette, and sank into one of the chairs, still looking anxiously round.

"Ah, well!" he sighed. "It's a long time since I gave up worrying about dissociations and sublimations. . . . I look after people with cancer, and heart disease and lung troubles. . . . The Port of London occasionally sends me compatriots of yours, seamen. . . ."

At that instant, from behind the green curtain, there came a sound that is never forgotten by any who have heard it—the scampering of a rat, a swift, dry sound accentuated by the hard claws of the feet. Suddenly I had visions of a dug-out which I once shared with James in a railway cutting.

"Hullo!" I said laughingly, "do you keep rats? That's something to stir up common memories for us!"

"Rats?" he said, rising with a look of displeasure. "How do you suppose there would be rats in a hospital? You're suffering from hallucinations, my boy. . . . I say, I'm awfully sorry, but we can't stay here. . . . It's time for me to go round my wards. Would you like to come with me? It might interest you."

I was now definitely embarrassed.

"Are you sure I shan't be in the way?" I said. "I can easily come back some other time."

"No," he answered, in a tone of mingled good will and irony. "No, you aren't in my way now. . . ."

He stepped quickly over to the sink, and taking a little soapy water, wiped a red smear from the edge of the basin.

II

SAINT BARNABY'S Hospital struck me as one of the least gloomy that could be imagined. The floors of the wards were tiled in black-and-white squares, the red beds were trimly ranged, the windows had their flowers; and oases of healthy freshness were set in this realm of sickness by the nurses, almost all of them pretty and kindly, in their blue print dresses. Each ward was ruled over by a ward sister, recognizable by the deeper blue of her belt.

"Nothing to report, sister?" James asked.

"I'd like you to have a look at number 216, doctor. The fever's not going down. . . ."

He went over to the bed. Turning over the case-sheet hung above the patient's head, he made an effort to remember the history of the illness, and ordered a change of treatment in a mournful, tired voice. In the women's ward, I was struck by his indifference. In myself the sight of a sick woman (especially if she be young and pleasing) has al- always inspired an ardent sense of pity, mingled perhaps with sensuality. I realized that a doctor entering these rooms would not, as I did, experience a sensation at once agonizing and grateful, a feeling of invaded intimacy and melting compassion; yet it surprised me to see how insensitive my companion was to the little blandishments of some of these dying women. There was one girl, deathly pale under her long, loosened hair, who attempted a smile as we passed, only to fall back upon her pillow, gasping for breath.

"Poor child!" I said to James.

"Which?" he said. "Oh, yes. . . . 318. No hope for her. . . ."

In the male wards several patients were out of bed, standing grouped in their red jackets round the beds or the flower-laden tables. There was a dock strike in progress at the time, and many of the patients were slightly injured men who stood there arguing politics and religion amongst themselves in the weighty tone of Hyde Park orators. I saw my friend's eyes soften as he spoke to one strikingly handsome lad of fifteen.

"Is that you, sonny?" he said. "No more giddiness? You can go out tomorrow. . . . Anything to report, sister?"

"I don't think 413 will get through the night, doctor. He doesn't open his eyes any longer."

James went over to a corner bed where an old man was lying. His thin cheeks and nostrils seemed to be sucked in toward the inside of his body. He was breathing very fast. His ruddy-white beard had not been shaved for several days. James took the sick man's pulse; he was unconscious and showed no reaction.

"You're right, sister," he said with sudden animation. "He won't last the night. . . . I'll warn Gregory. Don't bother about anything. . . . In any case I'll come in and see him during the day. Get him a little camphorated oil: it will keep him going until the evening."

I was taken aback by this sudden change in my friend. His excitement now seemed to equal his previous indifference.

"I must go and see the post-mortem clerk," he said. "Come along with me; that will interest you."

"What is the post-mortem clerk?" I asked.

"Forgotten your Latin? He's the assistant responsible for seeing to the autopsy of the corpse after a patient dies. Ours is a queer little man called Gregory."

We went down three flights of stairs. James pushed back a heavy door laden with bolts, and we entered an amphitheater capable of holding about twenty onlookers, the white walls coated with a shiny varnish, and with four dissecting tables in the center. The air was impregnated with an unpleasant smell of formaldehyde. I gave a start when a small figure of a man seemed to rise with diabolic abruptness from the middle of the amphitheater. He repelled me from my first glimpse of him. And yet his appearance was quite commonplace, the points of his waxed mustache twisting spirally up towards his gold-rimmed glasses. When James mentioned this clerk of the corpses I had imagined, for some reason or other, a sort of romantic executioner; and I was shocked by this polite, tradesmanlike vulgarity in conjunction with the idea of death.

"Morning, Gregory," said the doctor. "This is a French friend of mine who is going over the hospital. . . . I came in to warn you that we shall certainly have number 413 tonight."

"Very good, doctor," said the little man. "I'll come this evening. Everything will be ready. Ten o'clock?"

"Yes, about ten," said James. "A little earlier if you can."

"And by the way, doctor," asked Gregory in a lowered voice, "you aren't forgetting that you owe me for the last two?"

James looked all round with the same anxious glance that had surprised me in his room, and taking two notes from his wallet he handed them to Gregory. The latter eyed me through his spectacles.

"Perhaps," he said, slowly folding the notes, "the French gentleman would like to see our installation?"

I murmured some unintelligible remark. The smell of this room was beginning to give me qualms, and I was afraid of making myself look foolish by fainting.

"Our organization," the little man went on complacently, "enables us to deal, in this room and that next door, with as many as eight corpses daily. It is quite enough—except in midsummer, because the babies crowd me up then. . . . And yet, sir, with methodical handling, even in the busy season, I can keep up. . . . can't I, doctor? I've done as many as four on the same table. . . . Feet here and head there. . . . Hard work, I can tell you! No, no, don't go this way out, sir. You haven't seen the best. . . ."

He turned toward the iron door let into the varnished

wall, on which a notice was pasted: *"Professor Simpson wishes to have hearts intact. The greatest care must be taken."* Bolts creaked. Slowly the door turned. I was caught by a sense of mortal chill. I must have been rather pale, for James took my arm and gave me a close look. Going down a few steps, we reached a large, brick-walled cellar. In the center of the refrigerating room stood a metal apparatus which looked like a baker's oven, a boiler, or more exactly, with its long projecting rods, a gigantic waffle iron. Gregory gave me a glance, signed to me with an air of hidden understanding as if he were on the point of giving me a wonderful present, and then, with remarkable agility, opened two doors and pulled one of the rods. I almost cried out loud, for he had drawn forward to where we stood a long platform on which lay a naked woman.

How lovely she was, that dead creature! I shall never forget the unearthly whiteness of that body, on which the points of the breasts laid twin stains of pale pink. Her eyes were closed. A sad, lofty smile gave shape to a delicious mouth. How had such a woman come to die in an outlying hospital? One would have liked to know her, to console her, to help her. . . . Gregory and James stood motionless, eying me.

"Do you recognize her, doctor?" said Gregory. "It's that Russian girl. . . . They're waiting for the relatives to claim her. . . ."

He pushed back the rod with an abrupt jerk, thrusting platform and body into the black metal machine, and said with an air of pride:

"We can keep them indefinitely in this cold. . . . Would you like to see a man?"

"No, thanks," I said. "I'd like to get outside."

James took my arm again, kindly this time.

"I'll take you up to my room," he said, "and you shall have a glass of port. You don't look well. . . . And look, Gregory—is that fixed for this evening?"

At that moment a muffled bell sounded in the amphitheater: *tak-tak . . . . tak-tak-tak-tak. . . .*

"Two-four," said Gregory. "That's for you, doctor."

"Excuse me," said James, "I must leave you for a mo-

ment. . . . Yes, we all have our own signals on these bells.
Mine is two-four. . . . There are bells like that in every
ward and in our rooms too. . . . All I have to do now is to
telephone to the lodge, and they'll tell me where I'm
needed. . . . You wait here for me."

"I'd rather see you somewhere else, doctor. Will you dine
with me tonight? I'm staying in a delightful little hotel in
the city. . . ."

"Tonight?" he murmured absently. . . . "Tonight? Yes,
at a pinch, I can get someone to take my place. . . . I, too,
should very much like to have a talk. Only you heard just
now—I must be back at ten o'clock. If you're willing to dine
early, about seven, I can come."

"I'll expect you . . . . Johnson's Hotel. . . ."

High up in the amphitheater the buzzer was repeating:
tak-tak, tak-tak-tak-tak.

III

THE proprietor of Johnson's Hotel prided himself on having
installed neither central heating nor electric light; but a
huge fire of logs blazed in the hall fireplace, silver candle-
sticks gleamed on the dining-room table, the servants were
silent and respectful, and the visitor felt that to them he
was not a number but a man. I asked the head waiter to
give me for this dinner the small private dining room; I
liked its light oak paneling, and on coming in about seven
o'clock, I was struck by a sense of surprising intimacy. On
the mahogany of the table a vase of jonquils shone in the
soft light of the candles. When James arrived a moment
later, I noticed with pleasure that he too responded to the
charming simplicity of the setting.

"Ah!" he said, standing warming his hands in front of
the fire, "it takes a Frenchman to discover corners of old
England in the middle of London. What a good idea of
yours! I needed a rest so badly. . . . Strictly speaking, I
don't deal with the out-patients, but the list is so heavy on
Mondays that I give my colleagues a hand if I can."

"Why are there more patients on Monday?"

"Oh, that's easy enough! In our poor districts, Monday is the day when the rent-collector calls for the week's money. The women contrive not to be at home, and so as to have an excuse they bring their children along to us. You ought to see that some day; it's incredible! Some of them leave their brats on the benches and go for a drink at the pub opposite. After the consultation they have to be found and brought back, all drowsy with beer, and made to pick out one from the kids who've been left behind. . . . Besides, there are the Sunday accidents, fights, and of course my own patients. . . . It's a stiff day."

"Sit down, James. . . . We'll try to put the hospital out of your mind. Do you remember that Burgundy we used to drink at Amiens? I've ordered you the very same."

Wartime memories occupied us during the soup, and then James retired into an impregnable taciturnity. I remembered that he used often to emerge from such fits of abstraction with one of those dazzling, paradoxical speeches which had made me like him. So I remained silent myself, and waited.

"Tell me," he said suddenly. "There's one question I've never asked you. . . . even at times when it would have been very natural. Do you believe in the immortality of the soul?"

I was a little surprised, but quite pleased, for in this abrupt exordium I once more saw the James of my memories. I reflected for a moment.

"What a question!" I said. "You know, or rather you used to know, what my metaphysical 'position' is. . . . I believe I can see in nature the traces of an order, a plan—the reflection of divinity, if you like. . . . But the plan itself seems to me to be unintelligible to a human mind. . . . To answer you, then, I can fall back on no traditional doctrines. All I can honestly say is that I have never come across any visible sign of the survival of souls. . . . But to declare as a fact that the soul dies with the body strikes me as equally rash."

"You're very canny!" he said impatiently. "It is impossible that one of these hypotheses should not seem to you more probable than the other. . . . Do you live as if you believed or as if you did not believe in another life?"

"I certainly live as if I did not believe in a Day of Judgment; but that doesn't prove that I am sure of the non-immortality of the soul. It proves that I don't believe in the severity of a God who must at the same time be our Creator. . . . But if you give me a moment or two to think, I feel I can find arguments in favor of the hypothesis that the soul dies with the body. . . . Thought without body? It seems inconceivable. . . . Don't you think so? Our thinking is a tissue of images and sensations. . . . Sensations cease with the sentient organs, and the rebirth of images is bound up with the existence of a nervous system. . . . You know better than I do how certain physical deterioration of the brain cells causes an alteration, even a suppression, of personality. . . . It was you yourself who taught me that a man's thoughts can be transformed by the presence of spirochetes, the injection of certain glandular products. . . . All this shows a very strong link between the physical basis of our thinking and the thought itself. . . . And then, after all, there is syncope. . . . Do you remember, James, the day when my horse fell on me, in Flanders somewhere, and you found me unconscious in the meadow? I had been there for two hours, and I remembered nothing. . . . It did not look as if my soul had been living while my body was annihilated."

"That looks very poor reasoning to me," said the doctor, in a harsh, sarcastic voice. "I grant you that in your swoon you ceased for a period to be conscious of your personality. (Yet that is going a long way, for there are many patients who come round from a faint or an anaesthetic and remember extraordinary scenes, and sometimes describe the impressions of a soul set free.) But that your personality was annihilated, the very fact of your awakening totally disproves. . . . When you got up after your tumble from your horse, you weren't a different man—you were the same man. . . . If this experiment proves anything, it would rather be that your personality was able to survive when your body had seemingly deserted it. . . . But we can imagine better. Nowadays, when a heart stops beating and lungs stop breathing, we doctors say that the patient is dead. . . . Very good. . . . But suppose that means were found (and it's not at all improbable that they may be) for inducing a circulation of new blood in the dead man's head. Will not the man live again?"

"I don't know. . . . It's possible."

"If he is reborn, will it be with the same or a different personality?"

"The same, of course."

"Then we're agreed. . . . But where will that personality come from? Will you maintain that it is suddenly formed, with all its vast landscape of memories, with its passions and sentiments, in that newly reborn body? Or is it the dead man's old soul? And if the latter, are you not thereby granting that it did *not* die with the body?"

"Why, James? If our memories are linked with a definite structure of the brain, and if that structure has not altered, the memories are reborn identical. . . . To use a rough-and-ready image, but one that will give you some notion of my thought, it is as if you said: 'The ministry is empty all night, isn't it?' And yet when the clerks come back in the morning, they will busy themselves with the same matters. Therefore, the ministry has a personal soul which dwells there invisibly during the night?"

"An ingenious sophism!" said the doctor, as he poured out some wine. "But it has no substance. . . . For you're pre-supposing that the brain contains the outline of its images and memories just as the ministry contains its files. . . . Well, you must allow me my opinion as a doctor that we possess no proof at all of any such organization of the brain. The idea of cerebral localization is less and less favored by the specialists, and even were it true, it would not prove your assertion. . . . No, the more one studies the structure of the brain, the stronger is one's impression that it is, as your countryman Bergson says, a system of communication, a telephone exchange between the body and something else. Naturally, if you destroy the exchange your communication ceases, but that doesn't prove that the interlocutor never existed, nor that he vanished with the instruments. . . ."

"Quite so, James. But in the case of the telephone exchange, I believe in the interlocutor because a simple experiment will enable me to trace him by proceeding to him in the flesh, on foot, on horseback, or by air. Who has ever traced this soul-interlocutor of yours? Can you give me a single instance of thought without a corporeal basis?"

"Why certainly! You must see that if the body, the first cell, the first perceptible particle of protoplasm, were not preceded by a 'vital force,' a 'creative thought,' matter would never have been organized into a living body. . . After all, it is rather surprising that you yourself should have formed a *body*, the body I see before me now, with carbon, oxygen, phosphorus, and a few other insentient elements. . . . And it's still more surprising that you thus constructed a man, rather than a bear or a shrimp. . . . Where was the material basis of the thought from which you were born? From what brain were transmitted the inherited thoughts and ancestral images that make you *You?*"

"Are you talking seriously, James? Don't you believe simply that this material basis was within the fertilized cell from which my body sprang? Biology is not my strong point, but. . . ."

"I can't help smiling!" he said. "Where have you seen any scientific proof, my dear fellow, that your body and mind were prefigured in a certain cell thirty-five years ago? You said just now: 'I believe in the interlocutor because a simple experiment will enable me to trace him.'. . . . But in this case, what experiment have you made? What allows you to imagine that to enlarge a cell to a gigantic scale, beyond the power of any microscope, would enable you to discover in it the nose of your great-grandfather, or the puritanism of mine? And if you really believe so, do you think that such a belief is scientific? That would be a great mistake. . . . That notion, if you have it, is a religion, neither more nor less proven than another, surprising only in a man who has just been declaring himself emancipated from any doctrine. . . . I know very well that the nineteenth century strained every nerve to reduce the spiritual to terms of the material. But it failed. Observation in no way proves that the mental, the sentimental, life is contained within the material life, but on the contrary, that the former supplements the latter with a whole unexplored domain. . . ."

The plump, pink head waiter brought in our coffee. He looked pained. Guests at Johnson's, I dare say, did not usually argue heatedly on the immortality of the soul. I held my peace. James's arguments left me somewhat embarrassed. I offered him a cigarette, and for some time he smoked in silence.

"All the same," I said at last, "all the same. . . . Try the *reductio ad absurdum,* James. . . . Supposing that each single one of us has an immortal soul, where the deuce would the billions be who have lived? Where would the millions of billions go who have still to live? Where are the souls of brute beasts? If you were a theologian, you'd say they hadn't any. But you're a naturalist. Where are the souls of all the porpoises and kangaroos and crabs that ever existed? Don't you find such an idea inconceivable?"

"If I were a theologian, as you say, I should probably reply that those numbers which terrify you are as nothing in the sight of an all-powerful and infinite God. . . . But you're talking now of an eternal survival of all personalities. I'm not asking so much as that. Can't you imagine that every living body might have attached to itself a certain quantity of a force, the nature of which is unknown to us, but which, for convenient reference, we may term the 'vital fluid'? What's to prevent us from thinking that after death this 'fluid' returns to a kind of common stock? Why shouldn't there be a principle of the conservation of life, analogous to that of the conservation of energy? Grant me that, and I shall say I'm satisfied."

"Satisfied? But my dear James, why do you attach all this importance to such frail hypotheses?"

"That, my friend," he said, rising, "I shall explain to you in an hour's time, if you will do me the favor of coming back with me to the hospital."

IV

WHILST we had been dining, a thick fog had come down over the streets. The gleaming headlights of invisible cars planted it with rings of red and white light. Ludgate Circus was a landscape of nightmare. James bade me take his arm and guided me toward a bus. He had not spoken a word since leaving the hotel. When we were seated, I turned to him.

"What are we going to see?" I asked.

"Nothing perhaps. . . . You shall judge for yourself. . . . But in any case, you must realize that you're the first person to whom I am revealing my researches. . . . Besides, you'll understand. . . . But I'd rather not talk in here," he added, casting a hostile glance toward a lady in mourning who was sitting beside me.

The bus crossed the river in the midst of a veritable bank of yellow cotton wool. Factory fires on that baleful shore gleamed vast and pale through the flocculent gloom. The vibration of the bus made me drowsy.

"We get off here," said Dr. James abruptly.

We were in front of Saint Barnaby's. The lights of the hospital shone feebly in the enveloping cloud. With the sure movements of a man on his own ground, James led me across the quadrangles and under archways, and in a moment or two I recognized the iron door of the mortuary. For some time I had felt sure it was there that he was bringing me, and in spite of myself, I shuddered. My companion's nervous state seemed to be one of violent overexcitement. With what macabre exhibition did he propose to round off our evening? The door was shut and bolted, and James knocked once, then twice quickly.

"I'm here, doctor," came the insufferable voice of Gregory from inside.

I was annoyed with myself for my uneasiness, and could not overcome it. As a matter of fact, looking back on it in cool blood, I can now hardly find an explanation of its intensity. I had found this man Gregory distasteful, but I had no reason to think that he was anything but a harmless laboratory assistant. My acquaintance with James was of old standing, and nothing I knew of him could fail to fill me with confidence. True, he had greatly changed since the War, and I was not quite confident of his being in his right mind. But what could I have to fear? The sight of death? The years between 1914 and 1918 had accustomed me to that. Was I being made an unwilling accomplice? But an accomplice in what crime? I strained every nerve to make that effort at self-command which one made, ten years before, when a bombardment began, and I crossed the threshold, resolved on firmness.

"Good-evening, doctor," said Gregory.

Then he noticed my presence. He looked surprised, and, I thought, rather put out.

"Hullo, you've brought someone along, doctor?" he said.

And taking James aside, he whispered a few words which I could not hear.

"It makes no difference," said James out loud. "My friend is a Frenchman, a total stranger to the hospital, and a loyal friend of mine throughout the War. He will hold his tongue."

"I hope so," said Gregory, "I certainly hope so. . . . We'd both lose our positions, doctor, if the gentleman did any talking."

"All right, all right—I tell you he won't," answered James impatiently. "Have you got the man?"

Stepping aside, Gregory opened the dissecting table to our view. I then saw that a body was lying on it, completely naked, with its head flung back, and I recognized the man with the ruddy-white beard I had seen that morning in his death agony. I had been wrong in taking him for an old man. Sickness had left marks of wear on his face, but the body was youthful, handsome, and muscular, and in the pitiful limpness of death left one with a cruel impression of wasted vigor. The left thigh was tattooed with a device of two entwined serpents, and the chest displayed a bark with swelling sails.

"We're late," said James. "This fog. . . . How long has he been there?"

"The last breath was about nine-forty, doctor. . . . And it's ten-thirty now."

"That's all right," said the doctor. "There's a chance yet. . . . Quick, Gregory, the weighing-machine. . . ." And turning to me, he added: "Sit down on one of those benches. . . . Don't move; and not a word. . . . I'll explain later what you'll have seen. . . ."

Gregory had vanished under the tiers of seats. He returned bearing an apparatus which I identified, when he set it up, as a weighing-machine with a dial and pointer on top, very much like those to be seen in railway stations. Its platform was large enough to support an outstretched human body. With James's help the assistant laid the corpse of the red-headed man on it, and fixed a small mirror at the tip of the pointer. Then, diving once more beneath the benches, he brought up a cylinder mounted on a fairly tall upright support. I heard a spring being turned. No doubt he was winding up some piece of clockwork mechanism.

"Make haste, Gregory, make haste!" said the doctor impatiently. "Are you ready? I'll put the lights out. . . ."

He turned a switch. All the lights in the amphitheater went out. And I then saw that a luminous ray, reflected by the mirror fixed to the point of the needle, struck the cylinder, which was slowly revolving. By this means, any movement of the pointer was matched by the much more extensive movement of a luminous point on the cylinder. It was the classic method which I had seen used long ago, in the physiology class, to augment the sensitiveness of a galvanometer.

I understood nothing of the experiment I was witnessing, but the scene had assumed a scientific, and therefore familiar, aspect, which reassured me. I was now alive to its curious beauty. The blackness, that feebly gleaming ray, that naked body vaguely outlined in the dark, James's face picked out for an instant by the ray—it all recalled those pictures of Rembrandt's wherein the philosopher, the alchemist, toils in the brown shadows relieved only by a yellow light from the narrow, unearthly windows. For a few minutes the silence was complete, and then James's voice came out from the darkness.

"Are you beginning to grasp?" it said. "You gathered, of course, that the luminous spot on the cylinder indicates the weight of the body. . . . Well, now, look at the two phosphorescent marks showing the top and bottom of the cylinder. You see how the ray's point of impact is slowly dropping—the weight is diminishing. . . . The weight of a corpse always diminishes during the hours following death. . . . Why so? That's easy to understand: part of the moisture contained in the tissues is lost by slow evaporation, and there is no nutrition to replace it. . . . Observe that this drop is continuous, as you can see by noting that the luminous point falls steadily, and in fact there seems no reason why such evaporation should be anything but regular. . . . It is about an hour now since death took place. For half an hour more, within a few minutes, this phenomenon will continue without any change. After that you must watch the cylinder very closely."

There followed an extraordinary stillness. I could hear James and Gregory breathing. Slowly the luminous point kept sinking, and there this man lay, he who doubtless had once, to a wife and children, been the center of the world, now stretched on a metal platform, the object of an incomprehensible experiment. High up in the amphitheater the buzzer sounded—*tak-tak-tak, tak-tak.* . . .

"Twenty-five past one," said James, in a tone which again made me aware of the extraordinary nervous tension he had shown earlier in the night.

I kept my eyes glued to the cylinder. I could distinctly hear the tick of a chronometer, which James no doubt was holding.

"One-thirty," he said.

A few seconds later I saw the spot of light drop sharply. The jump was very small, but easy to detect.

"Did you see, James?" I exclaimed.

"I've seen better things than that," said the sarcastic voice, "I didn't bring you here merely to observe *that* phenomenon."

And with that he turned on the lights again. Slightly dazzled, I saw once again Gregory's waxed mustache, and the ruddy man lying there in one of those limp, clumsy positions assumed by corpses.

My calm had returned. I felt interested and curious; I had glimpses of what my friend was seeking. I felt passionately anxious to know his own interpretation of his experiment.

"Now you'll explain," I said.

"Wait," he answered me. "I must let Gregory get to bed. . . . Come up to my room and I'll let you see something else. . . . Thanks, Gregory. I'll be seeing you tomorrow."

"Shall I keep the heart for Professor Simpson tomorrow?" said the little man politely, taking the dead body in his arms to put it back on the dissecting table.

"Who cares about hearts?" said James with a shrug. "Yes, of course: just do what they told you."

And taking my arm, he led me away.

V

"WELL, James?" I asked, when he had settled me in his solitary armchair, with a whisky on my right and a cigarette box on my left.

"Well, my friend, I suppose you're expecting me to explain this session to you. . . . But first I should like to know what you yourself think of the things you've just seen."

"I? Well, what am I to say? Our talk during dinner, and the experiment I've just witnessed, seem to me to prove that you are in pursuit of—what shall I say?—of the human soul. . . . And also that, believing in the spirit, you are seeking it by material means. . . . Which, if you will excuse me, seems a contradiction. . . . But I'm wrong to pass judgment, as I don't even know what experiments you have made apart from this evening's. So it is up to you to talk and start off."

He was standing leaning against the mantelpiece. He lit up his pipe. Behind the green curtain a galloping of sharp claws sounded along a wooden board.

"James, tell me the truth. Those *are* rats, aren't they?"

" 'How now! A rat?' " he said with a smile. . . . "I must take you to see *Hamlet* again. . . . There's a new batch just now. . . . But we'll talk of rats all in good time. . . . Let's get back to men. . . . To begin with, I want to answer your first objection. You tell me that I'm seeking the spirit in the form of matter. But that's not quite right. . . . I am not seeking the spirit. I am seeking a certain form of energy which, when linked up with matter, will endow matter with that still unexplained property—life. . . . You will grant me, I think, that notwithstanding the claims of fanatical materialists, it has hitherto proved impossible to reproduce the reactions of living matter by any physical or chemical process. . . ."

"True. But there is a supposition that some day they will be explained. . . ."

"Oh, if you like!" he said impatiently. "One can suppose anything. . . . But there again, that is no longer science, but religion. . . . In any case, you will grant me that, scientifically or experimentally, I am entitled to say that we do not know what life is. . . . So there is no absurdity in seeking, as I am doing, the existence in living bodies of a form of energy different from all forms familiar to us. Observe, pray, that this search does not raise the problem of the soul in the religious or philosophic sense of the word; it transposes it, shifts it, sets it farther back. . . . Even if I succeeded in proving that in every living being there does exist a definite mass of 'vital fluid,' allowance would still have to be made, within that fluid itself, for spirit and matter, and then one would have to show how they are united. . . . I mention that in case any orthodoxy may make you distrustful a priori. . . ."

"My dear James," I said, "I have made my point of view in this connection quite clear, and I am listening in a critical but perfectly free spirit. . . . In any case, your idea of vital fluid is not a new one. Mesmer, who was one of the remoter causes of the French Revolution, had. . . ."

"I know, I know," said the doctor, pulling at his pipe. "What's more, he had a much more important successor, whom I dare say you know nothing about—the Baron von Reichenbach."

"You're right: I know nothing of him. Who was he?"

"He was an extraordinary character, put out of the way by the French police because he wanted to found a state. . . . A great chemist—it was he who discovered paraffin and creosote. . . . About 1860 he attacked the problem of the radiation of living bodies. He was the owner of several fairy-tale castles in Bavaria, some perched on mountains, others set beside lakes. And there he assembled subjects of peculiar sensitivity, people who could perceive in total darkness, round men and animals and flowers, a luminous fluid to which Reichenbach had given the name 'Od,' from a Sanscrit term meaning 'all-penetrating.' Reichenbach's subjects, in total darkness, saw emanations rising from bodies; they were neither smoke nor vapor, but resembled a sustained flickering. . . . A curious detail was that these emanations were reddish in color for the right side of the body, and bluish for the left. . . . As a matter of fact, I have tried to repeat Reichenbach's experiments. But I never found anything. When the three of us, you and Gregory and myself, were in total darkness just now, you didn't detect any 'odic flickering,' did you? And yet we were all in a state of extreme hyperaesthesia at the time."

"No, I saw nothing."

"And round the corpse?"

"Nothing."

"Nor did I. And it has always been the same. . . . But I have found something else. . . . This is how it was. . . . I once read an account, in a medical paper during the War, of an experiment made by a certain Dr. Crooks. He described how he had weighed the corpses of animals, and had observed that, after a period approximately regular in a given species, there was an abrupt drop in weight. . . . In man, he reckoned this fall as averaging seventeen-hundredths of a milligram. From which he concluded that the soul does exist, and that it weighs seventeen-hundredths of a milligram. . . . In that crude form the communication was regarded as absurd. The said Crooks was put down as a madman, and nobody read his paper with care. . . . For my own part, his account struck me by its sincerity of tone and by its remarkable precision in details. . . . All the same, I would never have tried repeating these troublesome and unpleasant experiments if—" (He broke off as if he regretted having started that sentence, and went on without concluding it.) "Last year, as circumstances and hospital routine placed corpses at my disposal, it occurred to me to verify the facts registered by Crooks; and with some surprise I discovered that he had told the truth. . . . Only, he had stopped the experiment too soon. In man the normal curve of evaporation is almost always interrupted, not once, but three times by sudden falls. . . . The first, which you have observed tonight, takes place about one hour and thirty-five minutes after death, and is between fifteen- and nineteen-twentieths of a milligram; the second and third, which I did not wait for because I now know them all too certainly, follow the first at intervals of twenty minutes and one hour respectively. . . . Were you going to say something?"

"Nothing important. . . . a mere comment. As you can never place your bodies on the scales except some minutes after death, you do not know, James, whether a phenomenon of the same category may not have taken place during those few minutes."

He reflected for a moment, and then said:

"Quite true. . . . But I come back to what I know. . . . Regarding the results of the experiment, no doubt is possible. . . . You have just seen them for yourself, everybody can verify them. . . . Let me add that I have repeated them with animals—whence the rats which intrigued you. And there, too, Crooks's results are correct. There is always a sharp drop, but its extent is very much less than in man. . . . In the case of a rat, it is so faint that it cannot be measured. . . . Such are the facts; the interpretation, of course, admits of argument. . . ."

His pipe had gone out. He relit it and looked at me. I was careful to say nothing. He continued:

"At this stage, this is what I put forward. It seems to me possible to suggest, not that the soul weighs seventeen-hundredths of a milligram, which would be oversimple, but that every living creature is animated (in your language you could almost say '*âme*') by a certain form of energy, still unknown, which leaves the body after death. That all energy possesses mass is something admitted by the post-Einstein physicists. You know that light can be weighed, and that theoretically light could be compressed in a receptacle. . . . Well, why not vital energy likewise? True, the weight of light is of a different order of size, something infinitely smaller than what we are observing here. But I don't see why that should be an argument against me. It merely proves that we are in the presence of a quite different phenomenon, which is not surprising. . . . States of matter are now known of such a kind that a ton of atoms reduced to their kernels could find room in my waistcoat pocket. . . . Do you follow me thus far, or do you think I'm quite crazy?"

"I find it very hard to accustom myself to these ideas, but your argument there is clear to me. . . . However, I will raise one objection. You apparently regard a human body as a living unity; but so far as we know, it is nothing of the kind. The different cells of the body don't all die at the same time. A heart lives longer than a brain. When I was in America I was shown in Carrel's laboratories how heart cells can be kept alive almost indefinitely by artificial means. I cannot remember the name of the scientist who once said that the cells of a body die like the inhabitants of a starving city—the weakest first. But if death is a series of stages, how is that idea to be linked with that of your sudden drops?"

"A very reasonable point: I had considered that myself. . . . The answer is, first, that I observe not one drop, but several; and then, that your idea of the individual death of cells is a hypothesis, but no more than a hypothesis. . . . If there does exist a certain force which may be the basis of what we call 'personality,' it is bound to disappear all at one time—doubtless at the instant of the heaviest fall; nevertheless, the personality of one of us is something quite distinct from the life of each of our cells. . . . A personality either exists, or does not exist. . . . Remember again, I have no wish to make the soul something material; but, as I explained just now, just as the soul is linked with the body for the expression of its thoughts and the perception of its sensations, so it is likewise possible that after quitting the body, it should be linked with this mysterious energy which we have just noted in the act of departure."

"You mean that personality could survive the body, if the vital energy of that body could remain grouped in one single place?"

"Exactly. . . . But for the moment I make no affirmations. . . . I merely say it is not inconceivable."

"But in actual fact this energy does not remain grouped."

"We don't know at all, but, as I said when we were dining, just as the matter from which a body is made up returns under various forms to universal matter, so, at the moment of death, our vital force returns to some vast reservoir of spiritual energy until such time as, reunited to certain atoms of matter, it once more animates a living being."

"In other words, you believe in an immortality of the universal soul, but not in the survival of the individual?"

"You have the real French taste for ideas, *mon ami.* . . . At the moment you are drawing me into the field of hypothesis; and that has no bounds. . . . For my own part, the problem interesting me is much more restricted. . . . If one could gather up the vital energy of a human being, would one thereby have fixed his personality? Would that assure him, if not of immortality (all problems involving infinity surpass the human mind), at least of some measure of survival? That is what I am trying to find out."

"A little crazy, James—but interesting. . . . Well, what next? Have you tried to gather up this 'something' that weighs seventeen-hundredths of a milligram?"

"I have not yet found a means of trying it with a man. . . . I have tried it with animals. During the weighing-machine experiment, I have placed certain animals underneath glass-bell jars—but what did I collect in them? Did they even collect anything? I have never been able to say. In the first place, I am obliged to lift the bell jar in order to withdraw the animal. Do its contents thereupon escape? I simply don't know. . . . Notwithstanding Reichenbach and his assertions, the vital fluid remains invisible; and that doesn't make observations easy. . . . Obviously experiments made with humans ought to give results more readily observed, as the quantities involved are greater. Three days ago I ordered a glass-bell jar of a size large enough to cover the body of a man. I shall have it next week. . . . We'll see. . . . Are you likely to be still here?"

"I have to return to Paris for a few days, but my work is far from being completed, and I shall be back in London on Friday, about seven in the evening. . . . Will you dine with me then?"

"No, I can't leave the hospital on a Friday. . . . But come here yourself, and perhaps. . . ."

He looked at me long and steadily, like an architect gauging with his eye the strength of a beam or a wall.

"Of course," he said, "you'll stick to your promise not to breathe a word about what you've seen here. . . . It would mean the loss of my position and of the opportunity to continue my experiments. . . ."

I shook his hand, and left. I had great difficulty in finding my way back in the fog, and it was three o'clock in the morning before I got back to my hotel. I could not sleep.

VI

I AM reaching the point in this story where circumstances led to my playing a larger part in it, and I must admit at once that, after my solemn promise given to James, I was blameworthy in talking to a French scientist, even indirectly, of his researches. But I had, I think, some excuse. In the first place, it was chance, and not my own intention, that during this period brought me into touch for the first time with Monestier. Further, as will be seen, the questions I asked him were such that he could not for a moment think that investigations of so strange a kind were really being carried out by a doctor. And finally, I am bound to say that the steps I took, rash though they may have been, enabled

James to make great strides toward the solution of the problem.

I reached Paris on a Saturday, and dined that same evening with some friends. Taking my place at table, I found that I had Monestier as my neighbor. He had long been an object of my admiration, for he is not only, after Jean Perrin and Langevin, one of the greatest of physicists, but also a perfect writer. And I was charmed by the man himself, with his eyes as blue and lively as a child's, the soft clump of his white hair, and his swift, youthful voice. He talked first, I remember, about the works of Esnault-Pelterie and the possibility of a voyage to the moon.

"I shan't go, myself," he said. "My son will perhaps go. My grandson certainly. . . . In any case, there will be hundreds of volunteers."

"How will they breathe?" I asked.

"They will have oxygen with them," said Monestier. "And later, when a colony of human beings has been settled there, an oxygen market will be opened where the housewives will go every morning to get their supplies of breathable air. . . . The life will seem quite simple to those who live it. . . . What would Christopher Columbus have thought. if the liner *Ile de France* had been described to him? Read your Jules Verne and Wells again. Almost all the dreams of the preceding generation have become the realities of today."

It was just then (and doubtless because he had sympathetically thrown the names of Jules Verne and Wells into the conversation) that a sudden and irresistible desire caught me to question him concerning the scientific value of Dr. James's investigations.

"I ought to tell you," I said to him, "that I am thinking of writing a fantastic story myself; and it is one on which, as I have the opportunity, I should be very glad to have a scientist's opinion. . . . Of course you'll think the subject quite absurd. . . . I know it is. But I'd like to know, supposing that a scientist was so foolish as to make certain experiments, what course he would take, what line of inquiry he would follow."

Whereupon I recounted to Monestier, as if it were a fictitious story, my conversations with James, and the experiments which I had witnessed. He listened with good-humored amusement.

"It is not really so very absurd," he commented. "Why shouldn't there be 'psychons' as there are electrons? We know so little, after all. . . . Then what exactly do you want me to tell you? What experiments your doctor could make? Well, in his place I should first try to find out whether certain rays do not make visible this energy which he thinks he has collected in his flask. . . . Have you ever seen how certain fluorescent substances, invisible in broad daylight, become visible in darkness under ultra-violet rays?"

"No, never."

"I can show you that some time; it's a very pretty sight. . . . Could you come to my laboratory tomorrow?"

"I should be delighted."

And the next day I found him in a new building, surrounded by shining and complicated apparatus. When I entered, he was standing before a glass tube in which, on coming nearer, I could see rings of woolly light, mauve-pink in color, pale and unearthly.

"Ah, good-day!" he said. "Look, here is a very odd phenomenon. . . . Look at this. . . . I pass a magnet right along the tube. . . ."

He was holding a small horseshoe of metal, and he shifted it slowly towards the right. Whereupon I saw the rings separate from each other, following the magnet and turning paler and more transparent. Then Monestier moved the magnet back toward the left; and the rings slipped into each other until they formed simply one small ring of a violet-colored substance.

"It is delightful!" I exclaimed. "But what is the explanation?"

"Ah!" he said, "that is what I'm looking for! I don't yet know. . . . But you came along to see the phenomena of fluorescence. I mustn't waste your time."

In one corner of the room stood an extended apparatus, completely black, looking rather like a large-scale camera, covered with the cloth which photographers use when they are focusing.

"This is the apparatus that produces ultra-violet rays," said Monestier. "Visible light is shut off as it emerges by a black disk which lets only the invisible rays come through. . . . Look—will you kindly switch off the light. . . . The switch is farther to the left. . . . Good. Now I set the apparatus in action in the dark. . . . You see nothing. . . . If you put your hand over the path of the beam you will see it turn partly luminous, and if you leave it too long, you'll burn yourself. . . . Good. Now I place in front of the apparatus a flask filled with water. Naturally, it is invisible. . . . But I pour a fluorescent substance into the water and—look!"

Suddenly two spots of steely blue appeared in the darkness, like planets hanging in the night. They spread out, curling in slow spirals, growing larger and fainter, nebulae becoming more and more attenuated. A liquid smoke filled the whole flask with an unreal, luminous cloud.

"How beautiful!" I said. "It is like being present at the creation of matter. . . . But why isn't all that visible in ordinary light?"

"My dear sir," said Monestier with a smile, "the 'becauses' of science are nearly always statements of observed fact. . . . You remember Molière's *'Quia est in eo virtus dormitiva.'* . . . Because there are fluorescent substances which are visible in ultra-violet rays. . . . But to revert to your story—and I dreamed a lot about it in the night—nothing prevents one from supposing that your 'vital fluid' is fluorescent. . . . The doctor in your tale could certainly borrow an apparatus in his hospital similar to this one. . . . Let him place one of his bell jars in the path of the rays and—who knows?—perhaps he will see the 'psychons' suddenly become luminous."

"Yes—a very good idea. . . . And do you think that the glass of the domes would not allow the energy which they contain to escape? Wouldn't he need metal ones? Or rock crystal?"

"Ah, that I don't know. . . . It all depends on the nature of your fluid, which is unknown to me. But I see no a priori reason why glass should be inadequate. . . . If it is, you can suppose that your hero tries a colloidal glass.

Then you'll have beautiful red flasks in your story. . . .
But I'll show you something else."

He showed me blades of soap, infinitely thin, in which
there were formed disks of vivid, changing colors, and I
did not venture to say more to him about "my story."

VII

I RETURNED to London on the Friday evening. A bad
crossing left me too tired to go out again the same night,
and it was not until the Saturday morning that I went to see
James at the hospital. He was not in his room, but the door
was open and I went inside to wait for him. The great curtain was pulled back. The shelves which this curtain had
hidden on my first visit held a small pair of scales, an inverted glass bowl, a few small bottles. Whilst awaiting my
friend's return, I looked at the women's photographs which
stood along the mantelpiece and on the writing table, and I
then saw (what I had not observed on the first day) that
they were all portraits of the same woman, a girl, almost
indeed a child. The expression of the face was gentle and
ingenuous, with charming features, and hair so very fair as
to seem almost white. In nearly all these portraits the young
woman wore costumes of bygone times. Was she an actress?
Did she like to set off her beauty with different adornments?
I was lost in that musing into which the enigma of a lovely
face always plunges us, when I heard footsteps. I turned
round. James was behind me. He laid a hand on my shoulder,
and himself glanced at the portraits for a moment.

"Well!" he said at last in his hoarse voice. "You've got
back, have you? And how did you find 'the Gay City'?"

"Very pleasant. . . . I don't know any city more charming than Paris in springtime. . . . But that's not the question. I believe, James, that I picked up some valuable suggestion over there for your researches."

"For my researches? How so?"

I told him of my indiscretion, making it plain that it could
entail no dangers to himself. I described what I had seen

in Monestier's laboratory, and gave him as clear an account as I could of what the scientist had told me.

"Do you understand, James? It seems to me that if you could pass a beam of ultra-violet rays above the body just when you think something escapes from it, you would perhaps be able to see the fluid become luminous. . . . Of course, it may just as well be the contrary—but couldn't you try? This hospital surely has an ultra-violet-ray apparatus?"

"Oh, yes," he said, musing. "The only difficulty would be to get it in the dissecting room. . . . But that shouldn't be really impossible. . . . Yes, thanks very much—it's a good idea. . . . I have often seen experiments in fluorescence; but I hadn't thought of applying them here. In any case, I can make a test in my own room on one of the small animals. Will you come over tomorrow night? We'll do this together."

I promised to come, but I asked him, if he had to kill a rat or any other creature, to do so before my arrival, as I greatly disliked such a sight. He laughed at me a little, and told me that the animals would not suffer, as he anaesthetized them beforehand with an injection.

. . . .

The state of excitement in which I found James next evening is past imagining. The sound of my step on the staircase brought him out of his room, and when I reached the landing he held out both hands to me.

"Look here, old man," he said in a low voice, "we've got a solution, thanks to you."

"What do you mean?"

"Come in and have a look."

The room was dark, but James guided me from behind with a hand on each of my shoulders.

"Be careful," he said. "The apparatus is in the middle of the room. . . . Keep a little to your left. . . . Farther. . . . Right. . . . Now straight in front of you. . . . Do you see anything?"

Over toward the fireplace I could discern a faint glow, about the size of a nut, but more elongated. Going closer, I saw that the interior of this luminous kernel contained darker currents revolving extremely slowly. The whole thing reminded one of the appearance of certain photographs of celestial nebulae.

"What have you got there?" I asked him. "It's curious, and rather beautiful in a way. . . ."

"I'll let you see it in the light," he said.

He moved away for a moment. The light in the middle of the room went on. I saw on the mantelpiece a small glass-bell jar, beneath which lay a dead rat stretched on its side. The warm glow had vanished. I looked at James inquiringly.

"You look very surprised," he said. "But I have applied the idea you gave me. . . . What you saw just now was a small mass of—I dare not call it matter—let's say, if you like, of the luminous fluid which appeared under the beam of the ultra-violet rays at the top of the jar, twenty-one minutes after the animal's death."

I was overwhelmed, scarcely able to believe what I had just seen and heard.

"But this is extraordinary, James. . . . Nobody has ever thought of this. . . . It is a great discovery—don't you think so? And where is it now, your fluid? I don't see anything in the globe."

"Quite true. Nothing is visible in ordinary light, and that explains why neither I nor anybody else ever noted the phenomenon before. . . . But your method, or that of your physicist friend if you like, is the right one."

"I'd like to see it again."

He switched off the light and turned on the apparatus. Instantly the tiny elongated kernel shone out with its soft nebular gleam.

"Really, James, I'm beginning to think that you are on the path of a wonderful and unforseeable future. . . . Do you think that the personality—no, one can't talk of the personality of a rat—do you think that the individuality of this creature persists in some form allied to this little glow?"

"I know no more than you do, old man. . . . All I can say is that it seems to me possible, even probable . . . and also, that I've decided to repeat the experiment on a man as soon as I have a larger bell jar. . . . And further, note that this fluid, luckily for us, is lighter than air and collects at the top, a fact which makes it quite easy to preserve even if the bowl has to be lifted to withdraw the body."

We stood silent for a moment or two in the darkness, gazing at this light which was perhaps the manifestation of a mysterious presence. At last James turned on the light again.

"How surprising it is," I said, "that such important and simple facts should hitherto have eluded mankind!"

"Why?" said James. "Isn't it the history of all scientific phenomena? The data of all the great discoveries have existed in nature for thousands of years. What was lacking was a mind to interpret them. When the cave-dweller dropped a stone into the stream beside his rocks he could have discovered, as Galileo did later, the laws of the velocity of falling bodies. . . . He didn't think about it. . . . Ever since the earth has been the earth, thunderstorms have provided wonderful experiments which could have shown all mankind the existence of electricity. . . . They were explained by the wrath of Jove. . . . Men have always been surrounded, and the atmosphere has always been traversed, by the rays of which our modern physicists make use; yet these rays remained invisible and elusive, like the vital force of my rat."

"Poor beast! Take it away, James. . . . I hate seeing that corpse amongst the photographs of that lovely woman there. . . ."

And after a moment's hesitation I added:

"Who is she?"

"Don't you know her?" said James. "That is Edith Philipps. The young actress, you know. . . . The whole of London is crowding to see her play Ophelia just now. . . . Haven't you been? I must take you one of these evenings."

"Take away the rat, James."

Carefully he raised the globe, and drawing the animal out by its long tail, he wrapped it up in a piece of paper.

"Now," he said, "we must see if our light is still there."

He repeated the experiment. The little ball of light was gleaming at the top of the jar.

VIII

MY VISITS to Saint Barnaby's Hospital became of almost daily occurrence. I continued my work at the British Museum because I was forced to, and because I could not spend the daytime with Dr. James, whose profession left him little freedom; but my friend's researches were of greater interest to me than my own. Every day I waited impatiently the hour he had appointed for me. In the reading room itself, instead of working, I kept watching my neighbors, a girl with tortoise-shell spectacles, a little Hindu with curly hair, and imagined them lying on Gregory's grim balance. And when the hour came round, I hastened over to the city of chimneys and wharves.

Twice a week, on Wednesdays and Saturdays, the thoroughfare leading to the hospital was occupied by the humble street market which I had noticed on the occasion of my first visit. I enjoyed stopping beside the open-air booths where they sold fish, and books at a penny apiece, and old boots. Sometimes I had a talk with the hawkers. One of them, Mr. William Slutter, was a favorite of mine, on account of his astonishing natural distinction and his handsome head, which was like that of an aged aristocrat. He sold for sixpence queer little cigarette-lighters on which a pig, with uplifted trotter, made the spark fly. "Wonderful joke!" he kept calling. "They never let you down. . . . I was sold out yesterday. I've only a few left." As a matter of fact I never saw him sell a single one. But he kept his good-mannered smile and an air of confidence in life. Nothing was further from my thoughts when I was talking with him one Wednesday about the difficulties of his trade than that he would be the subject during the very next week of the most extraordinary of experiments.

Yet so it turned out. Mr. William Slutter contracted a virulent pleurisy and was brought to Saint Barnaby's in a state that left no hope. That same day one of the big stores which prided itself on being able to supply anything, delivered to Dr. James the bell jar large enough to cover a

human body, as he had ordered three weeks before. That
evening, when I accompanied James on his round of the
wards, I was taken aback at finding William Slutter's usually
peaceful features there, ablaze with fever. "Wonderful
joke. . . ." he kept calling. "Only a few left. . . ." And the
next night, at midnight, I saw him again in the dissecting
room.

I was beginning to be inured to this macabre spectacle.
James, on the contrary, was in great agitation that night.
He had helped Gregory to hide the gigantic globe beneath
the rising tiers of seats, and was afraid lest the little man
might break it as he lifted it with our help on to the table
and set it over the corpse. The doctor had had to give up
the idea of using the weighing machine, as it would have
been difficult, if not impossible, to keep the globe balanced on
the platform. On the other hand, he had again obtained the
loan of the ultra-violet-ray apparatus. Gregory was not
aware of the nature of our new researches; he no longer
understood what the doctor was doing, and gave us only
clumsy and ill-humored help.

At last poor William Slutter lay outstretched under the
huge jar, and the contrivance was placed so that its top
should come into the line of the rays. These manipulations
took so long that we had only six minutes left until the
moment when, according to the now familiar timetable of
these experiments, "something" was sure to happen. James
had his eye on the clock and told Gregory to put the lights
out. I watched the invisible top of the globe, trying hard
not to lose its position. The waiting seemed endless.

"One minute," said James.

I began to count slowly. One . . . two . . . three . . .
four. . . . And I had reached fifty when I saw a faint
blue mist appearing. At first it seemed shapeless and as if
diffused over the whole width of the beam. But this stage
was so brief that I could not observe it. Immediately the
vapor became condensed in a milky mass, about four inches
long, the base of which was horizontal, with its rounded
top following the curve of the globe. This mass was neither
motionless nor homogeneous. Currents of lighter and darker
color were visible in it. I cannot describe it better than by

asking you to imagine the smoke of several cigarettes, of varying density and slightly different colors, superimposing their rings and spirals until they formed an object of well-defined outline.

"Doctor!" came the startled voice of Gregory. "Doctor! Doctor! Do you see that ball of light?"

"Keep quiet!" said James's grating voice.

I saw the doctor's head come into the field of the rays from the apparatus, and some of his features were for an instant lit up. Then he vanished into the darkness again. I could feel, though I could not see, that he was leaning, to watch it more closely, over the strange substance which he made his prisoner. I thought of William Slutter. . . . Did there really remain, under that glass bell, some fragment of what once had been that simple and contented soul? Was it possible that everything which had given life to that inanimate body was not concentrated in that tiny space? Were we holding there some impersonal force, or were we holding the individual William Slutter? Could he see us? Was he conscious of his incredible adventure? Was he thinking at that moment—"Wonderful joke. . . ."? And if the least chance of his consciousness existed, had we any right to keep a soul captive?

"Lights, Gregory," said James's voice.

I was surprised to see again the doctor, the little assistant with his waxed mustache, the apparatus with its black cloth cover, and there, under that inverted bowl now deprived of its gleam, the corpse of an old man with a white mustache.

.   .   .   .

James looked at me with a nod of his head. I felt that he was himself overwhelmed by the success.

"You saw that ball of light, sir?" Gregory asked me.

"We all saw it," said James in an impatient tone. "What I now want, Gregory, is for you to keep this bell jar for me without breaking it, and especially *without turning it up.* . . . Do you understand?"

"Yes, doctor," he replied humorously. "But don't give me another of these, for I shouldn't know where to stow it. As it is, if the students were to find it. . . ."

"I said nothing about another one," said James. "We'll give you a hand to carry this one underneath the seats."

And the three of us carried out this maneuver, not without difficulty, and then left Gregory. The little man seemed taciturn. When we were out in the hospital quadrangle under the starry sky, I said to James:

"I think you ought to give him some explanation. . . . You need him. . . . Now this evening. . . ."

"You're wonderful, my boy! What do you expect me to tell him? He knows as much as you and I do. . . . Can you yourself explain what we have seen?"

I told him that I could do no such thing, but that the experiment seemed to confirm all the theories he had put forward to me on the evening of our first dinner. If his hope had been to catch and preserve something of human beings after their death, he was on the track of such a possibility. I further admitted that I did not see what this success was leading to, for even admitting that he had the soul of poor William Slutter under his globe, he could not enter into communication with it. And I added that I was doubtful regarding his right to keep this unknown substance in captivity.

"For after all, James, suppose that the law of human nature really is that a vital fluid escapes from our body after death, to merge with some universal reservoir of life, why and how should we stand in its way? Your globes are not eternal, and a day will come when, despite you, William Slutter will cease to be William Slutter. And what will you then have done but vainly prolonged an existence, under conditions which perhaps are dreadful? You have made an amazing discovery, and one which will give you one kind of fame when you choose to make it public. . . . But you must confine the risk in these experiments to the bounds of strict necessity. 'There are more things in heaven and earth, Horatio. . . .' "

"That reminds me," he said, "that I must take you to see *Hamlet* one evening. . . . Good-night!"

IX

I COULD hardly have visited Saint Barnaby's Hospital so often without making the acquaintance of some of the medical staff. On several occasions James had taken me to a meal in the dining room of the resident members, where I had had some conversation with my neighbors, and I became particularly friendly with Dr. Digby, a mental specialist of the staff. I have always had a strong inclination, which I cannot explain very readily, toward the society of medical psychologists. . . . Experience of abnormal persons seems to give them a keener and more ingenious understanding of the normal. To myself, striving to be a writer and to understand mankind, their conversation always provided valuable lessons. Besides, I found Digby unusually congenial. He was a short bald man, with a look of wisdom in his eyes, who spoke in a very soft voice, with precision and intelligence.

On the day following the evening I have just described, I arrived in advance of the time fixed by James, and was strolling in the grounds of Saint Barnaby's, on the flowered terrace bordering the river, when I met Digby in a long white coat.

"Hullo," he said, "are you alone? Our friend isn't ill, is he? I didn't see him at lunch."

"I think he is all right, Dr. Digby, but he won't be free for a quarter of an hour."

He began to say something, stopped hesitantly, and then went on:

"Oh! Then this is just— No. . . . Yes. . . . As you have a quarter of an hour to spare, come into my room."

It was a very well-lit room, right on the terrace itself, and furnished with countless files and card-index cases.

"Cigarette? Whisky?" asked Digby. "No? Well now, listen. . . . As I've got the chance of seeing you alone for a moment, I'd like to talk to you about James. You're a friend of his; you're a stranger to the hospital; you can perhaps do us a great service."

"I should very much like to, if it is possible. But in what way?"

"I shall tell you. . . . But first of all it must be understood anything I say to you is confidential and cannot be repeated by you to any one, even to himself. . . . That's understood, isn't it?"

"Of course."

"Good. . . . Well, I have reason to think that you are in the know about certain mysterious experiments which James is said to be carrying on, to some quite incomprehensible end, and in which he makes use of the corpses of patients dying in this hospital. Am I right?"

"What an examination! I cannot answer, doctor. . . . And I must ask you not to take that reply either as an affirmative or a denial. . . . It merely indicates that I regard my friend's action as depending solely on his own conscience."

"I quite approve your attitude," said Digby with a smile. "But from my point of view I am convinced that I am doing my duty when I tell you that the hospital authorities have been startled. . . . So far no inquiry has been ordered, mainly because everybody here is well disposed toward James, and also because the experiments as described seem absurd, though harmless."

"It seems to me in fact," I said, "that if one can dissect a dead body, one can all the more——"

"Be careful!" he said. "You're going to say more than you wish. . . . Understand me. . . . If these rumors get round beyond medical men to those less tolerant persons, the board of management, our friend might well find himself in rather serious trouble. But that is my least important motive. I am chiefly afraid of— 'Oh!' you'll think, 'these specialists see their pet subject everywhere!' But never mind!—I am chiefly afraid that certain researches might prove a danger to James's mental welfare; and it is about his state of mind, if you will allow me, that I should like to have a word with you, because, I repeat, the circumstances seem to enable you to be of service to him yourself.

. . . To begin with, do you know anything of his personal history?"

"What do you mean by his 'personal history'? I got to know him during the War. Of what may have happened to him before then I know nothing. Nor indeed of his sentimental history since the War, for he is like all you English, not a man to talk much about these things."

"Well, I must tell you what I think it necessary for you to know. . . . In March, 1914, James married a young Danish girl of great beauty, who was studying medicine in London. I knew her quite well. She was a woman of surprising intelligence; candid, too, and generous, but in no way suited to English life; but she had never loved James. On the other hand, he worshiped her, and I believe that she must have married him out of pity for the violence of the feeling she inspired in him. . . . When James went out to France at the end of 1915, Hilda James felt herself completely stranded here and returned to her own country. There she met a young man more suited to her taste. She wrote to James telling him so, loyally but without trying to soften the blow. . . . She asked for her freedom. He rebelled, and refused. . . . One day, at the front, he learned that she had died in some obscure, dramatic circumstances, about which I know little. . . . He has never got over it."

"How mysterious people are, doctor! So when I was living in the same Flanders dugout with James, he had just gone through this drama—and I never knew it!"

"Yes. . . . That impotence of self-expression is at once the strength and the danger of our national character. . . . We keep ourselves to ourselves. . . . We 'repress,' as the layman now says with rather naïve pedantry. . . . It is not without dignity, but it is a dangerous thing for one's mental balance. . . . In James's case, which I have followed at pretty close quarters, I was genuinely alarmed during the first few years after the War ended. . . . He lived then in a solitude, a sentimental starvation, which a Frenchman like yourself, I suppose, could hardly imagine. . . . Had it not been for his work at the hospital, in which fortunately he was interested, I doubt whether his reason would have stood the strain. . . . Then, finally, when he was spending a holiday with his people in Wiltshire, he received an urgent call, in the absence of the local doctor, to see a young girl who was taken ill. She was an actress."

"Miss Edith Philipps?" I said.

"Ah! So he's spoken of Miss Philipps, has he?"

"No . . . at least, only just. . . . But I saw her photograph in James's room and asked who she was."

"So you know that she is very beautiful. But you haven't been in a position to observe, as I have, her close resemblance to the girl who was once James's wife. . . . That was certainly the reason why he became attached to her from the first day he set eyes on her, and with an intensity that has been constantly growing. . . . Do not imagine that she is his mistress. She is unmarried and lives with her father, Gerald Philipps, who was himself one of our leading actors. She would certainly be married were it not for her health, which is so frail that we medical men can hardly tell how she can possibly withstand the strain of her calling. . . . What does she think of our friend? Does she love him? Does she feel affection, or indifference, toward him? I have never seen them together, and all I know of them comes to me from third parties. I know only that he is desperately attached to her, that he spends all his free time with her, and that he knows her to be seriously ill and lives in terror of losing her. . . . That is what I wanted to tell you so as to help you a little in your relations with him. . . . I don't want to add any of the conclusions which I myself draw from these given facts, because you are too intimate with him, and I know from experience, alas, how dangerous it is to plant suggestions in a hypersensitive soil where they immediately become sources of infection. . . . Excuse my frankness!"

"I am grateful to you, Dr. Digby. But I don't altogether understand. . . . What do you want me to do? I have no authority over James; I do not know Miss Philipps; and besides, I shan't be staying much longer in England—even if I wanted to, I couldn't. When I leave, I shall probably lose sight of James."

"That is all quite true, and I am asking nothing definite of you. . . . I merely wished you to know the facts, so as

not to find yourself walking blindfold on difficult ground.
. . . Now it is for yourself to judge. . . . If you can bring
our friend within a reasonable interval to forsake this dan-
gerously heretical quest of his, I think you will have rendered him a service, and even a twofold service. . . . But go
along and see him quickly, for I've kept you more than your
quarter of an hour."

I left him. When I reached James's room, the buzzer was
ringing its two-four, two-four summons. . . . James had
been called down to a ward and I had to wait for him. And
I then observed that one amongst the photographs on the
mantelpiece, the largest, was that of a different woman. I
had noticed it the first time, because its resemblance to the
other woman whose portraits surrounded it was truly
astonishing.

X

I HAD not paid much heed to James's proposal, a few days
earlier, to go and see *Hamlet*. The days and nights I was
then spending with him, amongst his patients and sharing
in his researches, seemed to me as beautiful and as varied
as the greatest dramas. But after my talk with Digby I
was naturally fired with a desire to meet Edith Philipps,
and I reminded James of his promise. He told me he would
ask for seats on his first free evening.

On the way to the theater he explained that the company
was that of a theater in a working-class district. The critics
had been so enthusiastic in their praise of the young man
who played Hamlet, and of an unknown actor's Polonius,
and above all of the Ophelia of Miss Philipps, that a West
End manager had provided a theater for the players. Whereupon the whole of London had been rushing to see them,
Shakespeare became the fashion, and many people came
out declaring that they had just seen *Hamlet* for the first
time. This, said James, was certainly true of the majority,
but England discovered *Hamlet* in this way every fifty
years. His friend's father, Gerald Philipps, had himself

made his name half a century ago in the title part, and had "revealed" this unknown author, William Shakespeare, to the English of 1875.

To myself, as to the spectators at whom James had smiled, *Hamlet* was a new play that evening. These actors had shown a simple, but all too rare, discretion in playing Shakespeare's text without cuts. The young man who took the part of the Prince of Denmark played with vigor and straightforwardness. When he spoke the lines—

"How weary, stale, flat and unprofitable
Seem to me all the uses of the world. . . ."

he seemed as closely akin to our French selves as the youthful Barrès or Benjamin Constant. It was the young man of all time. And so too with Miss Philipps: from her first entrance I could see that she was the young girl of all time. In her opening scene with Polonius she displayed a blend of the demure, the artlessly forward, the childishly submissive, which I found enchanting.

"James," I said to him in the interval, "your friend is adorable!"

He seemed happy.

"You can tell her yourself shortly," he said. "I have told her that we would have supper together. . . . Are you pleased?"

"Delighted! It is excellent. . . . I've only one criticism— the Ghost. The Ghost disappointed me. Why make him speak from the wings? It is beneath the swords that Shakespeare's 'old mole' should cry his 'Swear! Swear!' Do you remember Goethe's comment on that point in *Wilhelm Meister?* Goethe thinks that the Ghost ought to disappear underground, and that a tongue of flame should spring from the ground to show where he is."

"The odic flickering?" said James, glancing at me with the faintest of smiles. . . . "I wonder what the ghost of William Slutter is doing at the moment?"

"I wonder indeed! Is he still in the bell jar?"

"Yes, I saw him still there last night; the glass prison is keeping him for us faithfully."

"Don't you want to restore him to liberty, James?"

He laid a finger on his lips. In front of us stood an attendant offering ices and boxes of chocolates. The bell announced the end of the interval. We were plunged once more into the world of Shakespeare.

It will no doubt seem surprising to find me speaking in such detail of a performance of *Hamlet* in the middle of a narrative so different in its subject. But I have two sound reasons for that. First, this was the evening when I made the acquaintance of Miss Philipps, who, as you will see, plays an important part in the secret which I wish to reveal in these pages. And further, I know not why, the atmosphere of *Hamlet* remains linked for me with the memory of Dr. James. It was the only occasion on which I could gauge the depth of hidden, desperate feeling which lay beneath that tragic but impassive mask. At the moment in the players' scene, when Hamlet feels the shame of his own calmness in contrast with the actor's feigned emotion—

> ". . . all his visage wan'd;
> Tears in his eyes, distraction in 's
>   aspect. . . .
> . . . What would he do,
> Had he the motive and the cue for
>   passion
> That I have?"—

I saw James lean forward and open his lips as if he were on the point of crying these lines aloud himself. During the scene of Ophelia's madness, for the first and only time in my experience of him, I saw a tear slip down his cheek. And there Edith Philipps, it must be said, was deeply moving. Her eyes looked forth upon a transparent world. Her voice came singing and speaking in a monotone, with infinite softness, and she held out invisible flowers: "There's rosemary, that's for remembrance; pray, love, remember. . . ." She turned my thoughts also to so many things past and beautiful.

"Do you know," James said to me in the interval, "what is the most admirable thing in her playing? It is this—she succeeds in giving the impression, which madwomen in real life will often give, that madness is an almost conscious refuge. . . . Ophelia no longer wishes to see this horrible world; she has created another, the world of flowers, and her memories, and she will go on talking of it in her soft, implacable voice, to the very end. . . . Really, there is nothing in the theater more deeply human than that!"

When the stage had been strewn with corpses, and the young Fortinbras had had the Prince borne off upon the shoulders of four captains, and the audience had applauded loud and long, and the orchestra had played *God Save the King,* we came out in silence.

"What a crowd of corpses!" I said at last.

"As in life," said James. "Will you come round the theater with me to meet Edith at the other door? She must be ready by now, for she has had time to change during the last act."

We found her ready, as he had said, and waiting for us with the stage-door keeper. She was a thoroughly simple young girl, ingenuously pleased by the few compliments I paid her, as if she had not already been told by every critic in London that she was an actress of genius. James took us to a little French restaurant. There, in the light, I could see Miss Philipps better. She was every bit as beautiful as her portraits, but startlingly pale. During supper she was very gay. I was a little disappointed by the quality of her remarks; but isn't one always disappointed in an actress whom one has just seen in a masterpiece? Unconsciously one has endowed her with the spirit of Shakespeare or Musset; one has wished, almost hoped, that she may prove in actual life to be Juliet, or Desdemona, or Camille. And one finds—a child. It calls for a gift of greater penetration than I then possessed to detect in her the poetry she really held. I can now see the traits in Edith Philipps that made her wonderfully Shakespearean. James himself had realized them long before. I was touched by the tender admiration he showed towards her. And we parted on coming out of the restaurant, as he wished to take her home to her father's before he returned to the hospital.

XI

IF I have succeeded in conveying any idea of James's character, you will have realized by now that when we met again, nothing further was said by either of us about Edith Philipps. I made several attempts to "start him off" on the subject, by taking up one of the photographs on the mantelpiece and looking at it with close attention. But I never succeeded. I regretted this, not only from curiosity, but because I believed (as I still believe) that my friend's unhappiness would have been lessened if he could have given utterance to the deep, bewildering passions which gripped him.

I had also tried several times, in accordance with my promise to Dr. Digby, to divert him from his researches. I pointed out to him that Gregory was now freeing himself from his influence, that the little man now only gave his help distrustfully and grudgingly, and that even the bank notes which James gave him more and more freely hardly brought forth a single word of thanks. The doctor likewise had observed these disturbing symptoms; but he did not make his visits to the dissecting room any less frequent. It must be admitted that his investigations had taken a very curious turn, and that I myself, though disapproving them, could not but follow them with intense interest.

In the first place, James had been struck with the difficulties involved in the handling and safeguarding of these huge glass-bell jars, and had conceived the simple but ingenious notion of having them fitted at the top with a small globe, about four inches in diameter, communicating with the large one by a glass tube. Observing events under the ultraviolet rays, we saw, as might be expected, that the fluid rose from the larger vessel into the small one. The latter then became almost entirely luminous, the bell jar itself remaining dark. It was a simple matter to cut the connecting tube with a blow pipe and seal it, and so to preserve the "matter" or "energy" which was our concern, in a much reduced volume. By welding a new tube surmounted by a small globe to the same bell jar, the latter could continue to be used so long as it was not broken by careless handling.

These small globes, which could be easily carried about, had been preserved by the doctor in his own room. To avoid confusion he had gummed on each a small label showing the name of the person from whom the contents had been obtained, and the date of the event which everybody else would have called their "death," but which James called their "metamorphosis." Globe No. 1 was that of William Slutter; No. 2 was an old eel-seller, Mrs. Prim; No. 3 was a Norwegian seaman. There were by now seven in all, set side by side on an empty shelf in James's room. I spent hours contemplating them. They looked like soap bubbles suddenly and miraculously solidified. Inside each there stretched shifting strands of mingling blue and green, which, one convex, the other concave, followed the curve of the ball. It was merely, I think, the reflected image of window, sky and trees in the two surfaces of the sphere. But sometimes I fancied I could see other and stranger shapes quivering within.

"Ah!" the doctor would say, when he found me in contemplation before the shelf, "you're having a look at my 'souls,' are you?"

"How I wish you would set them free, James!"

"Later on," he would say, "later on. . . . When I've found out all I can learn from them."

From time to time he made an examination with the rays, to be sure that his "souls," or rather as he used to say his "fluid ghosts," had not escaped through the transparent walls of their prison. He observed no change. Every time he found that same milky gleam, the same stirring of whirling shapes. An incomprehensible, but real, life was maintaining itself inside the globes.

James had discovered that the fluid exerted a distinct action upon certain external objects. If one brought a screen of fluorescent substance close to one of the globes, it was faintly lit up. For a long time I hoped that it might thus prove possible to enter into communication with the "ghosts." The luminosity of the screens subjected to the action of the globes continually varied; and by long or short periods of light a conversation might have been practicable. But all my efforts at interpreting these signs were in vain. James, for his part, tried to "bombard" the psychons, a first time with the help of X-rays, and a second time by making use of radioactive elements. These last experiments, besides yielding no results, were distasteful to me. I regarded them as at once useless and cruel. The word "cruel" may seem surprising—but what did we know of the effect of these atomic bombardments on a substance which might well be sentient? I had argued this matter quite frequently with James; and over the question of a much simpler experiment, yet one which seemed to me much more blameworthy, our arguments were resumed, but so fiercely this time that for a moment I almost thought they would put an end to our friendship.

I had been away for a couple of days, engaged in some library researches at Oxford. Visiting my friend on my return, I found him examining two globes added to his collection during my absence, bearing the numbers 8 and 9. No. 8, he told me, was Agatha Lind, a young dancer who had committed suicide with veronal; No. 9 a Russian, Dimitri Roskoff, who had died of cancer. I was surprised to observe that instead of cutting the tube, and so making the globes perfectly spherical, James had in each case left the tube on the globe, contenting himself with sealing the extremity.

"Hullo, have you adopted a new method, James?" I asked. "I don't like it. . . . You rob our soap bubbles of all their beauty."

"You don't know what I want to do," he answered. "I have my reasons—you'll see. . . . I even think you will be pleased with me, you who are always complaining of possible cruelty in leaving a soul 'imprisoned in solitude.'"

"What do you mean?"

"It's quite simple. . . . Suppose that I place these two tubes in communication, one of the two globes being upside down above the other, what will happen?"

"I don't know. . . . Probably the two fluids will mingle and fill the whole space."

"Just what seems likely to me, too. . . . But then you will no longer have one solitary soul; you will have two souls joined in a closer, more intimate way than is conceivable in any earthly union. . . . What's wrong? Don't you think that's so?"

"I don't know at all, James, but it seems to me a monstrous idea, and I cannot understand your conceiving it. . . . What! You would go and choose two beings at random who don't know each other, who would perhaps loathe each other, and you would force them, as you say, into a kind of union more intimate than any other, one that you yourself cannot even imagine? And you would do this for no reason, just from curiosity? No, not even from curiosity—because what will you ever know about the result of your attempt? Nothing—because, even granting that we are here in the presence of sentient and conscious beings, you are powerless to enter into communication with them!"

James looked at me solemnly, and even sadly.

"How unfair and passionate you are!" he said. "You know I am not a wicked man. . . . Very much the contrary. . . . I've had too many sorrows to be wicked. . . . I can understand other people condemning my researches, but you. . . . You ought to have realized long ago that I wouldn't occupy myself with these matters if I had not hopes of their possibly opening up great hopes, infinite vistas, for others. . . . Have faith in me. . . . I give you my word I will drop all research the moment I find what I am seeking."

"No, James, I implore you! Leave these things alone! Put them aside. . . . I'm going to tell you something that I ought not to tell you. . . . I assure you that if you don't abandon these dangerous paths of your own free will, you are going to be forced to abandon them. . . ."

"Oh? Have they been telling you something?" he asked eagerly. "All the more reason for getting ahead fast! I'm going to make this test immediately."

"I will have no hand in it," I said. "Good-bye!"

And I came away. But as soon as I was out in the street, I regretted my words.

XII

NEXT morning I received a message at my hotel.

Don't be obstinate [it read]. *I was not quite myself. I have set free your protégés. Come over—you are the only man I can talk to about these things, and I need to talk about them. In any case, you are burning to know what has happened.—Yours, H. B. J.*

I jumped into a taxi, calling "Saint Barnaby's Hospital," to the driver. When I got there, the hospital porter, who by now had become a friend, told me where I could find James; he had just been called over to one of the wards. I went up, and from afar I could see his face of anguish lighten at the sight of me. Coming over to me, he took me affectionately by the arm.

"Be easy in your mind," he said. "I have broken those two globes. . . . But I missed you badly; I'll tell you why later on. . . . Just wait for me a few minutes."

He stepped behind the cretonne screen which had been placed round the bed of a woman patient for an examination, and I stood waiting. After a few minutes he reappeared, and led me on to the terrace.

"Well, James? Negative results?"

"Negative? Oh, no, not at all! Very curious results, but depressing."

"Depressing! You alarm me. . . . What happened?"

"Nothing serious. . . . But you remember how we both supposed that the fluid of the two globes would fill the whole of the available space? Well, that was a mistake! When I put the combined arrangement of the two sealed globes under the rays, only one, the upper one, was luminous."

"Really! But how do you explain that?"

"I don't explain, I never explain anything, I only state the facts. . . . The whole of the fluid in both globes, you see, had merged within the upper one. . . . Good. Well, now, tell me—do you suppose that this globe was a brighter or duller one than usual?"

"Brighter, of course, because it brought together——"

"Well, it wasn't! And that's what I find so depressing.
. . . It was almost extinguished. . . . What is the deeper
meaning of this phenomenon? What spiritual or sentimental reality can it point to? Perhaps we shall never know,
either of us. . . . But faced with that wan, ashy light, those
enfeebled and slowed-up currents, I thought of your scruples, and I saw more cogency in them than I did at first. . . .
Even if there were only one chance in a million, I reflected,
that two beings should be in misery through my own fault,
yet that was ample reason for trying to save them. . . . You
can imagine the strange and rather painful hour I went
through. I kept repeating to myself the words of our
friend Hamlet—'To die; to sleep; no more. . . .' I kept
telling myself that after this hard life of ours, it is cruel
to refuse men sleep and rest. . . . And at last I took a
hammer, broke the tube, and turned the globe upward."

"And it emptied itself?"

"Of course."

"Bravo, James! I'm delighted! And I'd be even more so if
you promised to leave things there. It seems to me that,
having reached this point in your researches, and given
the degree of precision they have attained, you have only
two courses open: either you must make them public and
repeat them in the presence of other scientists, or you must
abandon them because you will be losing your position and
your friends to no purpose. . . . As regards myself, I fear
you will be losing me of necessity. My work is coming to an
end, and I can't spend my life in England. In a fortnight I
shall be leaving, and, believe me, I would leave with an
easier mind if you gave me your word. . . ."

"Don't get sentimental, old man. A fortnight in France,
and you will have forgotten me completely. . . . But you're
right when you say that to continue repeating these experiments is useless, because nothing will persuade me to make
them known. . . . I shall drop the whole thing. . . . Or at
least, I'll only do one more . . . if circumstances ever make
it possible. If that fails, the whole business will have been
a dream, a dreary one, and no more. . . ."

"And you will give back Mr. Slutter his freedom?"

"You shall give it him yourself, this very evening."

And it was indeed myself who broke globe No. 1 that same evening. Before bringing myself to the point, I held it for a long time between my hands. In cracking it, would I be putting an end to the second, and brief, existence of Mr. William Slutter? There was no means of knowing, and it still seemed the lesser risk to allow nature to follow her accustomed course. I dropped the globe into an iron mortar, and with the noise of the splintering glass there was mingled, I fancied, a sort of infinitely distant vibration, infinitely faint, and yet perceptible.

. . . .

When I saw Dr. Digby again I was able to assure him that James had abandoned the investigations which were disquieting the hospital authorities. Digby had already heard this from his informant, who was no doubt Gregory.

"I am pleased with this news," he said, "for we shouldn't have been able to shield him much longer."

I refrained from telling him that James had made a reservation in his promise for one eventuality. Yet I was almost certain that my friend, when he actually spoke those words, had a definite idea in his head, and, what is more, I thought I knew him well enough to have guessed at this idea. I had seen that the failure of that experiment in which he had tried to obtain the close commingling of two souls, or (as he would have said) two fluid "ghosts," had disappointed him profoundly, and that this disappointment was something far more than the disconcertment of a scientist whose hypothesis turns out to be unsound. It had long been noticeable that James's dominant emotion was an acutely painful sense of what the irremediable cleavage of death means for human beings. He had often spoken to me of those words one longs to have said, words to remain forever unspoken save to a dead body, blind and deaf. The possibility of a more enduring union between two souls was bound to attract him and touch him in his most sensitive spot. And now, instead of the enhanced vital force which he believed and hoped that he would find by producing that union in the strange world of his "ghosts," he had been

faced with the contrary—the quenching of the united pair.
But his desire was left unvanquished. He had certainly told
himself that the failure was due to the fact of the beings
thus brought together having been made to repel each other,
and not to commingle. Furthermore, he thought that if two
deeply united souls really could be combined, atom for atom,
a superior state would then appear. Under his outward
sarcasm, as I have already said, he was a sentimental. He
believed profoundly in friendship, and in love. The single
experiment of which he spoke would depend, I was certain,
upon whether chance ever brought him two people, in their
last moments, whose unity in life had been perfect: he would
try to unite them once more in death.

You will think that the chance of this happening was
small. I myself was not so sure. Unless one has lived right
inside the life of a great town, as is possible for the police-
officer or the doctor to do, one has little idea of the sorrows
and beauties it may hold. During the past two months I
had been watching so many extraordinary cases pass
through Saint Barnaby's that anything seemed possible.
But my own stay in London was almost over, and I knew
that if ever Dr. James carried out his last experiment, I
should not be a witness of it. During that fortnight I only
saw him once again. I was working hard. I had found an old
French friend, a secretary at the Embassy, with whom I
spent several evenings, and I did not return to Saint Barnaby's until the eve of my departure. I had telephoned to
James asking if I could meet him, and he had sent word by
the porter to come and see him in his own room about nine
in the evening.

.   .   .   .

He was not there when I entered, so I took a book and sat
down in the armchair. After a time, as there was no sign
of James, I drew aside the curtain concealing the "ghosts."
I hoped that he had completed their liberation, and I had an
idea, if he had not already done it, of asking leave to carry
out the act of release myself before leaving.

The globes were in their usual place, and to my great
surprise I saw that there was a new one amongst them, bear-

ing on its label the number "10-11," without any name. I
instantly realized that James had repeated the experiment
of fusion which had angered me, and I felt seriously annoyed with him. . . . "10-11.". . . No name. . . . Who
were these two hapless creatures? I was filled with a vague
sense of anxiety which I had difficulty in defining more
exactly. . . . Why wasn't James coming back? He had given
me a definite rendezvous, and to be seriously late was not
like him.

I was turning the mysterious ball over and over on my
knees, when I felt two hands laid on my shoulder. "Alas,
poor Yorick!" came a gay cheerful voice. I turned round,
and was astonished by the change I saw in James's face.
Never had I seen a human being so completely transformed
within a few days. The lines of his face, usually restless and
and twitching, had taken a look of soothed serenity. His
smile was no longer a sarcasm but a relaxation.

"What's happened to you, James?"

"Happened? To me? Nothing. . . . Why?"

"You look so happy. . . ."

"Oh! Is that so obvious then? Well the truth is that I am—
and I'll show you why. . . . Just put that globe you have
there on the mantelpiece, will you? How gloomily you were
gazing at it! That's right. . . . Now help me to get my
apparatus out from this corner. . . . Thanks. . . . Just a
bit to the left. . . . Will you turn the lights out?"

I turned the switch, and a cry escaped me in spite of myself. A sphere of light was gleaming on the mantelpiece with
prodigious radiance. It could hardly be compared with anything but that of a full moon in a perfectly clear summer
sky, in Greece or the East. It was a gleaming pearl, and
its depths moved currents more gleaming still, and a whirling nebula of liquid, flaming diamond.

"Marvelous!" I said. . . . "But what miracle——?"

For a few minutes longer he let me contemplate this amazing spectacle, and then, after putting on the lights in the
room, he told me the story. It appeared that in a neighboring
music hall, two acrobats, the Hanley Brothers, had been performing their flying trapeze act during the past fortnight.
James had not seen their "turn," but Digby, who had seen

it, described it to him, and later told me, too, about it. He had considered it as a spectacle of most uncommon quality and gracefulness. Ned and Fred Hanley were two very handsome young men, really brothers, whose resemblance was in itself a marvel. For their turn a backcloth of black velvet was dropped, and against this, during their terrifying spinning, their two white bodies stood out under the beams of the spotlight.

The brothers had enjoyed a great success, so great indeed that the management asked them to extend their engagement to another week. What happened on the first night of that extension? Nobody knew, and the police were making inquiries. Whatever the cause, one of the supporting wires of the trapezes had given, and the two brothers had fallen from a great height. Seriously injured, they were taken to the hospital and died there during the night, only a few minutes between them.

"Some of their friends came along with them," said James, "and I heard them talking about the extraordinary unison between these two lads, their work in common, and the strength of the affection that joined them, and I could not then withstand my desire to carry out in such favorable circumstances the final experiment I spoke about. . . . Don't worry—Gregory wasn't there: I had the help of a laboratory lad who understood nothing of what he was doing. . . . I came back to my room at three o'clock this morning; I united these two ghosts, and was able to contemplate the wonderful sight you have just been admiring yourself. . . . Do you now advise me to break that globe?"

"No, my dear James. I can only guess what is happening in it, but it would be surprising if such great beauty were not a sign of happiness."

And then, as the hour was getting late, I had to explain, notwithstanding my desire to stay, that I had come to say good-bye.

"True," said James. "Well, then, good-bye. . . . I don't know if I shall see you again. When life cuts apart it cuts deeply. But I shall always be grateful to you for these months during which you have been a loyal and discreet friend to me. . . . So loyal and discreet, indeed, that I am going to ask one last favor of you. . . . It won't be immediate—perhaps it will never arise. But it is possible that a day will come when I shall need your help. . . . Where I shall be, I know not, but I shall send you a telegram asking you to join me by the most rapid means, whatever your engagements at the moment. . . . You know me well enough to realize that I would not make such an extraordinary request if I did not have grave reason. . . . I give you my pledge to make only one such appeal to you in the course of your life, but for this single occasion I ask for your solemn oath."

"You have it," I said, moved by his deep earnestness.

"God bless you!" he answered.

He came with me to the door. It was a fine summer evening; but the moon in the starry sky shone with less brilliance than the light I had just seen on the mantelpiece, twofold and alive.

XIII

WHEN James said that I would forget him, I protested to the contrary. But he was not far wrong. During the next few years my work made heavy demands on me, and did not bring me back to England. Sometimes I thought about those strange weeks, but as one thinking of some fantastic tale rather than of a real memory. The first letter I had from James was early in 1926, to tell me that he had kept his promise and renounced the fuller pursuit of his researches; the second, in October, 1927, was to let me know that Miss Philipps had lost her father and that he was about to marry her. This did not really astonish me. I sent them a small present, and in her letter of thanks, Edith Philipps, or rather Edith James, told me that she needed a few months' rest in the south of France, that her husband was taking a holiday to accompany her, and that they would both be coming through Paris the following week. Unfortunately, I was in the country when this letter arrived, and I did not see my friends when they were passing through.

In December I had a card from James. He and his wife were at Cap-Martin. He asked whether I would not come and pay them a visit, if I had any thought of traveling that winter, or if not, whether a telegram from him would still find me in Paris. I replied that, barring unforeseen events, I was anxious to remain at home and work.

About the middle of January, 1928, a friend of mine, a man of letters, fell ill and asked me to take his place for a lecture which he had engaged to give at Copenhagen. To oblige him, I accepted; and it may be that the memory of Hilda James, whose story I had not forgotten, counted for something in my desire to see something of Denmark. My journey was only to take five days in all.

I arrived in Copenhagen in the morning, and had to speak the same night. As soon as I got out of the train, one of my welcomers handed me a telegram which had just arrived for me. I opened it and read: "Come. James. Florida, Cap-Martin."

I was bowled over. It had not occurred to me to let James know of my being away for such a brief time. But he had counted on my pledge, and my mind was made up to keep it, although circumstances would force me to do so more slowly than I could have wished. To the great surprise and annoyance of the organizers of the lecture, I told them my dearest friend was dying, and that I would have to set off home again. What time was the first train? There was none before the next morning.

I spent my day in scanning time-tables with the hotel porter. Even granted that there was no hitch, and that none of my trains on this long journey was late, I could not reach James until the third day. But his telegram, forwarded from Paris, was already twenty-four hours old; my friend would think me singularly careless. I inquired about the possibility of going by air, but the weather was bad and the winter service uncertain. All I could do was to send James a wire in my turn, explaining my delay and announcing my arrival. This I did. I lectured that evening, better than usual because of my high pitch of excitement; I did not sleep, and left Copenhagen in the morning.

During the long ensuing hours of Danish and German and

French trains, ferryboats, customs and passports, I tried vainly to foresee what I would find at my journey's end. I was filled with mournful and inevitable forebodings. The sole link of real intimacy between James and myself, and the one which made me, so far as he was concerned, irreplaceable, was that macabre quest of which I had been the witness. If he was urgently in need of seeing me, it could only be to help him in the course of an experiment of the same kind, and as his anxiety about it was such that he summoned me, it was not hard to guess what this experiment might be. Would I get there in time? Wouldn't James and I have difficulties with the local authorities? I remembered with relief that M. Raibaldi, the *préfet* of Alpes-Maritimes, was a friend of my father's. He might be useful. Down came the train, past the olive trees, alongside the pebbly streams. Beyond Marseilles, the vivid blue of the sea and the white sails seemed cheerless and frightening. And at last, under a summer sun, about half-past two in the afternoon, as I was in despair of ever arriving, the train stopped in the station of Roquebrune-Cap-Martin.

James was not at the station. This hardly surprised me, for he could not have known which train I would arrive by, so I took a cab and drove to his villa. It was a small pavilion ringed with palm trees, in a garden full of flowers. I remember my pleasure at a whiff of heliotrope that reached me when I was ringing the bell. A servant clothed in black appeared on the steps of the house. 'I seem to know this man,' I thought, as he came across the garden to open the gate for me. 'Where the deuce have I seen him?' And just as he reached me I recognized him. It was Biggs, an English soldier who had been the doctor's batman during the War, and whose services I myself had shared with James for several months.

"Good-day, sir," he answered. "Yes, my wife and I were here, with Dr. and Mrs. James. . . . I am sorry to tell you, sir, that the doctor is dead. Did you not receive my second wire?"

"No. . . . Dead? James? But when? I heard from him only four days ago."

"He was already dead, sir. . . . But come in."

He took my bag and carried it with him into the house. Then, seating me on a garden-chair, he told me his story:

"You know, sir, that Mrs. James has always been very ill. She had an operation shortly before her father's death. . . . When she became the doctor's wife, it was obvious to every one that she was dying, and of course to a medical man as he was, more obvious than to any one. . . . I always said, sir, that the doctor was a saint, and only married Miss Philipps to be better able to look after her. When he suggested that I should take service with them and come with them to France, I said to my wife: 'It won't be a lasting place, but we must take it. . . .' And we haven't regretted it, sir. . . . Nobody could have been nicer than the doctor and his wife. They were very fond of each other. . . . Never did I see people so easily happy. In the daytime, when the weather was good, they went and sat on the beach together, and in the evenings the doctor read aloud. . . .

"For the first couple of months Mrs. James was pretty well. But after that, from the middle of December, she seemed only to get paler and more silent. . . . It was obviously the beginning of the end. But happily the doctor kept her hoping right to the last that he would pull her round. He told her he was going to give her a new treatment he had invented. . . . And in one room he prepared some very strange contrivances for this purpose. There was a big glass bell which could be raised and lowered by moving a small lever, small flasks, and an apparatus covered with a black cloth. . . . His 'laboratory,' doctor called that room. . . . My wife and I never entered it. . . . What's more, he never used it himself, except— But I'm forgetting to tell you the most important thing, sir. Five days ago Mrs. James had a fainting fit and remained unconscious. My wife was with her, along with the doctor. About one o'clock in the morning he told my wife to go to bed, and that he would call her down if he needed her. He did not call her, and about eight next morning she came back into the room. . . . There she was startled to find that Mrs. James was no longer in her bed, and that the doctor had disappeared. On the table there was a large envelope addressed to me. . . . My wife was frightened and brought it to me in a hurry. I read the poor doctor's letter. . . . Here it is, sir. . . ."

Biggs drew two letters from his pocket and handed me one. I read it:

"Biggs—you are to do exactly what I am telling you, extraordinary as it may appear to you. Mrs. James died this morning, and I wish to avoid surviving her. Our two bodies are in the room I called my laboratory. Do not go in, and do not touch anything. Send off the telegram which you will find in the envelope; it is for the French officer who was with us at Ypres. He will come instantly and make all arrangements. So do not concern yourself with anything. Simply send off the telegram and wait. All will be well. Goodbye."

"But then, Biggs . . .," I began.

"Just a moment, sir. There was another letter, addressed to yourself, which I was to give you as soon as you arrived."

I felt a touch of reproach in his tone of voice. The letter he handed me was sealed. I tore it open and read as follows:

"I fear I shall cause you pain, and probably serious trouble; but I have your promise, and know that you will do what I ask of you. Biggs will explain what has happened—I had foreseen it for a long time. You will then understand (although I dare say you had already done so), why during the time you were in London, I was so feverish in pushing forward the researches which seemed so wild to you. In the house you are about to enter you will find a laboratory very much like that in which we worked together at Saint Barnaby's. Under the glass-bell jar in the center you will see two bodies—my wife's and my own. You remember the way in which the globe at the top of the jar is taken off. Do so with care. Then, after sealing up the globe, take it over in front of the black apparatus familiar to you. I hope that you will then have a glimpse of something of Edith and myself. If you find, as I hope, and believe you will, our ghosts mingled in the same way as those of the two brothers whom you doubtless remember, it is my wish that you should preserve them, and if possible that you should provide for their safe-keeping, by your children and your children's children.

*Naturally, I cannot hope for the very long preservation of so
fragile an object; but in my earthly existence I have had too
brief an enjoyment of my poor Edith's love. If, thanks to
you, I can find a few years' happiness in a world that is still
outside our conception, I think you will have done a good
deed. . . ."*

With that sentence I broke off reading, and eagerly asked
Biggs:

"And where are the doctor and his wife now?"

"At the cemetery, sir. . . . After sending you the telegram I waited two days. . . . And then as there was no
sign of you, my wife and I got frightened. . . . What could
we say if we were asked why we had left these two dead
people unburied? We're in foreign parts. . . . I only know
a few words of French. . . . I went to the *Mairie,* sir, and
showed them the doctor's letter—mine, not yours. A doctor
came up, and broke the glass."

"Broke the glass! Then everything's ruined, Biggs. . . .
But why break it, when you told me it was easy to lift?"

"I don't know, sir, I didn't understand what he said. . . .
I think that when he came in and saw these two bodies under
a glass cover, he thought it was a case of asphyxiation.
. . . Later on, after the post-mortem, he told me that the
doctor had taken poison. . . . At least, I think that's how it
was, sir—as I say, I didn't understand very well. . . . But
what could the doctor expect, sir? And if you had arrived
sooner . . . After all, he was dead—what *could* we have
done?"

Interrupting, I asked him to take me to the laboratory. I
clung to a faint hope that perhaps, by some miracle, the
globe had remained intact at the top of the bell jar. Alas, I
found the room strewn with broken glass. Of the jar and the
globe there remained nothing but fragments. Those who had
found the bodies had no doubt wanted to waste no time.
They could hardly be blamed: how could they have guessed
the strange nature of what they were wrecking?

"There is also this case, sir. The doctor had fixed a label
on it saying that I was to give it to you. So I hid it in my
own room when the men came from the *Mairie.*"

"What's in the box, Biggs?"

"I don't know, sir."

I opened it. On a layer of crumpled paper I found a glass globe just like those of Saint Barnaby's, and I picked it up with sudden hope. Then I saw that it bore a label which I knew well: "10-11, NED AND FRED HANLEY."

"Poor James!" I reflected. "So he succeeded in giving to others the survival he would so gladly have had for himself!"

I went over to the cemetery to lay some flowers on the graves of Edith and Howard Bruce James, and left for Paris that same evening, carrying on my knees the case bequeathed to me by my friend. I clung to the object with a superstitious care which was the greater for my vague sense of remorse. Certainly, I knew not what form of existence James had desired for himself and his beloved, but I had given him my word to secure it for him; and now, in spite of myself but still through my failure, he was robbed of the fruit of his researches. Endlessly I wondered what I ought to have done. Should I have warned James before I left for Copenhagen? There had been no time; and in any case, though I had always guessed more or less what he hoped from me, I had not fully realized it. It had not occurred to me that James would want to die at the same time as his wife. Was I to be solely responsible for that lack of comprehension? He alone knew his own designs, and could he not have anticipated more methodically all the opposing hazards in this unique event? Couldn't he have given Biggs exact instructions in the event of my not arriving? But doubtless he had thought that Biggs would grasp none of such recommendations, or would be a poor hand in carrying out a delicate maneuver. And in the end, as I reached Paris, I told myself that these broodings over the past were vain.

For a long time I deliberately refrained from thinking about the experiments at Saint Barnaby's and their tragic climax. But for some months I have been feeling ill and quite near death myself. I have felt it my duty to leave an account of the incredible and true facts of which fortune made me the witness. It is my only means of providing for the safe-keeping, with all the care I have always taken myself, of the globe containing the mingled ghosts of Ned and Fred Hanley. Last night, possibly for the last time, I had a fancy to look at them in the invisible beam of the apparatus which was the doctor's legacy. Their brightness has not dimmed since the day when it made me cry out in admiration, up in James's room. The amazing persistence of so beautiful a phenomenon only heightens my grief at having been unable to unite, in that same way, Edith James and her husband.

The glass globe will be found in the small cabinet, shut off by a blue curtain behind a grille, on the right-hand side of my desk.

BERNARD QUESNAY

(Translated by Brian W. Downs)

In Memoriam
J. A. M.

CHAPTER ONE

"Devant tant de sécheresse, Lucien tomba
dans une profonde rêverie."
STENDHAL

"MONSIEUR ACHILLE," said the notary, "I am ready."

"We are listening, Maître Pelletot."

The notary settled his glasses more firmly and began the office of the day:

"On this fifteenth day of March in the year one thousand, nine hundred and nineteen, there appeared before me, Maître Albert Amédée Pelletot, notary of Pont-de-l'Eure, the following:

"Monsieur Achille Quesnay, manufacturer, of the Château de la Croix Saint-Martin, Pont-de-l'Eure;

"Monsieur Camille Marie Lecourbe, Chevalier of the Legion of Honor, manufacturer, of Pont-de-l'Eure;

"Monsieur Antoine Pierre Quesnay, manufacturer, of Pont-de-l'Eure;

"And Lieutenant Bernard Quesnay, at present on active service with the fifteenth battalion of the *Chasseurs à Pied*.

"The aforesaid have agreed on the following articles and regulations of the partnership into which they are desirous of entering for carrying on the business of manufacturing and selling woolen fabrics under the style or firm of 'Quesnay and Lecourbe.'"

163

Bernard Quesnay studied the scene as a connoisseur of painting.

Opposite him, his grandfather's face, a vivid pink beneath his white hair, stood out against the dark tapestry with the clear brilliance, the sharp outline of a Holbein. To the old man's right and left his son-in-law Lecourbe and the elder of his grandsons, Antoine, minor figures veiled in shadow, listened resigned to the notary's rigmarole. The monotonous throbbing of the looms in the mill made faces and hands tremble with a mechanical vibration, giving these three men the passive appearance of machines.

"The decease of one or other of the partners shall not entail the dissolution of the partnership, which shall lawfully continue as between the surviving partners, and the widow or assignees of the deceased partner shall not be entitled to any payment over and above the sums placed to the account of the deceased at the stocktaking next preceding his decease."

'Nice talk,' thought Bernard, 'all it's concerned with is our dying. . . . However, the sacred fire must burn everlastingly beneath the boilers of the Family. This notary sets up one safeguard after the other, so that the continuation of the cult may be assured. . . . What would Monsieur Achille do if he knew he was condemned to die tomorrow? Without a doubt, he would dictate his letters and take the necessary steps for his "falling due" (as he would consider it).'

"The present partnership shall be constituted for a duration of twenty years, as from the first day of July, one thousand, nine hundred and nineteen. In the event of voluntary liquidation. . . ."

'Maître Pelletot is my grandfather's chaplain. . . . Here are we—for twenty years at peace with the gods; and here am I—for twenty years tied to this job. Am I doing right?'

". . . Done at Pont-de-l'Eure, in the registered office of the firm, this fifteenth day of March, in the year one thousand, nine hundred and nineteen. . . ."

'Buying wool, selling cloth—this then is to be my life.
. . . In twenty years' time, the game will be over, all hope
. . . My short and only life. . . . In twenty years' time, the
game will be over, all hope of adventure lost, every chance of
happiness gone. Every morning I shall go my round through
the work-rooms; of an evening, in the office, I shall dictate:
"In reply to your favor. . . ." The worst of it is, that I shall
not be unhappy. . . . And what for? What compels me to
sign?'

A heavy sadness enveloped him; he repeated to himself:
'My short and only life. . . . God! How ugly those
painted windows are! And that blue stuff on the walls,
edged with that red border, is just frightful. . . . All the
same, I ought to be listening. I am tying up my life by this
deed and I can't even get myself to take any interest in it.
Uncle Lecourbe really is preposterous. Even when he isn't
doing anything he keeps his self-important look.'

"And, the deed having been duly read, the aforesaid have
hereto appended their signatures with that of the notary. . . ."

In pronouncing the last phrase, Maître Pelletot's voice
rose like the scale run up by the last drops of water in
filling a vase. He stood up.
"Monsieur Bernard, permit an old friend of your family
to congratulate you on entering a business which has never
ceased to expand and to wish you that success, so richly
deserved, which has always fallen to the share of your
grandfather and your poor father."
Already, in order to sign the deed, the old man had gone
and sat down heavily in the armchair left vacant by the
notary.
Monsieur Lecourbe, affable and solemn, stroking his
square-cut beard, wished to explain the economic situation
to Maître Pelletot. A great reader of financial reviews, he
built up on shifting statistics theories which straightway
came to grief. The magnificence of his mistakes detracted
nowise from the authority of his prophecies.
"Trade," said he, "is about to go through a long period
of prosperity. That happens after every great war. As in

1815, as in 1871, the needs of Europe, crippled as she is, are immense."

"Immense," the notary agreed, sadly contemplating the shiny, greasy sleeves of his frockcoat.

"The foremost economists," said Monsieur Lecourbe, stroking his beard, "predict that this period of fat kine will last for thirty years at least. Consider, Maître Pelletot, that we have to set on their feet again the devastated regions of France, of Belgium, of Italy, not to mention Austria and Russia. Never before has such a task been presented to human activity."

Bernard and his brother Antoine exchanged a smile. Monsieur Lecourbe's eloquence amused them with the scientific form of its incoherence. His "up to a certain point and in a certain degree," his "in this connection, but in another realm of thought" were famous in the family. The Quesnays, a rugged, taciturn race, could not get over their surprise at having admitted this chatterer to their counsels and bosoms.

"The stocks of wool," Monsieur Lecourbe continued, "have been exhausted to make uniforms. In Japan. . . ."

Monsieur Achille was listening impatiently to this futile speech. His bony, hairy hand made a swift turn, as if starting up an invisible machine. At this crude signal, this sharp reminder of the rights of machinery over man, his docile grandsons and son-in-law at once vanished, as if a powerful cable had dragged them off to the mill.

CHAPTER TWO

MONSIEUR ACHILLE, an old man of seventy-two (and very rich at that), went in for business as old Englishmen go in for golf, religiously. To his grandson's question: "Why spend a short life in manufacturing textiles?" he would doubtlessly have replied: "Why live and *not* manufacture them?" But all talk which did not deal with the technicalities of his business was, for him, mere negligible sound.

A descendant of farmers who had turned weavers in the days of the First Empire, Monsieur Achille preserved the traces of that peasant origin in an unappeasable lust for work and an incredible distrustfulness. His maxims astounded with their fierce contempt of mankind. He used to say: "Every deal put to me is a bad one, for if it wasn't it wouldn't be put." He used to say also: "Nothing you don't do yourself is ever done." "All reports are false reports."

The roughness of his retorts terrified the wool-brokers, whose hands shook as they opened their blue parcels before him. He did not believe that amiability and solvency were compatible virtues. If a customer tried flattery, he cut down his credit. With foreigners, whom he used to call "Natives," without making any further distinction between Europeans and Kanakas, he refused all dealings.

Like all the great mystics, Monsieur Achille led an austere life. In his eyes, luxury was one of the first signs of indigence. In women he saw nothing but the fabrics in which they wrapped themselves. On his lips, a phrase like "I feel your dress: the stuff is very soft," would have been ingenuous, innocent of afterthought. Deprived of his clicking looms, he would have withered away at once. He grew old only on Sundays, and holidays would have killed him. His two sole passions were love of "business" and the hatred which he bore to Monsieur Pascal-Bouchet, his fellow mill-owner and competitor.

The high red roofs of the Quesnay mills towered over the country town of Pont-de-l'Eure like a fortress over the country it protects. At Louviers, a small town only a few miles away, the Pascal-Bouchet mills stood ranged on the bank of the Eure like so many broad-backed, gnarled cathedral naves.

In the face of the imperial industry of the German "Kartels" this French industry of the days before the war remained feudal and quarrelsome. From their neighboring strongholds the two manufacturers of the Valley waged a war of prices, wishing it were lethal.

A merchant who told Monsieur Achille that "Bouchet's price is lower" made him bring down his figure at once. An overseer of Monsieur Pascal's who announced "They want me at Quesnay's" got a raise at the end of the month. This feud cost the two rival houses dear. But Monsieur Pascal-Bouchet, in this respect like Monsieur Achille, looked on business as a martial sport and never spoke of the blows dealt him in each season's campaign except with pride.

"Pascal!" Monsieur Achille was wont to say after each stocktaking. "Pascal is a fool who will be ruined in two years."

He had been saying it for five-and-thirty years.

Monsieur Pascal dissimulated his equally violent feelings better. Younger and much less rustic than his hereditary enemy, he had that considerable classical culture proper to the French middle classes towards the close of the Second Empire, which he often used to compare with the "indigo base" without which no dye is "fast." His speeches, which he always adorned with Latin quotations, and his majestic presence had made him president of the Chamber of Commerce in Pont-de-l'Eure. He lived in style, had bought the charming château of Fleuré built for Agnès Sorel, possessed pictures, fine books, and hunted with the squireens of the Valley—frivolous tastes which his austere rival reprobated. The elder of his daughters, Hélène, had married the Comte de Thianges, deputy for Pont-de-l'Eure in the Chamber.

In one another's despite, the war had brought Monsieur Achille and Monsieur Pascal together. In 1917, Françoise Pascal-Bouchet had become the wife of Antoine Quesnay, who had been wounded and discharged—a diplomatic revolution more astounding than that which made France and England allies so few years after Fashoda.

After the reconciliation, these two old men, who had spent their long lives in patient attempts at ruining one another, found no greater pleasure than to meet of an evening at their children's house and there talk over the Heroic Age. Two formless heaps sunk in club chairs, each balancing the other on either side of the fireplace, after a curt enough commentary on the day's official communiqué, they immediately took up again the story of their textile warfare.

"Do you remember, Monsieur Pascal, those white flannels which you sold to Delandre at fifteen centimes below cost price?"

"I should think I do! I was in a hurry that day and forgot to add in the spinning. . . . But you, Monsieur Achille, will you explain how you were able to do that coating at five francs, of which Roch bought all those parcels?"

"I was *not* able to do it. I was throwing money away; but it vexed you a good deal, didn't it? . . . I thought so."

Monsieur Achille rubbed his hands as he contemplated retrospectively the image of Monsieur Pascal's fury. Monsieur Pascal laughed a dignified laugh in his beautiful white beard. At hearing his whilom adversary describe the then invisible aspect of events which had so strongly stirred his passions, each of them found the lively intellectual satisfaction which opposing generals—provided they thought well of one another—would experience after the conclusion of peace in making mutual explorations of one another's systems of lines and communication-trenches; and the recollection of difficult times afforded these feudal barons some small consolation for the insipid prosperity of an industry bereft of competition.

CHAPTER THREE

"HORATIO: *Hail to your lordship!*
HAMLET: *I am glad to see you well.*"

THE throbbing of the looms stirred the air with gentle vibrations. Through the open windows you could see, above the steaming tops of the limes, the long orange roofs of the mill. The azured mist of a Normandy morning floated over the Antoines' garden. Bernard relaxed his military soul. The suppleness of civilian clothes enchanted him.

"What a day!" he murmured as he dressed. "It would be jolly to get a horse and jump a few ditches."

Overtaken by the war at the age of twenty, in the army for almost seven years, he felt he would never now be a real

Quesnay. Accustomed to consider as comrades or superior officers the beings in whom his grandfather had never seen anything but a tradesman, a customer, or a "hand," he now classed them according to their courage and spirit, not, as a Quesnay should, by their credit or their work. Sometimes even he forgot that men were created for buying, wearing and selling textiles and caught himself envying the studious leisure of rich art lovers.

In the 15th *Chasseurs* he had chosen for his closest friend a young writer, at that time a sergeant like himself, and he had spent a sedate, delicious leave in the little Paris flat which this Delamain inhabited. In a whitewashed room, furnished with a chair and a frame-bed, he had tasted the acute joys of voluntary poverty. Delamain had made him read Stendhal, very dangerous reading for a Quesnay, because it inculcates the hatred of boredom.

'If I had the will or merely good sense,' he thought as he knotted his tie, 'I would tell Monsieur Achille this very morning that I was going, and I would settle in Paris. I would go in for mathematics, history, riding and fencing, and I would see Simone every day. That would be happiness. . . .'

"Bernard!" a woman's voice called from the garden.

He went to the window and saw his young sister-in-law on the sunlit lawn.

"Hello, Françoise, up already?"

"Already, Bernard? Why, it's ten o'clock. . . . Monsieur Achille will eat you. Antoine has been gone a long while. . . . Come down and have breakfast with me. . . . I have some haddock for you, I know you like that."

"But how nice of you, Françoise. I shall be ready in a minute."

He finished dressing very quickly and joined her in the dining room.

"How charming this is, this browny-grey tablecloth of yours with the violet border and that basket of wisteria and acacia! I do admire your taste."

"The Pascal-Bouchet taste," she said, gaily and provocatively.

She had really brought into the Quesnay family, until

then insensible to beautiful things, the Pascal-Bouchet taste
extolled by the keepers of old furniture shops in Evreux
and Nonancourt.

Bernard admired the rustic style of the woodwork, the
ceiling with its black and white beams, the great opening
on to the garden with its masses of bloom. But right at the
back of his mind a Quesnay ancestor protested against this
too perfect setting.

"But you are not looking at the most beautiful things of
all. . . . My Rouen ware. . . . Admire that!"

"I will admire it this evening. . . . You are right; I'm
terribly late."

He swallowed his cup of tea at one gulp, jumped at one
bound the six steps leading down from the house, careered
like a child over the lawn, which sloped down to the town
and the mill, and did not drop again to walking pace until
he was only ten yards off the Quesnay and Lecourbe works.

Monsieur Achille greeted him at the office by looking at
his watch, a mute reproach. Monsieur Lecourbe, stroking
his beard, square and grizzled after the style of President
Carnot's, had the morning's letters passed over to the ex-
soldier.

"You will find," said he, "trade first-rate and easy."

"Too easy," growled Monsieur Achille.

Absent-mindedly turning over the spread-out letters,
Bernard beheld all the peoples of the earth humbly implor-
ing the favor of buying. On the requests of "natives" Monsieur Achille had written in blue pencil: "No reply."

Bernard amused himself with guessing the psychology of
these unknown people by the printing of the headings.

"Who is Jean Vanekem, gentleman-broker?"

"Vanekem?" said Monsieur Lecourbe with pride. "He is
a second cousin of mine. He set up a commission agency in
1916, and now he occupies a whole house in the Rue d'Hauteville. Now, that's a fellow with a first-class brain! He has
an immense office, an office, my boy, as large as the Club
here!"

Bernard, standing close to the window, was watching
four men in the muddy yard, loading a dray with "pieces"
of cloth. Not knowing that they were overlooked, they

were joking and playing. One of them, however, noticed the bosses, said something in a low voice and the whole group became businesslike and serious. Bernard sighed.

"And our relations with the hands?" he queried.

"First-rate," said Monsieur Lecourbe, stroking his beard with satisfaction.

Starting up his invisible machine with a turn of the wrist, Monsieur Achille dispatched his grandsons to the work rooms.

Barrels of oil, bales of wool, bundles of yarn strewed in the mill yard. In the work rooms, Bernard met again the smells so familiar to his childhood: the strong smell of greasy wool, the mawkish smell of wet steam. Familiar faces called forth with a rapidity that surprised him names forgotten for seven years.

"Hullo, Quibel, have you gone lame?"

"Yes, Monsieur Bernard, since the Somme. . . . When they took off my left boot, the foot came too."

"And what about you, Heurtematte?"

"Me, M'sieur Bernard? I was discharged after the Dardanelles."

"Oh, were you? That must have been a pretty warm spot, the Dardanelles?"

"It was no joke. But Cairo, that's a fine town. Haven't you been there? Women like in Paris."

Through the spinning room, where the great jennies slowly maneuvered their large squares of white yarn, they reached the burling room, where a hundred women, seated at long tables, were drawing with tweezers straw and knots out of the wool. There the oldest and most loyal women in the mill fêted Bernard.

"Madame Petitseigneur! Madame Quimouche! How are you? How are you?"

"Oh, M'sieur Bernard! So you're back again, M'sieur Bernard?"

"This stuff doesn't look too good, does it?"

"Aye, you may say it. It's bad work, M'sieur Bernard. What we want is the work they sent us before the war. Now all they can do's holiday-making."

Behind these women, through the skylight, you could see

the red roofs of the mill, the green water of the reservoirs, the river, a line drawn by a bright blue paint brush, gleaming through the silver poplars, farther away the soft curves of the violet hills. The building was lofty, and the movement of the looms imparted to it a gentle seesawing, so that the landscape danced.

CHAPTER FOUR

MONSIEUR ACHILLE installed his grandson in his private office, a dark cavern encumbered by account-books a century old, and entrusted to him the checking of cost-prices. In these calculations, the most esoteric rites of industrial magic, the profane would only have seen common problems in arithmetic; the initiate knew the part which inspiration played. The genius of the Quesnays—no less!— in a kind of holy delirium dictated to Monsieur Achille his sudden decision to forget the usual charges in order to snap up a tender coveted by Pascal-Bouchet's or to raise his figure for weaving to insane heights in order to shun the dangerous favors of the "natives."

But Bernard, a vocationless novice, did not perceive the grandeur of his ministry. Before his eyes, the scaling bricks of a long building, all windows, took up the horizon. On to the clicking of the looms, always perceptible in the trembling air, he embroidered the opening of the *Pastoral Symphony;* then, with a shake of his head, settled to work again.

'12 kilos of warp at 56 francs . . . 672 francs . . . 14 kilos of weft at 27 francs . . . 378 francs. Weaving: 82,-000 picks at . . . at how much?'

He hummed the *Peasant's Rondo.*

'Delamain and his friends would still say that I have bad taste. But what does it matter to me that Beethoven repeats himself, if what he repeats gives me pleasure? No, it's merely because he's too rounded, too finished for them. . . . I can understand Stravinsky as well as they can, but that does not lessen Beethoven in any way. . . . And my costings . . . 82,000 picks. On Saturday Pierné is doing Wagner and they are playing Molière at the Vieux Colombier in the evening. I might have taken Simone. If I warned her in time, she could get rid of her husband. But that would mean leaving for Paris in the morning: fond hope! . . . the jolting of this table with the movement of the looms admonishes me to respect the laws of Pont-de-l'Eure. . . . On the glass panes of the door Monsieur Cantaert—who doesn't look at all pleased with me—beats with redoubtable hand. And here is Monsieur Cantaert in his white blouse.'

Monsieur Cantaert, the head buyer, was harsh with his young employer.

"Monsieur Bernard, you absolutely must talk to Desmares, the head of your spinning department; the man's off his head: three adjustable spanners he's wanted of me in the last fortnight!"

"Monsieur Cantaert, I will tell him so."

"Yes, you'll have to tell him so. And then, Monsieur Bernard, I'd trouble you to cast an eye over this packing-paper account. I ask you—can you possibly use up a ton of paper in ten days, when . . ."

"Monsieur Cantaert, the packers are criminals, and I'll let them know it."

"What I tell you, Monsieur Bernard, is in the interests of the firm. You look bored when I mention such details to you, but they're important all the same, they are."

"To be sure, Monsieur Cantaert."

"By the saving for which I'm responsible, I make my salary twice over. But to keep a firm hand, I must be backed up by the boss."

"You shall be, Monsieur Cantaert."

Monsieur Cantaert's white blouse disappeared round an archway. Bernard concentrated his attention and plunged into the costings-book.

'82,000 picks at 60 centimes, plus 10 centimes cost-of-living bonus . . . 65 francs. Burling, warping, sizing . . . 50 francs . . .' "Come in!"

Crimson with fury, Monsieur Desmares came in.

"Monsieur Bernard, is it true that you told Cantaert to slate me for wastage of tools?"

"It would be more exact to say, Monsieur Desmares, that Monsieur Cantaert came to me to complain. . . ."

"Monsieur Bernard, if you have no confidence in me, all I can do is to throw up the management of your spinning department. I don't eat adjustable spanners; if I ask for them, it's because I want them. That fellow Cantaert! I'll have nothing more to do with him!"

"Monsieur Desmares, you will only have to do with me."

"From you, Monsieur Bernard, I will take anything. But from him! . . ."

Tranquilized, he departed. The young man sighed.

'Governing men is a difficult business. To succeed in it you must be completely lacking in rigidity and obstinacy. The psychology of these heads of departments is the same as that of the heroes in Homer. The most useful book for an industrial magnate is not Taylor's Ready Reckoner, but La Bruyère's *Les Caractères*. After substituting the pursuit of wealth for the pursuit of court preferment, the chapter "Of the Court" would become a first-rate "Of Business."
. . . . In five minutes, Monsieur Achille will want that price of his from me. . . . Dyeing . . . 22 kilos at 6 francs . . . 132 francs. Dressing . . . 50 francs . . . General charges . . Oh! Who is it now? . . .' "Come in!"

There were two timid knocks.

"Come in!" he called louder. "Come in, for the Lord's sake!"

Trembling hands with difficulty turned the door-handle. Five old women entered: gnarled hands folded on their black aprons, honest faces pale with emotion. This Chorus of Suppliant Women formed itself into a line and stopped to take breath.

"Madame Petitseigneur? Madame Quimouche? What can I do for this deputation from the burling room?"

"M'sieur Bernard, we've come to you, because we daren't go to Monsieur Achille. I hope you'll not be vexed, sir, with us for coming to have a word with you the very day after you're back—but we can't go on, nohow. It's the country folk, M'sieur Bernard, it's the country folk who's ruining us. You go up to Pont-de-l'Eure market; a rabbit'll cost you four francs and five sous; peas, why you can't even think of them! The more you pay us, the dearer things get. The weavers, they get their eighty, their hundred francs, but us, we're always victimized. Us in the burling room, we're all more or less widow-women, but it's necessary for the manufacture, M'sieur Bernard. . . ."

He smiled at them, embarrassed; their anxious good faith was evident. He would have liked to distribute among them riches which would have astonished and delighted them, but the shade of Monsieur Achille, formidable and watchful, floated in the steam of the boilers that dimmed the office windows. He uttered some vague phrases: he had only just got back, hadn't picked up the threads yet, would have to consult his grandfather.

"Why, of course, M'sieur Bernard, take your time. Don't worry, we won't leave the mill and go out on strike, we won't. . . . We're not for playing the fool in the streets."

Hands folded on their black aprons, the Chorus of Suppliant Women departed.

CHAPTER FIVE

SINCE the death of his wife, Monsieur Achille dined every Sunday with the Antoines. He said little beyond two or three witticisms addressed to Françoise at the expense of her Pascal-Bouchet taste. After dinner he would smoke a cigar while casting hostile glances at certain objects he hated more than others: a green Sedan chair, the model of a frigate, an old barometer. The soft mauves of the Jouy hangings on the walls, the subdued straw-colored curtains at the windows seemed to diffuse a luminous serenity in the drawing room.

Antoine used to read *Le Consulat et l'Empire* or mend bells and electric-light plugs; he was happy only in the company of Thiers, Taine, M. de Tocqueville, or with a screwdriver or hammer in his hand. At the works, he lived in the engineering shop, inventing ingenious little improvements for the machinery. In his grandfather's presence, he seemed embarrassed and as if on the defensive. He looked at him every now and then; he saw that the old man was thinking: 'What a drawing room for my grandson, and what a wife!'—and suffered a little, in silence.

Françoise, absent-mindedly striking chords, would look at them in sad astonishment, which two years' experience had not mitigated. The dismal life of the Quesnays stifled her. In her father's house at Fleuré such evening gatherings were almost always gay and lively; there were guests and games, reading aloud or music. But, outside working hours, these Quesnays were like machinery out of gear. They were waiting for the moment they returned to the mill and only awoke to a spark of life when one of them called to mind some forgotten trifle: a dissatisfied customer, a sick hand, a spoilt piece of cloth.

'How different Antoine was while we were engaged!' Françoise thought. 'But he was an officer in those days and hardly saw his grandfather; he looked from a distance and with indifference at this mill, which I detest. He had time for thinking about me. He used to lend me books and explain them to me. He was nice and affectionate.'

She called to mind their trysts on the river-bank, halfway between Pont-de-l'Eure and Louviers. At that time she was very proud of reconciling the Montagues and Capulets of the Valley. Antoine had given her a lovely edition of *Romeo and Juliet,* bound in violet doeskin and dedicated "To Juliet." She had always loved the "parma" color. Only two years ago—and that delicious enthusiasm had brought her to evenings like this! Her fingers, softly gliding over the keys, sketched out an air of Schumann's.

" 'The roses, the lilies, the sun and the doves . . .' " Bernard hummed and smiled at her.

He got up, sat down at Monsieur Achille's side and retailed to him the burlers' visit.

"After all," he wound up, "they're in the right."

"They're in the right!" growled Monsieur Achille. "That's easy enough to say. . . . Everybody's in the right."

"We're not concerned with everybody," said Bernard, rather nervous. "If you grant these women twenty centimes per hour, the earth will still go round."

"Twenty centimes per hour per hand," said Monsieur Achille, "comes to a million francs at the end of the year."

"But again," said Bernard, "we are not concerned with the whole mill."

"You cannot raise some," said Antoine, relinquishing Thiers, "without raising others. The hierarchy of labor is sacrosanct. A fine-drawer asks more than a burler, a spinner than a weaver."

"But why?" said Bernard. "They have the same stomachs, the same needs."

"There is no 'why,'" said Monsieur Achille, shrugging his shoulders. "That's how it is."

It struck nine. He got up. He never said good-bye to anyone. Antoine went with him as far as the gate. Bernard remained alone with his sister-in-law; pivoting on the piano-stool, rather after the manner of Youth Set Free, she looked at him with a smile of friendship, almost of complicity. She had hardly known him before the war, but had seen him frequently since the armistice had made leave easy to obtain. She inspired in him a rather queer feeling, a mixture of admiration, of sympathy, and of fear. Fear of what? He couldn't have told. She always seemed on the verge of taking him for her confidant; it was that perhaps which he dreaded. He was very loyal to his brotherly faith. Moreover, once more, confidant about what? Antoine worshipped his wife; he was a perfect husband.

"Well, Bernard, how are you getting on?" she said, in English.

She had been brought up by an English governess and had always spoken English with her sisters. For her it was the language of mystery, of intimacy. Bernard, who had spent a year in London, liked using it too, and that had brought them together. Antoine understood English also, but with more difficulty.

"Well," said Bernard, "I am trying to accustom myself again to the ways of Pont-de-l'Eure. It isn't much fun."

"Fun?" she said indignantly. "Oh, no, Pont-de-l'Eure is no fun. And yet I was a bit prepared for it. Louviers is not so far off, and not so different. But you—if you marry a Paris girl, I shall pity her."

"You will have no one to pity, Françoise; set your mind at rest, I shall certainly never marry."

"What do you know about it?"

"Are you discreet? Can you keep a secret?"

"It is no secret, my poor Bernard; everybody here knows that you have a liaison and that you can be seen about Paris with a woman—a very handsome woman too. But a liaison doesn't last for ever."

"No, that's perfectly true—because I am mortal myself; but it will last for as long as she wants."

"Really?" said Françoise, excited and happy. "So you love her very much? Is she beautiful?"

"What do you expect me to answer? I am a partial witness. But, honestly, since I have known her, I have never met a woman comparable to her, except perhaps you, Françoise. . . . No, that's not a silly compliment—she is like you. I have often thought, how strange it is that the two Quesnay brothers should be in love with two women of the same type! Only, Simone has something daring about her which you have not got. In you, sweet resignation is rather the dominant trait."

'Do I give the appearance of sweet resignation?' Françoise asked herself curiously. 'I feel myself so little resigned. I should like . . .' "But, Bernard," she said, "why don't you marry her?"

"Firstly, because she is married. And then—I don't believe in marriage."

Françoise was looking at him, leaning forward with her elbow resting on her knee and her chin in her hand. It was her habitual attitude in reverie.

'Does he write to her? Every day? Can a Quesnay be romantic? Why at this moment have I the impression of being frustrated? Antoine loves no one but me. The only drawback is that I am bored. . . .' "But I am sorry for that," she said aloud, "I was counting on you to get me a harem-companion. You know, there's quite a conspiracy here to make you marry the Lecourbe girl, your cousin. . . ."

"Yvonne? But she's a little girl, isn't she? I haven't seen her for years. My last remembrance of her is seesawing with her in the Lecourbe's garden. She was very heavy."

"She isn't a little girl now. She is nineteen and quite exceptional. She knows all sorts of difficult things, has taken her matriculation and is reading for a degree in English. At the moment, she's at Oxford. . . . Queer, isn't it? . . . the two Lecourbe children have brains. Roger too is doing wonders at the university."

"But after all," said Bernard, "they are half Quesnays. . . . And what is she like? Pretty? Ugly?"

"That's hard to say; she has nice points, but she is very 'robust.' She goes in terrifically for games, you know; I think she is overdeveloping certain muscles. Intellectually, she has an air of authority that frightens me."

"What a portrait!" he said, laughing. "And she is destined for me?"

Antoine came into the room. His hands were black with motor-grease.

"I beg your pardon," said he, "I have been down to the garage. The car went up the hill very badly this evening and I wanted to have a look at her with Charles."

"And what was the matter?" asked Bernard.

"The petrol-feed was faulty."

For some time they discussed questions of air-mixture; then Bernard said good-night.

"Not much changed, Bernard," said Antoine, when he was alone with his wife. "When he was ten years old, during a strike, he asked: 'Grandfather, if I sold my bicycle, could you give them what they want?'"

"That was very sweet of him," said Françoise. "And what did your grandfather answer?"

"He told the story for ten years—I never could make out whether from pride or contempt."

"I should like to know," said Françoise reflectively, as she began undressing, "I should like to know whether he, Bernard, I mean, will be happy here after his long absence."

"He will have to be," said Antoine, looking at her a little uneasily.

Before going to bed, he spent a long time mending the hot-water tap of the bath. Françoise read a novel and, from time to time, looked at the clock.

CHAPTER SIX

THANKS to Bernard's firmness, the burlers were raised; the fine-drawers followed; the weavers, whose higher wages had annoyed the other classes of labor, in their turn put in a claim; for it was an important matter to preserve the ancient hierarchy of the callings and the distances between them.

The raising of wages once more carried with it a rise in the price of fabrics. Bernard Quesnay was commissioned to go to Paris and inform the customers of the firm of Quesnay and Lecourbe.

Old memories made him dread this mission. Before the war customers—august beings of whom one only spoke with respectful awe—imposed without difficulty their cruel caprices on an industry divided and always starved for work. At the least sign of rebellion a Quesnay would see himself threatened with a Pascal-Bouchet. A complicated diplomacy, sacrifice and prayer were necessary in those days for pacifying their ferocious taskmasters.

"Times have changed, Monsieur Bernard," said old Monsieur Perruel, the Quesnays' Paris representative.

And so it turned out. Monsieur Roch, of the house of Roch and Lozeron, whom Monsieur Bernard feared more than any other—he used to buy every year more than one-third of the Quesnays' output—received him with a meekness altogether novel in that man of wrath. Monsieur Roch's office was a kind of cube of planks, scarcely furnished, which hid itself with a sort of shame behind piles of stuffs mounting up to the ceiling. This warehouse had been built to. accommodate stuffs, and in it cloth forcefully asserted its predominance over mind.

"My dear Bernard," said Monsieur Roch to him, "(I can very properly address you so, I was on friendly enough terms with your poor father), my dear Bernard, I am not haggling with you, I shall never haggle with you. . . . But more than fifteen francs I cannot pay you for riding-habits. . . ."

"Our workpeople demand a raise, Monsieur Roch; we have to satisfy everybody. . . ."

"No, my dear Bernard, not everybody. . . . Never throw over old friends. Ah, if your poor father were still alive, I am very certain I should get my thousand pieces for fifteen francs. I can still see him, your poor father—sitting on the chair you are on and dressed in that great black overcoat which he never left off. . . . Ah, he had the business instinct, and that, you know—either you have or have not got it! . . . Come now, I will go down and see Monsieur Achille at Pont-de-l'Eure, and we shall come to an understanding, I make no doubt; we shall always come to an understanding in the end, your grandfather and I."

Monsieur Roch deeply depressed Bernard, who felt him impenetrable and powerful. He sighed as he walked away from his place.

Monsieur Delandre, of the house of Delandre and Company, gave a description of the manufacturers' dictatorship:

"I telephone to Lapoutre at three in the afternoon and ask the price for a little gabardine; they quote me 13 francs 32. I wait for my partner to come in and ask him: 'Must we close at that?' 'Yes, telephone again. . . . Now the figure's 13 francs 47' . . . Why? That's how things are!—But the worst of autocrats is your friend Pascal-Bouchet. He gives you an appointment for the twenty-third of July at 9:45; you are shown into a little office; at the stroke of 9:45 Monsieur Bouchet comes in. If you are on time, he says to you: 'Monsieur Delandre, I have allotted 48 pieces to you at 29 francs. Here is a pattern-book; I give you quarter of an hour for choosing your patterns.' A quarter of an hour later he comes in again and you have got to be ready. That's present-day business: you must own that it is preposterous."

Monsieur Perruel then took him to Cavé Brothers, who exported materials for Algiers and Tunis.

"The price doesn't much matter," said Monsieur Cavé senior; "What we need, Monsieur Quesnay, is a heavy, well-gummed cloth to replace the article which the Austrians used to make before the war for Arab burnooses."

"We could make it," said Bernard, "but at the moment we have so much work in hand. . . ."

"There you go! Always the same!" Monsieur Cavé cried in his indignation. "I often used to say to your father: 'All you are capable of doing at your mill is staring at your own navels.' "

"Upon my soul, Monsieur Cavé, that would perhaps be the best thing we could do. The sages of India used to find keen enough pleasure in gazing at theirs, so they say."

Monsieur Perruel gave his employer a nudge with his elbow. As they went away, he took him to task:

"Monsieur Bernard, you ought to take your customers seriously all the same. At the present moment you don't need them, but that may yet happen. Besides—if my years authorize me to give you advice—don't talk so much. There is always too much talking in business. The foremost salesman of the place, here in Paris, is an Englishman. He never says anything but 'Good-morning' and 'Good-bye.' He comes in with his case: 'Good-morning.' He spreads out his samples, slowly, before his customer. When you say 'No,' he packs up. When you give an order, he books it. He doesn't argue, he doesn't plead. He is a very smart fellow. The funniest thing is that he comes from Montmartre and does not know any English. Another thing: you always want me to tell customers the truth. Monsieur Bernard, customers do not like the truth."

"Alas, Monsieur Perruel, no one likes the truth!"

"Customers think they know all about it, Monsieur Bernard; you must leave them with that illusion."

He took him to the region of nobler houses. The Place des Victoires, the Rue Etienne-Marcel, the Rue Réaumur, the Rue Vivienne bounded the ancient fastness of the draper-aristocracy.

There noble merchants and their prudent, athletic sons held sway; on to their oaken ceilings Bernard would have liked to paint Courtesy and Friendship coaxing a smile from Commerce. Having explored the Fastness of Drapery all day, he remembered towards evening that he had promised his uncle Lecourbe to look up Monsieur Jean Vanekem.

This great man's offices were furnished in the Directoire style. Through a half-open door you could see other offices, fair-haired typists—all pretty—and calculating-machines, gleaming in red and black japan.

Monsieur Vanekem, a very young man with his hair brushed back and an altogether American zestfulness, received the provincial Quesnay with a mixture of good grace and superiority.

"You will pardon me a second?" said he. "It is the time for my meeting with my heads of departments."

He proceeded to turn rapidly the handle of a small house-telephone, issuing orders in curt tones.

"Monsieur Perrin, conference . . . Monsieur Durand, conference . . . Monsieur Chicard, conference . . . Monsieur Meyer, conference. . . ."

Through the three doors into the office there streamed in men in black morning-coats, magnificent and deferential.

"Statistics A," Monsieur Vanekem called out. "Hungary? . . ." "2,000 metres, sir." "England? . . ." "5,000 metres, sir." "Rumania? . . . You see," he observed to Bernard, "I know every day exactly what has been sold during the day, what I still have in stock in the different countries and the total of my commitments to the manufacturers. It is all mathematics."

'Yes,' thought Bernard admiringly, 'this is your true man of affairs. Perhaps I might take a liking to this calling if I had not to follow it in that second-rate office down at Pont-de-l'Eure, where Monsieur Desmares and Monsieur Cantaert have feuds over an adjustable spanner.'

"Who," asked Monsieur Vanekem, "looks after the Banat of Temesvar?"

When the chorus of statisticians had left the stage, Bernard timidly brought forward Monsieur Lecourbe's petition.

"Help you to find capital for starting a dyestuffs plant? Child's play, my dear sir! . . . How much do you want? Two million? . . . Ah, that's a more difficult proposition. A capital of two million, you will understand, hardly interests the banks. . . . Ask me for ten, twenty, thirty million, and you shall have them tomorrow. . . . But two! However, I will see what I can do. . . . Will you dine with me, Monsieur Quesnay? We will talk about that business of yours again; I am only waiting for a friend of mine, Liliane Fontaine, an actress who is not yet very well known, but has a great deal of talent."

"But I know about her!" said Bernard. "She came and played *Hernani* at home in the country. I shall be very pleased to come."

CHAPTER SEVEN

MADEMOISELLE LILIANE FONTAINE wore her hair drawn back and perfectly flat, had fine black eyes, rather a thin bust and a lemon-yellow handkerchief tied round her right wrist. Bernard told her how he had admired her when she played Doña Sol on tour at Pont-de-l'Eure.

"Pont-de-l'Eure? . . . I should think so. The Silver Kid Hotel? And the dirt of it! . . . And that audience of old ladies with real lace fichus, medallions, violet dresses and mantles. In the gods workmen convulsed with laughter. . . ."

"I must confess," said Bernard, "that the audiences of Pont-de-l'Eure are not very romantic. . . . But they found you excellent. It was the leading man who made them laugh."

"Now, who was that? Oh, yes, Ponroy . . . the old fellow who used to be at the Odéon. He certainly is a sentimental and melodramatic actor. And he spurtles! You may imagine how nice it is to have to harmonize 'You are my lion, proud and generous' with 'How I wish you wouldn't spit in my face!' . . . Ponroy is one of the old-fashioned sort who take an interminable time over everything and give significance to every phrase. It is awful. I have played *Le Cid* with him as Don Diègue. He left me at his feet for an hour; you simply don't know what to do."

Bernard liked this green-room chatter. As he listened to it, the throbbing of the looms which still rumbled in his head seemed to die away to nothing more than a low sough-

ing of muffled violins. Monsieur Achille, taciturn and uncouth, Monsieur Lecourbe, solemn and pedantic, Monsieur
Cantaert and Monsieur Desmares, brothers at feud—all
these highly colored figures that floated through his melancholy reveries—grew dim, the far-away characters of some
Balzacian *Scénes de la vie de province.*

"Look," said Mademoiselle Fontaine, "there's Sorel. . . .
Over there in the corner the Spanish *infante* with his two
old ladies. . . . And Suzanne Caruel with her Greek."

Bernard looked about him. At the table on the right two
couples, talking very loudly, were endeavoring to astound
each other by bandying Rolls-Royces, Delages, Monets and
Corots. At the table on the left two men, by themselves,
were preparing a deal. "Now listen closely to me, old man:
the Hungarian crown is worth three centimes. For ten million crowns I can obtain the concession for a gaming-house
on Lake Balaton. Over there, you can attract . . ."

"And our bit of business?" said Monsieur Vanekem to
Bernard. "I've thought it over. After all, there's no reason
why the capital should be limited to two million."

"Well, you see," said Bernard, "we have next to no
liquid resources. . . . Wool is so dear. . . ."

"What?" said Monsieur Vanekem, surprised. "You mean
to put your own money into this business? Never do that,
my dear man. . . . No, form a little company with a capital
of six million: three in founders' shares, which you and
I will hold between us. The public will subscribe the rest.
. . . Take the business of mine for the import of coconuts—
when I started it I fixed the capital at ten million, though I
had neither ships nor plantations. . . . We did very well
without."

Bernard, musing, admired the poetical genius of Monsieur Vanekem, who, out of ideal plantations and chimerical
coconut-trees, knew how to extract real necklaces for the
graceful neck of Mademoiselle Fontaine. The orchestra
played the *Relicario*: between the tables couples danced
cheek to cheek. With the jade fringe of her whirling skirt
a very beautiful woman, her eyes half closed as if in a
swoon, grazed a crystal glass which gave forth a sweet, soft
sound. The monotonous rhythm of the violins obsessed Ber-

nard, so that he fancied he heard, like a melancholy appeal, the far-away throbbing of his looms. Music always saddened him, by filling him with an acute sensation of the flight of time. The melancholy cynicism of the beings all around him shocked his ancestral Quesnay Puritanism.

Monsieur Vanekem, who knew the two men at the table to the left, had leaned over to them and begun a professional conversation. Bernard turned to Mademoiselle Fontaine's charming face.

"Do you not find," he said to her, "that music, even of the vulgarest kind, always inspires a desire for solitude? . . . How artificial this life is! Would you not like to live on some far-off island, in Fiji or Tahiti, where machines were unknown and money without power, but where happy, naked savages danced in a heavenly tropical climate?"

" '*Mon enfant, ma soeur, songe à la douceur d'aller là-bas vivre ensemble. . . .*' It can be sung too."

"Are you making fun of me? The moment I find myself, as now, surrounded by smart women, crystal lusters, overfed men, I experience immediately that 'something bitter which emanates from joys.' I have seen too many unhappy people."

"Are you a Bolshevist?" she asked.

"Oh, no," Bernard protested vigorously, "I have the strongest class loyalty; my ideal is the primitive Roman senate, or some few English conservatives who have a very strong sense of their duties. . . . But I am a fool and am boring you."

"Oh, no," she said, "but for me only one thing really exists: the theater. All the rest . . ."

At that moment Mademoiselle Fontaine's fine black eyes lit up:

"Look at that boy coming in," said she to Bernard. "Isn't he good-looking? Chérubin to the life. I should like to get him to play *Le Mariage de Figaro* with me on tour this summer. But the infant won't hear of it. His dream is *Polyeucte*. It's enough to make you die with laughing."

"A cigar?" Monsieur Vanekem suggested, proffering his case. "Fancy, among the American war-stocks I came across some marvellous Laranagas. . . ."

CHAPTER EIGHT

A VISIT of Monsieur Roch's to Pont-de-l'Eure was ordered in accordance with an invariable and meticulous ritual. At ten o'clock Monsieur Achille's victoria (he never could make up his mind to replace his old coachman by a chauffeur) went to the station. When the carriage drew up at the door, Monsieur Achille assumed an air of indifference and attentively studied a badly balanced pile of cloth.

"Ah, it is Monsieur Roch," he used to say, in a tone as if he had expected that day twenty personages of the same importance.

"Never get a day older, Monsieur Achille," Monsieur Roch replied with artificial good humor.

The visitor took a seat at one side of the table, Monsieur Achille at the other, and they would talk of the past and of their young days for a space of time which, according to the observations of Antoine, that man of precision, varied between twenty-five and thirty-five minutes. The same anecdotes were reeled off several times per annum. The first time that Bernard attended this entertainment he had marvelled that a man as sparing of his speech and time as his grandfather should waste the one and the other in conversations all the more futile in that they were always identical. In pondering over them, he had realized that they played the same part as passes with the *muleta* before the eyes of a bull fresh from the *toril;* their aim was to surprise and tire the beast and to draw out the fight. There was no train for Monsieur Roch to catch before four in the afternoon. His decision would not be taken until five minutes before his departure. It was essential to avoid bringing the steel into play.

About half an hour after his arrival, Monsieur Lecourbe had instructions to make his entry. He served the same purposes as the *picador's* horse, a wretched creature foredoomed to defeat, and the clown in a circus, who by the comicality of his antics produces a gay and sympathetic atmosphere. Monsieur Roch took great pleasure in his demonstrating, in the name of the foremost economists, contradictory theories before him.

As soon as the *picador*, his belly gored, beat a retreat, Monsieur Achille gave the sign to the darters of *banderillos*. Antoine and his brother were entrusted with this operation. They had to take Monsieur Roch for a walk through the mill.

"My grandson," Monsieur Achille would say, "would like to show you a new machine."

"Yes," Antoine responded, "your opinion would be very valuable to me, Monsieur Roch."

"I know, my boy," Monsieur Roch said, "that I owe that to your poor father. Ah, I still see him, your poor father, with that great black overcoat of his. . . ."

An hour later Antoine brought him back, worn out and sated for a year to come with gearing, cams, eccentric-wheels, almost ripe for the *stoccado*.

Lunch was served at Monsieur Achille's and always excellent. No allusion was ever made to the day's real objective. Françoise was there—which put a surprise attack out of the question. She began by making a great effort to be agreeable and then gave up. She was blind to what Bernard called the "Balzac side" of Monsieur Roch, an ex-commercial-traveler, who, become head of his business through the sudden death of his two employers, lacked culture but not subtlety. As soon as lunch was over, she cast off all constraint.

"I have done what you told me to, Bernard, I have re-read *Anna Karenina*. I can understand Anna's suicide very well. If Vronsky had been very cruel, and not good, she would not have killed herself."

"You are talking about the theater?" said Monsieur Roch. "Personally, I do not like present-day plays, but I am fond of going to the Comédie Française to see *L'Ami Fritz* or *Monsieur Poirier*. It isn't naughty like the Palais Royal, but it's good and gives you something to think about."

Françoise became reckless.

"Bernard," she said in English, "let's walk round the garden. He's too boring. I can't stand it."

"Be careful. He might speak English."

"Certainly not. Just look at him."

With a look Antoine besought his wife to keep calm. Monsieur Achille, without understanding, divined danger, inwardly cursed the Pascal-Bouchets and proposed that they should return to the mill on foot.

The two old men walked in front, blowing a little. Antoine and Bernard followed, admiring the reeds which massed their waving tufts at the bends of the river. Antoine thought how, when he was engaged, he had walked there with Françoise. That year she had won a tussore frock which had a blue foulard collar with white spots. How lovely he had thought her! . . . He thought her still as lovely, but what strange bashfulness prevented him from continuing to tell her so? Often he disapproved of what she did and said, and that he dared not tell her either. Why had she taken up that attitude during lunch? That very morning he had begged her to control herself. She was dangerous. He loved her.

Monsieur Achille continued to withhold the steel until the moment when the rolling up of the victoria announced that the time of the visitor's train was drawing near. Then he curtly rapped out the "bottom price" he had been keeping in reserve since morning, and Monsieur Roch, agreeably surprised, drew from his pocket an order-book. Bernard took him down to the station and returned pondering somewhat sadly over the banality of the day.

'What a farce!' he thought. 'Is it necessary? One ought to run a mill as one commands a regiment, without subterfuge and without self-abasement. This all might be so simple and even grand. What need have we of a Roch? Françoise had an attack of nerves. I don't wonder. . . . If I could persuade Simone to marry me, how would she endure Pont-de-l'Eure?'

Without knowing why, he had a vision of the little violet mules which she wore in the evenings on the only trip they had ever gone on together. Before going to sleep, she put them in front of the bed, symmetrical and neat, as in Carpaccio's *Saint Ursula.*

'Simone's mules under Monsieur Achille's roof . . . Oh, it's not possible. The pity of it!'

He thought of the linguistic crazes she had. She used "authentic" when she meant "sincere," and it was from her that he had caught the trick of employing the term "side." She would, for instance, have spoken of Antoine's "Louis XVI side" and of Françoise's "Marie Antoinette side." Another of her crazes was to talk music in the language of the studio and painting in musical language. She used "rhythm" and "sonorousness" to describe a landscape. All that gave Bernard much pleasure. The carriage drew up. They had reached the mill.

"Did he look pleased?" asked Monsieur Achille.

CHAPTER NINE

CALLED to Paris by Monsieur Vanekem, Bernard felt a wish to see Delamain again. He had not given him warning, but knew him for a stay-at-home. A carriage smelling of mouldy cloth took him to Montsouris. A tiny narrow staircase climbed from floor to floor. He rang, in great fear of not finding his friend in.

After a minute, however, he heard steps. Delamain himself opened the door and did not seem surprised to see him.

"Hullo! So it's you. I am glad. . . . Come in."

"I am not disturbing you, am I?"

"I am working, but it's nothing of consequence."

To Bernard the small room in which Delamain was writing seemed an enviable asylum, a forbidden dream. Standing up with his back against the mantelpiece, he looked at his friend with pleasure. Both smiled, to express a good will which words would have falsified. Bernard admired the sheets covered with a firm handwriting. Knowing that Delamain did not like small-talk, he talked to him about his work.

"What are you busy with at the moment? I have seen your article on Sainte-Beuve. It is very good . . . Have you read this Proust they're talking of now? . . . Personally, I like the man a lot."

"Yes," said Delamain, "it is wholesome reading. . . .

What, for instance, is there left of jealousy after Swann?
A morbid curiosity, without love. . . . And how true that
is !"

"Do you still see Denise?"

Delamain nodded affirmatively.

"And you, old chap?" he said. "What are you up to in
those provinces of yours? Your works are at Pont-de-
l'Eure, aren't they? Is trade good?"

"Trade is very good, but it is all one to me. . . . My
grandfather has been at work for fifty years; what happiness has he? I don't like this job of mine, Delamain. The
workpeople, whom I actively endeavor to give a square deal,
mistrust me, and that is natural enough. In the eyes of
the statesman and bureaucrat, the employer of labor is a
parasite, making a fortune out of the exertions of others.
No one sees his difficulties. No one considers his function.
You yourself, I am sure. . . . It's intolerable. And then you
do not know what business is. It's very hard, almost impossible, to avoid crooked ways. . . ."

"For instance?" said Delamain briefly.

"Well, for instance—a customer asks you your bottom
price; you honestly quote it him. . . . Do you think he ap-
preciates your good faith and refrains from bargaining?
Not a bit of it. He presumes a priori that you are deceiving
him. That's putting it mildly: he is furious if you stick to
your point. That kind of thing exasperates me."

Delamain gently shrugged his shoulders.

"It seems to me," said he, "that you are worrying about
nothing. All human relationships are governed by conven-
tions. If it is one of them that 'bottom price' in reality means
'bottom-but-one,' all you can do is to accept it. You are
working yourself up over scuples, Quesnay; confessors do
not like that."

Bernard opened his hands as a sign of helplessness and
then, pointing to the outspread papers, said:

"What will the book be about?"

"Oh, an arid enough subject. . . . The Resurrection of
Freedom. I shall describe the generation before ours,
crushed by too oppressive a fatalism; terrified by Darwin,
that mystifier of genius; inflamed by Marx, another of the

same kidney. And I hope to show that their 'iron laws' are
nothing but hallucinations which fade away if you will it
with sufficient force. . . . I do not know if it is very clear
to you. In short, I want to show that freedom and deter-
minism are true at one and the same time, are not contradictory. Do you follow?"

"Yes; but I do not think you are right. Now, in my particular case—my sensation at the present moment is that
of being crushed by a mechanism stronger than myself. This
overwhelming rise in prices, these changes in wage-rates,
this wealth which is bursting our coffers—what influence
can I have over all these things? It's the flowing tide; it's
the tide-race. . . . What can a swimmer do? And a bad
swimmer at that? On the other hand, to clear out, leave
the mill, in order to do what I want, when all my means
are derived from it—that would strike me as something
base. Don't you think so?"

Delamain put back a log into the fire, then raised it with
the tongs so that the flame could get better hold.

"I tell you again," said he, "it seems to me that in all
this you mingle too much moral solicitude. Where action is
concerned, we must conform to custom. The individual cannot put everything in question. And moreover, are you
sure you are not transforming into ethical preoccupations
what, at bottom, is nothing but pride? There is an almost-
virtue which consists in saying to oneself: 'I am so virtuous
that I cannot practise my virtue in the framework of society.' In that case one holds aloof. It is convenient."

"Perhaps," said Bernard meditatively. "Everything is
very difficult."

"The essential thing," said Delamain, "is to keep your
spirit free. Haven't you a little love-affair to make you
forget Pont-de-l'Eure?"

"On the contrary," said Bernard, "I have a big love-affair
which makes me hate Pont-de-l'Eure. Do you remember
Simone Beix?"

"That handsome woman who was about in Châlons in
March '18? The wife of the Railway Transport officer. . . .
Rather! She was delightful. At one and the same time she
looked like Joshua Reynolds' angels and that delicious Rus-

sian dancer, Lydia Lopokova, you know. She certainly took a fancy to you. Do you still see her? Do you love her?"

"I do not know," said Bernard, suddenly talking very fast. "I think her very pretty, of course, and she is intelligent, rather in the 'high-brow' way. She is very *'Nouvelle Revue Française'*-y, like you, more advanced even, and in music very *'Groupe des Six'*-y, but all that very gracefully. She paints, and I like her painting: it is very simple and straightforward."

"And Lieutenant Beix, what is his job in peacetime?"

"He is a banker—a big commercial bank. But his wife does not get on with him."

"And you? You haven't given me an answer. Do you love her?"

"What does it mean, to love? Do *you* know? My greatest pleasure is to be with her, but I cannot really love her enough, since I haven't the courage to give up my life to her and live in Paris. And yet I realize well enough that I shall lose her, if I go on seeing so little of her."

"But could you leave the mill?"

"Could I? . . . Obviously I could. I have merely to say: 'I am going.' No law on earth can compel me to live in Pont-de-l'Eure. I am young and active; I should get on anywhere. . . . But sometimes it seems to me that I have become two persons. One Me says: 'The essential thing is that your looms keep on working'; another Me replies: 'Are you mad? You are making me waste the whole of my youth.' I know that the second personage expresses my thought more truly, and, in effect, I obey the first. It is queer, isn't it?"

"And down yonder, at Pont-de-l'Eure?" asked Delamain. "Nothing?"

"Nothing . . . I have a charming sister-in-law, but she is my sister-in-law. . . . No, nothing."

"And marriage?"

"All young girls bore me. . . . Can you tell me why?"

He stayed with Delamain until two o'clock in the morning and returned to his hotel on foot, through a lovely night. He had not been so happy for a long time.

CHAPTER TEN

THE inspection of the pieces after weaving was made at Quesnay and Lecourbe's by Daddy Leroy, a terror to negligent workmen. Monsieur Achille had trained him in his youth.

"Ah, Monsieur Bernard," he would say, "smears of lubrication-oil again! I've told the foreman a score of times, but the young folks of today, they don't care about nothing nor nobody; they just stick to their own little bit of a job, over and over again. What I says is, when you do a job you mun do it."

In incipient old age this Leroy committed the imprudence of marrying a pretty girl, who worked under him and coveted his savings. His wife wore silk stockings and was cynical in her unfaithfulness to him. Ill-wed, ill-fed, ill-tended, the old man took to drink for consolation. He became dirty and wretched.

One morning, the two women who shared his duty with him saw this usually sober man come to work completely drunk. The night before, he had found his home empty, his wife gone off with a mason and the plate-glass wardrobe. He carefully donned his white coat, dusted his slippers, put them on and, quickly climbing to the top of a heap of pieces that were awaiting his inspection, pulled from his vest an old pistol bequeathed him by an uncle in the army and announced to the two women:

"I'm going to blow my brains out!"

"God A'mighty, God A'mighty!" they cried, their fingers in their ears. "Don't do that, Daddy, don't do that!"

"Aye, but I shall," he said. "My missus has left me, and I don't want her to have the last word. She'll read o' this in the paper, and it'll curdle the blood in her veins. . . . I'm going to blow my brains out, I am!"

" 'Tain't good sense, Daddy Leroy. . . . We mun find M'sieur Bernard."

Pistol in hand, but faithful to discipline, he awaited the boss. But as Bernard could not be found, the engineer Cazier, the veteran's oldest friend, came in his stead.

"Try and get hold of his revolver," the women called to him.

"You shut up. . . . Kindness does it. . . . A man the worse for liquor, if you cross him, he can do away with his-self. . . . Now, just you wait and see. . . . Women, why, there's plenty o' that sort o' thing! Myself, when I got back from the war, they told me mine had run away. . . . To begin with, I was fair upset over it. But when I was in court and saw there was more nor a dozen there for the same game, we stared and then made a joke of it. Do like me—tha's still gotten thy mates."

"No, no," said the veteran. "My wife's a harlot. I'm going to blow my brains out!"

But as he was groping for the trigger with rather a trembling hand, Monsieur Cantaert and Langlois, the trade-union secretary, came up at the double. The secretary, in his fine pathetic voice, appealed to the old warrior not thus to desert his old comrades. The manager, a man from the north and very pious, spoke of suicide with horror. The veteran gave them his ear. He shook his head and again raised his pistol. In vain big Cazier tried to take him in the flank. The drunkard saw him coming and threatened him with his weapon. At this moment Bernard arrived at last.

"What, Leroy," he said, "do you mean to kill yourself? And what will become of us without you? Who's going to inspect our pieces? And all this for a woman who isn't worthy to help you on with your coat. . . ."

"M'sieur Bernard, I'm sorry to leave you like this. . . . I'm sorry, specially as I know you can't find none to take my place. The young folks of today, they don't care about nothing nor nobody. But I've told that harlot I'm going to kill myself. I don't want her to have the last word. I'm going to blow my brains out!"

Monsieur Achille was just coming up on his rounds and received the tidings.

"What's all this?" he said severely. "I absolutely forbid

you to blow your brains out here. You'll leave marks on my pieces."

Then Daddy Leroy came down from his perch and was disarmed without any trouble.

Bernard told his story to Delamain, who was immensely pleased with it.

"It's a surprisingly exact symbol of your own existence," said he.

"Not exact in every respect," said Bernard.

But he remained a long time lost in thought.

CHAPTER ELEVEN

*"Hélas! Donner tant à celui qui de
si peu se contenterait."*
MME. DE NOAILLES

SIMONE BEIX had taken for three months, in the heart of the Basque country and in a still unspoiled village, an old house with carved wood balconies. Her husband, who had a liking for casinos and gaming rooms, had soon tired of such solitude. At the beginning of September Bernard Quesnay installed himself for ten days at the inn.

Every morning at eleven o'clock he called for his mistress at her house. The sea was not far away. Simone, in a skimpy bathing-dress, baked her slender body in the sun, so that it was taking on the beautiful tones of Etruscan pottery. Lying at her side in the sand, Bernard, half naked and burning on his own account, forgot everything except the sweetness of caresses under the Chinese umbrella. Towards noon they plunged into the water. Bernard was a good swimmer; Simone had more style. They lunched on the verge of red rocks, in a black and ochre inn with vast unsymmetrical roofs. Then Simone would seek out a corner to paint and Bernard watched her painting. As they made their way home, the ox-drawn carts were slowly returning to the farms; the lengthening shadows outlined more strongly the opulent curves of the hills.

For three days Bernard was happy. On the fourth morning, he rose early, with a feeling of impatience and anxiety.

At eight o'clock, the tam-o'-shantered postman delivered a letter to him from Antoine.

"We have no luck, my poor old chap; you only have to go for us to get into difficulties. It is everlastingly the rise in the cost of living. Several grades came yesterday to protest against the new wages. Going through the work rooms, I see nothing but discontented faces. Desmares tells me that good fellows like Heurtematte have complained loudly to him. The worst is that I had promised Françoise to go away with her for the week-end, and that cannot now be done. With a strike threatening on the horizon, grandpapa will not hear of it, and poor Françoise is bitterly disappointed. What a beastly business life is! On no account cut short your holidays, but we shall be glad to see you back."

He put the letter into his pocket and strode up and down on the high road between the inn and the beginning of the village. 'I pace backwards and forwards like a wild beast in a cage,' he said to himself. 'But what a nuisance it is to be so far away!' Perhaps by talking to Heurtematte or Ricard he might have been able. . . . They listened more readily to him than to Antoine. There was no reason for it, but so it was. . . . What could he do from a distance? Sit on the beach at a woman's feet. . . . The sight of the fair Basque landscape, all green hummocks, bored him. He felt as if inside him he had a kind of coiled spring vainly seeking to be released. He stretched himself, yawned and looked at his watch; it was only ten o'clock.

When it was a proper hour for him to ring at Simone's and she came down, he felt less dissatisfied with himself. She wore a frock of pink organdie with a little white Quaker collar, white cuffs and a white leather belt: 'How pretty she is,' thought Bernard, overcome, 'with something so clear-cut and so strong. . . .'

He went to take the little car out of the garage. He took a methodical and keen pleasure in silently manipulating the well-oiled gear-lever.

The moment he had stretched himself out on the sand his thoughts turned to the mill again: 'It is queer; I am experiencing again the sensations of war: you were on leave in Paris; you were coming away from a pleasant evening's entertainment, you bought a paper, read that things were going badly in the sector, and the evening was ruined. . . . What's wanted is a talk with Langlois, their secretary. One could prove to him . . .' "Yes . . ." he said out loud, absent-mindedly, in answer to a question of Simone's which he had not heard.

She looked at him in surprise.

After lunch, while she was painting, Bernard, very silent, seemed for long plunged in thought, then got up, came to see what she was doing, walked a few paces away, came back.

"What is the matter with you?" she said.

"With me? Why, nothing."

"But there is. You are all on edge today. Have you had a letter from your brother? Is there something rotten in the state of Pont-de-l'Eure?"

"Yes, that's it. How well you know me!"

"You are so transparent, dear; of all the beings I know you are the one that least knows how to conceal his annoyance. It is an endearing trait, though. It is the 'child side' of you. . . . Come now, what is it they want? Have they sent you marching-orders?"

"No, not at all; but they are in difficulties and I cannot help asking myself to what degree I am justified. . . ."

"Oh, you are terrible!" she said with a spice of passion. . . . "Yes, yes, terrible, I assure you. You are asking yourself whether you are justified in spending ten days with your mistress. It is almost incredible, you know."

"Why, no," said Bernard. "It takes all men that way. Your husband is very busy too."

"I do not love my husband: that is all one to me. And moreover that is not the point. I will readily grant a man may be busy. . . . In fact, I admire him for it. But I absolutely must feel that I too have a place in your mind. With you I know that the most insignificant occurrence in your mill takes precedence over the most important occurrence in our love. You must own that that is saddening and humiliating. Every now and then, you know, I have telephoned to you at Pont-de-l'Eure. Oh, if you could hear the exasperated tone of voice in which you speak back to me, because you are afraid of shocking your grandfather or the underling standing at your side. . . . Your shame of being affectionate, that is what I reproach you with . . . do you understand?"

"I understand," he said, surprised, "but I think you are wrong. The portrait you draw of me is preposterous and inaccurate. What you have just been saying, I tell myself too, and the mill is very often a vexation to me."

"No, no, dear; you only think so. . . . What you do is never a vexation, as long as you can act, give orders, in short think yourself of use. During the war, everybody in your regiment used to tell me that you were a model officer. Now you want to be a model employer. You have a 'Simon le Pathétique' side, a 'virtuous apprentice' side, you are 'upright'—it is not a crime, only it's boring. . . . Or, alternatively, I should like you to be equally conscientious where our love is concerned."

"But in love I have no need to be conscientious. I love you naturally, without effort."

She put aside her paintbrushes, got up and seated herself at Bernard's feet in the grass.

"You never succeed in anything without effort," she said. "I myself, I try to make every moment of my life a little masterpiece. I want the morning meeting to be beautiful, my dress to go with the weather and the time of day, the last words one says at night to make a good 'curtain.' And I bear ill will towards a partner who spoils my effects. . . . I have always been like that. . . . I remember when I was fifteen years old (I was very pretty at fifteen), I had a young cousin who was in love with me. One evening—it was a divine night—on the balcony of my people's house in the Boulevard Maillot, he told me that he loved me. The trees of the Bois were quivering in the moonlight. It was as it should be. . . . Then I thought: 'For everything to be quite perfect, he must send me some white roses in the morning.' And as I knew he would not do it of his own accord, I told him to. . . . When they came, they gave me as much pleasure as if I had not ordered them myself. . . . With you, beloved, the roses never come."

"Tell me what I'm to do."

"Precisely, I am telling you. This holiday at Cambo . . . it is the first time that we are spending ten days together. I am very, very ambitious. I want them to be (in modern terms, of course) as beautiful as all the great romantic encounters. . . . Yes, yes, it is possible. . . . Only, you must help me. Forget your looms, your customers, your grandfather for ten days. . . . You must tell me that it isn't nothing, ten days with a woman like me, who is doing all she can to give you pleasure. . . . Come, say something!"

She looked at him for a moment in a melancholy way. On their left there was a kind of heath, covered with bracken and heather, on their right a little wood of stunted, riven oaks.

CHAPTER TWELVE

BERNARD did not cut short his holidays. Monsieur Achille received him coldly. Wages were raised and peace reigned in the Valley again. The truce lasted for two months; then at Pont-de-l'Eure market Madame Petitseigneur and Madame Quimouche, better paid, saw eggs and butter rise, as if mysterious tubes, to keep them at a uniform level, had been laid in connection between these ladies' purses and their saucepans.

In his office Bernard beheld again the broken-hearted Chorus of Suppliant Women.

"We can't go on, Monsieur Bernard, we can't go on. . . . You must raise us again, just the least little bit."

"It is lunacy," said Monsieur Achille.

"Law of supply and demand," said Monsieur Lecourbe.

But the employers' federation granted once more what was demanded of them. They and their kind were living blissfully in a fool's paradise of insane prosperity. The more furiously commodities rose, the more the sheeplike herd ran after them.

"In my days . . ." growled Monsieur Achille.

He was dissatisfied with his grandsons. Françoise had so earnestly besought her husband to get her away from Pont-de-l'Eure, that, eventually and much in his own despite, he had taken her to Morocco. As a pretext he had alleged a voyage of investigation into wool. He had spent three weeks at Rabat, at Fez and at Marakesh, and brought home badly woven cloths which his wife extolled for their coarseness. Bernard often went to Paris, but seemed to be wasting his time there, since his customers complained that they never set eyes on him.

"Your heart in not in your job," Monsieur Achille would say to the two young men.

"Our job goes of its own accord," they answered.

"Your cloth is badly turned out."

"Everyone finds it all right."

"You overpay your hands."

"That is not their view."

For the workpeople, malcontent denizens of the fools' paradise, hoped to see (by means of a miracle, no doubt, and divine intervention) wages rise without end and the price of manufactured articles fall. They reached the point —quite unknown in that sensible Normandy of theirs—of violently hating their too steadily thriving employers. Their long prosperity, which by the novelty of its benefits had brought them together at first, had ended by sundering the two classes. As in certain too-happy homes, a wife, unnerved by tranquility, comes to wish for the death of a husband, who is over-considerate to her whimsies, these fellows, whose every demand was fulfilled, would turn into a griev-ance against their unduly wealthy masters a munificence which they felt to proceed from indifference more than from generosity.

In the trade-union, Langlois, a supporter of the principles of Proud'hon and '48, had been succeeded by Renaudin, a little, hard-faced man who talked severely to the middle classes, announcing their speedy end. The coming into force of the new Eight Hours Law provided him with a pretext for the fight he had longed for.

Monsieur Pascal-Bouchet, on behalf of the employers, offered to maintain the ten-hours-day wages for a working day shortened by one-fifth. Renaudin declared that that was not enough.

"But I say it is enough," Monsieur Pascal-Bouchet told him. "You want to work less and earn more? . . . You are crazy! If you are looking for a *casus belli* . . . you shall have one."

"Monsieur Pascal," said Renaudin, "pay good heed to what I say. . . . You have just used a word I do not like at all. . . . Tempers are up."

"I can't help that," said Monsieur Bouchet. *"Quod dixi . . . dixi. . . .* At most I might be able to grant you some slight concessions, if, by way of off-set, overtime on holidays were paid at the usual rates."

"What do you mean by holidays?" asked Renaudin.

"Why," said Monsieur Bouchet, taken aback, "Christmas, Easter . . ."

"Christmas was all very well in the days of Jesus Christ. Myself, I only know of one holiday: May Day."

A long snarl of indignation ran round the employers' table.

"Quousque tandem, Catilina," murmured Monsieur Pascal.

All the same, he gave way again over the question of holidays. But there was this peculiarity about the negotiations: the successive concessions brought no state of peace. All the time that they dreaded it, both parties wanted war. Like the peoples of Europe in August, 1914, they were tired of their own moderation. Just as occupants of a motor-car, seeing themselves driven to certain disaster by a drunken driver, from a sentiment of honor do not intervene to mitigate his speed, so Renaudin's inveterate determination and Monsieur Pascal's grandiloquence led two resigned flocks to a collision which both feared.

At the moment when everything seemed settled:

"And the stokers in the boiler room?" said Renaudin. "They demand . . ."

"Look here!" exclaimed Bernard Quesnay with a vehemence that astonished himself. . . . "Look here, don't you see that. . . ."

"You must not argue, Bernard," said Monsieur Lecourbe.

When a long period of drought and heat has accumulated in the stagnant air too great a reserve of energy, a storm must break. None of these mill-owners could have said precisely why in the end they denied the stokers what they had so readily granted to the other classes of labor. There was really no reason, but these successive onslaughts against the employers' patience had finally worn down their nerves. The storm burst.

"Very well," said Renaudin, with his biting voice . . . "Your stokers will not be at the mill tomorrow morning."

"They can stay at home."

"Good-bye for the present, gentlemen. You will have to give in."

Then, when the workmen had left the room:

"Well," said Monsieur Pascal, "we shall close down tomorrow, that is all. . . ."

Bernard interrupted him, vibrant and acrid:

"Close down a mill with a thousand hands on account of four stokers! What an idea, Monsieur Pascal. . . . If necessary, I had rather stoke myself."

"I should like to see you," said Monsieur Lecourbe.

"You will see me."

There was thunder everywhere.

CHAPTER THIRTEEN

"Vous avez donné pleinement dans cette folie de la première jeunesse qu'on appele le zèle."

                                                STENDHAL

THE stars were shining in a sky of black velvet when Bernard Quesnay, exhilarated by a pleasant enough sensation, passed through the sleeping town. The air was chilly. Sometimes, far away, a step echoed on the cobbles. When he arrived before the mill, he had difficulty in divining the black mass in the solid darkness.

As he was walking up the long yard, a voice issued from the night:

"Good-morning, Monsieur Bernard."

He recognized the hearty tones of the chief engineer.

"Good-morning, Cazier. . . . Well, are they going to leave us in the lurch?"

"Upon my soul, Monsieur Bernard, since they're not here, I am afraid they mean to, right enough. . . . They voted for striking by forty votes to thirty. Our chaps were against; but they daren't come. Though I don't belong to the union, I have a word with more than one that does. They're frightened of a boot in the backside. Shall I turn on the light? When there's a row on, it's a good thing."

He threw in a main switch. Immediately the works stood in a blaze of light. Although the machines were not working, the mill seemed alive at once, like a sick man whose eyes still preserve the luster of life. It struck five.

"They won't come," said the big engineer. "Crew of wasters! What shall we do?"

"Find casual stokers and carry on."

"I shall be surprised if you find any. . . . They're not a very bold lot, hereabouts. When they go for you, it's better hereabouts to shout 'Fire' than 'Help,' if you want to see heads at the windows."

"My brother and I will do the stoking, with some clerks."

"You won't do it for long."

Towards six o'clock, undecided groups began to form at the gate. Bernard went up to them. They bade him a subdued good-morning. Women nudged one another with their elbows and laughed.

"Is the mill working, Monsieur Bernard?"

"Why, of course it's working. . . . All we need is some willing men, to stoke. The engineers are at their posts. . . . You are not going to play, a thousand of you, for want of four volunteers? You, Ricard, you're not afraid?"

Ricard, a colossus who had won the Military Medal, turned very red.

"I am not afraid, but I can't take these men's jobs."

"Who's talking of taking their jobs? They'll get them again when they come back."

"It's not so much that as I don't want to have words with nobody."

"And if someone should say something! You're as strong as a lion."

"That's it, Monsieur Bernard, that's just it; I know what I'm made on, I'd be laying two or three on 'em out . . . that'ud be a bad look-out."

By dint of rhetoric he enlisted some men, who made their way down into the boiler room. But he saw clearly that their mates looked upon them, not as heroes, but as traitors. It made him uneasy, on their account as well as his own.

In the boiler room he watched the pressure rise.

"Will it take long?"

"No, sir, it's still warm; a few bundles of heather and the fire'll catch."

With the improvised stokers he learned the job. An hour later, the triumphant siren proclaimed the resurrection of the mill. Bernard hurried through the weaving room: it was all but empty. In a room of forty looms, three wavering women were in colloquy.

"Oh, lawk-a-mussy, it gives you the creeps to be so alone! If only everybody was come, we might have the heart. . . ."

"The heart, you say? But what are you afraid of?"

"What we be afraid of? Why, it ain't them as is used to the job that's on the machines. . . . If everything blew up. . . ."

Like the engineer Cazier they too feared and desired disasters at one and the same time, as, no doubt, the inhabitants of a town in an invaded district both fear and desire a bombardment.

"What an idea! The engineers are there; I give you my word they know all about the boilers."

"That makes no matter. . . . It'd be better if they didn't work at all than work like this."

An obscure but powerful class feeling rendered odious to them the wages they were about to earn. When Bernard went down into the middle yard again, Monsieur Cantaert

informed him that one of the crews had disbanded, overcome by remorse. At that moment Antoine came up.

"Antoine, shall we take on a boiler, the two of us?"

"Right you are."

Naked to the waist, in blue dungaree trousers, the two
brothers betook themselves to stoking.

CHAPTER FOURTEEN

WHEN, at dinnertime that evening, they came to table with
soft shirts, well brushed hair and ruddy faces, they were
extremely pleased with themselves. As a good soldier, who
has fought as best he can in his corner, fancies that the
battle is won, regardless of the insignificance of his part
and of the general catastrophe, they showed little interest
in the strike and, overcome by a wholesome fatigue, thought
only of exchanging their impressions, going to bed and
sleeping. Françoise played her part of Woman in Wartime,
admired the warriors and rewarded them with her praises.

"How tired you must be!"

"Not as bad as all that: if you are in training for games,
you are equal to anything. The only bad time is when you
clean up. . . ."

"And the hands? What do they say?"

"We don't know; we haven't seen a creature in our hole."

After dinner, when Françoise, at her brother-in-law's
request, had just begun the andante of *The Fifth Symphony*
("Don't call it 'The Fifth,' Françoise—you make me think
of Madame Verdurin.") and was sending forth those notes
which gently, gently sink like soft caresses on to a weary
brow, they heard in the grounds the little iron gate clang
noisily and then steps hurrying over the gravel. Françoise
recognized the signs of Monsieur Achille's approach. The
two young men got up.

"The old man? At this hour? What can the trouble be?"

His hat on his head and his stick in his hand, he walked
into the drawing room, followed by Monsieur Pascal-
Bouchet, calm and smiling as usual.

"So there you are, the two of you! At last! And what the devil have you been up to all day?"

"Don't you know? We have been stoking boiler No. 2."

"Ah, to be sure!" said Monsieur Achille ironically, flourishing his stick. "In your craft the captain's place is in the pantry, is it?"

"If there are no stewards, certainly," Bernard answered, furious.

Going softly up to Monsieur Achille, Françoise with an adroit gesture took the old man's hat from his head, his stick from his hands and pushed an armchair up to him. The only woman in this family, she played with the old chief the part of the Duchesse de Bourgogne at the court of Louis XIV. To entertain him, she would perform countless pretty little tricks, sometimes with success. At other times she hated him. Monsieur Pascal-Bouchet lit a cigar and began a discourse:

"To be sure, you have given proof of great energy, my young friends. . . . In principle, however, Monsieur Achille is right: *de minimis non curat prœtor.* . . . And, in effect, your enterprise has led to mischievous results. . . . We have just had a visit from one of my old workmen, one of the faithful, who was present at a meeting of the Trade Council at six o'clock this evening. Now, feeling has risen very high against you, against the firm of Quesnay and Lecourbe. . . . The stokers are furious that you have been able to carry on. . . . People are saying that you have compelled children of thirteen to work in the boiler room, that one of them has been badly burnt, that a steam-pipe has burst and Heaven knows what besides!"

"But that's tommy-rot, sir. We don't employ children; no one has been burnt and if you will come with me you can see for yourself that the boilers are in perfect order."

"I don't doubt it, you may be sure, but the mischief is done."

"The absurdity of all this twaddle is easily proved."

"No, my dear Bernard, no: nothing is more difficult to refute than what is utterly untrue. . . . Don't you know the affair of the soldier Vibulenus? No? Ah, these young men have got their 'indigo base.' Well, my boy, read it in

Tacitus before going to sleep tonight . . . And you will see how a Roman general got into the greatest trouble for putting to death a legionary who never existed!"

"Meanwhile," said Monsieur Achille, "they have decided to prevent our working tomorrow by every means, 'violence included'. . . . A word that has never been heard in Pont-de-l'Eure. Ah, you have done a fine day's work, the two of you. Why couldn't you let them have their strike, if they thought it a lark?"

"I regret nothing in what I have done," said Bernard, standing with folded arms confronting his grandfather, "and I shall do it again tomorrow. . . . In the last analysis, it is physical force which wins battles, and that is as it should be. If the middle class wishes to keep command, it must know. . . ."

Shrugging his shoulders and muttering, Monsieur Achille asked for his hat and stick. At the door he called out again to Bernard:

"And what's all this story too about your having stuck up a notice at the factory gates, bragging that you'll break the strike, if it costs you millions?"

"What's that?" said Bernard, flabbergasted. "I've simply had a notice put up to announce that we shall be working tomorrow."

"How was it framed, that notice of yours?"

"I can't remember now. . . . 'Messrs. Quesnay and Lecourbe hereby give their employees notice that, in spite of the stokers' strike, they have used all the means at their disposal to ensure the continued. . . .'"

Monsieur Achille lifted his arms to heaven.

"All the means at their disposal! All the means at their disposal! Ah, you've a rare gift of expression!"

And brandishing his walking-stick, he departed, furious.

CHAPTER FIFTEEN

AT THE gate of Quesnays' a great arc-lamp lit up with fantastic illumination a number of exasperated faces which stood out with strange brilliance against a background of seething mob in heavy shadow. Several hundred strikers, massed before the gate, were reviling the infrequent hands who obstinately desired to go on working. As they came up, the Quesnay brothers saw from afar in the sector of light a woman forcing a passage for herself and finally managing to get through, her shawl pulled off her shoulders, her skirt torn.

Pale and resolute, ready for the fray, they came upon these demonstrators. To their great surprise, however, as soon as they were recognized, the ranks opened out, the shouts died down: such were the laws of that warfare, the rules of the game. The boss was fighting his battle: it was his right. He was even honored for it. But the traitors to the laboring class had to run the gauntlet.

Bernard hurried through the almost deserted work rooms. The only arrivals were those workpeople who had so pressing a need for their wages that they had become indifferent to any humiliation: some unmarried mothers who had to rear their brats, some widows without savings, no more than three or four men, those eternally "agin the government."

"No use holding out," said Monsieur Achille, when he arrived at eight o'clock. . . . "Close down everything."

With his grandsons he set out on a tour of the expiring mill. The driving-belts were gently ceasing to revolve; outside one heard the scalding snort of boilers blowing off. Then a great silence set in.

Alone, in an immense room where the machines gleamed useless and the belting hung disregarded, the old millowner looked like a great spirit which, stricken by paralysis, gazes stupefied at its motionless limbs. Without a word the three men made their way back to the office, bowed down by a feeling of sadness and solitude.

'But why?' thought Bernard, walking along with bent head. . . . 'We have all this crowd against us. . . . How unjust! One day it too will find itself standing before motionless machines. Its strength will be ready to make them go, but the coal will not have come from England, the wool will not have come from Australia, because some delicate organism will have been destroyed, some old man's crown knocked off. . . .'

At that moment he heard his grandfather's voice behind him:

"Bernard, put this drum back straight."

Monsieur Achille was putting a row of them in order.

In the office they found Monsieur Lecourbe, excited and caressing his President Carnot beard with feverish strokes.

"The excesses to which these ringleaders go beggar description. Through the window I saw them seize hold of Ricard when he went out. They beat him and fastened a placard labeled 'traitor' on his back, and Renaudin invited the women to take him home, spitting on him all the way! Up to a certain point and in a certain degree, these brawls among the workpeople are no concern of ours; all the same. . . ."

Bernard, clenching his fists, burst out with a cry:

"No concern of ours, you say. . . . A brave fellow who, alone, put himself on our side? It is infamous! Let us close down for a month! Let us clear out! Let us leave Pont-de-l'Eure!"

"Don't talk nonsense," said Monsieur Achille harshly. "We're not at the play. . . . This whole affair has been badly handled. We must look out now."

Monsieur Cantaert came, bringing news: Renaudin had left in a motor-car for Louviers, where he intended to bring about a stoppage of the Bouchet mill.

"We must telephone to the prefecture," said Monsieur Lecourbe, "and have him arrested."

"You would do him a great service," said Monsieur Achille.

Monsieur Pascal-Bouchet, another master-magician, who arrived towards the end of the afternoon, was of the same opinion.

"Renaudin," said he, "has set a thing in motion that will greatly embarrass him before two days are out. Enthusiasm does not last. Next week, his henchmen will start calling him to account. If you make a martyr of him, you set him free of all responsibility. . . . And martyrs act as stimulants. . . . We must wait."

Then he began an interminable conversation with Monsieur Achille about the precautions required to prevent the abandoned cloth from rotting in the damp milling rooms.

"Beware of sun especially," said Monsieur Achille to him. "If the pieces are not shifted from time to time, the part exposed to the light bleaches. In the dyeing afterwards, it comes out in bright streaks."

"To be sure it will," said Monsieur Pascal. "I had an old foreman-finisher, who always used to tell of the terrible trouble he had with stains, when they were left overnight in the river. 'And ye may believe me or not, M'sieu' Pascal,' he would say, 'but it was a devil of a moon that streaked our bolts in t' watter.' "

With a movement of his wrist Monsieur Achille dispatched the young men to do combat against the hostile stars. The two old men remained alone: Monsieur Achille, as dry as a stick, a trifle yellow, Monsieur Pascal filling out his fresh-colored skin, his eternal rose in his buttonhole. Since the jerking of the looms had stopped shaking his office, Monsieur Achille seemed sick and sad. To divert him, Monsieur Pascal offered to take him along to Louviers and show him over his idle mill.

It was the first time that old Quesnay had penetrated into that mysterious retreat, which for so long had been to him the cave of the Spirit of Evil. He was astonished to find there old buildings like his own, the same smell of wool-fat and hot oil. But the factory was more up-to-date, the walls seemed freshly repainted, one caught glimpses of lavatories distempered with Ripolin and of cloak rooms with nickel-plated hat-pegs.

Monsieur Pascal-Bouchet, a worthy man and proud, moreover, of his kingdom, conducted the great enemy chieftain through it with affectionate complacency. Monsieur Achille, troubled by painful memories and vague fears, only stayed a short while.

Returned to the soil of his own tribe, he stalked the silent yard for a long time, voluptuously snuffing up the smell of *his* wool and *his* oil.

CHAPTER SIXTEEN

THE five days which the young Quesnays spent in lethargy at their mill seemed interminable. No peace in sight. Each side had pronounced so many vows that the word "conciliation" was considered infamous in both camps. Tumultuous processions marched through the astonished streets of Pont-de-l'Eure. Bernard, who watched them passing from the factory windows, admired the enthusiasm they evinced and regretted that he could not join in them.

In the front rank there marched Renaudin, arm-in-arm with two comrades, his face rapt in a kind of ecstasy. 'At bottom,' thought Bernard, 'he is perhaps not such a bad fellow, and this popularity must be intoxicating.' Behind him came a large bevy of pretty young girls, then, carrying a red flag, the big stoker Ricard.

"What's this, Antoine? Has that chap turned revolutionary now? I thought he was beadle at St. Louis's and bugler to the fire-brigade."

"That's right enough," said Antoine. "But he can't see a parade without marching at the head of it."

"It would be a pity if he didn't," said Bernard. "He is the drum-major type."

The crowd tailed off in order of decreasing enthusiasm, so that, towards the end of the procession, where the veterans and carts full of children trundled along, you did not quite know whether you were looking at demonstrators, passers-by, or objectors.

A group of militants which brought up the rear of the cortège struck Bernard because of the hardness of their faces: 'What Septembrist heads'; he thought. At that moment, one of these men noticed the two Quesnay brothers at their window, and said aloud with naïve sincerity: "What slave-drivers' mugs!" That threw Bernard into endless reflections.

Returning home, he met Heurtematte and bade him good-evening.

"Beg pardon, Monsieur Bernard," said the man, "but I

can't walk along with you. They'd say I'd been bought over. It's awful the bad blood there is."

Sunday came. After mass Bernard accompanied Françoise home. In the garden, the first roses stood chiseled out in their full, perfect forms. A vague musical murmur rose up from the little town that lay stifling in the blazing heat.

"How quiet it is!" said Bernard. "Who would think that this peaceful little hole could poison our life in this way! How fitting it is what you were singing yesterday: 'Ah God, ah God, simple and quiet is life over yonder. . . . That peaceable humming. . . .' Would you believe it, Françoise —at times I pine for the war! It is awful, if you like. You had a bad time of it; but, all the same, there was great happiness in feeling oneself 'at one.' I knew that my men respected me; I ran the same dangers as they, I was satisfied with myself. Here, I feel myself suspect, envied. And it is unjust. . . . A man like my friend Delamain, who only works for his own amusement, who has any amount of leisure, has the right to be a socialist, a friend of the people, and to have himself cheered if he wants to. And I, who really only take on this beastly job to allow the workpeople to go on working (you know how little I care about money), I am detested. . . . No, no. I abominate all that, I have had enough of it. I am not joking, you know. . . . I want to throw up everything, shake off my shoulders the burden of this mill, its bricks and its machines."

"And I?" said she. "Don't you think that I have had enough of it? I don't know, Bernard, but sometimes I get the impression that all this is one gigantic lunacy. Why do you all live as you do? Look at your grandfather: he will be dead in four years, or five, but what has he experienced, what has he made of his life? He is an unhappy maniac, a lunatic, I tell you, and Antoine is mad, and you, you will go mad, too. My little Bacot is already sacrificed, I know for a certainty. And I, I am wretched."

"You?" said Bernard, crossing his arms and looking his sister-in-law in the face. "But why? *You* have got no idle mill and hands on strike. You have everything to make you happy; you have your pretty children, a nice house, an easy life."

"You are extraordinary people," said she (and, doubtless, that "you" designated the whole tribe of Quesnays). "You believe that if you give a woman as much money as she wants and, every now and then, a kiss on the forehead, she must be happy. It isn't so. Your grandmother and your mother . . ."

"I don't believe, Françoise, that our grandmother was very unhappy. Mother—that was another matter, because she came from Paris. She never got accustomed to Pont-de-l'Eure."

"Your grandmother? She was buried alive. Your grandfather forgot she was there for whole evenings on end. The first year of my marriage, her existence terrified me. When I became bored, she was astounded: 'Why don't you do some work?' she used to ask me. 'In my day a young woman always had some needlework.' And really she made all those awful net sun-blinds over at your place. She had a drawing room which she never opened, because sun fades the curtains. She never went out. She had never seen Chartres or Dreux, which are within a stone's throw. When I said to her: 'Don't you long for anything? Have you no wish to see Italy or Egypt, in short, to enjoy yourself?' she would reply: 'Life is not made for enjoyment. I have helped my husband; I have brought up my children well; I shall not hold out empty hands in the Presence.' "

"And don't you think that very fine?" said Bernard, not without a touch of pride.

"Very fine? Perhaps. Only, I don't understand it. I want to be happy."

'(They are all the same),' thought Bernard, '(Simone would have used the same phrases).' "But don't you think this appetite for happiness in young women of your generation is rather a weakness, a sign of inner poverty?"

"You are like Antoine," she said, a trifle annoyed. "You allow yourself the right to be dissatisfied, and you decree that for women all is well."

Behind them the gravel crunched. They turned about.

"Ah!" said Françoise, happy, "here's the Pasha."

That was the name which the Pascal-Bouchet children gave their father, whom they greatly loved. He came up to them, smiling, with an enormous rose in his buttonhole.

"What faces on the two of you! What's wrong, young Bernard?"

"Do you want anything more, sir?" said Bernard.

"What's that? Oh, this strike! In a week's time we shan't remember anything about it. . . ."

"How can it be settled? Each side has sworn. . . ."

"Sworn? Where should we be landed, my dear boy, if we had to perform all we swore to? . . . 'We shall never compromise!'—that means: not in the next five minutes, not today. . . . But tomorrow! . . . Everything comes out all right."

"How, sir? . . . If it does, so that we go on waging a sort of subterranean feud with our workpeople, I had rather become a taxi-driver. . . . I want to be loved."

"A master," said Monsieur Pascal, "is neither loved nor hated. . . . He is a master, that is to say responsible. . . ."

"Well then, let us say, if you prefer, that I no longer wish to be a master."

"Most happily, your wishes are not consulted," said Monsieur Pascal, patting him on the shoulder. "Françoise, my dear, where are Bacot and Micheline? You see, Bernard, I turn the strike to account by seeing more of my grandchildren. *Renaudin nobis haec otia fecit.*"

CHAPTER SEVENTEEN

AT THE beginning of the strike Simone Beix had deeply sympathized with Bernard. She had written to him that she could imagine his cares, that she loved him very much, that she was thinking of him. Bernard had replied with a little note of two lines in the tone of a general tossing off a bulletin in the heat of battle. Then he had completely forgotten his mistress's existence. The emotions of this struggle rendered him incapable of experiencing any others. Entirely given up to seeking out means for the overthrow of Renaudin, he neglected those for keeping Simone. She was confident that he would come to Paris to see her, if only "between trains." As a matter of fact, the idea never even occurred to him.

At the end of ten days, such indifference had stung her, and Bernard received a somewhat ironical letter:

"I am not very clear now, beloved. In the days when your mill was working, you could not get away, because it was working; nor now, because it is not working. Why are you not on strike yourself? I picture you sitting on a heap of wrecked machinery. . . . Bernard Quesnay on the ruins of Pont-de-l'Eure . . . or perhaps planted on a stump at the street corner, rallying to their work a crowd vanquished by your eloquence. But no—you would not be successful as a public orator. You would rather lack the mellowness and nonchalance. . . . Seriously, dear, what are you doing? You must come to Paris on Tuesday. I shall be free, absolutely free; I can meet you at the station, if you come by the noon train, and spend the whole day with you. Wire to me at the studio what time you arrive."

As he read it, Bernard had said to himself: 'Why not?' It was perfectly true that he was not doing anything. For the first few days he had spent some hours in taking precautions for the preservation of the cloth and in stopping certain consignments. Customers, in ignorance of the strike, had continued to write. They had to be answered. At the end of a week the correspondence had become thin, then nonexistent; but the habits of the Quesnays had so strong a dominion over them that they still arrived at the office by eight o'clock. There they stayed till lunch, returning punctually at two o'clock and not leaving again until the evening. These long days passed in vain and interminable conversations. Monsieur Lecourbe elaborated theories about wages; Bernard betrayed violent sentiments, which Monsieur Achille ridiculed with a growl. They discovered a charm in this anxious indolence. Like a soldier placed as sentinel at a post of no great danger, but yet an honorable one, the Quesnays did not feel themselves on the square with their consciences but by denying themselves the right to go away. They sat at the bedside of this moribund mill as at that of a sick man, who can no longer speak, whose last breath is awaited by the family with a mixture of impatience, sadness and pity, and whose more distant relations, talking, bored and subdued, in the next room, realize perfectly well the uselessness of their presence, but would think it disgraceful to desert.

Sometimes a visit from Monsieur Pascal, or the mayor, or the police-superintendent would for a moment embellish the monotony of the days. At the beginning, Bernard and Antoine had attempted to read, but Monsieur Achille had said "Books at the office!" in such a way that they had given it up. The sacred character of these high places appeared to them more clearly in days of trial.

Bernard put Simone's letter in his pocket without disclosing any emotion. A little later he murmured with a feigned negligence: "I shall perhaps go to Paris on Tuesday. . . ." Neither Monsieur Achille nor Monsieur Lecourbe nor Antoine gave any reply; all three were contemplating with gloomy attentiveness the blue tapestry which covered the walls. Bernard should have stopped there, but an obscure feeling of guilt made him continue: "After all," he said, "there is nothing to do here." To this Monsieur Achille retorted, raising his thick, shaggy eyebrows: "There is always something to do"; and Bernard comprehended forthwith the infamy of his project. The really shameful thing was to think of his pleasures in the midst of his country's misfortunes. He was extremely cross with Simone for occasioning this lack of tact. At noon he sent her a wire: "Regret impossible leave mill. Love. Bernard."

Towards five a small telegraph-boy came into the Quesnays' office and asked: "Monsieur Bernard?" Bernard read: "You, sir, are king; I weep, but you remain. Bérénice."

He made a movement of impatience, crumpled up the telegram and put it in his pocket. The others looked at him inquiringly and reproachfully. To receive telegrams at the office without saying something about them was not countenanced by the Quesnays. He thought: 'I certainly won't go.'

When he took his refusal to the post office the telegraphist of Pont-de-l'Eure smiled; she followed the amours of Monsieur Quesnay with interest and had wondered several times since morning whether he would give way, but was quite baffled when Bérénice, a new female, became mixed up in the intrigue.

CHAPTER EIGHTEEN

BERNARD was not sorry that he had stayed, for the Tuesday was marked by a little drama. About ten in the morning Monsieur Cantaert entered the office, very much agitated and puffing, since he was stout and had been running.

"There's a man dead, Monsieur Achille."

Everybody stood up.

"What? Dead?" said Bernard.

"In the weaving-shed down by the water-side, Monsieur Bernard. It's Leroy; they've killed him."

"Who did? The strikers?"

"Yes, Monsieur Bernard. . . . That Renaudin. . . ."

He explained. In this weaving-shed, an old building in the Louis XV style, overgrown with roses, there remained a few hand-looms, of which Monsieur Cantaert had wished to make use for weaving samples against next season. He had found some old weavers retired into the country and had engaged them. They belonged to an age where unions and strikes hardly existed; they had come with enthusiasm. Daddy Leroy, the old inspector whom Monsieur Achille had saved from suicide, supervised them. For the first fortnight Renaudin had not known of their presence. The steam-engine was stopped; no one gave a thought to the hand-looms; the smoke-stack, shorn of its crown of smoke, was a guarantee. Then, without doubt, the noise of the looms or a spy had given them away. Suddenly, that Tuesday morning, a crowd of fifteen hundred strikers had surrounded the shed, jeering at the "black-legs" and throwing stones through the windows. The veterans, surprised, had stopped their looms and endeavored to get out. Their appearance had been greeted with catcalls and a volley of abuse. At that moment old Leroy had collapsed. The shouting did not cease straightway, because the old man's fall had passed unobserved. Then, seeing him motionless and the others bending over him, the demonstrators had become alarmed and held their noise. The gatekeeper had ventured to come up and had said, stupefied: "Eh! Eh! But he's dead!" The front ranks heard and, like a flock of scared crows, the rowdies fled away from the corpse.

"You have seen him for yourself? You are certain he is dead?" asked Monsieur Achille, distrustful of all second-hand reports.

"Absolutely certain, Monsieur Achille. Besides, I've sent for the doctor."

"A death," said Bernard. "The business is getting serious. This time, that Renaudin. . . ."

"Renaudin?" said Monsieur Achille. "Renaudin has perhaps got nothing whatever to do with it. Besides, I cannot make head or tail of this affair. What did he, what did Leroy die of? Did anyone touch him?"

"Oh no, Monsieur Achille. He was ten or twelve yards away from the demonstrators."

"Someone must have fired on him then?" queried Bernard.

"Fired!" said Monsieur Achille. "Did anyone fire, Cantaert?"

"Oh no, Monsieur Achille. He must have died of a stroke."

"That does not alter the fact," said Bernard, "that it was the excitement which proved the immediate cause of his death. . . . It is Renaudin who killed him. . . . It must be shouted from all the housetops and placarded on all the walls of Pont-de-l'Eure."

"You had much better go and look," said Monsieur Achille.

Bernard went. Through the door of the shed he saw Dr. Guérin buttoning up a shirt. He went up and gazed at the dead man's face. He was a fine old man, with white moustache and imperial. In a tree, a bird sang. Bernard uncovered.

"What did he die of, doctor?"

"I don't know, my friend. He was a stranger to me. . . . I can find no trace of a wound or a bruise. Cardiac casualty, I suppose."

The police-superintendent came on the scene and asked if he should telephone to Evreux and have a magistrate sent down.

"What for?" said the doctor. "It isn't a murder. . . . Have him taken to the hospital, and I'll make the post-mortem."

In the evening Bernard went to inquire the result of his investigation; he nourished a vague hope that he might be able to prove Renaudin's guilt.

"Well, doctor? What about our man?"

Dr. Guérin rubbed his hands with the air of a collector who had just come across a good specimen.

"A superb coronary angina," was his satisfied reply.

As he walked away, Bernard saw that the walls of the infirmary were covered with big red posters. He went up and read the headline in enormous letters:

EMPLOYERS' VICTIM

"Capitalist greed has at last claimed a victim. An unhappy octogenarian. . . ."

CHAPTER NINETEEN

ON THE following morning Monsieur Pascal received a telephone message that the prefect desired to see him.

Monsieur le préfet Caumont, a great artist in administration, a great expert in men, had been ready for some days past to proffer his mediation; but, as English bishops keep a lookout for a falling barometer before ordering Prayers for Rain, he had waited before intervening until the storm had produced its beneficent results.

Enthusiasm is only maintained by change—which makes the agitator's task a hard one. In wartime, the heads of the ministry command a thousand ephemeral attractions for rekindling the nations' zeal: entry of new allies into the arena, minor attacks, diplomatic notes. Renaudin, for his part too, did all he could to keep his troops at a high pitch. At the start, processions and singing had sufficed. The *International* had caught on; then people had got sick of it. For want of something better, they had come to singing

"Ho, for a student's life, Mother" and, as a last resort, *La Madelon*. A few days of bodily rest and oral violence had thoroughly calmed the nerves. The vehement eloquence of orators sent down from Paris had displeased the peaceful masses of Pont-de-l'Eure. The workpeople wanted to get back to their jobs and the masters to their office. It was now only a matter of saving their face.

For this purpose the Prefect of the Department of the Eure was truly admirable. Long experience had taught him the salutary effects of solemn eloquence. Two parties at issue and believing that they hated one another, made aware by this inimitable orator of their common ground of humanity, had to recognize that they were men and that their sensibilities were susceptive to the same accents.

Having assembled, at a table shaped like a horseshoe, the employers on his right, the workmen on his left, he delivered a short speech from the throne. A mere administrator, lacking technical knowledge, he would take good care not to grapple with the fundamental question. If he had thought it his duty to intervene, it was in the interest of the innocent victims of a conflict between interests of equal consideration; women and children ("hear, hear" from the labor side) would shortly be exposed to the horrors of starvation. . . . At a time when the country, already sorely tried by cruel losses ("hear, hear" on the capitalist side), required all the active strength of the nation . . . he was assured that devotion to these sacred duties would prevail over the impulses of violence ("hear, hear" on all sides).

Nevertheless, the real question—that of the stokers— still awaited solution. Renaudin, having said "15 per cent or nothing," wished to beat a retreat, but couldn't. Monsieur Pascal-Bouchet, having declared *"Quod dixi, dixi,"* wished to concede 7 or 8 per cent, but did not know how to do it without appearing ridiculous. For the prefect it was child's play. These wages, which the one wished to get and to which the others could not agree—he awarded them without awarding them, he withheld them without withholding them. He withheld them under the name of wages, but he awarded them under the name of bonuses. He withheld them without hurting the pride of Labor; he awarded them without undermining the masters' authority. He withheld them while lauding proletarian moderation; he awarded them while exalting the good will of the bourgeoisie.

His proposal traveled many times backwards and forwards from masters to men and from the men to the masters, but it was as the budget travels from the Lower to the Upper House; everyone knows from the beginning of the ceremony that, after some bridling of an affronted old prude, the high assembly will accept some "working formula."

In a short closing discourse the prefect congratulated the captains of industry on their fecund and large-minded enterprise, the working classes on the intelligent comprehension of their corporate interests.

All round the table there were embracings and shakings by the hand. Renaudin, all smiles, shook Monsieur Pascal's hand, saying:

"No ill feeling."

" 'Let us be friends, Cinna,' " replied Monsieur Pascal.

. . . .

The following day, happy to resume their familiar life after such a romantic holiday, the workpeople returned joyfully.

Peace was signed: they came with outstretched hands. Their candor disarmed Bernard's ill will. He found it hard to believe that these men were the same who, the day before, had howled at the gates of the deserted mill. He questioned those whom, up to the strike, he had taken for real friends, who had gained his esteem and whose confidence he had thought he deserved.

"Now you, Heurtematte, why did you leave us like that, on the second day? You have seen enough of us to know that we're not the men to compel children to work or to risk blowing up the mill, now haven't you?"

"Oh me, Monsieur Bernard, I didn't believe a word of all that. . . . Only, to make no bones of it, I didn't want to be no more of a scab than my mates."

CHAPTER TWENTY

IN JUNE, 1920, Françoise asked her husband with gentle insistence to take a villa for her at Deauville. Her sister, Madame de Thianges, was going to spend the summer there; she had hardly seen her since the war; the sea air would be good for the children; and she herself needed a change of air.

Antoine struggled for long. He would only be able to go to Deauville on Sundays; he loathed all that fashionable life; no Quesnay had ever removed his household in that manner far from the hallowed shade of the smoke-stacks; Monsieur Achille would think the idea scandalous. But Antoine's greatest fear was that in other surroundings Françoise would conceive a disgust for the life of Pont-de-l'Eure.

"But why?" he kept on repeating dejectedly. "The children are all right in the country. They look perfectly well."

"Shall we say, if you prefer, that I would like it? . . . Isn't that enough?"

Because he was weak, he gave way in the end, but so tardily and ungracefully that she did not even feel he did it to give her pleasure. Monsieur Achille shrugged his shoulders; he had made up his mind to consider the case of Françoise as hopeless. She went off at the beginning of July.

. . . .

Since the strike the mill had adopted the system of a weekly half-holiday, and Antoine had promised to be at Deauville every Saturday by five o'clock; but he had a new car to which he had fitted so many improvements that, in the end, it wouldn't go at all. On the first Saturday he arrived at seven o'clock, covered in mud. On the apple-trees with their belt of white palings, on the pink geraniums the rain was falling, steady and hard.

"There you are at last!" said his wife. "You'll only just have time to dress; we're dining at Hélène's."

"Oh, I say!" said Antoine, "I'm fagged out. I haven't seen you for a week. I was looking forward to playing with the children. No; telephone to her that we're not coming."

"That's out of the question; we shall wreck her whole table. Besides," she continued, in a tone of the most winning reassurance, like a mother comforting a child, "you'll see, there'll be a very amusing little party there: Lambert-Leclerc and his wife . . . *he's* Under-Secretary of State in the Victualing Department, *she's* Sabine Leclerc that was, who was at boarding-school with me. It's jolly seeing Sabine again, she's delightful, a bit outspoken. Then there's Fabert, the playwright, you know, the man who wrote *The Steppe*, also with his wife, and, besides, a young musician, Jean Philippe Montel, who is a marvel. He does parodies at the piano; you'll see, it's too funny for words."

"How frightful!" said Antoine, terror-stricken.

But Françoise's good humor was not to be shaken; ever since morning, she had been repeating to herself: "I must be nice to Antoine. . . ." She was happy, she was having a good time, she was grateful to him for it, and she wanted him to share her pleasure.

"At the Casino I'll show you the most delicious little Spanish women, all powdered and painted, and the beautiful Lady Diana Manners. . . . This morning at the *Potinière* there were some lovely dresses; people admire mine a lot, you know, specially the white and red. I don't look too much like Pont-de-l'Eure; you won't have to blush on my account."

Antoine listened to her in utter despair. His most secret apprehensions were justified; he had foreseen that she would take a liking to this kind of life. It was natural: she was so pretty, she must feel an intoxicating pleasure at being noticed in such a crowd of women. But he, Antoine, would have wished to bury himself with so much beauty in some hidden retreat. He felt himself unworthy to keep her, if, in order to please her, he would have to sustain comparison with brilliant men. Perhaps he would have done better to tell her all this candidly, but he was timid, and his timidity drove him to the garage and the workshop. Realizing that the game was up, he sighed and went off to dress.

. . . .

Although the Thianges' villa was quite close at hand, they had to take the car to get there, because Françoise was wearing silver shoes. Antoine was gloomy and silent. He always had the impression that his brother-in-law Thianges treated him with rather a contemptuous condescension. He was wrong: Maurice de Thianges had a patronizing tone of voice which he could no more change than the shape of his eyebrows. Hélène was not so good-looking as Françoise, but was much liked because of her natural wit, gently mocking and void of malice. She had many friends in the most diverse circles; she collected celebrities. Antoine found Lambert-Leclerc pretentious and Fabert disappointing; the young musician Montel, whom everyone called Jean Philippe, he disliked particularly, because, in so little time, he seemed to have become great friends with Françoise.

At table he found himself between Madame Lambert-Leclerc and Madame Fabert; they both terrified him. The minister's wife was young, intelligent and caustic; the other was a fat, well-meaning lady, but wanted to talk about actors he'd never heard of. He listened and never said a word. The rapidity of the conversation made him rather giddy. These people seemed to have read everything, seen everything and knew the whole world. One of them had an anecdote to tell in connection with every new name which a chance phrase brought into play. The moment a man's voice was silent, Hélène de Thianges' clear little voice set out like a kind of shuttle, carrying across the table the thread of the conversation to him who was to throw it back. Lambert-Leclerc talked about the Foreign Debt and told amusing stories about the Peace Conference. Then, without Antoine's being able to notice "how it was done," Jean Philippe was found in possession of the stage, with his paradoxes about Negro music, which Thianges followed up with Negro sculpture.

"No one," said he, "has the sense of three dimensions more than the Negroes."

'Good God!' said Antoine to himself. 'And why?'

But, during the second in which his attention had wandered, the chase had gone off on a new scent. They were now talking about the way in which artists received their inspiration.

"The subject of *The Steppe?*" Fabert was saying. "It is an anecdote I heard when I was sixteen and which I fostered slowly with everything I experienced. As a general rule, you do no good with a theme unless it has gone through the normal period of gestation in the mind. A novelist makes use of his childhood or his youth, rarely of his years of discretion. The novel of old age has never been written 'from inside'. . . . It hasn't the time to mature."

"And the musicians?" said Hélène, throwing the shuttle to Jean Philippe.

"Oh, that's quite different. A theme is provided for you by chance, or by nature. Now, that tune from my operetta," he continued, turning to Françoise, "which I was playing to you last night and which you liked, I picked it up one day on the boulevards, walking past the Café Napolitain. Two saucers fell down and spun round on the marble top of a table; it sounded like 'tu-lu, tu-lu, tu-lu' . . . I'd got my theme. It's all very queer."

"But do you remember?" said Françoise. "Wagner tells how the *cor anglais motif* for *Tristan* was given him one night in Venice by a gondolier's cry?"

And she smiled at Antoine, as if to apologize for herself. 'She too!' he thought.

She was utterly different from the Françoise of Pont-de-l'Eure or Fleuré. She seemed to open out like a flower that has found favorable surroundings. Antoine would have liked to rejoice at it, but his own silence exasperated him. Not that he lacked culture; he had read much, more perhaps than any of the men present, but it was his habit to think slowly and in solitude. And now that he pondered it, that question of inspiration, he too could tell a tale or two. Flaubert, for instance, had got the idea for *L'Education sentimentale* one day at a funeral. . . . Meanwhile the conversation went its way: romanesque cathedrals, English poets, Chinese vases. When Antoine again paid heed, having polished his anecdote, it was too late; they were talking of love.

"I believe," said Fabert, "that we are returning to much simpler manners, much closer to those of the Ancients. At the seaside, men and women are once more adopting the habit of living naked—which makes desire less active and less dangerous. We must not forget that this extraordinary mixture of modesty and provocativeness, instinct and sentiment, which we call 'romantic love,' is quite a novel combination: it has been in existence for eight hundred years and will perhaps vanish very quickly."

"That will be a pity," said Hélène.

"Oh no," said Jean Philippe, "we shall not even notice it. Our descendants will find it as natural to separate desire from affection as we to combine them."

"It's very pleasant, all the same," said Françoise.

Fabert leaned over and murmured a few words in a whisper to Hélène de Thianges, who burst out laughing.

"You make me blush," said she.

Jean Philippe was talking with Françoise. Antoine's anger was so obvious that his sister-in-law cast him a glance of reproach and attempted in vain to make him talk. His sulky silence was embarrassing the whole table. Françoise felt it and was ashamed.

'Really,' she thought, 'Antoine is impossible! He does not make the slightest effort to please me. I have been very happy the last five days, away from Pont-de-l'Eure and from him.'

As soon as they left the table, she went to sit with Jean Philippe in front of the piano. Antoine came up and propped himself on his elbows without speaking to them. Françoise got up. Fabert, who had watched the scene, came to her rescue and led her away to a divan.

"I must ask you a question," said he. "I am curious to know if there is a heroine in fiction with whom you feel you have traits in common—an affinity?"

"Certainly," said Françoise passionately, "Anna Karenina!"

"What I was thinking," said Fabert with a kind of compassion.

He talked to her for some time. The moment he had gone, Antoine took his place.

"What has he been saying to you?"

She looked at him angrily:

"He has told me things about myself which have surprised and frightened me."

"Let us be off! Come along!" said Antoine curtly.

"What? But we've only just left the table and we're all to go and see Fabert's play at the Casino."

"I am not feeling the thing; I can't stay. Do you hear, Françoise; I *can't* stay."

He looked so upset that she feared a scene in public and gave way. Their departure left the Thianges and their guests astonished and saddened.

A little later Jean Philippe spoke of them to Hélène de Thianges:

"How different from your sister her husband is!"

"Yes, isn't he? He was unbearable this evening. We have never understood what she wanted to marry him for. There were family difficulties, but she was mad about him. Of course, he's a good-looking man, and at that time he was an officer in the army, and also, precisely because our families were at odds, Françoise thought the match romantic."

"Shall we see them tomorrow?" said Jean Philippe.

"Now," said Hélène with a laugh, "you leave her alone."

CHAPTER TWENTY-ONE

ANTOINE remained a long time in the little drawing room of the villa without daring to go to Françoise in their room. In a corner there was a small library in which he found *Les Origines de la France contemporaine*. He read several chapters or, at any rate, turned over the pages in an attempt to calm himself.

' "These staircases at Versailles so wide that eighty ladies in panniered skirts . . ." It is out of the question,' he thought, 'I cannot leave her here by herself: God knows whom the Thianges' won't yet have at their house before the summer is out. The freedoms of this Parisian society are dangerous, yes, dangerous. François is straight: she will understand. . . . *Will* she understand? She is so changed already. Oh why hadn't I the necessary will to prevent her coming here!'

At last, about midnight, he made up his mind to go upstairs and talk to her.

'Perhaps she'll be asleep.'

He wished she might be, but she was not asleep. She had gone to bed, had kept the light on, however, and was waiting without even reading. Her face had a very serious expression: she had been crying.

"You are not tired, are you?" said he. "I may have a talk with you?"

She looked at him fixedly without replying. He continued: "I have been thinking it over. I fancy you will agree with me. It isn't suitable for you to remain at Deauville alone. Your sister will be having a whole heap of people at her villa—bachelors, artists. . . . She has her husband about and that is perfectly all right, but you. . . . without meaning to be, you will be compromised. . . . I should be too uneasy about you. . . . We should have no difficulty in subletting the villa for the month of August."

"Have you gone mad?" said she coldly.

"What makes you say that?"

"You believe that I shall return to Pont-de-l'Eure in August, deprive myself of society I find entertaining, yes, entertaining, simply because you are not brilliant and are jealous? Never, do you hear, never! Now I am going to make you another proposal, Antoine: I too have been thinking it over during the last two hours. I am sick of passing my youth buried in the country, tied to a man to whom I am of less account than his chimney-pots and his looms. I still have a few years of youth left. I want to live. Give me my freedom: I will bring up my children; you will be quite taken up by your cloth and your wool, since nothing else in the world exists for you."

The discussion became very violent. Françoise painted a portrait of the Quesnays, terrible, unjust and truthful. A flood of petty grievances seemed to gush out with irresistible force from these two tormented hearts.

'What am I saying?' Antoine kept thinking, 'what am I saying? How did this all start?'

But he could not hold in his words. At last the truth appeared clearly to both of them: they hated one another, they had nothing more in common. They fell silent.

Antoine mournfully passed his hand over his forehead: "My head is too bad; I must take a turn outside; I want air."

He went out; the rain had stopped. An immense starry sky covered the sleeping villas. It was certainly very late. At the Normandy a few lights still outlined the drawn blinds; only the Casino blazed out, a liner on the high seas. Antoine turned his back on it and walked towards the sea. The tide was coming in with a slow, soft lapping. The beach was deserted. He lay down on the sand. In the distance, over towards Le Havre, a lighthouse revolved. 'One, two, three, four, five—flash . . . One, two, three, four, five—flash.' This rhythm tranquilized him somewhat; then, stretching himself out backwards, he had the sensation of plunging into the midst of the stars. He called them by their names: 'The Little Bear, the Pole Star . . . That sort of chair, I have forgotten its name. . . . The Pleiades winking. How beautiful it is!' The silence did him good, and also the immensity of sky and sea, their indifference. It was as if he had before him some gigantic companion, tender and dumb.

'And now,' said he, 'what has happened? What was the starting point? All this is childish. It is like an absurd dream. I love Françoise dearly.'

He thought of her little crazes, her love of flowers and of old stuffs, of certain delicious expressions she had when looking at the children. 'Everything,' he thought, 'I love everything about her, even her "Pascal-Bouchet" side, as Bernard would say. Perhaps that especially. I am grateful to her for being different from me. . . . But how about this evening? . . . When I got here, at seven o'clock, she was as usual . . . It was afterwards . . . at that dinner-party.'

He closed his eyes, trying to remember. The sound of the breaking wave was like a caress.

'No, all this lies farther back; she has been drifting away from me for the last two years, and the fault is mine. When

I married her, she admired me; I represented a force in her eyes, first because of my tales of the war, and especially because I braved my family in marrying her. . . . That's it. . . . I raised hopes in her of a great, heroic love. And I haven't stayed the course, on account of the Quesnays. The moment I am inside the works, I am dominated, impotent. Up against grandfather and even Bernard, when he speaks to me in a particular way, I have no courage. Some women require an immense surrender; Françoise has discovered pettiness in me. . . . I have felt it and have not dared talk about it, and I have fled to this life of reading and tinkering. . . . And, all the same, I should have been ready to die for her. . . . Yes, certainly. . . . I must. . . .'

He stood up and started walking rapidly over the sand towards the villa.

'There is going to be a change in all this. . . . But how could I ever think that the mill, that Grandfather Achille are things of greater importance than the sky, the sea and, in particular, than Françoise? I really must have gone mad.'

On nearing the house, he started to run. A lighted window stood open; coming up, he saw Françoise leaning out. "Is it you?" she said. She had been frightened. On seeing him go out into the night, she had imagined absurdities, possible suicide, death; and then she too had found a gigantic, tender companion, who had put everything back into its true perspective. Had she been absolutely in the right? Had she not a spice of coquetry to reproach herself with? During the week preceding Antoine's arrival she had been much too intimate with this Jean Philippe. She knew quite well that if he stayed a few days longer he would become enterprising. The other day already, at the piano, his hands . . . During that time Antoine was toiling at Pont-de-l'Eure, and toiling for her and the children. At bottom she loved him very much. He had taught her everything really solid and serious that she knew. He was very good, very simple; if she could have torn him away out of his grandfather's influence, he would have been perfect. Poor Antoine! How miserable she must have made him!

She went back to bed; when he came in, he dropped down on his knees near the bed without saying a word and took

Françoise's hand, which he kissed with a sort of fervor. Then she raised herself a little and, with her left hand, softly stroked his hair. He saw that he was forgiven.

"Now tell me what you want. We will live in the way you like."

"No, no," said she, "I want nothing. If it can give you any satisfaction, I will leave Deauville tomorrow."

"What an idea! Not a bit of it! Stay all the summer; I will come over oftener. Grandpapa can make a rumpus. . . . Much good may it do him!"

She smiled.

"I love to see you like that; one thing I ask of you: try to belong to me more than to them."

"I will try," said Antoine and kissed her. Under the pink silk of her nightdress she was warm and unresisting.

.   .   .   .

They woke up at daybreak; for they had left the window open. It was a blue morning. On the horizon sea and sky merged in a silvery mist. Monsieur Achille had announced that he would come over to spend Sunday. The pleasures of indignation attracted him in these abodes of offence. Antoine said to Françoise: "If it bores you, I will look after him. You can stay with your sister." She protested: "Why, not in the least. On the contrary, it will be most amusing to see Monsieur Achille at the *Potinière*."

He arrived about eleven o'clock, driven by Bernard. The sea was grey, slate grey and dove grey, the sky spanned by a flight of pink clouds; the yellow, coral, flame-colored dresses made gay spots of color on the drab sands. Monsieur Achille refused to take a chair. A voice behind him called out cheerfully: "Monsieur Quesnay, your humble servant!"

Turning round, he beheld a young man with his hair thrown back by a graceful movement, whose very wide-open shirt afforded a view of his smooth chest. The idea that this androgynous apparition could pretend to his acquaintance filled him with violent fury. He hurled a black look of surprise at the creature. But the low-necked being remained unmoved: for it was Monsieur Jean Vanekem.

He had taken at Deauville a villa embowered in geraniums, which sheltered a whole harem of typists. Thence he dispatched to the markets of the world orders for triumphant purchases.

As he had pronounced his own name, Monsieur Achille regretfully put out a finger to the proffered hand and grunted a hostile good-morning.

"Well, Monsieur Quesnay," said the athlete familiarly, "do you believe in the rise now? Combed is up to a hundred francs."

"Don't rely on it too much," growled Monsieur Achille. "The old ewe isn't dead yet. There'll be a general break sooner than you think."

"You won't take things seriously," said the other with regret. "I am coming to see you one of these days at Pont-de-l'Eure. I have a splendid proposition to put to you. . . . The Ko-Ko-Noo paper-mills . . . A factory in the heart of Africa . . . Labor for nothing and forests of raw material. . . . See you later, then. . . . Remember me kindly to my cousin Lecourbe"

Between two pretty girls, each complementary to the other—a blonde in a violet jumper, a brunette in a straw-colored jumper—Monsieur Vanekem disappeared with elastic step along the plankway.

"Who's he?" ask Françoise astounded.

"That?" said Monsieur Achille contemptuously. "That's my greatest debtor, walking about with his chest bare."

Standing with his alpaca jacket gleaming in the sun, he watched with sarcastic mien the tennis-players arrayed in white flannel, the women, whose breasts made little peaks under the stretched material of their bathing-dresses, and the brilliance of this swarming, useless crowd. Françoise thought that he looked like some old magician to whom all these mad folk had forgotten to send an invitation and who, with a gesture, was about to transform them into toads.

CHAPTER TWENTY - TWO

ANTOINE got into the way of not returning to Pont-de-l'Eure before the Monday. In his eyes the life of the mill had, all of a sudden, become as it were far-away and monot-

onous. He was like a man who has for long had magnifying
glasses before his eyes and who, suddenly dropping them,
sees objects recede from him and assume their true size.
'What?' he kept saying to himself. 'Is this all?' He was
already thinking of next Sunday. He experienced again a
sensation of his young days when he was a soldier and the
week went by in the expectation of leave. In those days Sundays alone counted; so now—the post, the round through
the work rooms, the purchases of wool became compulsory
exercises, as tiresome and futile as bayonet practice, and
real living was confined to the few precious hours in which
he was with Françoise again.

Towards the end of July, as he was leaving the mill with
Bernard, a wool-broker called out from a distance: "Wool's
down in London, gentlemen." In the same way, six years
before, a friend on opening *Le Temps* had said to them
negligently: "Hullo! They have murdered the heir-apparent
of Austria."

At that moment the madness of buying was at its apex,
and the speculators, intent on their game, did not see the
mountains of wool accumulated beyond the seas in the
Argentine *haciendas,* in the Australian farms, ready to
topple down over Europe.

The slump at London was slight, an undulation hardly
visible in the rising curve of prices, but it fell into a market
so loaded with stocks that it dampened every ardor, just as a
speck is sufficient to precipitate a supersaturated solution.
The merchants who had overbought lost their heads at the
first onset and asked for their orders to be canceled. Monsieur Lecourbe received them proudly. "There will still remain enough of them."

But the contagion was rapid, the epidemic formidable.
The newspapers proclaimed a speedy return to pre-war
prices. A conspiracy of thrift leagued the consumers against
the producers' greed. To wear a worn-out jacket, to have a
shabby overcoat turned, became a mark of virtue. From
snobbery the newly-rich ceased their squandering. Vanekem's friend, Liliane Fontaine, wrote Bernard Quesnay:
"Could you send me some beige gabardine? I want to make
myself a little frock." On every side stocks emerged like

rats on a sinking ship. Came the Antwerp sales. There prices rushed down the hill at full speed.

Like a train coming to a stop over an obstacle (and the first splintered coach becomes itself a danger to the second, against which the third is smashed to pieces), so the militant zeal of the shopkeepers came to nought against the stolid obstinacy of the consumers; against the overflowing shops the force of the factories vainly dashed itself, and the factories, energetically applying the brakes, received the unavailing impact of the wool-producing countries.

The transition from prosperity to want, like all the great tragic catastrophes, was made in the sharp, theatrical manner that Fate commands. At the beginning of a month, an excessively flourishing and wealthy industry was disdainfully refusing orders for which it had no use; at the end of the same month, that industry felt its back to the wall, with a stoppage imminent. As on the morrow of defeat a routed general contemplates his battered line, examines one after the other the points on which he believed he could rely and comprehends in a flash that all this apparent strength was nothing but weakness, each of the fortified posts being of use only with the support of all the others, so the two Quesnay brothers, turning over their order-books devastated by blue-pencil fire, found on all hands the too-certain foretokens of the crash.

"It is a serious business," Antoine said to Françoise. "If this goes on, we shall be ruined."

She received the news very cheerfully.

"It is all the same to me," said she. "I shall set to work. I'll make hats and dresses. It would be fun."

In the Fastness of Drapery woebegone customers showed Bernard pile upon pile of stuffs, gigantic and redoubtable.

"Give you work for your looms? . . . My poor man, just look for yourself! My cellars and attics are full of cloth. . . . and I have three thousand pieces of it yet to come. . . . I have fabrics to last me two years!"

"Those piles," exclaimed young Saint-Clair, whom the Quesnays loved for the vigor and directness of his language. "Those piles! They fairly put the wind up me. . . . If some bloke comes piddling round in the morning to buy three yards of blue cloth, he sends 'em back again in the evening, on the pretext that he thought it was yellow. . . . And the damned piles are as they were."

Monsieur Roch, on his dignity, received the ambassador from Pont-de-l'Eure with no great graciousness:

"Is this some joke of yours, my young friend? I myself hold stocks to the value of twenty millions. What do you want me to buy for?"

"Monsieur Roch, it is no deal I am putting to you, but a service that I ask of you. I have a thousand hands, and they must have their livelihood. . . . You were my father's best friend. . . ."

"Of course, of course, my boy . . . But your father has nothing to do with the case. . . . The point at issue is not a question of sentiment, but to discover whether or no I can meet my creditors. Business is not carried on by dint of family souvenirs."

To Monsieur Cavé senior Bernard proposed to manufacture the heavy, well-gummed materials desired, for their burnooses, by the Arabs of Algeria.

"Too late, Monsieur Quesnay. Algeria is no longer in the market. They have had a bad harvest over there; the Arabs are suffering from a corn famine. . . . It is your fault. . . . If you had deigned to turn out the article at the time I told you to, you would have established a position for yourselves, but all you have ever been capable of doing at your mill is staring at your own navels."

For two long days Bernard explored Paris, astonished at his own ardor in pursuing buyers who eluded him after all. As happens with lovers, the difficulty of the undertaking began to give him an appetite for it.

CHAPTER TWENTY-THREE

HE HAD a rendezvous with Simone at five o'clock in a studio she had taken and where she often received him. At noon he got a telephone-message from Pont-de-l'Eure that Monsieur Roch wanted to see him again and would expect him at five o'clock sharp.

'What a bore Roch is!' he thought. 'I have seen him this morning. What can he want? I won't go . . . or I'll go tomorrow. . . . But tomorrow they're expecting me at the mill, and I have promised Monsieur Cantaert to see that boiler-engineer with him. All the same, Roch is a very important matter. . . . How you vex me!' he said to himself, 'you trouble all my pleasures. . . . Perhaps Simone will be free earlier. That would settle everything.'

At half-past three he rang at the studio door. She opened and said: "But how nice of you to come early!" and was, all of a sudden, very gay, very animated. On an easel stood the outline of a fair woman in a black dress with a narrow belt, striped red and bright blue.

"What a pretty dress!" said Bernard.

"I am glad you say that; it is the dress that I wanted to paint. At the moment, I am mad on stuffs, on hats. It seems to me that there is a whole poetry in them which has not yet been expressed. I have even amused myself painting the shop-windows on the boulevards. Look. . . ."

"Yes," said Bernard. "Excellent! But are you not afraid that it might turn into a fashion-plate?"

"With due proportion, dear boy, it is as if you had asked Monet: 'Are you not afraid that Chartres Cathedral might turn into a picture postcard?' One must never be afraid of the commonplaceness of a subject, if it really moves one. Do you think that before Berthe Morisot and Monet people would have dared paint household utensils, garden seats, railway engines? At the first Utrillos you see you say to yourself: 'What a funny idea; that is all far from beautiful.' And then, all of a sudden, in a Paris suburb, you find yourself in love with a school or a hospital or a café and observe: 'Look, an Utrillo. . . .' You, who are a Norman, haven't you seen in the Rouen gallery that delightful canvas of Blanche's, representing a London shop?"

"What I like about your art," said Bernard, "is that you paint very straightforwardly. I don't know the technical terms, but I mean to say that it isn't jarring, doesn't go out of its way to be crude. In nature transitions always appear to me as gentle, and it seems to me that many painters, sometimes the greatest, refuse to see it, in order to be more powerful. Do you understand what I mean to say?"

"Of course. I am like you; I am very susceptible to the 'smooth side' of things. . . . Only, you must be careful: there are two sorts of smooth—that of Vermeer and the great Italians, which overlies an expressed relief and is authentic, and then there is that of Bouguereau or of Cabanel, which is smooth because it is flat. . . . As for me, I do my best. . . . Look, I am pretty well satisfied with that woman's shoulder. . . ."

Bernard, who was behind her, softly placed his lips on the nape of her neck and slipped down her dress, uncovering her shoulders striated with violet-colored ribbon.

"Darling," he said, "how lovely you are!"

.   .   .   .

Half an hour later he softly lifted up Simone's head, which was lying on his shoulder, raised his wrist above his mistress's body and gently turned it. She opened her eyes.

"You're looking at the time? Already?"

"Yes," said Bernard, somewhat shamefacedly. "I did not dare tell you: I have to go earlier."

"I guessed that some time ago. . . . You came at half-past three. . . . Well, to whom am I to be sacrificed?"

He explained, very precisely.

"And you weren't able to put off this Roch until tomorrow? It is I then who always have to take a back seat? Oh, you are hateful at times. Be careful, Bernard, my boy, one of these days it will all be up. I shall not warn you in advance; you will get a letter, and that will be the end."

"That will prove that you do not love me."

"No, I don't love you. It is only a well-played comedy. I shall get on very well without you. Why should I love you? You are neither amiable, nor amusing, nor attentive. I know a hundred men more seductive than you. If I had not met you during the war, at a time when I was in need of being loved and when, moreover, you were quite different, I should not have noticed you."

Bernard looked at her, a little uneasy; the Quesnays were

bad at understanding irony. She enjoyed his surprised look for an instant, then folded herself in his arms.

"But I do, I do love you."

Monsieur Roch waited that evening in vain. But when he caught his train back to Pont-de-l'Eure, Bernard felt very dissatisfied with himself. 'That's not going to happen again,' he thought.

CHAPTER TWENTY-FOUR

"YES," said Monsieur Achille, "too many idiots have made money: we must have a cleanup. One country hasn't room for many big fortunes. Before the war industry was a difficult undertaking. With much labor you hardly got five or six per cent for your money; the idlers went smash. That was as it should be."

With his son-in-law and his grandsons he examined the means by which they might go on working. One by one the orders remaining on the books were subjected to a severe scrutiny.

"Boisselot? We must cancel him. He won't be able to get out of it. He has got stocks to the tune of eighteen million, on which he will lose six million. No pre-war capital. Done for! . . . Pity, a good chap. . . . Bemma of Castres? Yes . . . he'll leave his feathers behind, but he will get out of it. . . . His war damages will be a nice feather-bed for him. . . . Fabrics Limited? . . . Registered address . . . A managing director . . . No confidence. Cross them off. . . . Cernay? He will lose a lot, but he knows what work is. We shall have to take the bull by the horns and ask him how he stands. . . ."

The incoherence of such metaphors beguiled Bernard's anguish. Monsieur Lecourbe was lavish of them: "The tail is eating up the head. We must put our rifle to the other shoulder. We shall swallow up all we've got, but we shall land on our feet."

"What is the upshot?" Bernard interrupted. "How long will our orders last us?"

"A month."

"We must get hold of more, then, or close down," said Monsieur Achille.

"Close down! . . . And the hands? . . . A stoppage at the onset of winter?"

Monsieur Achille turned over the leaves of the order-book in silence, then went on:

"We can go on working at cost-price . . . certainly. . . . We can help the hands in a stoppage with canteens and the like . . . certainly. . . . But we cannot accumulate stocks. . . . To fail helps no one and nothing. If you want to keep your employees, find markets. You are young."

A swift movement of the bony, hairy old hand dismissed the meeting. Bernard was the first to leave. In the mill yard, where the bundles of yarn and barrels of oil already stood sparser, he met his sister-in-law.

"Good-morning, Bernard. . . . I am looking for Antoine. I require some flannel for the mites in my crèche."

"Antoine? I have just left him; he will still be busy with the post."

"With your grandfather? No, thank you. I am not going there."

"Are you afraid of Monsieur Achille, Françoise?"

"Afraid? No. . . . But when he sees me in the mill he always looks as if he thought me the temptress who will lure away the two of you from the Paradise of the Quesnays. . . . That man has no soul, Bernard."

"All the same, he is a great force. . . . Where should we be today without him?"

"Poor Antoine is in an awful humor. . . . Are things really going so badly for you?"

"Listen to the looms. . . . Monsieur Achille declares that when he comes into the mill he knows his position at once by that rhythm. When the work is urgent, the workman isn't: money is easy to make, jobs easy to get. They stop for a word with a neighbor, to eat a bite. One end of the room stops running, another starts off again . . . as in those modern symphonies, you know—those in which the calls of the instruments rise in unexpected spasms. . . . But when the market is dull, when the master, at his wits' end with accumulating a ruinous amount of stock, wants to produce as little as possible, then the workman works for all he's worth. We are in a very bad way."

"So these poor folk will soon be playing, will they, Bernard?"

"I am afraid so. All the same, I have got together a good exhibit. Come and look at it."

By staircases and bridges he took her along to his office. On a long wooden counter he spread out innumerable bundles. There were rough tweeds there, flecked with red, green and blue; soft wool saxonies with their delicate shades shot by brightly colored silks—orange, violet and red—at one and the same time effective and invisible.

"That is very pretty, Bernard; I should much like a tailor-made of that silvery-grey. . . . Are you proud of it?"

"Well, to be honest, I am. After all, a beautiful material is as beautiful as a beautiful piece of tapestry or even as a beautiful poem. It is always a matter of selection, arrangement and proportion. And then, to have made something yourself—that's happiness, don't you find?"

"Perhaps," said Françoise sadly. "I try to think so. You see, I am busying myself with this crèche; I have taken on your grandmother's good works; I do what I can."

"I do see it and I am very glad of it," said Bernard. "I have never said anything about it to you, but I have thought that your life had an æsthetic side which was not altogether authentic. . . . Of course, to have the finest curtains and the finest plate is jolly while you are about it, but after that it is a very negative pleasure. What we need is to forget our own existence. I often get here at eight o'clock in the morning and, when the hooter blows at twelve, I feel as if I had been at work for five minutes. So life goes by."

"It goes by perhaps without one's having properly relished it."

He spread out his arms a little way and pulled a disdainful face.

"Do you think so? What is there to relish? '*A tale told by an idiot.*' . . . No we must not think about it."

"Monsieur Bernard," a clerk came to say, "Monsieur Jean Vanekem wishes to see you in the warehouse."

"Please excuse me, Françoise," said he.

CHAPTER TWENTY-FIVE

MONSIEUR JEAN VANEKEM, a little vexed at having to wait, was pacing the warehouse with a nonchalant air. He was dressed in a light-colored overcoat, drawn in under his bosom like ladies' dresses in the days of the First Empire, had a felt hat of a delicate grey on his head and, on his feet, boots of pale buckskin. He adorned his face—the face of the juvenile lead in an American film—with a condescending smile when Bernard Quesnay joined him.

"Good-morning, my dear fellow. I asked to see my cousin Lecourbe, but your clerks told me he was away, and I took the liberty of disturbing you. Besides, what I have to tell him concerns you equally. . . . Are you keeping well? Have you seen Liliane in *L'Adventurière?* She is charming in it."

Bernard took him to the office, which he measured with a sweeping and rather disdainful glance; he let himself sink very gracefully into an armchair.

"My dear fellow, you know as well as I that the present state of things has put the best houses in a bad way. Although my dealings have always been perfectly sound, the accumulation of stocks on the one hand and stagnant markets on the other hand make it impossible for me to meet my engagements with all the exactitude I could wish. I know that with the terms on which we are, you and I, these things are of no consequence; nevertheless, in view of the fact that I owe you a pretty considerable sum, I thought it, with possibly exaggerated scrupulousness, my duty to put you *au courant* with the exact state of my affairs. . . ."

Bernard listened to him with surprise and suspicion.

'What is he driving at? Has he come with all this assurance and grand manner to inform me that he is filing his petition? In that case, this display is very much out of place. . . . He owes us nearly a million. Monsieur Achille will laugh. . . .'

"Indeed?" he said out loud. "I do not altogether understand what you mean by the state of your affairs."

'"Yet it is very simple, my dear fellow. There is nothing disquieting about my position: I have it well in hand, provided I can make a valuation of my goods and securities at cost-price. And here's my balance-sheet. . . ."

He took out of his pocket a little piece of paper, which he handed to Bernard.

"You see," he said, "the position is altogether healthy and, provided I am given time to liquidate. . . ."

Bernard raised his eyes and gazed with stupefaction at Monsieur Vanekem's handsome, plump face wreathed in smiles.

"Your position is altogether healthy, you say?" he remarked. "Why, sir, you are virtually bankrupt!"

Monsieur Vanekem appeared more grieved than angered by such regrettable lack of tact.

"Bankrupt! . . ." he said indulgently. "You must imagine that we are living in the time of Balzac, my dear fellow. People do not go bankrupt nowadays. I may perhaps be compelled to apply for the voluntary liquidation of my concern, but I do not think I shall. I imagine that my creditors, among whom I take at once pleasure and concern in reckoning yourself, would find it to their advantage to accept by amicable arrangement a dividend of thirty to forty francs in the hundred. Do you not agree with me?"

"It is not my business to take any decision in this matter. . . . I shall explain the position to my grandfather this very evening, and I will let you know. . . ."

Monsieur Vanekem appeared a trifle put out.

"As you please; but you will understand that I absolutely must know where I stand. If all the world has to be consulted, maneuvering becomes difficult. So I shall rely on you to write to me this evening."

"What are the Ko-Ko-Noo shares worth?" said Bernard,

exasperated. "They represent an important part of your assets and, moreover, thanks to you, we are shareholders ourselves. . . ."

"Ko-Ko-Noo," said Monsieur Vanekem, "is a first-class enterprise, but it is not in full swing yet. The small capital hitherto subscribed has served primarily to pay for certain financial and political co-operation and to send out some exploratory expeditions into the Lower Congo to determine sites for the factories. The latter are not yet built. We are shortly to increase the capital by four times the old amount, and those who hold shares already will be entitled to four new shares at the issue-price: a gift. . . . Upon which note, my good friend, I will leave you to your labors. I must go over to Louviers to see Monsieur Pascal-Bouchet, whom I equally have the pleasure of counting among my purveyors."

He held out a hand gloved in supple reindeer-hide. Bernard accompanied him as far as the gate of the mill. A chauffeur in a white rubber cape opened the door of a fine low coupé with long straight lines.

"A Cadillac from war stocks," said Monsieur Vanekem modestly. "Yes, it's a nice little car."

As he looked upon the noble cloud of dust in which Monsieur Vanekem was enveloping his form divine and the last days of his gilded glory, Bernard thought not without hilarity of the certain fury of Monsieur Achille when the Twilight of the God was announced to him, and of the lecture to which Monsieur Lecourbe would have to listen for having made the Quesnays pull an oar in that galley.

He knew that his progenitor was on his rounds in the spinning-mill by the waterside and lay in wait for him.

"So there you are. . . ." said Monsieur Achille. "On the road I passed that Vanekem's car; he drives like a lunatic. Has he been here? What does he want now?"

"He does *not* want to pay the six hundred thousand francs he owes us. He showed me an altogether delightful balance-sheet . . . with charming unconcern."

"Ha! ha!" said Monsieur Achille in triumphant tones which clearly signified, "What I foresaw has happened with a vengeance," "Ho, ho! So Vanekem is done for? Well, he owes Monsieur Pascal close on two million. He told me so himself. That's a fine business!"

And, rubbing his hands, he went off with great strides, to seek out his son-in-law, fretting and fuming on principle, but completely consoled for his own loss by the satisfaction of having foretold it and by the much heavier loss of his friend and crony.

CHAPTER TWENTY-SIX

IN THE Paris train Monsieur Lecourbe and his nephew Bernard met Monsieur Pascal-Bouchet. The morning sun made the silver roofs of the farms sparkle; a rich brown mist enveloped the trees as in a landscape by Turner.

Monsieur Lecourbe, who was depressed, talked about "the situation."

"It is frightful. The best houses are in jeopardy. . . . Do you know that Cavé has called together his creditors? He is asking for five years in which to pay; his stock amounts to thirty million. A house dating from 1805? A man who couldn't get collars high enough for him! . . . And Roch and Lozeron—people are talking about them too. But who isn't being talked about? My cousin Vanekem, a boy who hadn't a penny before the war, who had the chance of making a fortune, is going to lose it all again, idiot that he is. However, I must in justice give myself the credit of always having sized him up properly. . . . What do you expect? Everybody has been pulling too hard at the string, and it has snapped. Up to a certain point and in a certain degree, we had to be prepared for it."

"The string has not snapped," said Monsieur Pascal. "This post-war Europe of ours is more like a violin-chord that has been plucked too roughly: it is in vibration. We have got no farther than the first oscillation; for twenty years we shall witness ups and downs, ups and downs of decreasing magnitude. Then everything will remain calm again until the next upheaval. Everything settles itself."

"Nothing settles itself," said Monsieur Lecourbe. "Depression begets depression. The only consumer is the working man, and now he is earning nothing. The peasant has money, but the country never buys; it hoards. We are heading for disaster. The foremost economists expect a world-wide cataclysm. Besides, it was the same thing after all the great wars: in 1817, in 1876. . . ."

"The world has not come to an end," said Monsieur Pascal. "At present, production is very low. You are hardly working at half-pressure; I am like you. Soon demand will be great. There are still people who wear clothes."

Through the door-window Bernard gazed at the immense plain, which a man and horse were slowly crossing. At hearing the lamentations of Monsieur Lecourbe, infallible in error, he took heart again.

"We are living in sad times," said Monsieur Lecourbe tragically.

"Sad times?" protested Monsieur Pascal. "I don't agree with you; I find these times capital. Before the war, the businessman of genius was unemployed. Today, in order to survive, a man must have intelligence and a cool head. You say we are living in the full blast of the gale? Yes, but we can swim. We are in the trough of the wave? That very fact proves that we shall rise again. . . . Fools sell when everything is falling and buy when everything is rising, and wonder when they are ruined. . . . Listen, Bernard, my lad, you are young, you are a nice boy, I'll tell you the secret of success. . . . Always do the opposite of the others. . . . As the majority of men are fools, you are sure to prosper."

They were nearing their destination. Already five-storied houses rose up isolated in the bare fields, like toothing in an unfinished citadel. Watteau was ceding to Cézanne. Beneath the June sun suburban odds and ends of terrifying beauty were throwing hard, angular shadows. Asnières station, self-important and ridiculous, encircled the train with its endless platforms.

"Ah," said Monsieur Pascal, "here we are. . . . We shall shortly behold our worthy customers once more."

"The situation," said Monsieur Lecourbe, putting on his overcoat, "will have to be stabilized, one way or the other."

CHAPTER TWENTY-SEVEN

BERNARD was to spend the evening with Simone, whose husband was away. He had not seen her for some weeks; for he had left the mill very little since the situation had become dangerous. On several occasions he had promised her to come up; unforeseen difficulties, an urgent piece of work to finish, the whims of Monsieur Achille (whom events were making irritable), had compelled him every time to postpone the meeting already agreed upon. He had suggested seeing her on Sundays, but that was the only day on which it was quite impossible for her to be free. She had written him an ironical, witty letter, not in the best of humor.

'How will she welcome me?' he asked himself as the taxi was taking him to the studio. . . . 'I can understand her point of view perfectly well. She has a bore of a husband, who dislikes going about. She needs a companion who will share her tastes . . . go out with her, take her to concerts or the theater. . . . Only, she maintains that I could live in Paris and that only the will to do so is wanting. That is not the case. A business like ours cannot be run unless one is on the spot. . . . She would reply that a mill is not the purpose of life. That may be so, but then one has to make a choice. What is intolerable hypocrisy, is to assume the privileges of a class without assuming its functions. I would rather . . .'

He noticed that he was talking out loud in the taxi. 'Now, keep calm,' he said to himself, and tried to call up Simone's delicate features and the tone of her voice, which was at once clear and slightly veiled, like the high notes of a piano, when you gently press the pedal.

. . . .

She did not look too greatly annoyed. She did not mention the canceled meetings. She had prepared a funny little supper, which she served herself and shared with him.

"Now," she said, "I'd like you to sit for me for an hour. I have always said that I would like a picture of you."

"Why, what an idea!" said he. "Why this evening? You can't see."

"I can see enough for an outline-drawing. Don't move too much."

During the sitting she described a tea party at which she had been that afternoon: "Madame de Noailles was there; she was charming and talked about Barrès very well too. Then Jean Cocteau, the Pitoëffs. . . ."

She had a very great gift of mimicry; not only did she reproduce voice and gestures, but she would also improvise perfectly congruous tirades for all her personations:

"There was a Spanish poet there too; he recited sonnets to us. Would you like me to recite a Spanish sonnet?"

"But do you know any Spanish?"

"Not a word, but neither did anyone there, so it will come to the same thing; I shall get the atmosphere."

"He certainly is a very great poet," said Bernard when she was silent again. "Let me see your sketch."

"Another five minutes. Your mouth is difficult."

"How delicious you are!" said Bernard suddenly, with obvious and ingenuous sincerity.

"You think so?" she said. "Really and truly? You would miss me if you lost me?"

"But I shall not lose you."

"But supposing you did lose me? Would you think of me? For long? How long? Three months? I am not even sure of that. You have no memory. But I—in thirty years' time I shall be able to draw you, to imitate your gestures. After all, you are not an artist. . . . But I love you, just as you are. I wouldn't change anything about you, not even your nasty character. Don't try to look at your watch; this evening I mean to be pitiless. There is no one at home, and I can come in at four o'clock in the morning if I want. . . . Oh yes, I know you get up early. Well, you'll have to be tired."

She kept him till daybreak. In the Rue Jouffroy they found a taxi on its way home.

"24 Rue de l'Université," said Bernard.

She lived at Number 14, but always stopped her cab some way off. As they crossed the Seine Bernard shivered. Simone was nestled close up to him, very silent. He shut his eyes. The taxi stopped. He helped Simone to get out. It was a grey, melancholy day. Ashbins stood in a line along the pavement. The street was empty.

"When do we meet again?" said Bernard.

She hastily pulled a letter from her bag, held it out to him and ran off. A moment later, a heavy door shut with a bang. Bernard remained for a moment on the pavement, surprised; then, getting back into the cab, said to the driver: "Terminus St. Lazare," and opened the envelope.

"This, Bernard, is a letter of farewell, a genuine one; you won't see me again. Do not try going to the studio, you won't find anybody there. Don't write to me; I shall not read your letters. I have been too wretched and don't want to be so any more. I do not believe you have understood how greatly I have loved you. Some of the fault is mine; I loathe melodrama and the emphatic, and I took refuge in raillery when I was too unhappy. What is terrible with you, is that one has no hold. Your true life is elsewhere, and I cannot bear it. And yet I love you. I love you for reasons which will greatly surprise you. I love you because your shoulders resemble those of Egyptian statues, because you are unsophisticated and boyish even in your scruples, which seem to me so silly. I love you because you have spoken some very pretty phrases to me about my beauty, which you have certainly forgotten, but which I shall remember all my life. I love you, my dear, because enjoyment suits you. I could love even your coldness, but what exasperates me, what is driving us apart is your wishing to convince yourself and others that this emotional coldness, this devotion to your calling are virtues. They are natural to you, dear, that is all. You love telling yourself that you were born to be an idle philosopher, that you accept all activity like a martyrdom. It isn't true. You love it. You were born for it. You have described your grandfather for me: you will be like him, and before long. You may trust me: I see very clearly where you are concerned. Your renunciation is a form of egoism, only it is a prettier word.

"I was anxious to tell you this, because I like you to be what you are, but you can't run with the hares and hunt with the hounds. After a very long time, if you haven't completely forgotten me (with you, one never knows: it's a possibility), you will perhaps begin to understand that you have spoiled a great love, and that that is always a misfortune. You will marry some little girl in the country. She will be horribly unhappy. Perhaps she will notice it less than others, because she won't know what happiness is like. I shall miss you for a very long time, but a slowly diminishing sorrow is better than the life of doubt, waiting and deception I have lived since I have known you. Goodbye, my dear, dear love; I am glad that I have had the courage for this, I have never loved anyone but you, I love you."

Bernard read this letter three times over, then found himself at the door of his hotel. He went upstairs to his room, stretched himself out on his bed without undressing and cried a little. . . . Then he fell asleep. He dreamed he was going through a weaving room and one of the work-girls came up to him. She showed him a number of *L'illustration* containing reproductions of pictures. "Do you see, Monsieur Bernard," said she, "this picture I've made of you; they have turned me down because I am only a mill-hand." Bernard looked at the portrait and thought it very good; the face was vigorous and kindly—just as he saw himself. 'Of course,' he thought, 'if it were Françoise or Simone who had painted that picture, everybody would admire it; but because she's a mill-hand, they turn it down. . . .' "Don't worry," he said to the woman, "I shall write to the President of the Republic." She returned to her loom full of confidence.

. . . .

He woke up at eight o'clock. When he left the hotel, it was a fine, cold morning; people were walking quickly, with a cheerful air. Bernard had a yearning to be doing and working and suddenly felt very much alive. 'But how can this be?' he said to himself, 'I have a great sorrow, I adore

Simone, my life has lost all its meaning.' Great troops of young girls were coming out of St. Lazare Station; he looked at them with pleasure; some of them were running, clumsy and graceful. He too went off town-wards, with a brisk, resolute step. At nine o'clock he was at Monsieur Roch's.

CHAPTER TWENTY-EIGHT

ANTOINE QUESNAY was president of the Pont-de-l'Eure Discharged and Wounded Soldiers' Club; on that account he was compelled once a month to go out alone after dinner to a meeting. A tradition had established itself that on these evenings Bernard dined with the Antoines to keep Françoise company. The latter looked forward impatiently to these evenings, because Bernard always took the opportunity to inform her of new occurrences in his emotional life. Her brother-in-law's liaison entertained Françoise; she loved to think of this very Quesnay Quesnay's attention being diverted from his work by a woman; she found, too, in this adventure a happiness rather like that which a novel affords. Sometimes Bernard had nothing to tell her; he would talk about the mill, about music; Antoine would come home about ten o'clock without Simone Beix having been mentioned, and Françoise would go to bed disappointed. But when Bernard had any confidence to make, she guessed it during dinner; for in that event he would remain very silent, take no interest in any subject of conversation, look impatiently at his watch and do what he could to hasten Antoine's departure.

One of these dinners followed almost immediately upon Simone's ultimatum. As soon as they had left the table Bernard proceeded to walk backwards and forwards in the library, picking up a book, turning over the pages in it, then abruptly putting it back on its shelf. Antoine lingered, smoking a cigar and looking at the garden in silent bliss. He wanted to talk and found the two others tongue-tied. At last he got up. "Well," he said, "I must be off, whether or no; I have a good mind to send in my resignation."

"Good-bye," said Bernard promptly.

"Au revoir, dear," said Françoise cheerfully. The door was shut with a bang (all the Quesnays shut doors violently) ; they heard the engine of the car, the slight grinding of the gear-changes, the friction of the tires against the gravel of the drive.

"A cigarette for you?" said Françoise.

"Thank you very much. . . . Shall we take a turn in the garden, Françoise? It's a lovely evening."

They went out; the sun was sinking on the axis of the long rose-walk. The dogs came to meet them, overjoyed; they stooped to stroke them, then went off without a word to the orchard. Françoise turned to Bernard and smiled; a gentle, warm breeze almost imperceptibly lifted her hair. Her face had a happy, questioning expression.

"Well?" said she. "What great news have you to tell me?"

"How do you know that I have great news to tell you?"

"Because you are of all men the least able to hide things of that kind. . . . You wanted to drive poor Antoine away the minute you got here. . . . Now, what is it? What is afoot? Are you going to marry her? That would be a jolly good thing."

"Marry whom?"

"Whom? Bernard! . . . Your lady, of course!"

"It's exactly the other way about, Françoise. She has left me. . . . Yes, the day before yesterday, when I took her home, she gave me this letter. . . . I brought it for you to read."

Françoise took the letter and stopped under an appletree. Bernard, standing by her side, tried to follow her impressions on her face. When she came to the phrase, "I love you, my dear, because enjoyment suits you," she sighed. She turned the page, he put his hand on her shoulder in order to read with her. He was surprised by the sensation of pleasure which the warmth of her gave him through the silk and took away his hand quickly enough. Françoise had made no movement to get away. Having finished the letter, she handed it back to him.

"Well," said he, "what do you think of it? Will she come back to me?"

Françoise had resumed their stroll along the path.

"That's very hard to say. . . . I don't think she will.
. . . She seems very proud and won't want to abase herself. . . . Besides, she doesn't love you. . . . That letter
of hers isn't the letter of a woman in love. . . . No, no,
she writes too well and she has got the courage to leave
you."

"But I think you are wrong," said Bernard. "It is always
silly for a man to say of a woman: 'She loves me.' It sounds
incredibly fatuous—but, really, I have reasons to believe
that this woman did love me. If she didn't, why, for so
long past . . . The moment I had an hour to spare, she
was at my disposal. . . . And then, I can't explain to you.
. . . No. Only, it is my fault, I have been a beast; I put
her after all else in my life, after the mill, after customers.
. . . God! What a fool I have been at times! One day I
tore myself away, and not gently either, from that beautiful
creature, to go and have a talk with a master-spinner. . . .
During the strike I didn't even write to her. I answered
her four-page letters with telegrams! If she had not loved
me, she would have written me this letter two years
ago. . . ."

"If she had loved you, she would never have written it.
. . . Yes, Bernard dear, you must be a horrid lover, with
your cold manner, your theories, your systems, your ethics;
but a loving woman can put up with much worse. . . . Now,
if I loved a man . . ."

" 'If I loved,' Françoise? But you do love a man, I should
hope. . . . What about Antoine?"

She shook her head impatiently.

"You don't understand women, Bernard. You will never
understand them. . . . Yes, of course, I am married, I
dearly love my husband, I dearly love my children, I dearly
love my home. . . . And that will always be Life to me.
But, come, do you imagine that I don't know there's something else . . . a feeling so strong that family and pride
and point of honor are all swept away? You are surprised
at hearing me say such things; I know you don't like it; you
are shamefast; you are a Quesnay. . . . But that's hypoc-

risy. . . . After all, you know what desire is for you, for a man? Well, for a woman, dear boy, it is exactly the same thing, and where that exists, I believe there is nothing to be done; and if your Simone cared about you, you could have humiliated her, neglected her, betrayed her—she would never have written you that letter. . . . Never. . . ."

To get from the orchard into the kitchen-garden the path narrowed between two hedges, and their bodies found themselves close; against his folded arm Bernard felt the firm contact of a young bosom. He prolonged this contact a moment longer than was necessary. When open ground separated them, he took a deep breath. A long border of white pinks filled the air with strong perfume. The sun had disappeared, and the bats were wheeling in the twilight.

"And you?" said Françoise, bending down over the pinks . . . "Do you miss her?"

"I don't know. . . . I feel I have lost something very beautiful and very precious. . . . The moment I am alone I conjure up her form. I tell myself: 'I shall never see it again,' and I can hardly believe it. . . . I need her, horribly. . . . And yet, at the same time, I have as it were a sensation of relief. . . . I am free. . . . In Paris, when it gets towards five o'clock, I shall now no longer say to myself: 'I shall be late, Simone will be cross.' . . . I can do my work quietly, with nothing lurking at the back of my mind. . . . If she agreed to start seeing me again, she wouldn't find me changed. . . . I should be just as unbearable. . . . I should be the same. . . ."

"But why, Bernard—since you *know* that it is absurd?"

"Simply because I cannot be otherwise, because a job must be properly done. . . . Do you remember that story of Kipling's, *The Man Who Would Be King?* You don't? But you must—the English adventurer, you know, who becomes king of a small Himalayan people and has their respect until such time as he wishes to take to himself a wife. . . . Then his subjects become aware that he is a man. . . . That's the story. . . . Yet a last circumstance: I dared perfectly well say to Simone: 'I shall not come up on Saturday, because my grandfather requires me at Pont-de-l'Eure.'

I should never have dared say to Monsieur Achille: 'I shall not be back on Monday, because my mistress requires me to lunch with her.' Do you grasp the subtle difference?"

He could hardly see her on the path, but often in passing a rather thicker gooseberry-bush he could not help brushing against her. She stumbled a little, caught herself by his arm and remained clinging to it.

"No," she said, "I do not understand. . . . You say that a job must be properly done. But why that at Pont-de-l'Eure especially? There's no reason. . . . Is it decreed that you are tied to Pont-de-l'Eure for all eternity? . . . You were born there, that is all. It is an accident. . . . If it wasn't you, it would be another. . . ."

"That's no argument," said Bernard.

The tour of the garden had brought them back to the narrow passage between the bushes, which, under the vault of the lime-trees, was like a black tunnel. They advanced into it. Bernard, having struck a branch with his forehead, put out his hand, encountered Françoise's body and suddenly felt a mad desire to press her to him. He felt a head fall on his shoulder. He put out his lips at haphazard and met the delicious, humid freshness of other lips. He straightway forgot the world.

"Hoo-oo!" cried a voice in the distance.

It was Antoine's familiar call to Françoise. She slowly disengaged herself and replied without any embarrassment, quite naturally: "Hoo-oo!"

Then she went on more quickly. In the distance they heard Antoine's footsteps on the gravel. He called out:

"Where are you?"

"Here we are," said Françoise. "Come across the lawn."

Bernard marched behind, furious with himself, and thought: 'What has come over us?' So as not to see Antoine again in the light, he said good-bye out in the dark and refused to go back again into the house.

CHAPTER TWENTY-NINE

AT QUESNAY and Lecourbe's the weavers were only working three days a week. As a good physician rejoices to hear
the heart beating, however feebly, Bernard, on his round
through the rooms, took delicious pleasure in listening to
the sound of the rare surviving looms. Too well aware of the
real strength of the mill in its extremity, he thought of the
exiguous quantities still to manufacture before the fatal
stoppage.

'Those looms will be able to weave gabardines for another fortnight. . . . I still have a hundred pieces of
Serbian uniforms over for these women. . . . After that,
nothing. . . . They have no conception by how slender a
thread all this hangs. What is to be done? Where is one
to go seeking?'

The hands watched him pass with a look of interrogation
and trustfulness, like civilians meeting an officer in a town
under bombardment. In peacetime they have often judged
him harshly; they have looked on his uniform with memories of strikes and barracks. Now, happy in seeing him,
they hope he will be able to defend them. This change of
attitude, so impressive and far-reaching, gave Bernard
great satisfaction.

All his strength was bent towards one little goal, which,
in days gone by, he would have considered paltry: to find
buyers, to go on working. In France—nothing doing. But
in America, in Eastern Europe, in the countries of the
"Northern exchanges" perhaps the situation was better.
He mentioned it to Monsieur Achille who gave him an
indignant stare.

"Natives? Never! Rather shut down!"

In vain did Bernard for several weeks attack his progenitor.

"No, no," he would reply, "we have never done it."

"But look here," Bernard said, "England, the United
States are not populated by savages or brigands. They do
business in milliards. What are you afraid of? That you

won't get your money? There are law courts over there just as here."

"People we don't know," growled Monsieur Achille.

Adventures frightened him more than death. At last his grandson found the serviceable weapon.

"Monsieur Pascal is working five days a week. He has got very big orders in Holland and Rumania."

"Pascal!" said the old man, pricking up his ears. "So he's working five days a week, is he? He's never said anything about it to me."

The next day, without Bernard having again broached the forbidden subject, the old man himself began timidly:

"After all, Holland is not so very far away. . . . You could always go over and have a look."

.   .   .   .

Before setting out Bernard had to go and say good-bye to Françoise. He had not seen her again since that kiss in the night. The fact was that he had fled. Twice he had refused to have dinner at her house; at the mill he had seen her from a distance, but, instead of going up to the crèche to meet her, as he always used to do, he had escaped to the burlers' room on the fourth floor and had not reappeared on dangerous ground until after a long tour of inspection. He did not know what to say to her. What was she thinking? Was she expecting that haphazard act to mark the beginning of a real love affair? Was she wishing for more evenings like that, for meetings of greater secrecy, or, on the contrary, had the event taken her, like him, by surprise? 'What has befallen us?' he said to himself over and over again. . . . 'Never has any act of mine had so little to do with me. . . . I am not even capable of remorse. . . . At no moment did I think: "Now I am going to kiss Françoise." All of a sudden I discovered that the kiss had taken place.'

And yet he had been a little guilty. During the whole evening he had wished for and sought those imperceptible, but delicious contacts. But was that a crime? Was that disloyal? Hardly. What would have been disloyal, would have

been consciously to carry on what had been begun without
either realizing it. The thing to do was completely to forget that moment. It had no connection with the rest of his
life; it could be taken out of it without destroying anything. Unhappily, he discovered so keen a pleasure in calling it into his imagination that he would often dream
about it in the midst of his work. All of a sudden, in the
middle of a row of looms, between the milling-machines.
from which yellowish water was running, he would feel the
humid freshness of those lips and that body folded in his
arms.

What surprised him also was his feeling himself no different in Antoine's presence. He had made no effort to be
natural. Antoine, his brother, and Françoise, his sister-in-
law, seemed to have no connection with the personages in
that duodecimo adventure. He continued to discuss with
Antoine supplies of coal to get in before the rise, the new
winter exhibit, cost-prices, with no uneasy conscience. And
that was the genuine article, the close-knit union of the
common task, of all that long fraternal existence, the alternating lamentations over the folly of Monsieur Lecourbe,
the worries of bad trade, the mill. The garden-path in the
dark, that amorous young woman—they were dreams whose
furtive image would sometimes rise again in the midst of
reality and which a smile dispelled.

He feared Françoise. His grandfather's obscure rancor
against the Pascal-Bouchet breed hovered, without his being
conscious of it, round the idea he had fashioned of her. A
foolish, frivolous, unreliable breed. Did she share the Quesnays' firm doctrine of loyalty? Perhaps she was saying to
herself: 'We love one another, what does the rest matter?
. . . Antoine? . . . I do not love him any more and, besides, Antoine need know nothing about it.' Love. . . .
Women were always using that word as if it explained
something. But what is love? There is desire, which is very
strong, but which one can master; then there is affection,
friendship, conjugal and brotherly faith. How is social existence possible, if you cannot trust your brother or his
wife? To be sure, every obligation encounters resistance
from the body; but what is a man incapable of entering

into obligations, and is there anyone more contemptible?

When he embarked on this current of ideas he detested Françoise.

On the day before his departure for Holland Antoine said to him:

"I suppose you'll come to say au revoir to Françoise? She wants to see you. Will you come to dine?"

"No, thank you very much; I want to pack this evening, but I'll try to look in at your place about five o'clock."

She received him with gentle sadness. While he was talking, awkwardly enough, about his journey, about Holland, about his hopes of bringing back work to do, she looked at him with a melancholy, questioning mien and made no response. At last she said to him:

"I had got a letter waiting for you, Bernard . . . to explain to you. . . . Then I tore it up—it's too difficult."

"You did rightly," said he.

Then he talked to her about her children, relentlessly. She seemed unhappy, but made no effort to return to the subject.

CHAPTER THIRTY

BERNARD departed for Holland.

Amsterdam: substantial gabled houses catch reflections of themselves in the smooth waters of the canals. On an immense barge a waterman transports one tiny chest of tea. Massive wooden doors, gleaming with long-continued rubbing, bar the way to age-old "counting-houses."

The Kalverstraat, an opulent hurly-burly, calls to mind oriental bazaars. The smell of spices in a dark shop, a mulatto type glimpsed at the corner of an alley, the photograph of an exotic branch-establishment in a shop window recall to mind that these burghers were the first to possess the empire of the Indies. The riches of Java have furnished those houses.

The Dutch representative makes excuses in advance for poor business:

"Lot of stock. The slump is scaring buyers. The Germans
are coming back into the market. This is the Nederlandsche
Maatschappij . . . a tremendous concern . . . lot of stock.
Their buyer, Monsieur Loewekamp, is a friend of mine: I
play billiards with him at the café every evening . . . good-
morning, Mijnheer Loewekamp . . . *De heer* Quesnay from
Pont-de-l'Eure . . ."

"*Wij koopen niet*," says Mijnheer Loewekamp, a stout
man with shaved head.

Then, in laborious French mingled with English, he makes
polite excuses:

"*Situation difficile . . . Plus tard* . . . Another time."

Bernard smiles amiably; the stout man smiles too. The
gleaming door opens again.

His parcel of samples under his arm, the young Frenchman resumes with buoyant steps his progress along the
gleaming canals. The Dutchman speaks:

"We love the French in this country. I know Paris myself: the Rue Blanche; do you know the Rue Blanche? . . .
On this house there is a tablet in honor of a Frenchman:
'Here lived René Descartes. . . .' Who is Descartes? Do
you know him? . . . Really! . . . And Monsieur Langlois,
the commission-agent in the Rue d'Hauteville, do you know
him too? We go in here. . . . Export-Maatschappij. . . .
Very big business . . . But heavy stocks . . . We'll just
say good-morning; their buyer, Monsieur Groninghem, is a
friend of mine: I play skittles with him. He has got a handsome wife."

"*Wij koopen niet*," says Mijnheer Groninghem, a decent,
kindly man with shaved head. . . . "Later. . . ."

Once more canals, stairs, substantial counting-houses;
tramcars boarded at full speed; charming courtyards;
Drapers' Syndics in the flesh, feeling with expert hands the
cloths woven by Norman women; merchants distrustful and
good-natured, disdaining indifferent wools.

"Quality in this country. . . Not price . . . And dark,
plain designs. . . . Here you have got to work for the fashion of the country. The skirts your Paris dealers send
us . . . ! Our women's hips split them. . . . Big women in
this country, very fond of sport. . . . Will you come and

have a curaçao, at Focking's? Everybody goes, bankers and cabmen. . . . Afterwards, we'll look up Sijthof. . . . Tremendous concern. . . ."

From that solid country Bernard carried away promises void of deceit, a little work for the immediate future. The girl Duval can rear her brats by weaving trousers for the gardeners of Haarlem; Daddy Leroy's successor can inspect the white flannels with which fair skaters of Amsterdam will envelop their brawny chests.

Distrustful and uneasy Monsieur Achille saw his cloth depart for so many unfamiliar addresses:

"Loewekamp? Groninghem? Sijthof? Are you sure they are old established houses?"

For the tenth time Bernard described those sturdy merchants, so like his grandfather. Besides, the checks came in almost at once. The names of the familiar banks tranquilized Monsieur Achille.

"May I go to England?"

"Good business!"

That was his way of wishing him God-speed.

. . . .

London. The red splashes of the motor-omnibuses, the bluey blacks of the policemen ('all that black cloth—where does it come from?' thinks Bernard) enliven the grey of the city. From the top of a bus he admires the old houses of the Strand. Trails of black and white smoke, transforming the narrow stone houses, turn the city of commerce into a city of dreams. At his side, his "agent," an ex-officer and a gentleman, catalogues, with some erudition, the ancient taverns, the famous signs.

No touching of one's hat when one goes into the shops, more crammed with wares than those of Paris. An old draper, with comic but charming dignity, bends his short side-whiskers and tortoise-shell eyeglasses over the French fabrics.

"Well, sir. . . . This will perhaps interest me, not for the home trade, but for Canada and Japan."

Fascinated by the fine wool—as others of his race love fine wood or fine leather—he fondly fingers a soft ratine.

"Very fine, indeed. . . . I'm sorry I can't buy now. Come and lunch at my club, Mister Quesnay."

Over a table of massive mahogany ("look at that table, Mister Quesnay, it is three hundred years old") he forces Bernard to drink several glasses of '56 port. ("Look at the portraits of our chairmen, Mister Quesnay. That one is by Reynolds; this by Sargent.") By these libations the old gentleman acquits himself, without the peril of buying, of what he thinks he owes to friendship with France.

After lunch, the "captain in the army" takes Bernard for a walk through the big shops, wonderful in their orderliness and profusion, Isles of the Blest. The saleswomen, as pretty as Gaiety Girls, smile at the French accent. The buyers are more encouraging.

"Serge? . . . Gabardine? . . . All right. I dare say we shall be able to buy."

From the deck of the boat taking him back to France, Bernard, rejoicing, sees Dieppe, the houses of Le Pollet, the towers of the Casino, the slender wires of the semaphore rise up out of the mist and focus themselves on the screen provided by the limpid sky. Invigorated by the keen, salt air, he imagines vividly his return to the mill.

'Three hundred pieces! . . . Not so bad for the time being. Monsieur Achille will condescend to give a grunt of satisfaction. Antoine will be delighted. . . . And Citizen Renaudin will say that we are doing our utmost to prolong short-time working! Human beings really are pretty comic. . . . Another quarter of an hour.'

Setting his cap firmly on his head, he pulled the waterproof rug about his knees and tried to go on with his book. It was *The Prince,* which, for some time past, had become a favorite with him.

"*Of Cruelty and Clemency, and whether it is better to be Loved or Feared.*—Passing to the other qualities above mentioned, I say that every Prince should desire to be accounted merciful and not cruel. Nevertheless, he should be careful not to abuse this quality of mercy. Cesare Borgia was reputed cruel, yet his cruelty . . ."

In spite of himself his thoughts returned to his three hundred pieces.

'Fifty at Selfridge's . . . a hundred at Scott's . . . a hundred at Debenham's . . . fifty at Robinson's. . . . That makes three hundred all right. I'll have the serges done in the women's weaving room and the blue moleskin on the waterside looms. . . . Monsieur Cantaert will be able . . .'

In vain did he try to come back to more general ideas.

'Simone. . . . The only beings who can really love are those who give all their lives to love. . . . But is that natural? . . . I don't think it is. . . . Fifty at Selfridge's . . . a hundred at Scott's. . . .'

The boat was gliding along the pier. The tarred timbers were thickly coated with green, smelly moss.

'Fifty at Selfridge's . . . a hundred at Scott's . . .'

Bernard was mumbling his breviary.

CHAPTER THIRTY-ONE

"MONSIEUR DESMARES, you can tell the foreman dyer that I am sick of it! . . . Here are ten pieces thrown upon our hands in the United States, because the color isn't fast. . . ."

"It isn't his fault, Monsieur Bernard. . . . The dyes nowadays are good for nothing. No one can turn out those pink greys and beiges."

"I don't care. I am not a dyer. All I can do is to pronounce on the results. Monsieur Leclerc, I have had a Rumanian customer complaining this morning of faults in the weaving of your gabardines. I have told you I won't have more than three faults per piece. If you have weavers who don't know their job, they can go and learn it elsewhere."

"I know the reason, Monsieur Bernard. . . . There's a length of bad yarn. . . ."

"I don't care; your business is to examine the yarn when it comes in. . . . What I need is good pieces. Besides, henceforward, I'll look for myself. The competition in all foreign markets is terrible. The English and the Germans are everywhere. There is only one highroad to success: that is to turn out good stuff. And then, I must have my pieces promptly. During a slump, customers ask for nothing better

than an excuse for canceling; orders must be delivered on
time."

"Have urgent jobs prompt, Monsieur Bernard? It's easy
enough to say, but you're not on the job. You stick up a
ticket with 'Urgent' on to the piece. In the scouring room
they are put into a machine four at a time, and your ticket
has to be taken off. . . ."

"It's very easy to stick it on again afterwards."

"It falls into the hands of a chap who doesn't give a damn
for it or who can't read. You'd have to be standing over
them all day. In the dye-house the chap from whom you
want a grey has his vats full of blue or green: do you think
he'll hold up everything for one urgent piece? Why, Monsieur Bernard, it would be wrong of him if he did! Oh no,
it is *not* easy."

He sighed, tired and nervous.

('At bottom,' thought Bernard, 'he's right.') But aloud
he said: "I don't care in the very least, Monsieur Leclerc. I
must have my pieces; the rest is your business."

.   .   .   .

"He's getting into his stride," said Monsieur Leclerc, as
he left the office.

"Yes," said Monsieur Desmares, "what's bred in the bone
comes out in the flesh."

They too, indulgent during the years of plenty, because
they met with the same treatment, were becoming strict
about the quality of the work and were amazed to find the
hands, who yesterday were still recalcitrant, amenable to
their demands.

"It's a queer thing," said Monsieur Desmares, "you can
ask things of them which, six months ago, would have
caused a revolution. . . . No one lifts a finger. . . . They
like it. . . . We think we control everything, but it's work
drives us."

.   .   .   .

Bernard saw, to his happiness, the cloud of hostility,
which, since his joining the firm, had enveloped his activities
and his intentions, disappear into a now almost invisible
past.

He experienced an absurd and intoxicating joy in feeling on his young shoulders the weight of this huge machine, by which so many men got their livelihood.

The downfall of Monsieur Vanekem, the fall in the price of wool, the panic on the Bourse had made an enormous breach in the Quesnays' fortunes. But the loss of an artificial wealth, drawing them closer to average humanity, restored to them the sweetness of common sorrows and misfortunes shared. The hands, suddenly deprived of part of their wages and the relative prosperity in which they had been living for some years past, found active consolation in their distress by imagining that of their masters.

"Aye," Huertematte would say to Bernard, "for them as has millions of money and thousands of tons it must mean summat, this bad time must."

"It's pretty hard," said the master proudly (like a wounded soldier showing his wound), "but it must be harder to bear for you. What are your weekly earnings now? Fifty or sixty francs in place of a hundred and thirty. That's a hole in the family budget!"

"Aye, that it is. . . . Them as has seen this coming an's laid something by, 'll manage, but the others . . . I've a sister-in-law, Monsieur Bernard, a widow, who's got to keep her bairns in bed all day, because she hasn't a shirt to cover them with. I help her as I can, but my missus is expecting her seventh. . . . Not the time, you'll maybe say. But you know how 'tis. . . . You think you're doing one thing and you are doing another. . . . Then, you know, with three days' pay, it don't go very far. . . . When all's said and done, the working man has had good times; he has had a taste of things he didn't use to. . . . It's always something good to remember. . . ."

Both of them, unconsciously relishing the delight of concord regained, forgot in perfect good faith that the next wave of prosperity would bring dissension with it and enjoyed the sweetness of spontaneously believing in the sentiments which the diminishing wealth of man engenders, in the same way as the ebbing tide liberates the smell of algae and seaweeds.

CHAPTER THIRTY-TWO

IN THE days of the Fools' Paradise, Monsieur Achille and Monsieur Pascal had ridiculed at length the senselessness of their former bitter competition. "France is a big country, there's room for everybody." Suddenly and with marvelous facility they had come to agree about all the points on which, for so many years past, they had been divided.

By common accord they had reduced discounts, disallowed credits, refused free samples. They had congratulated one another on the firmness with which in a few months they had managed to put an end to antiquated abuses.

Above all, they had agreed not to contend with one another for certain customers who, in the almost forgotten days before the war, had played off the one of them against the other.

"To what purpose?" said Monsieur Achille.

"*Quid prodest?*" said Monsieur Pascal.

A convention thus had been entered upon by the two old lords of wool, a convention by which the kingdom of cloth was, by them, divided into inviolable "spheres of influence." In particular, Monsieur Achille was to sell to Roch and Lozeron, while Monsieur Pascal kept Delandre's. They expected great benefits from this understanding.

However, Monsieur Roch, a suspicious and sagacious observer, had soon noticed that, with astonishing persistence, the Pascal-Bouchet prices remained a shade higher than those of Quesnay and Lecourbe. As long as he needed "those gentlemen," he took good care to hold his tongue and bided his time. When it came, that clever strategist repeated against the two allies Napoleon's favorite maneuver and separated them in order to overcome.

In the spring, the women, in accordance with their sex's custom, had adopted a uniform. It was a tailor-made of plain woven black and white, a material hard to manufacture, a triumph of Monsieur Achille's. Monsieur Roch, who wanted to order a hundred pieces of it, came to Pont-de-l'Eure and found the price too high.

"You know, Monsieur Achille, that I do not haggle with you, but pay good heed to what I say: I can get very fine plain woven at two francs under your price."

"Impossible—unless it be some shoddy without the finish of the Valley."

"I beg your pardon," said Monsieur Roch, with an air of mystery, "it's an article as like yours as two peas and made not so very far from here."

"Pascal-Bouchet?" asked Monsieur Achille, raising his eyebrows and stung by a sudden, frightful suspicion.

Monsieur Roch drew his hands apart and gave a discreet smile: it was an ingenious way he had of insinuating false-hood without lying. Monsieur Achille saw red.

"That man's incorrigible," he said bitterly. "His father was a rogue; his grandfather was a rogue. There's nothing to be done with him. . . . He's quoting you two francs less, is he? . . . Well, tell him from me that, whatever his figure may be, mine is ten centimes below it."

That very evening he wrote to Monsieur Perruel, his Paris representative, to go and show his catalogue of patterns to Delandre, Monsieur Pascal's private customer on Monsieur Pascal's private preserves.

It was the end of that long truce. As soon as Monsieur Pascal learned of what he could rightly consider as a piece of treachery—since he himself was innocent—he immediately saw that his pre-war grievances were not extinct beneath the ashes, but burning with a smoky flame. The sweets of hatred and the love of fighting exhilarated that old campaigner. An obscure story of coatings, a fearful drama of flannels rose up again in his dreams, woke him up in the middle of the night panting with fury and speaking his mind to a spectral Monsieur Achille, who vanished with the dawn. He took train for Paris, hastened to Roch and Lozeron's and offered them a thousand pieces at their own price, no matter what it might be.

Soon Françoise had to listen to the alternating plaints and abusive conversation of her father and Monsieur Achille. Each of the two old men arranged it so that he came to the house when he knew that the other would not be there. If chance brought them together, both beat a retreat.

Passing bravely from one camp to the other, she attempted to restore peace. In vain did she say to Monsieur Pascal:

"I assure you there is a misunderstanding. I have questioned Antoine and his grandfather; they have acted in perfect good faith and believe, indeed, that it is you who broke the undertaking. . . ."

"Arcades ambo," said Monsieur Bouchet. "I'll show 'em the stuff I'm made of."

In vain she besought Monsieur Achille:

"My father declares it to be your fault that the fight has broken out again. . . . He seems sincerely convinced that he is in the right. Cannot you come to an explanation with him? May I invite you both to dinner?"

"No, no," growled Monsieur Achille, "I don't need any of his explanations. I have known your father for forty years: that's enough for me."

After the progenitor's departure Françoise looked for long at her husband with that air of intense seriousness that always frightened Antoine.

"Why didn't you say something?" she asked at last.

"What do you expect me to say? You know grandpapa."

"Yes, but . . . After all, you know the Pasha too, you know perfectly well that he's the most honorable of men alive. He is incapable . . ."

"Of course he is. . . . The Pasha's A-1; I still care for him as much as ever. . . . Nothing is altered there."

"Why did you not say so?"

He got up, went down on his knees in front of the little low bookcase and set about arranging books.

"I can't," said he, with false airiness, "find that book of Siegfried's: *Le Tableau politique de la France de l'Ouest.* Have you . . . ?"

"Antoine," said Françoise passionately, "I can't bear you when you show lack of courage."

He turned round, still crouched on the floor.

"What's the matter, what's the matter?" he said. "You're awful. Why do you want to turn everything into a drama?

. . . In what way are these business affairs of any consequence to you? . . . Don't worry about them. . . . We shall see your father over at his place at Fleuré; it comes to the same thing . . whereas, on the other hand, it is very unpleasant for you to be present when he and grandpapa are quarreling. Much better keep them apart as far as possible. . . ."

"I won't have it," said Françoise. "It seems to me stupid and cowardly—" (she was standing up now, looking like an Amazon brandishing a small javelin and very beautiful: Antoine saw all that)—"yes, cowardly. . . . In this dispute some one must be in the wrong; I want to know who; I want the guilty party to make a polite apology, to have it politely accepted, and us to be able to live in peace, without your grandfather, and even Bernard, seeming to look at me as if I were the daughter of a monster."

Antoine sighed and said nothing; then, having found the book for which he was looking, he sat down in an armchair and tried to read. On these hard, rounded characters, on Bernard and Françoise, he felt he had no hold. . . . Strange, this theory of Siegfried's about the super-position of the political map upon the physical one, strange but sound. In this way, at Pont-de-l'Eure . . . He circumspectly lifted his pupils to see what Françoise was doing. He was thinking of the lighthouse of Le Harve, which he had seen appearing and disappearing that night at Deauville on the sands, under the stars. How sweet he had found that heroic self-abasement!

'She isn't really reading, she's too upset. . . . I must say something to her. . . . How shall I begin?'

He realized very well that the longer the silence was prolonged, the greater would be the importance which the quarrel assumed. But she did not raise her eyes; he found no "opening," and they went to bed without having discovered any way of exchanging a word, although both wished to do so. Next morning Françoise was agreeable, even cheerful, and made no allusion to the evening's discussion. But after Antoine had gone out, she telephoned to Bernard to come to lunch.

.   .   .   .

The wind was bowing the black skeletons of the rose-trees under the driving rain. Underfoot, the sycamore and lime-leaves, rotting already, formed as it were a carpet of gold felt. Pulling his waterproof cape about him and leaning forward to protect his streaming face, Bernard slowly threaded the long drive.

After lunch, his sister-in-law came and seated herself by his side on the sofa, while Antoine slowly lighted his pipe.

"There is a matter, Bernard, I wished to talk to you about. It is this stupid misunderstanding between my father and the lot of you. I do not know who is in the wrong and who in the right, but it seems to me all very childish. . . . And you can understand how awkward and even painful it is for me."

"Poor Françoise," said Bernard with a smile, "Trojan captive in the midst of Greeks! You are charming, daughter of Priam, but your father has provoked us. He'll have his work cut out for him. . . . No, seriously, Françoise, all this alters nothing in our affection for you, but business must be kept out of the sphere of the affections . . . in the interest of the affections themselves."

His tone strove to be that of agreeable banter, but she knew the spirit of the Quesnays sufficiently to understand that she was wasting her time.

Tired of the complaints of the hostile captains, she went and sat down at the piano. A fantastic, broken, melancholy air expressed her ironic sadness.

Stretched out in an armchair, Antoine was turning over the pages of a catalogue of machine-tools. Bernard, standing near the window, looked in a vague reverie at the meadows bordered with black apple-trees which gently sloped down towards Pont-de-l'Eure.

Suddenly, from the high top of the smokestack a thin jet of white steam rose towards the clouds; the drawn-out whistles of the mill drowned the music of the piano. Bernard stepped forward, tapped his brother on the shoulder and, without realizing what he was doing, with a swift turn of the wrist started up an invisible machine.

CHAPTER THIRTY-THREE

FRANÇOISE spoke no further about Monsieur Achille's inflexibility or Bernard's coldness; she preserved a polite and unvarying melancholy. But Antoine knew that behind that curtain of good manners hostile shapes were moving in silence. At Christmas he proposed that he should take her to Paris for a few days. She accepted joyfully.

"So your sister is coming to Paris?" said Jean Philippe Montel to Hélène de Thianges. . . . "If you do not invite me to dinner, I shall never speak to you again."

Hélène laughed and promised. . . . But to avoid a painful evening with Antoine Quesnay she took a box at the Opéra-Comique, where *Pelléas* was being done. They arrived late, all in a fairly bad temper. Françoise was vexed with Hélène for letting a tactless invitation revive her forgotten memory of a quarrel; Montel's presence gave her no pleasure. Antoine, believing the opposite, was wretched. Thianges did not like that kind of music. Hélène alone was placid and cheerful. She had no violent passions and looked on life as a show.

The whispering necessary for arranging the seats got on Antoine's nerves.

"Take the chair next to Françoise," murmured his sister-in-law, "I have seen this seventeen times."

"Oh no," said Antoine and Françoise together, each of them slightly vexed at the "Oh no" of the other. At last Antoine took the chair, because the audience in front was turning round angrily.

The music was a very sweet threnody, underlining the melancholy of the words. *"I am not happy here,"* sang Mélisande. In the half-light of the stage her profile, framed by her fine hair, strongly recalled Françoise. *"I had rather let you know today, lord, that I am not happy here."* Antoine had preserved the extreme naïveté of men who rarely go to the theater: he did not know the name of the actress, or even the subject of *Pelléas*. A fair-haired woman was singing, with a childlike, despairing unhappiness: *"I am not happy,"* and he reflected that he too was keeping prisoner in a hostile house a more beautiful and sadder Mélisande.

What ought he to do? What ought Golaud to have done? The music created a simple, clear world, in which the major virtues seemed easy. Above all, one must be pitiful and loving. *"Ah, come, be reasonable, Mélisande. Is it me you wish to leave?"* Antoine sighed. Françoise looked at him furtively. *"Oh, no, it is not that. I would like to go away with you. It is here I can no longer live."* Why had he not thought of that? To leave Pont-de-l'Eure. . . . Then perhaps he might find her again. But what a decision to take!

The curtain fell. The noise of the applause built up a hard, closed world again. Standing at the back of the box, Thianges was looking for familiar faces. "Look, Françoise —over there in the stage-box—Madame Debussy. . . . And there, that man standing up by the orchestra talking to Marthe de Fels, that's Léger, Briand's cabinet-secretary."

"It is curious," said Jean Philippe, "that in one way this dates very little, and, more particularly, that in spite of appearances it has inspired nothing. There have been no disciples."

"But how can you say such a thing?" said Françoise, who was bent on contradicting him. "All modern music derives from this. I was trying to play *Petrushka* on the piano yesterday; I kept finding harmonies all the time that are Debussy and nothing else."

"Certainly," said Montel, "but I do not believe in the least that a Russian had any need to borrow them from Debussy. The fact of the matter is that this music and Russian music have a common Oriental source."

An old gentleman came into the box and kissed Hélène's hand.

"Well," said he, "would you have believed that it would date like that? When I think that twenty years ago I would have done battle in defence of Debussy. . . ."

Antoine listened to them, bored. He himself still heard repeated the sad, slow phrase: *"I am not happy here."* . . . What ought he to do, to save Mélisande? Françoise's bare, polished shoulders gleamed softly; she was wearing a plain white frock, a young girl's frock without a color or a jewel.

She alone was capable of such wise audacities and of attracting glances by modest means. The lights were dimmed again. Antoine allowed himself to be carried away by the current of the music.

Françoise too was dreaming on her own account. The scene at the window made her think of Bernard. What a queer boy—perhaps he was right in shunning her. *"I love you, my dear, because enjoyment suits you."* What precisely had that woman meant by that? She could still feel Bernard's hands on her bosom. How wondrous that minute had been to her! All that evening she had felt such desire to be pressed between strong arms. Antoine was so weak; she was sorry for him; she would not have wished to hurt him; but she would have liked him different.

It was the scene between Golaud and the child. *"My uncle Pelléas. . . ."* *"Do they kiss sometimes?"* *"Do they kiss? No, father dear. . . . Oh, yes, yes, once. . . ."* Oh yes, yes once . . . And there would be no second time. She imagined Bernard alone with her in her room, closed her eyes and listened.

Mélisande is at the point of death. So frail in that great bed, so infantile. . . . How guilty Antoine feels! Since to this we all must come, why destroy those whom we love? What *is* important in life, if not to bring happiness into a pretty face? The smell of waves in the night. . . . The lighthouse revolving and its thin beam of light. . . . Self-abasement, sacrifice of egotism, sacrifice of everything to the joy of perfectly understanding one being. *"I have done you so much hurt, Mélisande, I cannot tell the hurt that I have done you."* I have done you so much hurt, Françoise. . . . An obscure hurt, difficult to define. . . . A hurt of omission, inflicted by neglect . . . but I have done you so much hurt. *"Do not stay here, Golaud; it must have silence now."* *"Ah come, man, come, 'tis terrible, but 'tis not your fault. She was a poor mysterious little being, like all of us."* Like all of us. . . . No necessity for trying to understand, no necessity for arguing. What for? In an argument Françoise was in the wrong, Monsieur Achille and Bernard in the right. No necessity, however, for arguing. The one thing needful was love. Looking at those closed eyes between their fair tresses in the great bed, Antoine swore to himself to take Françoise away from the tyranny of the mill. From the violins purled the sound of harps. Old Arkel lifted up the dead woman's child.

The lights, going up for the last time, revealed to Françoise Antoine's eyes glittering with tears, which he wiped away vigorously. She knew very well why he was crying.

"Now, that child," said Thianges, standing up. "Was it Golaud's or Pelléas'?"

"Are you staying in Paris for long?" said Montel to Françoise, as he helped her on with her cloak. "Shall we be seeing you again?"

"No," she said, curtly enough. "My husband is leaving tomorrow, and I do not want to let him go back home by himself."

The Thianges' gave Montel a lift in their car, as he lived in their neighborhood; the Antoines took a taxi. They were both very silent. In the dark Françoise gently passed her fingers over Antoine's eyes to see if he was still crying. She wiped away an invisible tear, then put her hand against her husband's lips.

"Poor Golaud!" said she, while Antoine eagerly kissed her hand.

CHAPTER THIRTY-FOUR

"They came, the brothers, and took two chairs
In their usual, quiet way;
And for a time we did not think
They had much to say."

THOMAS HARDY

WHEN they had finished with the letters, Antoine said to Bernard:

"I should like a word with you. Will you come to my office?"

A private conversation between the two brothers was so rare that, as he walked silently by his brother's side, Bernard thought: 'There's something amiss. . . . What can it be? . . . Antoine looks very tragic this morning; Françoise has been so queer this last fortnight. At bottom, Antoine has made a bad marriage. A great man of affairs ought perhaps not to be married at all. He would have to be jealous of himself. The greatest, all the same. . . . It all depends on the woman; she must be passive, or collaborate. Françoise is antagonistic.'

In Antoine's office there was a large photograph of his wife, and her influence was noticeable in countless details. Of all the Quesnay offices his was the only one to have a carpet; the furniture was antique, and the old engravings on the walls illustrated the processes of the woolen industry in the eighteenth century. In them you saw girls weaving in panniered gowns and delightful children in round vests working hand-presses.

Bernard took an armchair, played mechanically with a ruler and, as his brother would not begin, said in a somewhat gruff tone:

"Well?"

"Well," said Antoine, without looking at him, "I simply want to ask you one question: Would it vex you a great deal if I left the firm?"

"You?" said Bernard, with genuine stupefaction. "Why, what an idea! Are you cracked?"

"No; yesterday evening I had a talk with Françoise, which lasted the greater part of the night. . . . The poor girl is at the end of her tether. She has always found our mode of life very gloomy and grandpapa's tyranny very oppressive. She has borne it a long while and made effort after effort. And now, the row with her father puts her in an impossible position. . . . Don't shrug your shoulders, Bernard, I beg of you; we must have a little imagination. The great fault of us Quesnays is our incapacity to perceive what is real to other people. A woman has not, like you, constant activity to prevent her thinking about herself. Incidents which seem very minute to you assume enormous importance in her eyes. She is made wretched by innumerable little rubs which you would not even feel. You say: 'No.' But it is not a debating-point, it is a question of fact.

. . . In any case, as far as I am concerned, I do not want my wife to be unhappy. Neither do I want to put you in an awkward fix. I will stay on as long as necessary, but I want it to be understood as a general proposition that I leave the firm as soon as it can conveniently be done."

"This all seems to me highly exaggerated," said Bernard, twiddling the ruler he had in his hand. "You are taking a serious, final decision because of an accidental state of affairs. If it is our quarrel with her father which is worrying your wife so, I will gladly shake hands with Monsieur Pascal and wipe that whole business off the slate."

('The conversation must not be allowed to take that turn,' thought Antoine. 'Everything seems capable of arrangement by words, but far-reaching difficulties will crop up again at the first occasion. . . . My choice is made. . . . Françoise. . . .')

"No," he said aloud to his brother, "it is not only that; there is incompatibility of temper between Françoise and the house of Quesnay. There must be a divorce. You may also put upon the last pleadings that I, as I have become during the last six months, am no longer minded to be the sort of man required here. I do my work without any satisfaction to myself, and badly, I know; I have lost faith."

"Yes," said Bernard, "you certainly have greatly changed. All the same, you know the technical side of the manufacture through and through and were still being of great use. Who is to take your place?"

"You'll soon be having young Roger Lecourbe."

Bernard pulled a face.

"A first-class Honors man!"

"He will do better than I. Day by day, I give you my word, I feel myself less suited to this job. It doesn't interest me any more; I am sick of it; I can't do anything about it either."

"And what do you mean to do? You know that, away from the mill, you won't be well off. . . . With the fall in the franc, the funds you hold aren't worth very much, and, moreover. . . ."

"Oh, we've thought of all that; we've made our plans. We mean to buy a house in Provence and spend the greater part of the year there. . . . I personally like being warm and, as long as I have a car and a gun, I am happy. . . . Françoise will have the children, a garden, flowers; I'll keep a tiny *pied-à-terre* in Paris, so that Françoise can hear a little music in winter and see her friends. . . ."

"You'll be horribly bored."

"I do not think so. . . . It is you, Bernard, who are always bored. And it's that which makes you so active and successful. . . . But I, you know, am easy to amuse; perhaps I shall write a *Life of Tocqueville*. . . . And then, I tell you again, my wife is everything to me. . . . That, however, you will never be able to understand."

"Never!" said Bernard, almost ill-naturedly.

He went to the window and looked at the lorries in the long yard, the workmen laden with pieces, all the familiar and, for him, so intelligible activity of the mill. A mechanic in a blue jacket was carrying some castings, which Bernard knew were destined for a new hydraulic press. A fuller passed, carrying on his shoulder a nasturtium-colored remnant and a bright blue remnant, which made a bright contrast. Farther on, Monsieur Desmares and Monsieur Cantaert seemed engaged in a furious argument, and Bernard knew why. Over the orange roofs of the factory, on the hill, you could see Pont-de-l'Eure cemetery in the middle of the bare trees.

('How can Antoine be so blind as not to see that this activity is the life of a Quesnay? I cannot even conceive the possibility of myself turning my back on all that. There is nothing more beautiful, more obvious, more necessary in the world. Terrible, a man who is tied to the apron-strings! Antoine is done for.') "What shall I answer?" he said aloud. "I cannot keep you here against your will. I disapprove of your scheme, and not merely from the narrow point of view of the mill; no, I believe that what you are doing is a very serious thing: if the middle-class is bent on seeking enjoyment before all, it is lost as a class. Besides, I believe that you will regret it. Having said my say—do what you wish. I feel equal to steering the bark all by myself."

"That is all I wanted to know," said Antoine coldly. "It will be the very devil talking about it to grandpapa."

"I'll prepare him," said Bernard.

Then, dropping the ruler and suddenly more animated:

"Tell me, by the way: what have you done for the looms by the waterside? You were talking of having them driven by separate motors. Would it be a saving?"

Antoine mustered up a little zeal again to talk of gearing and transmissions. In front of him, Françoise's portrait, that charming, melancholy face, denied the seriousness of these problems.

'But what is serious?' he was thinking, as he estimated transmission losses.

CHAPTER THIRTY-FIVE

"Hamlet est un mauvais prince, parce qu'il médite sur un crâne."

ALAIN

"GOOD-EVENING," said Delamain. "Good-evening, O wise man, who knowest how to keep thyself rare and precious. Fools think it necessary to see one another once a week. But really one changes very little."

He drew Bernard towards the light and bestowed a long look upon him.

"You are altered, all the same. Turn round. How amusing! You are getting the 'captain of industry' look."

"By what can you tell that?"

"Ah, my dear Quesnay, one would need to be a Balzac. . . . Something precise and authoritative . . . the soft collar, the well-tailored coat, the strong boots. . . . And, above all, that sad, relentless, gentle expression of Vigny's soldiers. . . . What have you been doing with yourself? The last time I saw you here, you reported that you were overwhelmed by business."

"Yes," said Bernard joyously. "I was seeking. . . . I was seeking something intangible in a direction where there is nothing to be found. I wanted to be 'just.' That isn't possible. It doesn't even mean anything. You can be loyal to your calling, to your associates; you can keep your word, that is something good to begin with, but it's all. . . . I understand the game now, Delamain, and the professionals are kind enough to tell me that I am an honorable partner. . . . The strange thing is that that does not prevent my remaining, at bottom, the timid and undecided young man you used to know, a great reader and a great simpleton. . . . But—the moment it is a question of woolens, a Quesnay ancestor inside me takes command and knows what is to be done, without hesitation. . . . I am the pilot's son, I know the channels. . . ."

Delamain wagged his head.

"I recognized the existence of that Quesnay ancestor a long while ago," said he.

They smoked for a time in silence.

"One thing, however, you must understand," Delamain said at last, "namely, that your solution is valid only for yourself. You used to torment yourself with certain scruples —you have allayed them with certain sophistries. You have sacrificed part of your mind to the unity of your Ego. That is absolutely as it should be. It is certain that, in order to live, we each of us need to construct a system which allows for our existence. . . . That is absolutely as it should be, on condition that you do not forget that at the same time a Ramsay Macdonald, a Romain Rolland are, in their turn, constructing diametrically opposite systems, which to them seem every whit as stable, every whit as noble."

"As noble, maybe," said Bernard, "but not as stable."

"Oh yes, they are," said Delamain. "You have sketched out for yourself a certain ideal type of middle class, at once military and industrial, and you are trying to turn yourself into a living exemplification. You are justified. But someone else has sketched out for himself a type of ideal revolutionary, and he is justified, just as you are. . . . However, I am doing wrong in telling you this."

"Why?" said Bernard. (And at that moment the image of Simone passed through his mind: 'She too used to think that I lived for a system which is not necessarily true. But Delamain, like Simone, is fundamentally ignorant of real life; which admits of but one truth.') He continued: "How-

ever, the beauty does not lie in the doctrine; it lies in a
certain attitude. . . . Your beloved Stendhal clearly recognized that. . . . Look here: I must at some time have
spoken to you with horror of the cold greed of business
men. Well, my friend, man is a more complex animal than I
used to believe. . . . I have told you of the hoary vendetta
between the families of Quesnay and Pascal-Bouchet? . . .
Since the great crisis it has broken out with greater violence. . . . Monsieur Pascal declared the War of Velours
Cloth against us, a war, I assure you, that would deserve as
much renown as the Wars of the Roses or the Hundred
Years War. . . . Do you know what Velours Cloth is?"

"I think I do," said Delamain, ". . . it is a grey or drab
stuff that women make cloaks of. . . . Denise has one."

"The color is immaterial," said Bernard with the slight
irritation of the expert in the presence of a layman. "It
is a fabric whose face is combed into a nap which is then
sheared, and it's the great post-war success. The lower middle class has no money, the cost of living is high, the women
cover up the shabbiness of their dresses with these light
cloaks trimmed with artificial fur. The French textile industry is turning out nothing else, and the competition is
terrible; but for a long time we Quesnays shared with Monsieur Pascal-Bouchet a monopoly of the finest velours. The
finish of the Valley is celebrated: we were able to make a
living. . . . Only—it happened in consequence of family
quarrels, which had already resulted in my brother's leaving
the mill. . . ."

"Your brother Antoine?" said Delamain. "Has he left
you?"

"Yes, didn't you know? He has bought a house in the
South, where he has been living for some months now. Oh,
I can get on without him; he wasn't much use. . . . Well,
Monsieur Pascal, feeling himself free from all obligations
towards us after his son-in-law's departure, began hostilities by offering the Louvre a superb velours at a quite
ridiculous figure. 'Very well,' said my grandfather, 'if
Pascal wants to play that game, he will find me the
winner in the end. I've more staying-power than he.' So
we counter-attacked the next morning and won the battle

of the Galleries Lafayette in brilliant fashion. Then the campaign continued with varying fortunes, at the Printemps and the Samaritaine. The battle of the Bon Marché remained undecided, each side claiming the victory. At the beginning both sides would have liked to delimit the area of hostilities, but that is impossible. Prices quickly got about. A tariff was set up. We got to the pitch of selling everything under cost-price. When the December stocktaking came round, Monsieur Pascal-Bouchet had lost several millions. We, of course, had lost as much, but he was harder hit, as he had no reserves. Before the commencement of hostilities, he was badly weakened by the collapse of a Mr. Vanekem, by the break in the Rumanian exchange and by enormous expenses incurred in restoring his château at Fleuré, which belonged to Agnès Sorel. . . . You should have heard my grandfather's exposition of all this and talking of Agnès Sorel, with a perfectly inimitable movement of the shoulders! In spite of everything, Monsieur Pascal flourished and was confident of the future. A local bank was backing him; one good season could put him right again.

"Unhappily the banker himself had the most pressing need of money and was obliged to demand the immediate repayment of an advance. Monsieur Pascal asked for time; the other could grant none. . . . In the end, a few days ago, it looked as if the Pascal-Bouchet concern was doomed to suspend payment at the end of the month. A tragic enough conclusion, beneath its apparent commonplaces, when you consider that Monsieur Pascal is sixty-eight years old, that he has worked all his life, that he has rightly been looked upon as the most honorable of men, in short, that it was a sad and undeserved end for his career. For my grandfather, on the other hand, it was the fulfilment of all his prophecies, the downfall of the hereditary enemy, the grand victory.

"But in his extreme peril Monsieur Pascal did the last thing one would have foretold. He asked for a conference with my grandfather, to whom he had not spoken for many months, explained the situation to him and told him that he relied upon his support."

"Napoleon on board the *Bellerophon*," interrupted Delamain. " 'I come, like Themistocles, to seat myself at the hearth of the most powerful, the most steadfast and the most generous of my foes.' "

"Exactly. . . . But my grandfather behaved much better than the English. In the first place, he betrayed no exultation, he did not even say—what would have been legitimate—'I always predicted it!' He remained silent all the evening and even somewhat gloomy. The next morning he went over to Louviers and was closeted with Monsieur Pascal. When he returned, he said to us: 'I have seen the last balance-sheet. It is quite possible to save the business. They need four million; we can manage that.' And he has put on his legs again this competitor whose annihilation he has been prosecuting for forty years. . . . What do you think of that?"

Delamain looked at his friend with amused attention.

"I think," said he, "that you are thorough representatives of the military tradition. . . . People fight for four years, thirty years, a hundred years; then the whole world is ruined, and the victor lends the vanquished all he has. . . . At bottom, you know, the great mistake which the old economists from Ricardo and Bentham to Marx made was in believing that people go in for business in order to make money. The aim of people like your grandfather is not to become rich, but to become so while fighting a rival. If the rival disappears, the game is over. . . . As that Englishman . . . Russell, I think . . . says: 'If two football teams came to an understanding, they could score many more goals, only there would be no more football.' "

"You understand perfectly," said Bernard. "But it's a pretty melancholy game."

"All games are melancholy," said Delamain. "Really light-hearted people do not play games."

"Don't make paradoxes," said Bernard. "I have been working all day, I am tired."

He looked at his watch. He was dining with Liliane Fontaine. She had begged him to be punctual, as she made her first entry at nine o'clock.

Delamain's stairs were narrow and badly lit. . . . This

dinner? . . . She would talk about her career. . . . Yes, and it was undeniable too that she was becoming a celebrity. "In my generation," Liliane Fontaine would say, "there are only Falconetti, Gaby Morlay, Blanche Montel and myself. . . . There is room for everybody." She would say also: "It's a pity the Comédie Françoise pays so badly, because I should like to play *Phédre*. . . ." She did not really love Bernard. She thought only of her career. It was the same with him. She had a delicious body. That was absolutely as it should be.

CHAPTER THIRTY-SIX

DURING the four following years the management of the firm of Quesnay and Lecourbe was the scene of slow and far-reaching changes. Monsieur Achille was growing old; his memory was not so good as it used to be; every now and then a day would come on which his mouth was slightly twisted, and he then had difficulty in speaking. At the same time he was becoming irritable and used to criticize the decisions Bernard had made, without, however, being capable of suggesting others. People got into the way of hiding disagreeable events from him. Power was ebbing away from him. That distressed him. "Why do you shut up when I come into the room?" he would say.

Bernard seemed to live for nothing but the mill now, and did so with a sombre and taciturn ardor. Once a week he went to Paris to see his customers. Perhaps he devoted an evening to his pleasures. People said that he was thinking of marrying. Françoise, who returned every summer to spend some weeks at Fleuré with her children, held that her brother-in-law was gloomy and embittered, that he had sacrficed the only woman he would ever love and that he lamented the loss of her from the bottom of his heart. Antoine did not think so at all. "You don't know him," he used to say, "women play no part in his life."

At Pont-de-l'Eure Bernard was in his office every morning at eight o'clock; an hour's fencing in the evening was his sole recreation; he went to bed early. When he thought of himself, it was always as a young man, but at the same time others decided that he was aging and assuming a great air of authority. The clerks knew that Monsieur Bernard's orders alone were important. They had always considered Monsieur Lecourbe's as eloquent soliloquies. They recognized clearly that Monsieur Achille's were no longer, as aforetime, the last word.

A son of Monsieur Lecourbe's had "come into the business" in October, 1921. His cousin had at first judged him with unjust and summary severity. First, because he was a Lecourbe, then, because he had taken his degree (in moral sciences and law), and, chiefly, because on his first day he had criticized the methods of the firm and announced intentions of reforming them.

"You are making no profits at all," he had said, turning over the balance-sheets. "Your money would bring you in as much, if you simply had it 'carried forward' every six months. . . . And in gold francs (which is the only real way of accounting) you are getting poorer every year."

Bernard had begged him to put on a blue overall and had sent him to the wool-sorters. He spent several days among them, sitting on a high chair in front of a greasy tray piled with fleeces and facing a sly old sorter, whose diagnosis Monsieur Achille came from time to time to inquire.

"He does his best, Monsieur Achille," the old man would say, "he does his best, but he bain't very bright. This very morning he left notches in a first quality."

But Roger Lecourbe was a type of young man very different from those which Antoine and Bernard's generation had produced. He talked Political Economy, like his father, but was always well informed. He drove his Bugatti to admiration and did bends faultlessly at seventy-five miles an hour. He could do five foot six at the high jump, twenty foot nine at the long jump and the hundred yards in ten and two-fifths. He got it into his head to be champion wool-sorter and became it in a fortnight. Old Ursin, his preceptor, marveled: "He's better than me, M'sieur Bernard, 'tain't to be believed."

Then Bernard, who wanted nothing better than a disciple,

adopted his cousin and straightway entrusted him with little missions of an educative nature:

"Roger, these borders are twisted; have Monsieur Desmares on the carpet and tell him this must stop."

"I don't mind," young Lecourbe would say, "but I know what the upshot will be. He will take his magnifying glass in his right hand, raise his left to heaven and affirm that this cannot be due to the weaving. And, no doubt, he will be right."

"That, indeed, is likely. Then you will send for Monsieur Leclerc and tell him that it is the fault of the dressing."

"Another song-and-dance. He will retort: 'Monsieur Roger, if you can explain to me how the dressing can produce such a result, I shall be most interested to hear you. . . .' And I shall be most embarrassed."

Bernard laughed outright.

"Yes," said he, "the only thing is that when you have unjustly blamed the whole mill, twisted borders will disappear. You must make a fuss."

"You are terrible, Bernard," said Roger Lecourbe. "Monsieur Achille and you, at heart, are Spartiates: that is to say, first-class fighters and quite unbearable."

"Come, come," mumbled Bernard gruffly, but well enough pleased.

He got into the way of having this young man about him, faithfully following him on all his rounds. Sometimes he would ask himself: 'What does Roger make of me? Am I for him what my grandfather was for me, that is to say a useful, efficient creature, rather ridiculous, however, rather one-idea'd? Very likely. And yet it seems to me only yesterday that I came back from the war.'

When he saw himself in a mirror, he saw Bernard Quesnay the schoolboy and, later, the soldier, whom he had always known. What did the others see? A sad memory cut through him then like a sharp pain. "Do you love yourself?" That was what his dear Simone used to say when she caught him in front of a looking-glass. "Oh, not in the least," he used to answer, "but I am so surprised at myself."

That remained true.

CHAPTER THIRTY-SEVEN

A MAN-SERVANT came to the office to say that Monsieur Achille was ill and keeping to his room. At lunch-time Bernard went to get news. He met the doctor on the stairs.

"Anything serious?" he asked.

"Serious?" said Dr. Guérin. "It isn't very serious this time, but it is a serious warning. He mustn't do any more work."

Monsieur Achille had had a slight seizure. He was lying on a sofa, his face a trifle too red and wearing that air of gravity which the approach of death and the exertions of the struggle impart. He was breathing rapidly and raised restless, glassy eyes to intruders.

Bernard contemplated the bedroom, in which he had never been since his childhood. His grandmother's bed was still there. The furniture was covered with garnet-red plush. Large buttons punctuated the upholstery of the easy-chairs. There were daguerreotypes on the walls, on the chimney-piece a bronze presented by the hands to Monsieur Achille on his wedding day. This bronze represented a naked man driving a plough. There were also shells and painted pebbles, souvenirs of Dieppe and Etretat.

"Good-afternoon, grandpapa," said Bernard.

"Good-afternoon," said a curiously feeble voice. "Any news?"

"Nothing much. Everything is going all right. A nice order from Brazil has come in this morning."

"The pound?"

"Over one hundred francs."

"Wool?"

"Dear."

At that moment Monsieur Lecourbe and his son came in on tiptoe.

"Any news?" the old man asked wearily.

"Nothing," said Roger. "Prices go up and up. I was shown some two-seventy at eighty francs this morning. But I have got to have it all the same."

"For gabardines?" said Monsieur Achille.

And he almost smiled, happy at being able to remember.

Then all fell silent. Sitting round the head of the family, they sought in vain for a subject to take him out of his suffering. 'Morocco?' thought Bernard. 'No, it means nothing to him. . . . The miners' strike in England? No. . . . Now, what did I go and see in Paris yesterday? Shaw's *Saint Joan?* He'd respond finely to that! . . . Queer, perhaps he is dying, and yet it seems inconceivable to talk to him tenderly or even naturally. . . . I think he cared for me. Poor old chap! . . .'

A rapid review of ideas suddenly provided him with a subject of certain interest to the invalid.

"Monsieur Pascal's fuller has told one of our men that their new season's coatings are a failure."

"Ah ha!" said Monsieur Achille, with a feeble smile of his twisted mouth. "He never understood fulling, Pascal didn't, never!"

"The burlers are asking for a raise," said Monsieur Lecourbe.

"And they're in the right," murmured Roger Lecourbe.

Bernard gave him a look of displeasure.

"They're in the right!" said he. "That's easy enough to say."

At that instant, the sound of his own voice reminded him that his grandfather had answered him with the same phrase, the very same, six years ago, and he blushed. Monsieur Achille had shut his eyes. All went out on tiptoe.

CHAPTER THIRTY-EIGHT

MONSIEUR ACHILLE had his third seizure, of which he died, in December. Antoine and his wife came over from Saint Tropez for the funeral. They stayed at Fleuré, but came to lunch with Bernard, who found his brother altered. A 'Bonjour, Monsieur Courbet side,' thought Bernard. Françoise was pregnant and seemed happy, more placid than she used to be. Her face showed a tendency to fill out, but she was still very beautiful.

She felt herself a complete stranger in Pont-de-l'Eure,

and things assumed for her a novel character she had never discerned in them.

"Oh, how old Bernard has got!" she said under her breath to Antoine, while Bernard was at the telephone.

"He has just been through some very heavy days."

"Yes, but his hair is grey and he is wrinkled: two strongly marked lines between nose and mouth. You look much younger."

"I see what you are driving at," he said and smiled at her tenderly.

Bernard, standing receiver in hand, saw that smile from afar, and it annoyed him.

'That life in the south. . . .' he thought. 'Waking up, very late, under the mosquito-curtains. . . . The papers. . . . Breakfast in the sun on the balcony, Antoine in pajamas, Françoise in a kimono. . . . The children on the beach. . . . Siesta, with a novel. . . . Tea, English and Russian friends from Cannes . . . toast, a slice of cake. . . . Happiness to turn your stomach.'

When he joined them again, Antoine asked him for news of the mill.

"Are you busy? And wool? Dear, I suppose. All that must be very difficult."

"Wool?" said Bernard. "It rises and falls—we are beginning to get used to it; we have given up speculating; we buy from day to day; one day we make a mistake, another we do well; that's not of great importance. No, the serious factors are the exchange and, above all, taxation. . . . All that is so obscure and unsystematic. . . ."

"And the hands? No more strikes?"

"No; we have a system now of automatic increases in wages as the index-figure for the cost of living rises. It's all perfectly above-board. At bottom, the hands are decent folk. When you play the game with them, they appreciate it. That is all much simpler than we used to think. . . . My chief concern is our new undertakings."

"Yes, I know," said Antoine, "your wool business at Roubaix and your spinning-mill in the United States. . . . You must have an appalling lot to do."

"Oh no; Roger is a great help. . . . He has turned out

first-rate. . . . And then I like work. What are you to make of life, if you don't work? You think of yourself, indulge in self-analysis, are a torment to yourself. It is splendid to come home at night, dead-tired, go to bed at nine and sleep like a log."

Françoise, who was listening to this conversation, said with some asperity:

"But isn't that the philosophy of an unhappy man, Bernard?"

"Not at all," retorted Bernard defiantly.

The sight of her still gave him pleasure, but there was now, as it were, a latent hostility between them. She felt it, and when she found herself alone with him for a minute, she looked at him with much coquetry:

"It's funny, Bernard, to see you turned into a big man of business. Everybody says you are one."

"Don't you believe them. It's all a game."

She had the fugitive impression that he was lifting a mask and was about to show her a truer face; but at that moment Roger Lecourbe came in, escorting his sister.

The Lecourbes had summoned Yvonne from England for the funeral. Bernard had not seen her for a long time. At first sight, people found her massive, all the more so as she dressed with almost monkish inelegance. She had fine, rather short-sighted eyes and a pretty voice. She was serious and precise, but not at all pedantic. A trait of hers which greatly pleased Bernard was her never affecting grief that she did not feel. She obeyed all the proprieties, but stopped talking almost at once about the death of this old man, whom she had hardly known, in order to explain labor conditions in England to Bernard and her brother.

"I think," said Bernard, "that their great mistake has been their determination at all costs to maintain the gold value of the pound. As the result, their wages are almost twice as high as ours and they cannot export."

"That is perfectly correct," said Yvonne Lecourbe, "and the depression in their trade is due to that. They are very proud of their financial rehabilitation; in the last analysis, it is nothing more than a bonus granted to wealth already made."

"I don't agree with you," said Roger. "We must all come to the crisis of trade depression one day or another. . . . Look at Germany. . . . The English have got over their illness earlier; perhaps they were right; it's less danger-ous. . . . It's like measles—better to have had it. . . . Then, at the moment, we in this country are exporting right enough, but below world prices; and we are slowly devouring our substance."

"That is not altogether true," said his sister. "A price is made up of two elements: the raw material which, bought with gold, must be sold for gold; and then the labor. If, with his smaller wages, the French working man can live as well as the English working man, that does not impover-ish France, since our food is produced in the country."

"But it does," said her brother. "Look here, Yvonne, push the argument *ad absurdum*. The paper franc falls to nearly nill. . . . Good, the French peasant continues to feed the French weaver, who sells his labor for nothing to Eng-lish or American customers. . . . That amounts to saying that the French become a nation of slaves in the service of the pound and the dollar."

"The wise thing, obviously," said Yvonne, "would be to call a halt and stabilize the franc. . . . Shall we have the courage for it?"

She spoke with great animation, from time to time cross-ing her legs with a quick movement which exposed her grey woolen stockings as far as the knees.

The economic discussion continued for long on this note. When the young Lecourbes had gone, Bernard said en-thusiastically to Françoise:

"She is splendid, that Yvonne! She's like a good car; you can flog her, but she responds magnificently."

"What a queer way of dressing!" said Françoise.

And she sighed.

Then she spoke of her house:

"I have got fig-trees, Bernard, and orange-trees, roses between the olives and an Italian garden with great jars of brown earthenware. . . . You must come and look us up."

CHAPTER THIRTY-NINE

*"The terrible thing is that there
is nothing terrible."*
TURGENIEV

AN IMMENSE multitude followed the funeral procession.
At eleven o'clock, sirens and whistles had proclaimed the
closing of the works in the Valley. All the workmen had
come. On violet ribbons you could read: "The staff of the
spinning department in the manufactories of Messrs. Quesnay and Lecourbe," "The Staff of the Waterside Weaving
Department," "The Directors of the Louviers Carbonization
Works to their Chairman," "The Fire-Brigade to its Bene-
factor."

Pont-de-l'Eure cemetery lies on the hill overlooking the
town. On leaving the church, the long black cortège set out
on the steep road that leads past the Quesnay works. Bernard, who, up till then, had been walking with bowed head,
lifted up his eyes and contemplated the hearse covered with
flowers. Then, unconsciously, he occupied his mind with
identifying the buildings. Here and there an open door
afforded a glimpse of piled-up pieces, teasels, drums, yellowish runlets. 'The spinning room . . . the burling room
. . . the milling room . . . the scouring room! . . Why,
the dye-house is still steaming!' In front of him the coffin
glided slowly along, as if it were passing them in review,
those silent work rooms. Monsieur Achille was going his last
round.

Monsieur Pascal-Bouchet gently took Bernard's arm,
who looked at him. That fine pink face had aged, the white
beard was now planted amid deep, bluish ravines. He too
would soon be going the same road. With a sweep of the
arm he drew Bernard's attention back to the great factory
and said: *"Vanitas vanitatum et omnia vanitas,* my dear
Bernard." The cortège stopped abruptly: the master of the

ceremonies was changing the pallbearers: "His honor the Prefect of the Eure! . . . His worship the Major of Louviers! . . . The President of the Chamber of Commerce! . . ." Monsieur Pascal-Bouchet dropped Bernard's arm.

With a great effort of the horses, who slipped on the frozen surface of the road, the hearse got under way again. Those behind resumed their progress. Roger Lecourbe looked at Bernard, who was walking alone, slightly ahead. He debated internally whether his cousin was feeling any grief. 'I think,' he said to himself, 'he must rather be feeling that he has come into his heritage, that from now on he is the boss, and that it is a very heavy burden. . . . He hasn't said a word since morning, except to give instructions. . . . And yet one cannot say that Bernard is another Monsieur Achille. He is much more conscious of what he is at. That perhaps is a pretty fine thing in the men of today—this faculty for standing outside themselves, of resigning themselves to the ensuing friction. The marionettes have come to understand the play, and yet go on playing. What is that phrase of Barrès': "To savor even to madness the stinging joy of feeling yourself different from yourself. . . ." No, it is much better put: "*I* savor even to . . ." '

They were passing into the cemetery. The narrower roadway dislocated the procession. Behind Roger Lecourbe strangers were now walking. "No, no," an old gentleman was saying, "I can't live in that Einstein universe of yours. The notion that space is finite hurts me." "Keep calm, Edouard, keep calm," a voice replied, "you may have your infinite space." He also heard: "As long as you increase the speed of cars without at the same time improving the roads. . . ."

Then the movements of the multitude carried towards him a young man's voice: "She's a pretty little piece, but her legs are beastly." Roger thought of his lady—hers were divine. She was a cultured and complicated Swede whom he had known at the Ecole des Sciences Politiques. A sudden surge of desire swept over him. He closed his eyes for a second and then, opening them again, was surprised to see graves and thousands of black-gloved hands. He had lost ground and Bernard was now separated from him by a whole field of bare heads.

When he succeeded in coming up to his cousin, now standing motionless in front of a tomb inscribed "Quesnay Family Vault," the ceremony was almost over. Monsieur Cantaert was delivering an oration: "In the name of the staff of the firm of Quesnay and Lecourbe, it is my melancholy privilege to bid a last farewell. . . ." He was no doubt experiencing an involuntary consolation in the thought that, from his oaken box, the terrible old man could make no retort. Bernard turned round for a moment and gazed at the crowd around him, then at the high chimneys gently smoking. Lines and colors were clear. A trace of snow emphasized the black branches of the trees. The flat roofs of the Quesnay works, the cement tanks full of cold blue water, the long metal sheds in which the wool was stored formed as it were protecting barbarian citadel over the town.

Roger Lecourbe again watched Bernard, who was very pale, and thought: 'Some day, no doubt, I shall be in the front row here and some one will be saying: "Farewell, Monsieur Bernard, farewell. . . ." What sort of a life will he have had?'

For long the crowd filed past. Strong hands a thousand times crushed Bernard's, who bowed mechanically and said: "Thank you, Heurtematte. . . . Thank you, Quibel. . . . Thank you, Madame Quimouche. . . . Thank you, Ricard. . . . Thank you, Monsieur Leclerc. . . ." Customers had come. Monsieur Roch murmured: "Ah, my dear Bernard, your poor grandfather. . . . I shall always see him sitting in front of that table. . . ." Many of the old women from the mill were crying. For a long time Bernard hoped he would see Simone. There was no reason for her to be there, but every time that, turning his head to the left, he saw at a distance fair hair or a young woman, he said to himself: 'It's she. . . .' When he looked to the right he saw, a little farther on, the firm, serious profile of Yvonne Lecourbe, her short-sighted eyes protected by large tortoise-shell-rimmed spectacles. Françoise had stepped back a pace and was standing behind the family leaning upon her husband's shoulder. About one o'clock the end of that interminable frieze of heads and black neckties hove in sight. Monsieur Cantaert came up, hat in hand.

"Monsieur Bernard," he said in a low voice, "Monsieur Roch wishes to know whether you will be at the mill at two o'clock."

"Of course," said Bernard.

NOVELETTES AND
SHORT STORIES

HARPIES ON THE SHORE

FROM THERESE TO ANTOINE

Evreux. October 8, 1932

WELL, my dear, like the rest of the world I've been reading your book. Don't worry; I thought it very fine.

In your place I should now begin to wonder: "Does she think it is fair? Did it hurt her?" But of course these questions never even occur to you. You will be so sure not only of being just to me but of having tempered your justice with mercy. That paragraph about our marriage!

"So eager was I for the ideal woman, the helpmate and the mistress in one, perhaps I overlooked the real woman. I was sure that the first days of my life with Thérèse would unfold the vision I had expected, with a little of the unpredictable too. I was a plebeian and an artist; Thérèse was the great middle class with all its worthiness and all its weakness. She was faithful, forbearing—even brilliant, according to her lights. But alas, no one could have been less equipped for the lifelong struggle of a spiritual crusade."

Sure of that, Antoine? In spite of my parents, I gave in to your entreaties. We were married. Was that the start of your spiritual crusade? For me, certainly, it took a little courage. You were unknown then and your ideas of the world clashed with mine—frightened me even. I left a wealthy and united family to embark on the perilous journey of a lifetime. I didn't protest a year later when you told me you couldn't work in Paris and led me off to your own grim, empty corner of the country. That frightened little maid we had was the only creature lonelier than I was. I accepted it all. For quite a while I even pretended to be happy.

But what woman could really be happy with you? I laugh now — bitterly, to be sure — when the papers harp upon your "strength," your "moral courage." Strength! Antoine, I have never met a man weaker than you. Not one, ever. I am not speaking in hatred. The time for that is gone, and since we parted I have found peace. But this is something you ought to be told. Your never ending tension, your phobia of people, even as you hungered for their praise, your childish fear of illness and death — those are not strength, even though the novels which are their fruit may fool your worshipers.

Two or three times in your life, I admit, you have stood up for a principle. But only after you had cold-bloodedly calculated its final acceptance by the world. A long time ago, in one of your rare moments of candor you made an admission:—

"As a writer ages," you told me, "his opinions ought to grow more and more radical. It's the only way to keep a hold on the new generations."

Little did your young idolators, so naïvely and frenziedly drunk on your *Messages,* suspect the synthetic passion, the satanic care, with which you had composed them.

You are not strong, not even healthy. Sorry to be cruel, but that has to be said. You were never a lover, Antoine, my dear. After we were divorced, I found the peace, the fullness of physical love, in those beautiful long nights when a woman sleeps fulfilled between the arms of a virile man. As long as I lived with you I saw only sorry mockeries, a few pitiful parodies of such love. I was too young and ignorant to miss it. I believed you when you said that an artist should sublimate his passion. But I should have liked to sleep beside you if only to keep warm; if only to be granted a little tenderness, a little pity. But you slid from my arms, then my bed, then even my room, never guessing my despair.

You lived only for yourself and your reputation and that Byronic personality which so titillates your lady readers but which is not your own, *and you know it.* An adverse notice in the book reviews upset you more than the suffering of the woman who loved you. The only evenings you thought of me were when politicians or critics who mattered had promised to come for dinner. Then you wanted me to shine. A day ahead, you would forget your all-important work and

lecture me half the day: what I should (or should not) say;
which dish excited the palate of this senator, or which theory
the enthusiasm of that doddering but important critic. On
those evenings you wanted our household to seem Spartan,
from principle, but our board Lucullan; because, after all,
great men are only human.

Then Antoine, do you remember when you began to make
money? Real money? You liked that because in the bottom of
your heart you are a peasant, grasping for a square of earth;
but at the same time you were a little embarrassed, because money has no place in your philosophy. I had to smile
at those blindfolds which your greed bound over the eyes of
your conscience. "I shall give almost all of it to the Cause,"
you used to say. Well, I handled the accounts, so I knew what
you gave away and what you kept.

Sometimes, so ingenuously, I'd exclaim: "Why, Antoine,
you are really getting very rich!"

Then you would sigh: "I hate the whole system, but as
long as it exists, you have to adjust yourself to it."

As fighting the system was the fashion, the more you
fought it the richer you became. What a cruel fate, my poor
Antoine. Still, I must admit that where I was concerned you
were impeccably orthodox. When you became a millionaire
I did venture to hope, like all women deprived of love, for a
few luxuries, for furs and jewels. Then, I admit, you de-
nounced the Golden Calf with all your heart.

"A sable coat? Pearls?" you cried in horror. "Can't you
see what my enemies would say if my wife grew into one of
those bejeweled country-club wives whose caricatures have
made me famous!"

I did see. I understood that the wife of Antoine Vence
should be above suspicion. I acknowledged my indecency. To
be sure, you had real estate and securities for playthings.
But bank accounts are invisible, while diamonds sparkle in
the accusing sun. As usual, Antoine, you were right.

So I resigned myself again to that and everything else;
even this last book. All my friends praise the young, true,
unflinching courage of its theories; its kindliness (you are
one of the few really mean human beings I have ever
known); its generosity towards me. Either I don't answer

or I agree: "Yes, he has been very fair, and I have no reason to complain." But am I right to play up to you? Is it wise to nurse this glittering legend of which you are the hero? Should youth be allowed to follow a man who I know is not a man? I ask, but have no answer. I shan't even write the expected but useless apologia, for you have made me disgusted with words.

Good-bye, Antoine.

FROM ANTOINE TO THERESE

Paris. October 15, 1932

Just like old times, your efforts to hurt me. Cheer up, you have succeeded.

Thérèse, you don't understand yourself. You are so invariably the victim — it's almost masochism. It took even me a long time to understand you. At first I accepted your version of the crushed violet, but little by little your cruelty and your deceit entrapped me. Just because the beauty of your sister and the vulgarity of your parents humiliated you in youth, you dedicate the rest of your life to avenging yourself on those unlucky enough to love you. When I met you, I had confidence in myself. You determined to undermine it, and assaulted it in my beliefs, in my soul, and in my body. You made me ridiculous in my own eyes. Even now that I am rid of you, I am ashamed to remember the secret wounds which your "candor" inflicted.

Your cold and implacable eye! "You are a small man," you would say, "very small."

True enough, I was short and, like most men who work with head instead of hand, had a little more fat than muscle. Was that a crime? Or even a defect? You never let me forget that it was at least something to laugh at. Love abhors constraint and distrust. When a couple strip off their clothes, they strip their fears, their tension, and their shame. Stretched out beside me, you were not a wife but a hostile judge, master of your senses, eyeing me with your cold clarity. Perfect love casteth out fear. How could I be the perfect man when I met in you, my mate, only constraint

and prudery? You accuse me of avoiding your bed. Are you
sure you didn't drive me out?

"For me, certainly," you write, "it took a little courage
to marry you." But didn't you know at the beginning that
I should soon rise from obscurity? You had chosen me because you had found in me something real and alive, unknown in your own people. Perhaps a little because you felt
you could wound me, and to wound is your dearest, your
only delight. I can hardly remember what kind of man I
was when I met you; but I believe I was unusual enough to
have faith in my own ideas — no, I'm going to say "my
genius."

You did all you could to kill that man. You murdered my
happiness with pity. Strange thing! You had married me
for my strength, and it was that very strength which you
set yourself to destroy. But I must not look for logic or even
design in your actions. Like so many women, you are the
wretched slave of your nervous and sexual system; warped
by an adolescent dream, furious at its failure. As long as
you lived with your parents you poured out on them that
liquid venom which you harbor; when I became your husband, you spat it upon me.

"A brand-new platform," you are thinking, "knocked together especially to answer my letter."

And you will proudly pass my book around, open at the
passages you so carefully underlined. "My wife was faithful,
forbearing, brilliant."

Take a grain of salt with this overgenerous recommenda-
tion. Now that I must use any weapon, as my back is to the
wall, I confess that this sentence was a lie. I wanted the
book to be sportsmanlike, but I was wrong. The least hypocrisy spoils any work of art. Bitterly, relentlessly, I should
have exposed you as a monster, as the destroyer of my soul.

"Faithful?" Before we parted, I knew you were no longer
so. Yet why should I blazon it in a public page, and give you
at my expense the prestige of the adulteress? "Forbearing?" You have the devil's pride, and the passion to dominate and dazzle lies behind your every word and action.
"Brilliant?" Yes, even now many people think you brilliant;
in fact, you have become so. But do you know why? Be-

cause I formed you. Because for over twenty years you received from me everything you lacked: your thoughts, your knowledge, your very vocabulary. Today, after our long separation, you live by the breath I infused into you, and that letter by which you hoped to finish me off owes what vigor it has to me.

Am I vain? No, proud; though I need to repeat my self-belief, like a rosary, to break the spell of your evil. I shan't take up your letter point by point — it would play your game to torment myself in vain. But one more word. "I laugh now — bitterly, to be sure —" you write, "when the papers harp upon your strength. I have never met a man weaker than you."

Thérèse, you know quite well that you attack me there on two different scores which you pretend to confuse. That is not fair. What my character was in our own relations is between ourselves alone. I agree with you now that in that struggle I was too weak. Weak out of pity; and pity is not always untainted by cowardice. But you pretend not to know that a man can be weak in the affairs of the world and yet create power; that often, in fact, his work is vigorous because his life is weak. You may be sure, Thérèse, that what Youth sees in my work is really there.

And on second thought perhaps I ought humbly to thank you for the suffering you have caused. To your unwavering hatred I owe an enormous part of what I have accomplished.

Before everything you are a Destroyer. That is the form your rancor has taken. Because you are unhappy, you hate happiness. Because you are frigid, you scorn passion. Spite has made you a penetrating and mordant observer, like those X-rays which reveal in the steel the straw which threatens the beam's stability. You make unerringly for a man's vulnerable spot. You see straws in every triumph. A remarkable gift, Thérèse, but a curse. I own to those weaknesses which you so cruelly point out to me. You have seen clearly and well. But they are bound in a matrix so heavy, so tough, that no human strength can break it. You have shattered yourself against it, and my work and my soul have survived your sinister reign.

"But what woman," you write, "could really be happy

with you?" I want you to know that I too have discovered love since we were divorced. At last, with a simple good wife I have found peace. I can see you smiling, "Yes, but what about her?" If you could see Sabine for a moment, you would not doubt her happiness. Not all women need, like you, to kill in order to live.

Whom are you killing now?

FROM SABINE TO THERESE

Paris. February 2, 1937

MY DEAR MADAME BERGER:—

You must be surprised to receive a letter from me. We are supposed to be enemies. I do not know how you feel; but I, far from hating, have a sort of unwilling sympathy for you. Long ago, at the time of your divorce, you may have been the adversary whom I had to drive at any cost from the heart of the man I had chosen. But after our marriage you soon became an invisible friend. Doubtless Bluebeard's wives, half-dead, often meet in the memory of their common husband. In spite of himself, Antoine used to speak of you. I would try to picture you in company with that exacting and strange being, and often felt that your discipline had been a wiser prescription for him than my patience.

Since Antoine's death I have had to sort out his papers. I have found many of your letters among them. One in particular impressed me: the one you wrote him five years ago after the publication of his Diary, in which he mentioned you. I often told him that page would offend you and begged him to omit it. But that weakling was surprisingly obstinate — or bold, if you will — where his work was concerned. Your answer was cruel, but I must say I found it just. Are you surprised?

Please do not think I am betraying Antoine now that he is dead. I loved him; I am still loyal to him. But I know him and I cannot lie. As a writer he had the talent and the conscience of genius. But you were right about him as a man. Antoine was not a crusader; or at least, though he may have seemed so to his followers, he never fooled us who were his wives. He had always to surround his actions, his social theories, everything, with a halo of sanctity; but we know that the motives behind them may sometimes have been petty.

He made a virtue of his hatred for society, but we both know that the cause was his neurotic fear. Towards women he was a watchful and considerate comrade; but, as you wrote him, that was less real tenderness than weakness. He shunned acclaim, but because of pride and forethought rather than modesty. All in all, he never made a sacrifice without getting a reward, and we two were the victims of his affected crusades.

I truly believe, madame, that he never knew his real nature; and that Antoine, so penetrating and so severe in judging others, died in the belief that he was honest.

Was I happy with him? Yes, in spite of so much disillusion, because he was an enormously interesting human being, with something always new to watch. The very double life I have just described made him a walking riddle. I never wearied of listening, asking, and watching. His weakness was most touching of all. In his last years, I grew to feel more like an indulgent mother than a woman in love.

Ah, well, if one loves a man, what matter how? Whenever he left me I cursed him. The moment he returned, I was his slave again. At least, he never knew my anguish. What could have been the use? I concluded that he would have hated any woman who unmasked him and forced him to the mirror, and that even then he would not believe what he saw there. After all, you yourself didn't attempt this until after knowing you would never meet him again.

But what an impression you had left! After your divorce Antoine did nothing but rewrite the history of that separation with me at his elbow. You were his only heroine, the central figure of all his books. Again and again, under different names, I met in their pages your Florentine page haircut, your slow gestures, your aspiration, your aloof purity, and the hard brilliance of your eyes. He never portrayed my character or my person. He tried once or twice, to please me.

But, ah, if you knew what I endured each time to see the woman whom he modeled on me evolve in spite of her creator into a woman who was unmistakably yourself. One of his stories, "Sabine," he named for me, but who could help seeing that its remote and virginal heroine is you all over again? Many is the time I have cried as I copied out the chapters where you are first the mysterious Beloved, then the Wife, faithless but adored, then the Enemy, hateful and vile but still desired.

Yes, after you left him he lived on his memories, those evil memories you had left him. At first I tried to make him lead a calm and healthy life devoted wholly to his work. I wonder now if I was right. Perhaps a great artist ought to suffer. Perhaps monotony is worse for him than jealousy or hatred or suffering. I cannot deny that when Antoine and you were married he wrote the richest and most *human* of his books; that bereft of you he could do nothing but relive the last months of your marriage. Even the cruelty of your letter did not cure him of his passion. He spent his last years trying to answer it in his heart and in his books. His last book — unfinished; I have the manuscript here — is a sort of relentless confession in which he destroys himself in self-defense. Ah, madame, I covet the coldness which could so awake him!

Why am I writing you this? Because I have so long wanted to say it. Because you alone, I believe, can understand it. And because my honesty will, I hope, induce you to do me a favor. You know that since Antoine's death a lot has been written about him. What they have said about his work is neither very accurate nor very profound, but I shall not correct it. Critics have the right to make mistakes. Posterity is the final critic, and I believe that Antoine, as a writer, is among the immortals. But I cannot be so casual when his biographers distort his character and his life. Only you and I, madame, have really known their intimate details. After much hesitation I have decided that it is my duty to make our memories permanent.

So I am going to write a book on Antoine. I know I haven't the talent, but this is a case where fact is more important than form. And at least I shall have made a start; some day, perhaps, a great historian will use it in the ultimate biography. For some months I have been trying to assemble all the information I need. But I am short on one period; the time of your engagement and marriage. It may be unconventional, or overbold, but at least I think it straightforward and loyal to come directly to you for help. Probably I should not have ventured this unless I had that curious but heartfelt sympathy for you which I mentioned at first. Though we have never met, I feel I know you better than anyone else. So won't you write me where and when I can meet you to explain my scheme?

No doubt it would take you a little time to find and sort out the old letters — if indeed you still have them; but at any event I should love to have a talk with you as soon as convenient. I want to tell you how I plan the book; you will see that I shall not be hard on you, or even one-sided. On the contrary, I promise to use every device I can in your favor. I know, of course, that you have built a new life, and shall be very careful not to quote or relate anything that might be awkward. Let me thank you in advance for what I am sure you are willing to do to make my task easier.

                                        SABINE ANTOINE-VENCE

P.S. This summer I am going to Uriage, where Antoine met you, so that I can describe from real life the background of your encounter on the terrace of the Hotel Stendhal. Then I should like to visit your parents' estate and make the acquaintance of your beautiful sister.

P.P.S. I haven't much on the affair of Antoine with Madame de Vaulges. Do you know more than I? He always spoke of you, but never about that youthful adventure. Is it true that he met Madame de Vaulges at Modane in 1907 and made a trip through Italy with her? Was Antoine's father's mother named Hortense or Mélanie?

FROM THERESE TO SABINE

                                   Evreux. February 4, 1937

DEAR MADAME:—

To my great regret, I cannot be of the slightest help. In

fact, I have decided to publish a life of Antoine Vence myself. You are of course his widow, bearing his name, so that
a short volume of memories would be appropriate. But we
must be frank with each other, madame; so let us admit
that you hardly knew Antoine. You married him at a time
when he was already famous, when his public life over-
shadowed his private. On the other hand he was mine during his formative years as a writer, when the legend was
born; and you yourself were kind enough to admit that the
best of his work was composed either with or in memory
of me.

Besides which, no real life of Antoine could be written
without the documents which I have: two thousand of his
love (and hate) letters — not counting my answers, the
best examples of which I have kept. For twenty years I
cut out all clippings about him and his books, and classified
them whether by his friends or by unknown admirers. I
have all his speeches, his letters, his articles in the *Temps*.
The Director of the Bibliothèque Nationale, who has just
inventoried this treasure (for I plan to leave it to the
nation), tells me: "It is an incomparable collection."

For instance, you ask me the first name of his grandmother from Bordeaux. I have a whole folder on this Hor-
tense-Pauline-Mélanie Vence, as well as on all Antoine's
forebears.

He loved to call himself a man of the people. That is not
true. At the end of the eighteenth century the Vences owned
a vineyard at Graves, small but excellent; and Antoine's
maternal grandparents boasted a hundred hectares near
Mérignac. In the time of Louis-Philippe his grandfather
was mayor of his village. One of his great-uncles was a
Jesuit priest. The Vences, though sturdy vintners, were
bourgeois in a way, and I shall prove it. Not that I want to
emphasize the reverse snobbishness which was one of poor
Antoine's weaknesses. I shall be unbiased, even indulgent.
But still I must be accurate. There, madame, lay the most
venial fault of the great man whom we two loved and
judged.

Towards you I shall be no less kindly than you have
generously proposed to be towards me. Why should we not

be united? From letters which I have before me it is clear that you were Antoine's mistress before becoming his wife, but I shall not quote them. I abhor scandal for others as well as myself. Besides, however just my grievances against Antoine, I am still a faithful admirer of his genius and shall exalt it as best I can without thought of self. Possibly, since our two books will appear so closely together, it might be well if we exchanged our proofs, so as to avoid any contradictions for the critics to cavil at.

You know more than I about Antoine's last years, and his decline after his first stroke. That period of his life I leave to you. I shall end the book at the time we separated. Why bring up the quarrels which ensued? But in an epilogue I shall relate your marriage, then my own; and tell how I heard the news of Antoine's death when I happened to be in America with my second husband. In a newsreel one day I saw flashed across the screen his last portrait, his state funeral, and a picture of yourself, madame, coming down from a stand on the arm of the President of the Republic. It would be an apt end.

But I am sure your own little book will be delightful.

FROM SABINE TO THE PORTICO PUBLISHING COMPANY

Paris. February 7, 1937

I have just learned that Madame Thérèse Berger (who was, as you know, my husband's first wife) is getting out a book of memoirs. To get ahead of her, we must publish as soon as possible. You will receive my manuscript July 15. I am glad to hear that options have already been requested in Brazil and the United States.

FROM THERESE TO SABINE

Evreux. December 9, 1937

MADAME:—

On top of the American success of my book (it was chosen by the Book-of-the-Month Club) I have just received from Hollywood two long cables on which I ought to consult you. An agent for one of the big producers suggests filming a life of Antoine Vence. You are aware that Antoine is widely read in the United States among the liberal and intellectual sets and that his *Messages* have become classics.

This popularity, and the almost crusading quality which the person of our husband has taken on, make the producer eager to give the film a stirring and noble character. At first, some of his conditions startled me. But on second thought I believe that no sacrifice will be too great for us if we can assure to Antoine that consecration with the public which in these days the movies alone can give. We both knew him well enough to be sure this would have been his own answer; and surely historical accuracy was the least of his worries when publicity was at stake. Here are the three most ticklish points:—

1. Hollywood insists that Antoine must be a man of the people, desperately poor, and wants to picture his early struggles in a tragic light. This is false, we know; but it is the reading which pleased Antoine and we cannot be more exacting than the hero.

2. Hollywood wants Antoine to take violent sides in the Dreyfus case, and to have risked his whole career for the captain. Historically this is wrong and chronologically impossible; but it couldn't harm his memory. Quite the contrary, in fact.

3. Finally, and this is hardest of all, Hollywood thinks it awkward to have two women in Antoine's life. His first marriage having been for love (made specially romantic by my family's opposition), the strange creed of the cinema demands that it should be happy. Therefore the producer asks my permission to "fuse" the two into one. For the last of the film he would use the description in your book, but give me your personality at the time of Antoine's illness and death.

I can well picture your qualms, and in fact at first refused the last request. But the agent has cabled again with an unanswerable argument. The part of Madame Vence will, of course, be played by a star. Now no great luminary of the screen would agree to appear in a film if she had to disappear after the first reel. He gave me an instance: in *Mary Stuart*, to persuade a famous actor to take the part of Bothwell, they had to present him as the love of her youth. Idyllic but quite anachronistic. You must admit that if history can accommodate itself to the needs of the screen in such well-known events, it would ill become us to display a ridiculous pedantry in regard to our own humble lives.

I might add that (a) this composite wife would have neither your features nor mine, since the actress who would play us will be the one with whom the producer has a contract at this moment, and who resembles neither of us; and (b) the sum proposed is very high (sixty thousand dollars, or over a million francs at the present rate), and that, of course, if you accept the proposed versions, I should liberally reward the great help your book has given.

Please wire your answer, for I must cable Hollywood myself.

FROM SABINE TO THERESE

SUBJECT TOO IMPORTANT FOR CORRESPONDENCE. TAKING TRAIN PARIS 2.23. ARRIVE ÉVREUX ABOUT 6.00. BEST REGARDS.
SABINE ANTOINE-VENCE

FROM THERESE TO SABINE

Évreux. August 1, 1938

Here I am again in this small cottage which you know and are kind enough to like. I am by myself as my husband is away for three weeks. Why don't you come down and make me a visit, for as long as you can? I should love it. You can read, write, or work, for I am so busy with my new book that I shall have to leave you to your own devices. Take my car whenever you want to tour the countryside. But in the evening, we can talk over our memories—and our business.

With love and best wishes,
THÉRÈSE BERGER

AFTER TEN YEARS

(Translated by Eileen Lane Kinney)

To John Erskine

"BERTRAND, do you know who called me this morning?"

"How should I know?"

"Intuition. A woman whom you loved very much."

"Is there, besides yourself, another woman whom I've loved very much?"

"What ingratitude, Bertrand! And Beatrice?"

"Which Beatrice?"

"Which Beatrice? You *are* an actor! You don't remember Beatrice de Saulges?"

"Ah! Beatrice! I thought she was in China or Japan. . . . God knows where. . . . Isn't she making a world tour?"

"She did. But she arrived last night at Le Havre."

"And why the devil did she call you this morning?"

"Just to get in touch with us. It's only natural that she wants to see her friends after such a long time."

"I didn't know we were friends of hers."

"Bertrand! When I think that I almost left you because of that woman! Yes! I asked myself, 'If he no longer cares for me, if he wants someone else, why should I hang on to him?' We had no children. I thought it my duty to leave. I even went to my friend Lancret to ask how one could get a divorce without publicity or scandal. Lancret listened to my troubles and advised me to be patient. For a long time I thought it over. . . . I hesitated. . . . In the end the sacrifice seemed too great. . . . I stayed."

"Luckily!"

"Yes, luckily! But who could have foreseen, darling, that you would be cured so quickly? Have you forgotten that ten

313

years ago you could not be happy one hour away from Beatrice; how you waited every morning for her telephone call; how on one word from her you broke any engagement, no matter how important, forgot any promise? Oh! that ring every morning. . . . I can still hear it. . . . My heart beat faster each time. And Amelie, if you happened to be in my room, would announce with a clumsy and guilty air, 'Someone wants Monsieur.' You would look embarrassed, but naïvely proud. . . . It was dreadful."

"Ridiculous, I should say."

"No doubt. But I was too unhappy to see the comic side. Do you remember, Bertrand, you were no longer interested in anything but Beatrice? If her name was mentioned in conversation your face changed. It was touching but depressing to watch you. You liked people because they knew her; things because she liked them. You, the most reasonable and unsuperstitious of men, suddenly became interested in fakirs, fortunetellers and miracle-workers. . . . Together, you attended meetings of strange cults. . . . You had forbidden me to have animals in the house, but spent hours choosing a Persian cat because she had expressed a desire for one. You were completely under her spell. She ordered you about like a pet dog."

"You exaggerate."

"I do not. You changed your plans three times a day because she was capricious. Our vacations were canceled to suit her. One summer, knowing I detest cold more than anything, you dragged me to the North Cape because Beatrice had gone to Norway on the James' yacht, and you hoped to meet her by chance in some port. How I wept during that voyage. I was cold, ill and desperate. You didn't even notice it. What are you thinking about?"

"I'm trying to recall my feelings at the time. It's true I was mad about that woman. But why, really?"

"Don't be a cad, Bertrand. She was charming; she still is."

"Thousands of women in Paris are more beautiful."

"Perhaps. . . . But she had a serious charm, almost childlike — something individual. Besides, she was amusing."

"Do you think so?"

"It was you who told me so."

"But was I a judge? When I see her now I don't know what to say to her. It seems to me that she is made up of about ten clichés gotten from me and a few stories from Salviati. . . . She irritates me."

"Don't you remember, Bertrand, the day she was operated on by Gaulin? You were pale and miserable. . . . I felt sorry for you. . . . I tried that morning to rise above it all. I, myself, telephoned the hospital three times for news. The news was encouraging and I told you, I remember, 'Don't worry, darling, it is not very serious.' "

"I have forgotten."

"What a pity! The most noble action of my life, and not even remembered! Tell me, dear, have you also forgotten that when she ran away with Salviati you wanted to kill yourself?"

"I couldn't have wanted to very much, since I didn't do it."

"But you thought of it. You even started a letter explaining your decision. One day going through some papers you gave me. . . . Would you like to see it?"

"Certainly not."

"Yes, I insist — you must see it. Wait, here it is: *'My dear little one, I know that I am going to cause you great pain. I ask your pardon. I no longer have the courage to face life. But I want, before the final curtain, to explain certain things which you have not understood. It seems to me that I can lessen your sorrow by telling you that our marriage was never what you imagined it to be.'* "

"Isabelle, this is painful to me."

"Do you believe I found it agreeable? . . . *'The reason for my attitude, which often must have seemed strange to you, was that when I first met you I was already in love with Beatrice de Saulges. Why then did I seek you out, court you and marry you? Because Beatrice had married someone else; because I hoped to forget her; because I found in you an affection which Beatrice had never given me; also because man is not simple, and I sincerely believed. . . .'* "

"Enough, Isabelle. . . . Burn that letter!"

"I never burn anything. Besides it makes good reading — good for both of us. For your sake I shall skip two pages. But listen to this: '*Your great fault, Isabelle (because you also have been to blame in this affair), your worst error was that visit to Beatrice, asking her to discourage me and give you back your husband. That day, my poor Beatrice, you succeeded only too well. You inspired remorse in a woman who is fundamentally good. You took her from me — and you lost me. It was after that visit, of which I knew nothing for a long time (but which I sensed in a thousand ways), that I felt Beatrice drawing away from me toward Salviati. It is because of that visit that I am going to die.*' "

"How theatrical and disgusting!"

"Absurd, Bertrand. But I want you to hear the last paragraph: '*Don't regret anything. My life, from every standpoint, is over, and I never wished to live to a ripe old age. Look on this act of mine as I do, with severity. You will be loved, Isabelle; you deserve to be. Forgive me for not having known how to make you happy. I was never made for marriage, but I have had a very real affection for you. No doubt, if circumstances had permitted me to live, I should have grown closer and closer to you through the years. One thing more — When Beatrice returns, alone or with Salviati, be friendly toward her. And if . . .*' "

"Let me see that paper. . . . Did I really write such nonsense?"

"Of course, Bertrand. You can see for yourself."

"Strange. . . . I assure you I can't even remember the man who thought those things. 'Never wanted to live to a ripe old age,' and here I am on the verge of old age."

"Discontented with life?"

"No, happy to live — with you."

"Which proves, Bertrand, that one should not die for love, nor despair because of one conquest."

"Do you believe that in affairs of the heart examples are proofs, Isabelle? Anything is possible. Your visit to Beatrice succeeded. It could have gone awry; it could have caused my death."

"It's necessary to take risks, and you are very much

alive. But you haven't told me what to say to the lovely lady."

"What does she want?"

"To see us. . . . Dinner or luncheon with us. . . . Which do you prefer?"

"She will tell us about her tour. . . . Bali. . . . Angkor . . . . Honolulu. . . . What a deadly bore. Find some excuse."

"That is impossible, Bertrand. She would think me spiteful. Besides it will amuse me."

"What pleasure can you find in seeing a woman who, you say, caused you so much pain?"

"The same pleasure one finds when stepping on land after a dangerous voyage. Looking at Beatrice, I shall remember my unhappiness; that will make me more conscious of my present security and happiness. Also, I find your friend very charming."

"You hate her."

"I hated her when she chased after you; when she upset you; when she took my place. . . . Now, I find her a very attractive woman, and that you showed excellent taste. . . . that pleases me."

"You know, Isabelle, I'm very tired, and I detest this useless conversation. Don't bother me with it."

"I won't annoy you any more; only grant me this one thing. . . ."

"You don't mean to tell me, Isabelle, that it is for your sake I must see Madame de Saulges?"

"But, of course, darling."

THE GUARDIAN ANGEL

WHEN Jeanne Bertaut died at thirty we all thought Victor Bertaut's career had ended. A hard worker and one of the best orators of his generation, Victor seemed born to succeed in political life. Those of us, however, who had been his classmates knew his weaknesses too well to think that he had the makings of a statesman. His faults were as spectacular as his abilities. He was too fond of women and had a naive confidence of his powers of seduction. In a debate he was so sure he was right that he was incapable of weighing the arguments of his opponents. Also, he had fits of rage that often made enemies of the very men he needed.

For these reasons, in spite of his great intelligence, I thought he would go just so far—until the day when, to my great surprise, he married Jeanne. The surprising thing was that he appreciated her. She was as calm as he was violent, as moderate as he was fanatic, as kind as he was harsh, as reserved as he was garrulous. She had undeniable charm, blooming health, a frank glance and a gay smile.

From the moment that Jeanne married her great man, they were never separated. She worked with him, went to the Chamber daily, followed him to his constituency, and, tactfully, so he could not take offense, gave him advice.

As for Bertaut, powerful senior statesmen no longer said: "Bertaut? . . . Very intelligent and a good orator, but crackpot." Now they nodded approvingly: "Bertaut? . . . Yes. . . . A bit young but ripe to be an Under Secretary." Once in a while a fit of rage would bring a tirade, but Jeanne immediately intervened, and smoothed everything over. As for amorous escapades, he was in love with one woman only—his own.

All this was cut short by the death of Jeanne Bertaut. I remember coming back from the cemetery with Bertrand Schmitt, the novelist, who had been one of the couple's best friends, and his saying: "She made him over. . . . She protected him from himself. . . . Without her, he'll revert. We can only wait and see—whether or not he will return to his old ways—to dissipation."

.   .   .   .

In October, when the Chamber reconvened, Bertaut appeared at the Palais-Bourbon. He was greeted with sympathy, but his colleagues soon found him as difficult as before. More difficult, even, for now there was a new and icy bitterness mixed with his rages. I, however, had nothing to complain of. We dined together once or twice a month; he treated me with moody affection. He never spoke of his wife and assumed a cynicism that seemed to me a defense.

In December the Ministry resigned, and the newspapers announced that B——, entrusted with forming a new Cabinet, had offered the office of Postmaster General to Victor Bertaut, Deputy from Drôme. When the official list was issued, I went to congratulate Bertaut. I found him in one of his bad moods.

"Keep your congratulations," he said. "I have been to only two Council meetings and I shall probably resign. . . . I had violent arguments with both Finance and Public Works. . . . Besides, this Ministry is a mess. . . . Everyone gives orders there but me, the Minister."

For a few days I expected to hear of Bertaut's resignation. It did not take place. The following week, I met Bertrand Schmitt, and of course we spoke of our friend.

"Did you hear about his strange experience?" he asked—and continued:

"It's a beautiful subject for a novel. B—— is easy-going, but his patience has its limits. . . . When Bertaut insulted poor Chéron, the President was just about to ask for our friend's resignation. Then something dramatic happened! . . . . To the surprise of all his colleagues, our uncompromising Victor voluntarily apologized to Chéron and showed himself so repentant and so sincere that Chéron himself went to plead for him with B——. So everything has been fixed up."

"And how do you explain this sudden change?" I asked.

"Victor explained it himself," said Schmitt. "The day after the unpleasantness with Chéron, his secretary handed him a letter marked *Personal* which had just arrived. With surprise, emotion and even terror he thought he recognized Jeanne's handwriting. He tore open the envelope. The letter was indeed from his wife. Jeanne had written:

'*My dearest, you will at first be very upset at receiving a letter from me. Be reassured, this is not a letter from beyond the grave. Before going to the hospital, not knowing whether the operation would be successful, my only thought was for you. I tried to imagine what would become of you if I did not survive. I know you, darling, better than you know your own self and I am a little afraid for you—of your inner self . . . I am far from being your equal, dear, but I acted as your brake. A brake is very useful on a racing car. I said to myself, there is nothing to keep me from remaining with you in spirit, so I wrote this letter for you. I am going to entrust it to a discreet friend, asking him not to send it to you unless certain events actually take place as I foresee them. In that case, you will find things written here that I would have spoken if I still could. That this letter is in your hands is proof that my little prophecies were correct. So, stretch out beside me; take my hand, darling, put your head on my shoulder and listen, as you used to. . . .*' "

"Are you making this up, Bertrand, or are you quoting?"

"I'm doing my best to quote, but even if the words are not exactly Jeanne's, the thoughts are hers."

"Are you sure you aren't the discreet friend?"

"Don't say that, I beg of you," exclaimed Schmitt. "However, to come back to Jeanne, she had foreseen for her husband both honors and quarrels. She advised generosity, moderation and straightforwardness."

"That is why he went to Chéron?"

"That's why he apologized."

"What a beautiful story! I hope you'll write it, Bertrand."

"I may some day. Now I have no right to do so."

When I saw Bertaut the following week he confirmed what Schmitt had told me. His guardian angel, brushing him with her wing, had affected him deeply, and it seemed to me that the hard cynicism of the past year was falling away. His colleagues also commented on the beneficial effects of the message.

. . . .

For some months, everything went well. Bertaut restored order to the Department of Posts. All France praised him. Then the Cabinet fell and Bertaut went to Morocco for a holiday. There he became infatuated with that strange person, Dora Bergmann, explorer and poet. None of us had wanted our friend, still young, to remain forever true to a memory, but his choice disturbed us. Dora Bergmann was beautiful in her own peculiar way, but her reputation was doubtful. She had had a number of affairs, always with officers or high-ranking Colonial officials. Some thought her a foreign agent. That may not have been true; but in any case nothing was more likely to ruin the chances of a man in public life than an intimacy of this sort.

When Bertaut returned to Paris, bringing Dora Bergmann, some of us tried to talk to him. He was infuriated, and dropped us, one by one. His liaison began to be mentioned in parliamentary circles and it did him tremendous harm.

One evening, I said to Bertrand: "There's only one hope. . . . that Jeanne foresaw something of this sort as well, and that a warning written by her will reach Bertaut. . . . . I think she alone has enough influence over him to make him aware of his peril."

"I'm positive that such a warning will come," said Bertrand.

"Bertrand, you know something."

"I swear I don't. But she could have guessed that a woman of a certain undesirable type might get Victor in her clutches. So she well might have left a letter to be sent in just such a situation."

The facts soon proved the novelist correct. One morning we were glad to see Victor leave hurriedly for his district. He left no explanations. He buried himself in his small country house. Dora Bergmann pursued him; he refused to see her. She insisted, stormed, was unsuccessful and withdrew. Victor was saved. When he came back to Paris, he received me cordially.

It was then he told about the second letter from beyond the grave. He had found it in his mail one morning. Jeanne advised him to go away that very day, in case an imprudent amorous adventure was seriously endangering him. *"I know you, my darling,"* she wrote. *"If you stay, if you see this woman again, you will act from a sense of honor, from desire and pride. At a distance, your own intelligence will regain control. You will suddenly perceive what you missed seeing by being too close. So do not hesitate. Fold up this letter, put it in your pocket, pack your bag and leave for Drôme immediately."* He had obeyed her.

"I had such faith in my wife's wisdom," he said.

I thought: Will he be protected all his life by this dead woman?

Two years later, when he was hesitant about remarrying, Bertaut received a third letter that approved the idea and determined his decision. Did Jeanne leave any others? Or, in her strange prescience regarding her husband's life, did the first wife abdicate before the reign of her successor began? We shall never know.

Bertrand Schmitt says that once, later, when Bertaut, as Minister, had a delicate problem of conscience to decide, he found him in front of Jeanne's picture as if in prayer. He had hoped for guidance from his guardian angel, but this time no message came from beyond the grave. Bertaut made his decision alone and was wrong. That was the end of his political career.

However, he does not seem unhappy in his country retreat. He rules his small family domain, his second wife gives him a child each year, and perhaps that was the very sort of happiness that his departed advisor had desired for him.

B O N S O I R , C H E R I E

(Translated by Eileen Lane Kinney)

To François Mauriac

"WHERE are you going, Antoine?" Françoise Quesnay asked her husband.

"To the post office to mail this letter and walk Mowgli. . . . It has stopped raining; the sky over Menton has cleared; the storm is over."

"Don't be too long; I've invited Sabine Lambert-Leclerc and her husband for dinner. Yes, I read in *L'Eclaireur* that they are at Nice for a few days. I wrote a note to Sabine."

"Oh! Françoise. . . . Why? His political ideas are detestable, and as for her. . . ."

"Don't fume, Antoine. You can't tell me that Sabine displeases you. You were practically engaged to her when I first met you."

"Quite so. I don't believe she has ever forgiven me for not marrying her. And then, I haven't seen her for fifteen years. She must be a fading dowager by now. I can't think of anything more disagreeable than meeting a grandmother whom one has loved as a young girl."

"Sabine is no grandmother," answered Françoise. "She is exactly my age. Besides, it is too late to discuss it. Sabine and her husband will be here at eight o'clock."

"You should have asked my opinion," he grumbled.

"Have a nice walk," she said lightly, and quickly left the room.

Antoine felt frustrated. That was her usual method, to walk out on a discussion. Strolling along the path between the tall and angular pines, he ruminated.

'Françoise is becoming impossible. She knows very well I don't care to see those people. . . . She was very careful not to tell me of her plan. More and more she uses the

323

tactics of the *fait accompli*. And why does she invite Sabine
Lambert-Leclerc? Because with me and the children she is
bored. But who wanted to live in this place? Who forced me
to leave Pont-de-l'Eure, my business, my family and, while
still young, retire against my will?'

Once he started the review of his grievances it continued
for a long time. Antoine had loved his wife passionately, he
still loved her sensually and one might say aesthetically. At
forty she was still so beautiful! During the long evenings,
he never wearied of looking upon her face with its delicate
features, fine nose and clear but mocking eyes. But how irritating she was at times! Certain habits, which long ago he
found enchanting, now grated on him like false notes.
Françoise had perfect taste in the choice of clothes, furniture and flowers. But with people she lacked all tact. At
times he trembled when she hurt one of their friends. He
felt both responsible and helpless. For a long time he re-
monstrated with her, but she took it with ill humor and
paid not the slightest attention, sure that all would be forgotten in the evening when his desire for her returned. At
last, he came to accept her as she was. After twenty years
of marriage, he knew that she would never change.

"Here, Mowgli!"

He went into the post office. On the return walk his meditations on Françoise became more bitter. Was she even
faithful? He thought so, but certainly her flirtations often
had gone to the point of imprudence. Would he have been
happier with Sabine Lambert-Leclerc? He recalled the garden in Pont-de-l'Eure where the adolescent Sabine used to
meet him. The whole town spoke of them as engaged. They,
without ever speaking of it, were convinced that they would
marry.

'She had a warm temperament,' he thought, remembering
how she had clung to him when they danced together.

She was the first young girl with whom he had been bold,
no doubt because he sensed her unspoken consent. Then
Françoise appeared. Suddenly, all other young girls ceased
to exist for him. Now he was tied to Françoise. Twenty
years of life together. Three children. The race was run.

When he returned and found her in the salon, so fresh in a gown of gaily flowered mousseline, he forgot his rancor. Micheline, their daughter, who would soon be eighteen, was ravishing, but not more so than her mother. Except for the white streak in her hair which for some reason known only to herself Françoise refused to have tinted—it would be difficult to tell them apart. And yet, it was Françoise who had made this home, this garden envied by all visitors. . . . It was Françoise who had forced him to leave Pont-de-l'Eure and the factory a few years before the crisis of 1929. Weighing everything, she had really chosen fortunately.

"Are Micheline and Bacot having dinner at the table?" he asked.

He hoped so, preferring the conversation of his children to that of strangers.

"No," she said. "I thought it would be nicer—just the four of us. Straighten your tie, Antoine."

Nicer, a word he detested. 'No, it will not be *nicer*,' he said to himself, arranging his tie before the mirror. 'Sabine will be sarcastic; Françoise coquettish with Lambert-Leclerc; the minister dogmatic and authoritative; himself, Antoine, silent and heavy.'

"Nicer!"

They heard the car in the driveway; it skidded on the gravel to a sudden stop. The Quesnays assumed an air of negligent activity. A moment later a couple entered. Sabine's hair was black, slightly frizzy, her shoulders fat, but her eyes were beautiful. Lambert-Leclerc had become very bald; several hairs lay across his pate, like barriers across a course. He seemed in bad humor. No doubt, he had been forced into this dinner also.

"Good-evening, darling," said Françoise embracing Sabine. "Good-evening, Monsieur le Ministre. . . ."

"Ah! No, darling!" Sabine interrupted. "You are not going to 'Minister' my husband. You call me Sabine; call him Alfred. . . . Good-evening, Antoine!"

.   .   .   .

The evening was so warm and humid that Françoise had the coffee served on the terrace. Conversation during dinner had not been easy. The women were bored. Antoine, petulant and annoyed with himself, imprudently contradicted the minister, who made every point.

"You are an optimist because you are in power," said Antoine, "but the situation in France is alarming."

"No, my friend, not at all. . . . The question of finances is never alarming. The budget in France has shown a deficit during six centuries, and it is a good thing. True, it becomes necessary at times to wipe out investors. Without doing so, where would we be? Imagine the fortunes invested at interest since the time of Richelieu. . . ."

"The British budget is balanced," grumbled Antoine. "It even shows a surplus, and I know that the English are none the worse because of it."

"My friend, I have never understood the mania of the French for comparisons between two countries which have different histories, morals and requirements. If France wished a balanced budget we would give it to her tomorrow. She doesn't want it. Or, to put it another way, she does not want it enough to accept the methods. The preparation of a budget is not a question of finance, it is a political question. Tell me which majority you want in power and I shall tell you which budget you want. The services of the Minister of Finance are at your disposal, to give you a socialist budget, a radical budget or a reactionary budget. . . . It is only necessary to raise your voice. It is all so much simpler than the layman believes. . . ."

"Is it so simple? And do you dare say that to your constituents?" Antoine demanded brusquely.

Françoise recognized the imperceptible signs—a slight narrowing of the eyes—of her husband's mounting anger.

"Antoine, you should take Sabine down to the cloister to show her the view."

"Let's all go," said Antoine.

"No, no," Sabine interjected, "Françoise is right. It is better to separate the families. It's more amusing."

She arose. Antoine was forced to do the same, and follow her, but not without a furious glance toward Françoise, which she disregarded.

'Just what I feared,' he thought. 'Here I am alone with

this woman for a whole half-hour. Will she take advantage
of it by demanding an explanation for which she's been waiting these twenty years? That will be gay. As for Françoise,
does she want that sexagenarian to flirt with her?'

"What is that divine odor?" asked Sabine.

"Just the orange blossoms," answered Antoine. "The pergola where we were sitting is surrounded by orange- and
lemon-trees, Chinese Glycine and roses. But the roses are
growing wild. We shall have to regraft them."

"Aren't you, yourself, growing a little wild in this solitude, Antoine?"

"I was always somewhat of a savage. Can you see in this
darkness? On both sides of the pool there are masses of
cineraria. The garden is planned with an eye for contrast—
the somber blossoms, blues and purples, against the vivid
notes of yellow. At least, that was Françoise's idea. Here,
around the bridge, she wanted to create a sort of *maquis*:
Genista, mastic trees, cystisus, king's spears. . . ."

"I am so glad to see you alone, Antoine. I'm very fond of
your wife, but after all we were such close friends before
you knew her. Do you remember?"

Prudently, he slowed his pace so as not to walk too close
to her.

"Naturally, Sabine. . . . How could I forget? No, look
ahead! Cross the small bridge; here is the cloister. The
flowers between the flags? Only pansies. . . ."

"Do you remember the ball at the club—my first dance?
You took me home in your grandfather's carriage. My
parents were already in bed. We went into the small drawing room; without a word you took me in your arms and we
started dancing sedately."

"Didn't I kiss you a little that evening?"

"A little! We embraced one another for an hour. It was
thrilling. You were my hero then."

"How I must have disillusioned you!"

"On the contrary. At the beginning of the war you
dazzled me. . . . You were wonderful! I knew your cita-
tions by heart. I still remember them; can still repeat them.
Later, when you were wounded and became engaged to
Françoise Pascal-Bouchet during your convalescence, I

was disillusioned. What could you expect? I admired you so much. When you married that girl whom I knew well, who was my classmate at Saint-Jean, who was charming but rather stu . . . stupid (pardon me, Antoine), I was surprised and saddened. And not only I, but the whole town."

"But why? We came from the same circle, Françoise and I, and were perfectly congenial. Look, Sabine; that wall with the lights playing on it. It is the rock of Monaco. Don't lean over too far; this terrace is straight above the sea. Look out, Sabine!"

With an involuntary gesture he caught her by the waist, and with surprising quickness she turned and kissed him on the lips.

"*Tant pis*, Antoine! I wanted to so much. It's difficult to remain distant with someone with whom one has been familiar. Do you remember our kisses on the tennis court? Oh! I'm shocking you! You are still the same—very Quesnay. I'm sure you have been a very faithful husband."

"Absolutely faithful. . . . Immaculate."

"For twenty years? Poor Antoine. And have you been happy?"

"Very happy."

"Then everything has been for the best, my dear Antoine. But it is curious—you don't seem happy."

"Why do you say that?"

"I don't know. . . . Something impatient about you, irritable, discontented. You are, after all, a Quesnay of Pont-de-l'Eure. That is to say, a man of action, a leader. I know that you gave it up for your wife's tastes. But it is impossible that you have had no regrets."

"Perhaps in the beginning I was unhappy because of the change. . . . But I have found new occupations here. I always liked history. I work. I've even published a few books which have had a certain success."

"*Certain* success? But they were very successful, Antoine, and they are remarkable. Especially your *Louis XI*."

"Have you read them?"

"Have I read them? Ten times! First, because I also enjoy history; and then I looked for you in them. I have remained very curious about you, Antoine. I believe you are a good writer. No, I don't exaggerate. I must say I was surprised during dinner that Françoise did not refer to that part of your life. Several times my husband tried to bring up the subject of your books, but each time Françoise interrupted. It seems to me she should be proud."

"Oh! There is no reason to be proud. But it is true that Françoise is not interested in that sort of thing. She prefers novels. But she is an artist in her way. Her clothes, her garden. . . . Do you know it was she who planned this garden, down to the least clump of flowers? Since the depression struck Pont-de-l'Eure our income has been reduced. Françoise does all the work herself."

"Françoise has done it all. Françoise has perfect taste. That is amusing. You are too modest, Antoine. I knew Françoise as a young girl. She had less taste then than today, rather she had the cluttered taste of the Pascal-Bouchets—gimcracks and ornaments—rather affected. It is you who have formed her taste, taught her the beauty of simplicity and order. Also you have given her means to indulge those tastes. The dress she is wearing tonight, perfectly chosen, comes from Schiaparelli. That makes it hard to go wrong."

"Don't be fooled, Sabine. That is a dress which Françoise and the *femme de chambre* concocted at home."

"Ah! no. Don't repeat such nonsense to a woman. . . . There is line, the perfection of the cording. . . . And besides the print is exclusive with Schiaparelli. Those periwinkles and buttercups can't be had elsewhere. It makes no difference anyway."

"Unhappily, it makes more difference than you think. I have already mentioned that we have less money than before. Indeed, much less. Pont-de-l'Eure sends me nothing at present, and Bernard writes that it may continue this way for several years. . . . My books sell well enough. . . . I write a few articles. Just the same, poor Françoise is unable to buy from the great couturiers."

"Then, Antoine, it is extraordinary. Unbelievable, but extraordinary! I must take your word. Besides, I have always had a sort of weakness for Françoise. That is why I have never understood why people don't care for her."

"Don't people like her?"

"They detest her. You didn't know? I found it is the same at Nice as it was at Pont-de-l'Eure."

"What do they find wrong with her?"

"Oh! Always the same things: egotistic, flirtatious, catty with women, very deceitful. . . . And then her lack of tact. But I have always defended her. Even in the days when we were schoolmates at Saint-Jean, I always said: 'Françoise Pascal-Bouchet is much better than she seems. It is only her affected manner and disagreeable voice which make people dislike her.' "

"Do you find her voice disagreeable?"

"Antoine! True, after twenty years perhaps you don't hear it any more. . . . Besides it is not her fault. I don't hold it against her. What I can't forgive her is to have a husband like you and . . ."

"And what?"

"No. Nothing."

"You have no right, Sabine, to start to say something, which seems full of innuendo, without finishing it. Do your informers say that Françoise has had lovers?"

"Are you speaking seriously, Antoine?"

"With a terrible seriousness, I assure you."

"You know, my dear, that is said of every pretty woman. Who knows? It is possible to have smoke without fire. Françoise is indiscreet. That shocking voyage with Montel was, no doubt, perfectly innocent."

"What voyage?"

"Their trip to Seville last spring. You are not going to tell me, Antoine, that you didn't know of it?"

"I knew that Françoise was in Spain."

"People criticized her for taking her daughter along. I said, 'On the contrary, that proves her innocence.' But you know how women are. When I think that at Pont-de-l'Eure they went so far as to accuse her of being your brother's mistress."

"Bernard's?"

"Yes, Bernard's."

"Completely idiotic! Bernard is the soul of loyalty."

"That is what I have always said. Françoise will never

know what a staunch defender she has in me. What is that white cluster gleaming over there?"

"Bindweed."

"It is ravishing. Aren't they the biblical lilies of the field?"

"No, I don't believe so. Should we join the others?"

"You are in a hurry, Antoine. . . . I would gladly spend the whole night with you here in this garden."

"I am a little chilly."

"Give me your hand. You are right; it is frozen. Do you want half my cape? . . . Say that we should have lived like this, close to one another. . . . You have never regretted it, Antoine?"

"What would you have me say, Sabine? And you? Are you happy?"

"Very happy. . . . Just as you are, my poor darling— with a depth of despair. I follow the road before me. I can be frank with you. For a long time I wished to die. It is better now. I have become calmer, just as you have."

"What insight you have, Sabine. In twenty years you are the first woman who really understands me."

"Don't forget that I loved you once, Antoine. . . . That makes for understanding. Give me your arm, will you? This slope is steep. . . . Tell me, Antoine. when did you discover what Françoise really is: when did you see her as she is? When you married her you were mad about her."

"I'm afraid you have misunderstood me, Sabine. I want you to understand me. I still have, today, a great affection for Françoise. . . . Affection is a ridiculous and feeble word to express what I mean. I love Françoise. . . . But, as you have said, the first two years of my marriage were a period of absolute adoration, and of love which I had every reason to believe was mutual."

"Now?"

"Why, *now?* Ah! no, Sabine, you go too far. You can't rob me of my memories. Françoise gave me evidence of love that even a blind man could see. We lived for one another. We were only happy when alone together. You don't believe me? But after all I know of what I speak. I was there, Sabine; you were not."

"I was there before you, my friend. I've known your wife since childhood. I grew up with her and her sister Hélène. I can still see Françoise in the school yard at Saint-Jean, a racket in her hand, saying to Hélène and me, 'I must marry the eldest Quesnay, and I will marry him.' "

"That is impossible, Sabine. The Pascal-Bouchet family and mine were always on bad terms. Françoise did not know me. We met by chance in 1917, during my convalescent leave."

"By chance! That was what you were supposed to believe. But I can still hear Hélène recounting the affair. The truth is, when the war started, their father, Pascal-Bouchet, was ruined. He was a pleasure seeker and a collector: two expensive hobbies. His daughters always called him 'The Pasha,' and he deserved the name in more ways than one. The restoration of the Château de Fleuré was the final straw. 'My daughters,' he said to Hélène and Françoise, 'there are but two alliances in this region that can save us: the Thianges and the Quesnay.' The girls succeeded; both of them."

"Who told you all this?"

"I have already told you; the two sisters, themselves."

"And you didn't warn me?"

"I couldn't denounce a friend. And then I didn't want to ruin her only chance. There wasn't a person in Louviers nor in Pont-de-l'Eure, but a naïve Don Quixote like you, who would have married her. Normand families do not relish bankruptcy."

"But Monsieur Pascal-Bouchet was never a bankrupt."

"True, but why? During the war the government carried him along because of the influence of his other son-in-law, Maurice de Thianges, who was a deputy. After the war, you know better than anyone else, your grandfather came to his rescue. That was what he had counted upon. . . . Ah! Again, that divine odor. We must be near the pergola. Wait a minute, Antoine, I'm out of breath."

"Because you have talked while coming up the hill."

"Feel my heart, Antoine. . . . It is thumping. . . . Wait . . . wipe your lips on my handkerchief. Women are terrible; they immediately discover the least trace of lipstick.

No, not *your* handkerchief, foolish! That would be seen. If you were not such an exemplary husband you would have known these things long ago. And dust off your shoulder. I might have left a trace of powder. Good. . . . Now we are ready to appear in public. . . ."

A short time later the guests departed, and the two women bid one another an affectionate good-night.

THE UNEXPECTED ALWAYS HAPPENS

(Translated by Eileen Lane Kinney)

To Robert Poumier

"AT ELEVEN o'clock the Radical party held a meeting. They returned a unanimous vote of confidence for their president and instructed him to co-operate with the other major parties of the Republic to bring the Cabinet crisis to an end as soon as possible. At midday the Socialist party . . ."

Lucille sighed. How could she be interested in this Cabinet crisis? If she listened at all, it was simply to hear another human voice in her solitude. In that dilapidated château in Perigord where, for economy, her husband had installed her and the two children, she was languishing of boredom and loneliness. Yesterday, during a storm, a part of the roof fell in on the great stone staircase. Now the rain was pouring into the vestibule, and, with Gilbert away, she did not know what to do.

"At three o'clock," said the voice which became lost at times in the thunder of a distant storm, *"the President of the Republic called the President of the Chamber of Deputies and instructed him to form a cabinet. Monsieur Herriot asked permission to consult his colleagues. We will now give you the foreign news. . . ."*

Foreign! She suddenly thought of that trip to Spain she had taken with Gilbert. How happy they had been in Toledo—in that inn where they were served a delicious luncheon warmed by the sun under an arbor. And now Toledo was in ruins and their happiness . . . No, their happiness was still intact; only shaken by poverty, by Gilbert's long absences and by anxiety.

"PRAGUE.—*This morning near Nedzec in the Bohemian mountains a French plane crashed and the two passengers, a man and a woman, were killed. A secretary of the French Legation is on his way to the scene of the accident to identify the bodies. . . ."*

The static became unbearable. She turned off the radio abruptly, and the silence invaded the *salle de garde* with its whitewashed walls hung with tattered tapestries, where Lucille sat because it was the only habitable room besides the bedrooms. The plane accident gave her a sudden start of pain, even though Prague was well off Gilbert's route. He was a pilot for the line between London and Paris. But did one ever know where Gilbert was, what he was doing, what he was thinking?

How different he seemed, after four years of marriage, from the young man she had loved so much. When she had known him first, an army aviator stationed near Strasbourg where she lived with her parents, she had been fascinated by his courage and his eloquence. Handsome? Was Gilbert handsome? Of no importance; he was brilliant, virile; he was attractive. In those days she could listen by the hour when he talked of what should be done to cure the world's ills. He formed military, economic and social plans. At times his violent and radical views shocked her parents—both from old families of functionaries—but she was inspired with hope and confidence. Gilbert believed himself destined to govern France one day. And who could be more worthy?

Old Leymarie with trembling hands (he had already suffered four attacks and it was folly to keep him, the only man in that enormous château), came to announce dinner.

"You may serve me here," said Lucille, "and put another log on the fire."

While eating the boiled chestnuts she continued her meditations. Gilbert's courage. It was the one trait in which she had not been deceived. Gilbert's courage sometimes bordered on foolhardiness, which seemed to stem from disgust with life and from despair. But his physical courage was not accompanied by any moral courage. Gilbert was disorganized. He was unable to plan his life beyond the most immediate and simple actions. His weakness in the face of temptation. . . . The radio, for example—three thousand francs to be paid in monthly installments, at a time when Lucile did not have money to furnish the children's room! He proudly brought it home one night from Paris, and during his leave danced with her to jazz from London and gypsy music from Budapest. It was charming and gay. Then Gilbert departed; it was up to Lucile to manage the payments. Often she went without a fire to economize, small as it was, while Gilbert lived in comfort in Paris and London.

All during the night the wind whistled in the chimneys. She did not sleep well, and early in the morning turned on the news. The ministerial crisis was not settled. Monsieur Herriot had refused the charge of naming a Cabinet. If Gilbert were there this news might have held her attention because he showed such interest in politics. Descended from a long line of Perigordian gentlemen, he often spoke of "going over to the people," to stand for election on the Socialist ticket.

"Ah! Lucille!" he would say, "You will see. . . .We'll do great things."

She no longer believed, besides she did not wish him to do great things. She would have preferred a little security, a little comfort, some advantages for the children, and that she could more often be with the man she loved. With Gilbert away, of what interest was the news from Paris? She knew that sooner or later a Cabinet would be formed, and her life would go on as before.

"PRAGUE.—*The bodies of the two passengers in the plane which crashed yesterday in the Bohemian mountains have been identified. They were the aviator, Gilbert de Peyrignac and Madame Moreau-Verneuil, born Vera Bezoukov. . . . LONDON.—The troubles in Palestine had repercussions in the House of Commons yesterday. . . .*"

It seemed to her that some invincible force gripped her heart in an attempt to stop its beating. *"The aviator, Gilbert de Peyrignac . . ."* There could be but one—her husband. But how could Gilbert have crashed in the Bohemian mountains? It was impossible. Of course it was an error, some mix-up in papers. Madame Moreau-Verneuil? . . . She had never heard the name. But Gilbert. . . . She must know. The only way was to telephone. She must go to the post office (there was no telephone in the château) and call the Paris office of Air-France.

She rang. After an interminable wait the old man with the trembling hands appeared.

"Leymarie," her calm astonished her, "bring me my raincoat. . . . I'm going out."

Outside the rain came down in swirls. The wind beat against the gate and swept the courtyard. The wet clay in the path was slippery but Lucille ran unheedingly. When she entered the post office, water streaming down her face, the postmaster let out a cry:

"Ah! Madame la Comtesse, you already know. . . . I was just about to send the boy to the mayor with the official telegram. The poor comte! I always warned him that those airplanes were dangerous. He laughed. . . . And now!"

Lucille fell to the floor.

. . . .

When she revived, old Leymarie, the postmaster and Doctor Leclerc, Mayor of Perigord, were bending over her. Her bruised body ached and blood was streaming from her head. But with the return of consciousness, her courage and resignation commanded the doctor's respect. He had received a telegram from the Minister of Foreign Affairs announcing the death, under rather mysterious circumstances, of the Comte de Peyrignac, and requesting that Madame de Peyrignac, if able to travel, come to Paris as soon as possible.

"But naturally," said Doctor Leclerc, "because of your fall and this concussion, you cannot travel today."

"Why?" she asked. "I want to know. I must understand. . . . And there might be an error. . . . In papers. . . . In name."

"Alas, madame," said the doctor, "there is little chance of that. The minister would not have notified us before checking the information."

"The minister can be mistaken. . . . My husband. . . . No one knew my husband. . . . No! I shall leave by the eleven o'clock train."

The necessity for action, the valise to pack, instructions to the children's nurse, the trip to the station kept her going. But alone in her compartment, she fell into a terrible revery. . . . Gilbert dead. . . . Looking out on the hills of the Limousin, the wet meadows and the slow-moving peasants in the fields, she could not believe that this familiar world could be the same with Gilbert dead. . . . She could hear his voice: "Ah! My little Lucille! This country. . . . How beautiful. . . . beautiful. . . . If I were Minister of Public Works . . ."

A young officer got on the train at Châteauroux; an aviator. . . . Gilbert dead. . . . And under what incomprehensible circumstances. . . . Incomprehensible, but not unbelievable . . . Very soon, she had discovered that being married to Gilbert meant taking risks. Strange boy—yet so attractive. How he had awed her, a young Alsatian, tranquil and sentimental. Gilbert had loved adventure, taking chances; she liked the stability of her parents' way of life. Gilbert craved violence and passion; she had sought in love, confidence and repose. She had entered upon matrimony with a small fortune and simple tastes; Gilbert was both extravagant and parsimonious. For three years, without admitting it, she had been living in fear of some such awakening as this.

At Aubrais she bought the evening papers. There were a few lines about the catastrophe:

"Gilbert de Peyrignac, twenty-nine, excellent pilot, last week requested and was granted leave of absence for eight days from Air-France. His leave would have expired tomorrow. Madame Jacques Moreau-Verneuil, his passenger, was the wife of a Parisian professor. She was born in Russia, the daughter of Colonel Bezoukov. The modern long-range plane had been purchased by her a few days ago. The reason for the voyage is not clear."

So Gilbert had requested leave without telling his wife. During eight days, while she believed his absence due to his duties, he had been living in Paris and having his comrades post his letters from London. Then he departed, piloting this strange woman to Central Europe. What could be the secret of this mysterious adventure? Perhaps the stranger had offered him a large sum to pilot her to Prague. Gilbert, always short of funds, was perhaps tempted. . . . But why so secretive with his wife? . . . Was the woman his mistress? In that case, why the absurd flight?

Two men met her at the station, one her husband's superior in Air-France, the other an official from the Quai d'Orsay. They were deferential and helpful. She asked the questions which obsessed her. Had Gilbert informed the company of his plans? No, the company had given him leave and believed him to be at home in Perigord. Who was the strange passenger, and was it known why she was making the trip? She was the wife of Moreau-Verneuil, a professor at the Lycée Fontanes, a man of promising future and very highly regarded by the University. The minister had informed the husband, who had been as surprised as Madame de Peyrignac and who knew nothing of his wife's plans. She had left home two days ago, saying she was going to visit friends in the country. She had not told Moreau-Verneuil of the purchase of the plane, nor of her departure for Czechoslovakia.

"But what was her relationship to my husband? A passenger—a friend?"

"We are sorry, madame, but we know no more than you. The inquest will, no doubt, clarify all that. Right now, it is for you to decide whether you wish to go to Prague to identify the body of Monsieur de Peyrignac and bring it home. In that case, the company will defray all expenses. Or would you rather have the Legation take care of these sad details? Monsieur Moreau-Verneuil has decided to go to Prague. He leaves this evening at ten o'clock from the Gare de l'Est."

"If it is possible, I shall do the same."

"It will be better that way; your presence may perhaps

be useful at the inquest. We shall make a reservation for you. . . . You will have several hours in Paris. . . . Where do you wish to go?"

"I want to see no one. . . . I must buy some black clothes."

At ten o'clock on the platform at the Gare de l'Est she found the engineer from Air-France who conducted her to her compartment and spoke with sympathy of her husband.

"Peyrignac was an excellent pilot, very popular with his comrades—generous and original."

As he was speaking, she saw the official from the Quai d'Orsay accompanied by a man dressed in black, evidently Monsieur Moreau-Verneuil, who raised his hat in passing. His hair was snow-white, but his face was very youthful. She thought he had an air of distinction and generosity. Seeing him bowed by sorrow, Lucille's heart went out to him.

.   .   .   .

After a restless night she fell asleep at dawn. Waking up, she had trouble realizing where she was. She called, "Gilbert," then remembered. Was it a nightmare? Raising the heavy leather curtain she looked out upon a mountain scene. Swiss or Bavarian wooden chalets, clocks of surprising shapes . . . No, she had not dreamed; she was a *widow*. The word, dawning upon her for the first time, seemed strange and menacing. She wept for a long time, then, sobbing, started to dress. Just as she finished there was a rap on the door. She opened it and the porter handed her a visiting-card.

"Pardon, madame, but this gentleman asks if you would see him for a few minutes, at any time you find convenient. He says you will understand."

She looked at the card: "JACQUES MOREAU-VERNEUIL."

"What time is it now?"

"Eleven o'clock, madame."

"Tell him I shall see him in twenty minutes."

When he entered she was again struck by that quality of

generosity which she had observed at the station, and she felt comforted.

"Madame," he said, "you might think my request surprising, but we find ourselves in such a sad situation, it is perhaps natural. . . ."

"Make no excuses," Lucille interrupted. "I also wished to speak with you. I have, as you, a desire to understand. Do you know how your wife and my husband came to be on this voyage together?"

"No, madame . . . I heard the name of Monsieur de Peyrignac for the first time yesterday morning on the telephone. But if you will allow me, I shall tell you all that I know. You do the same, and perhaps together we can discover (he sighed) . . . some clue which might aid us to understand this tragedy. My wife, madame, was Russian and very beautiful. She came to France with her parents at the time of the Revolution. When I first met her she was seventeen, but already ravishing. . . . Pardon me, madame, but I can't, even now, refer to her without admiration. But nevertheless . . ."

He stopped.

"Nevertheless, she has—unintentionally, of course— caused me much anxiety. In the first place, my love for her upset my life. My mother and brothers resented my marrying a foreigner with no money. We are an old and solid bourgeois family of Paris. My brothers are merchants; I am a professor. Mademoiselle Bezoukov was certainly of good family, but she had something fantastic and bold about her which repelled my family. This terrible ending proves that they were not mistaken. I wanted to make a Frenchwoman of Vera, a Frenchwoman of my family. That was never possible. My mother, who was unsympathetic towards her, did nothing to win her. I was occupied with work on my thesis on Procopius. . . . My wife sought companionship in a Russian milieu which I did not know, and I had little control over her actions in that circle. Although an exile from infancy, she always retained a curious nostalgia for Russia. . . . She learned to speak Russian, to read the Russian poets with a pleasure which I thought almost neurasthenic. Several times I came home to find her surrounded by a group of young men whom I didn't know, speaking with great animation in that beautiful but difficult language. I would ask what they were discussing. She would hesitate, seem troubled, and answer, 'Nothing of importance.' The others only smiled. I always acted as though I believed her. . . ."

He sighed, took a photograph from his pocket and said: "Look, madame, and you will understand why I was so indulgent with her—and credulous."

Lucille took the photograph, and with deep emotion sorrowfully looked upon the likeness of the stranger.

"Oh! She was beautiful! And she seems so young and frank."

"Yes, that youth and candor were my downfall—and hers. Looking on that childish face dispelled my suspicions which were aroused by her absences from home and long silences. . . . Human beings are very mysterious. I lived with my wife for seven years; I was madly in love with her. I now ask myself if I ever knew her."

Lucille looked for a long time at the stream which followed the road at the bottom of a ravine.

"It is true," she said at last. "I lived four years with a man whom I loved, but never understood. Now he is dead, without my knowing what he was, what he wanted, or why he lived. . . . This trip to Czechoslovakia, for example . . . He never mentioned that country to me. . . . Have you any idea?"

"None, madame. I got in touch with Vera's family yesterday and saw her brother before I left. I asked myself (one turns towards such unreasonable speculations, when torn by doubt and anxiety) if the Russian relief organization for which she worked could have sent her to Russia on some secret mission. It appears there is nothing to that explanation. Her friends were as surprised as I; they are even worried because it seems that she was in possession of some papers which they will have difficulty finding because of her disappearance. No, I have passed all night turning over each and every possibility. They are all absurd and distressing. Poor Vera! I can imagine her with naïve bravado embarking on some foolhardy adventure, discovering the dangers too late, and continuing through an exaggerated sense of honor."

"That," said Lucille, "is exactly how I imagine Gilbert's part in the adventure. He was also a foolhardy person with an exaggerated sense of honor."

They talked for a long time, finding a strange comfort in examining together all the aspects of the drama which, without their volition, had united them. Nevertheless, when the time for luncheon came, a sort of timidity, which they would have found difficult to explain, made them separate and eat at different tables in the dining car.

.   .   .   .

At Prague they were met by a secretary from the Legation, who took them in the same car to the hotel where they left their luggage. For him they were actors in the same administrative drama and he found it natural that they were together. The minister, Monsieur de Boissier, was waiting for them at the Legation. He was a courteous man and a fluent talker. He said he had wished to spare them the painful trip to the scene of the accident, and had ordered the caskets brought to the Capital.

"Also, any further identification seems useless. The passports, the photographs, leave no doubt. One of the secretaries, the one who met you, brought back the papers found in the cockpit. Here they are . . . Their contents are such that I wished to see both of you before sending them to the Department. In the first place, the passports which are intact contain no visas."

"It couldn't be otherwise in the case of my wife," said Moreau-Verneuil, "because she would have had to have my authorization to obtain a visa. But I knew nothing of this voyage."

"And you, madame, of your husband's plans?"

"Absolutely nothing," Lucille answered.

"That is most curious, since this trip had been planned for a long time. This is how we know . . . Among the papers found in the plane were two written in Russian. I had them translated. . . . One is a contract for six years, engaging your husband as test pilot for one of the great Soviet aviation factories. . . . The other is an order from the Commissar of Defense, dated at Moscow fifteen days ago, instructing all Russian authorities to allow the French engineer, Peyrignac, and his companion, Vera Bezoukov, to land on Soviet territory and to give them every assistance and direct them as rapidly as possible to the factory mentioned in the contract."

"A contract is a safe-conduct in Russia?" said Moreau-Verneuil with evident incredulity. "But that is impossible! If my wife were affiliated with any Russian organization (and I have reason to believe she was) it would have been an organization of White Russians."

"You believe so," said the minister, "but the facts are here. Were it not for the fatal accident, the two runaways would have landed in Russia. How could they have hoped to be received if the Soviet authorities had not looked upon them with favor?"

The conversation continued for a long time. In spite of the tact of the diplomat, his interpretation of the drama became clear. He believed that Madame Moreau-Verneuil and Peyrignac were lovers; they wished to flee together without leaving any trace of their whereabouts; a flight by air was the only possible way for Madame Moreau-Verneuil to cross the frontiers without a visa; Russia was the only country in the world where it was possible for the pair, with the aid of the authorities, to disappear and commence life under new identities. Madame Moreau-Verneuil through her knowledge of the language, and perhaps through acquaintances unknown to her husband, had been in contact with the Russian Embassy in Paris; the competence of the aviator made him acceptable. All in all, but for the tragic accident, their ingenious plan would have succeeded. All this was said with diplomatic finesse and circumlocution. Nevertheless, he told them—while the two victims of the tragedy listened dejectedly, without interrupting except for an occasional monosyllable of surprise. He finished by saying, if it was their wish, he would request the Department to keep the facts secret and declare the inquest closed. The role of justice, he told them, was not to create unnecessary scandal, but to hush scandal when possible.

Monsieur Moreau-Verneuil bowed his head and said he

did not believe there was any scandal involved, but a mystery which would never be cleared. Nevertheless, he agreed that silence was the better way. It was arranged that the Legation would arrange with the Czech authorities for a train to take the bodies back to Paris, and the departure would be set, if possible, for the day after the morrow. If, in the meantime, the minister could be of any service to them he was at their disposition. It was a polite dismissal.

Madame de Peyrignac and Monsieur Moreau-Verneuil found themselves alone in the streets of Prague. They were both overwhelmed by surprise and despair. An instinct of self-preservation kept them together. The sun shone in a clear sky. They walked through the modern city, then suddenly came upon the old Jewish cemetery where the aged tombstones plunged them into long and silent revery. They crossed the beautiful bridge, ornamented with allegorical figures, and walked through the streets of the old town. While passing a time-worn church Monsieur Moreau-Verneuil, free-thinking professor, started to explain to his companion the Hussite movement in Bohemia in the fifteenth century.

"John Huss," he said, "was a preacher, a disciple of the Englishman, Wycliff. . . . His crusade was religious and nationalistic at the same time. He was burned alive in a field which could not have been far from this spot. They say that when an old woman brought a fagot for the fire he called out, 'Oh, Godly simplicity!' . . . This castle which overlooks the city is the *Hradshin* where Châteaubriand saw Charles X, 'like a phantom dominating ghosts.' "

Lucille had always been interested in history. She listened, even asked some questions; then suddenly remembering her sorrow, was silent.

"We must go back," she said at last.

.   .   .   .

The trip home from Prague left them all their lives with a feeling akin to remorse. The train which took them across Germany carried the oaken caskets containing the mutilated remains of the two whom they had loved so ardently. Yet, several times during the voyage both were conscious of a guilty but unmistakable sentiment of hope; for the dead, however dear, had been slightly feared. Never could one live close to them and enjoy their exciting presence without fighting a confused anxiety. The attraction of their beauty and their power was always mixed with sinister presentiments. But as Lucille de Peyrignac sat across the table in the dining car, she talked with Moreau-Verneuil and felt a curious sense of security in spite of the sad topic of their conversation.

"And what will you do now?" he asked with solicitude.

"What shall I do? I shall try to rent Peyrignac which is too large and in bad repair, where it would be too terrible to live alone, and I shall move to Paris to raise the children there."

"You are fortunate, madame, to have your children in your sorrow. Vera never wanted children. But life in Paris will be more difficult for you—more expensive. That does not frighten you?"

"No, I shall work. . . . If I find nothing I shall return to Alsace to my parents. . . . But I believe that I can find something in Paris . . . perhaps as a secretary. I have a degree in philosophy, and was specializing in English when I met Gilbert. . . . Naturally, I gave it up after our marriage. It was impossible to work at Peyrignac; I was so far from the libraries—everything. Then I had too many responsibilities. . . . But in a short while, if I see my way clear, I should like to start my studies again."

"If ever I can be of any help to you I shall be very happy."

.   .   .   .

It was in an old officer's kit that Lucille found Vera's letters. There were almost a hundred, written in a clear precise hand. She had been searching for the property deeds which the notary had requested when she came across the bundle tied with a ribbon. At first she told herself she would not read them, then a few phrases caught her eye. She could not resist the terrible desire to know.

Throughout one whole night, in the same hall where she

had first heard of his death, she watched an unknown Gilbert come to life. Her husband had been for her the "lord and master," demanding, unreasonable and formidable. In that other life Vera dominated, fascinated and enslaved him. Following the dates of the letters and some easily decipherable notes in a memorandum book, Lucille reconstructed the love affair which had paralleled her married life, and of which she had never had the least suspicion.

At dawn, shivering, she went up to her room where she continued to mull it over in her mind. 'I was married to a man who did not exist—unless there were two Gilberts. . . . In Peyrignac, at night in my arms he was sincere. . . . He drugged himself with his own words until he believed what he said. I am the widow of an unknown man. Now, it is up to me to raise his sons. . . .'

By dying for another, Gilbert had succeeded in breaking the cord of sentiment which united Lucille to him. Delivered of her tormented love, she was calm and felt free; while Moreau-Verneuil, still pervaded by the personality of Vera, felt a confused sense of guilt about becoming familiar with another. Although Lucille was unhappy she suffered less than he. Her discovery had released her from a vow, freed her from an oath. She wore mourning for her broken home, but the certitude of the infidelity had liberated her from the past.

At first she thought it would help Moreau-Verneuil to show him the letters, for he continued to vindicate the phantom couple with naïve and chivalrous obstinacy.

"I begin to understand," he said, "Vera left me so as not to betray me. She could not stand hypocrisy. Certainly, nothing could have been easier than for her to have been unfaithful to me in secret. The idea of the mad flight came to her because it was the only form of romance compatible with her frank nature."

Lucille asked him: "Among your wife's papers didn't you find the least note from Gilbert? Is it true that you know nothing?"

"I don't want to know anything."

"Just the same," replied Lucille, "knowledge can be comforting."

"Perhaps," said Moreau-Verneuil. "But *know* . . . What do you know after all? You did not know Vera. . . . You judge her from the standpoint of a reasonable French-woman. But before all—she was Russian. Yes, in spite of exile, in spite of the Revolution. . . . My folly was to believe that I could change the heroine of a Slavic legend into a little bourgeoise Parisian. Know! Do you know what your husband was for her? Nothing—no more than an aviator who could make it possible for her to return to a country for which she had a burning nostalgia."

"What? You don't believe that she loved Gilbert?"

"Of course not! How could she love a Frenchman? She made use of him."

Lucille said no more. Why destroy the image to which the man clung so desperately? Later she asked herself if it were really possible for Moreau-Verneuil to be the dupe of his own arguments. But what difference did it make? When her mental explanations of the man ran from obstinate to noble and then to heroic, she realized that she was singularly attached to Jacques Moreau-Verneuil.

Unpleasant details, common to both of them, obliged them to seek one another often for consultations. The plane had been bought in the name of Madame de Peyrignac and the order had been signed in that name. It was necessary to prove it was not Lucille's signature. Moreau-Verneuil generously identified the writing as Vera's and assumed the debt. A short time later Lucille was sued for the unpaid rent on an apartment in an exclusive modern building which had been furnished for Peyrignac the year before by a famous decorator. She found there an assortment of tailor-made uniforms, a bar filled with empty bottles and a large portrait of Vera in evening clothes, very décolleté, painted by Jacovleff. To help her dispose of the contents, Moreau-Verneuil met her there several times where they had long conversations.

In the beginning Gilbert and Vera were the subject of their talks. Both had been so strange, one could recall without end their actions and their words. . . . How could Vera, hostile by birth and tastes to the new Russia, approach the Embassy and obtain a safe-conduct? . . . How

could Gilbert, who loved his country and his children, resolve to abandon them to live among strangers whose
language he did not speak? . . . Jacques and Lucille discussed these things during one whole winter. Their thoughts
traveled on two distinct planes which were complementary.
Lucille, observant and analytical, would bring up precise
facts which Moreau-Verneuil with his habitual generosity
would interpret without malice.

When spring came Jacques Moreau-Verneuil would propose long walks through the old quarters of Paris, and
Lucille was surprised to discover that she enjoyed them.
Could it be that she was in love with her companion? No,
that feeling of serene confidence, of friendly peace, was not
the same burning but tormented sentiment which Gilbert
had inspired. It was, nevertheless, a precious and incomparable support in her solitude. She knew that on his side
Moreau-Verneuil was attached to her. He discussed his
thesis with her, asked her to do some research for him, and
showed a genuine fondness for her children. So slight were
the transitions which led to their marriage, that when they
made the decision it seemed perfectly natural.

   .   .   .   .

Twelve years have passed since their marriage, and their
home is one of the happiest to be found in the world. It is the
sort of happiness which some might find monotonous and
dull, for it is built on work done together, vacations in the
country, serious and tranquil conversations; but they are
completely satisfied. They remain faithful, without bitterness or regrets, to the memory of the two stormy beings who
long ago passed through their lives like meteors. Sometimes
in summer, strolling together along some forest path, the
memory of their extraordinary adventure will come back to
them.

"I am always reminded of the story told by Goethe in
Die Wahlverwandschaften where the two couples discover
in horror that only through an exchange will they find
contentment."

"Yes," answered her husband, "but our case is more

astonishing because I didn't know you at all. If destiny and death had not entered our lives, I might never have known you."

Both of them pondered how sad that would have been, but dared not voice the thought for fear of awakening errant and jealous shadows. For some time they walked in silence, looking into the distance where streaks of sunlight had pierced the clouds.

THE EARTH DWELLERS

FRAGMENT FROM A UNIVERSAL HISTORY
PUBLISHED BY THE UNIVERSITY OF
* * * IN 1992.

(*Translated by Hamish Miles*)

BY the end of 1970 friendly relations had been established
between the Earth and most of the major planets, and terrestrial scientists became anxious to compare their own
hypotheses and doctrines with those of their colleagues in
other worlds. But such comparisons were often difficult, because, as is well known, the eminent physicists of Venus,
Jupiter and Mars had no perception of either light or sound,
and lived in a world of radiations of which we had hitherto
been quite ignorant. But the theory of sensorial equivalents
made rapid progress, and at the date of writing (1992) it
may be said that we are capable of transposing every language of the planetary system into Earth language—except
Saturnian.

One of the most interesting discoveries due to this new
philology was that of books written about ourselves, the
Earth Dwellers, by the scientists of foreign planets. Mankind had not the slightest idea that for millions of years
past he had been under observation, thanks to instruments
very much more powerful than his own, by the naturalists
of Venus, Mars, and even Uranus. Terrestrial science lagged
far behind the science of neighboring bodies, and as our
organs were insensitive to the radiations utilized by these
observers, it was impossible for us to know that, in the
most secret moments of our lives, we were sometimes within
the field of vision of a celestial ultra-microscope.

Nowadays these works can be consulted by any scholar

351

in the library of the League of Planets. They provide most commendable reading for young men eager to devote themselves to the learned sciences not only because of their great intrinsic interest, but also because of the sense of humility which they cannot fail to evoke. To observe the incredible errors made by beings of such high intelligence and so wonderfully equipped for research, one cannot refrain from reverting to a number of our own human affirmations, wondering whether we have not observed plants and animals very much as the Martians observed us.

One case in particular strikes us as worthy of careful study: that of the Uranian scholar A.E. 17, who published his book, *Man and His Life,* in 1959.[1] Until the War that book was the standard work not only in Uranus, but also, in translations, amongst the inhabitants of Venus and Mars. To ourselves it is readily accessible because, alone amongst our fellow-planetaries, the Uranians share with us the sense of sight, which makes their vocabulary approximate closely to ours. Moreover, the experiments carried out by A.E. 17 were such as completely to upset the Earth throughout a period of six months; and we have access to the terrestrial account of these events in the newspapers and memoirs of the time.

We propose here:

(a) To describe briefly a few of the events noted on our own planet in the year 1954;

(b) to show what interpretation the eminent A.E. 17 put on his own experiments.

The Mysterious Springtime.

In the month of March, 1954, numerous observers throughout the northern hemisphere gave surprising reports of atmospheric conditions. Notwithstanding fine and cool weather, storms of the utmost violence were bursting suddenly within strictly limited zones. Ships' captains and airplane pilots reported to the Central Meteorological Bureau that their compasses had for several seconds behaved quite wildly for no conceivable reason. In several places,

[1] Original Uranian edition, 1959. First terrestrial edition, 1982.

under a clear sky, people saw what appeared to be the shadow of a huge cloud passing over the ground, although no such cloud was visible. The newspapers published interviews with the eminent meteorologists, who explained that they had anticipated this phenomenon, which was due to sunspots and would come to an end with the equinoctial tides. But the advent of the equinox only brought stranger happenings in its wake.

The "Hyde Park Hill" Incident.

On the third Sunday in April, the crowds of men and women listening to the open-air orators on their pitch at Marble Arch, suddenly saw passing overhead the shadow of an invisible obstacle mysteriously interposed between the Earth and the sun. A few seconds later, from the Park railings to a point some three or four hundred yards inside the Park, there occurred an abrupt upheaval of the ground. Trees were uprooted and pedestrians tumbled over and buried, whilst those who were on the edge of the disturbed area were dumbfounded to observe that a great funnel at least three hundred feet deep had been scooped out, the soil from which had been thrown up to form a hill of corresponding height.

A policeman, giving evidence next day at the inquest on victims, said: "It all happened just as if a giant had been wielding a spade in the Park. Yes, it was just like someone using a spade, because the outer edge of the cavity was trim and smooth, while the edge on the side where the hill came consisted of crumbling loose soil, with half-cut heads and bodies protruding from it."

Over three hundred citizens walking in the Park had been buried alive. Some who had only been covered with a light layer of earth managed to extricate themselves with some difficulty. Some, too, suddenly lost their senses and rushed down the steep slope of the new hill uttering dreadful shrieks. On the summit of the mound there appeared the upright figure of a Salvation Army preacher, Colonel R. W. Ward, who, with astonishing presence of mind, still shaking the dirt from his hair and clothing, began to bellow: "I told you so, brothers! You have sacrificed to false gods, and now the Lord God is angered with his people, and the hand of the Lord God has fallen heavy upon us. . . ."

And indeed this inexplicable event bore such a likeness to certain divine punishments as described in Holy Writ, that sceptics amongst the bystanders were instantly converted, and began lives of practising religion to which they have from that moment been steadfast.

The episode enabled people to appreciate the virtues of the Metropolitan Police. Three members of the Force were amongst the victims, but a dozen others, arriving instantly on the scene, set to work on digging with great courage. Telephone messages were sent out at once to the military authorities and fire stations, and General Clarkwell, the Commissioner of Police, took command of the rescue forces, and within four hours Hyde Park had resumed its normal appearance. Unfortunately, the dead numbered two hundred.

Scientists gave the most varied explanations of the disaster. The theory of an earthquake, the only reasonable one if the supernatural were ruled out, did not seem plausible, for no shock had been recorded by any seismograph. The public were fairly well satisfied when the experts informed them that it *had* been an earthquake, but an earthquake of a very special sort which they had labeled a "vertical-montiform seismic variant."

The House in the Avenue Victor Hugo.

The Hyde Park incident was followed by a considerable number of similar occurrences, which attracted much less public attention because they caused no human fatalities. But at different points these strange mounds were seen taking shape with the same swiftness, each of them bordered by a precipice with sheer, clean-cut fall. In certain places these hills are still in existence: as for instance the one in the plain of Ayen in Périgord, that of Roznov in Wallachia, and that of Itapura in Brazil.

But the mysterious spade which was thus apparently wielded on bare land was now, alas, to attack human erections.

About midday on April 24, a strange noise, compared by

some who heard it to that of a whizzing blade, by others to that of an extremely fine and powerful water-jet, astonished the passers-by in the region of Paris bounded approximately by the Arc de Triomphe, the Avenue de la Grande Armée, the Avenue Marceau, and the Avenue Henri Martin.

People happening to be opposite the building known as 66 Avenue Victor Hugo saw an enormous oblique cleft appear across it; the house was shaken by two or three tremors, and suddenly the whole of the top storey, occupied by the servants' rooms, seemed to crumble away as if under powerful pressure. The frenzied inhabitants appeared at the windows and on the balconies. Fortunately, although the building was literally cut in two, it did not collapse. Halfway up the staircase the rescuers came upon the fissure produced by the invisible instrument. It looked exactly as if a blade had cut through the wood of the steps, the carpet, the metal balustrade, following a line at right-angles to these. Everything in its path—furniture, carpets, pictures, books—had been cut in two with a clean stroke, very neatly. By a miracle nobody was injured. A girl sleeping on the third floor found her bed sliced obliquely across; but the cut had just missed her. She had felt no pain, but did experience a shock like that of a weak electric battery.

In this case, too, there were numerous explanations. The word "seismic" was again produced. Certain newspapers accused the architect and proprietor of the building of having used faulty materials in its construction. A communist deputy raised the question in the Chamber.

The Transportation Phenomena.

Like the Hyde Park occurrence, the accident in the Avenue Victor Hugo was followed by several almost identical in kind, which we shall not recount, but which ought, as we now see, to have convinced observant minds of a hidden will engaged in the furtherance of a definite plan. In numerous countries, houses, great and small, were sundered by an invisible force. Several farmhouses, one in Massachusetts, another in Denmark, another in Spain, were raised into the air, and dropped back on to the ground, smashed to pieces with their inhabitants. The French Building in New York was cut in two. About fifty men and women met their deaths in these occurrences, but as they took place in very different countries, each isolated case being responsible only for a few victims, and also as nobody could provide an explanation, very little was said about them.

It was different with the subsequent series of happenings, which kept the whole planet in a ferment of excitement throughout May and June, 1954. The first victim was a young Negress of Hartford, Connecticut, who was leaving her employers' house one morning when a postman, the sole witness of the accident, saw her suddenly soar into the air uttering terrible cries. She rose to a height of three hundred feet and then crashed to the ground. The postman declared that he had seen no aerial apparatus of any sort overhead.

The second case of "transportation" was that of a customs official at Calais, who was also seen rising vertically and disappearing at high speed towards the English coast. A few minutes later he was found on the Dover cliffs, dead, but with no visible injuries. He looked as if he had ben laid gently down on the ground; he was blue, like a man hanged.

Then began the period of the so-called "successful transportations." The first victim to arrive living at the end of his journey was an aged beggar, who was seized by an invisible hand when he was begging for alms in front of Notre Dame, and ten minutes later was deposited in the middle of Piccadilly Circus at the feet of a stupefied policeman. He had not suffered at all, and had the impression of having been conveyed in a closed cabin to which neither wind nor light could penetrate. Eye-witnesses of his departure had observed that he became invisible immediately after he was raised from the ground.

For several weeks longer these "transportations" continued. Once they were known to be quite harmless, they were regarded as rather comical. The choice of the invisible hand seemed to be completely whimsical. Once it was a little girl of Denver, Colorado, who found herself set down in a Russian steppe; another time a Saragossa dentist turned up in Stockholm. The "transportation" which caused most talk was that of the venerable President of the French Senate, M. Paul Reynaud, who was picked up in the Luxembourg gardens and deposited on the shore of Lake Ontario. He took the opportunity of making a journey through Canada, was triumphantly welcomed back at the Bois de Boulogne station, and this unsought publicity was probably largely responsible for his election as President of the Republic, in 1956.

It should be noted that, after their journeys, the subjects of "transportation" were smeared with a reddish liquid that stained their clothing, for no ascertainable reason. This was the only inconvenience of these otherwise harmless adventures. After about two months they ceased, to be followed by a new and still stranger series which began with the famous episode of the "Two Couples."

The "Two Couples" Episode.

The first of the two famous couples was a French one, living in a small house close to Paris, in Neuilly. The husband, Jacques Martin, was on the teaching staff of the Lycée Pasteur, a sporting and scholarly young man, and the author of a remarkable biographical study on Paul Morand. He and his wife had four children. On July 3, towards midnight, Mme. Martin had just fallen asleep when she heard that steamlike whistling which we have already mentioned, felt a slight shaking, and had the impression of being very rapidly raised into the air. Opening her eyes, she was stupefied to see that the pale light of the moon was flooding her room, a whole wall of which had vanished, that she was lying on the edge of a bed cut in two, and that on her left hand, where her husband had been lying a few seconds before, there was a bottomless gulf, above which the stars were glittering. She flung herself in terror towards the still solid edge of the bed, and was amazed (and at the same time reassured) to find that it did not wobble, although it was left with only two legs. Mme. Martin felt that she was rising no higher, but was being moved very fast in a straight line; then she was made aware, by a feeling in the heart like that which one has in a lift descending too quickly, that she was dropping. Imagining that her fall would end with a crash, she had already closed her eyes in anticipation of the final shock. But it was gentle and elastic, and when she looked round her, she could see nothing. The room was dark. Her own narrative continues:

"I put out my arm; everything was solid. The abyss had apparently closed up again. I called my husband's name, thinking that I had been passing through a nightmare and feeling anxious to tell him about it. My groping hand felt a man's arm, and I heard a strong unknown voice say in English: 'Oh, my dear, what a fright you gave me!' I started back and wanted to turn on the light, but I could not find the electric switch. 'What's wrong?' said the unknown. He himself turned on a light. We both uttered simultaneous cries. In front of me was a fair-haired young Englishman, with a small short nose, rather short-sighted, and still half-asleep, in blue pajamas. Down the middle of the bed ran a crack; sheets, mattress and bolster were all cut in two. There was a difference of three or four inches in the level of the two portions of the bed.

"When my bedfellow had recovered his wits, his demeanor in these difficult circumstances gave me a high opinion of the British race. After a short but very excusable moment of confusion, his correctness was as complete and natural as if we had been in a drawing-room. I spoke his language and told him my name. He told me that his was John Graham. The place we were in was Richmond. Looking round, I saw that the whole of one half of my own room had accompanied me: I recognized my window with its cherry-colored curtains, the large photograph of my husband, the small table with books beside my bed, and even my watch on top of my books. The other half, Mr. Graham's, was unknown to me. On the bedside table there were a portrait of a very pretty woman, photographs of children, some magazines, and a box of cigarettes. John Graham looked at me for a very long time, examining the background against which I had appeared to him, and then said with the utmost seriousness: 'What are you doing here?' I explained that I knew nothing about it, and pointing to the large portrait, I said: 'This is my husband.' Pointing likewise, he answered:

'This is my wife.' She was delightful, and the disturbing thought came to me that she was perhaps at that very moment in the arms of Jacques. 'Do you suppose,' I asked him, 'that half of your house has been transported to France at the same time as half of ours has come here?'—'Why?' he said. He annoyed me. Why, indeed? I knew nothing about it at all. . . . Because this affair had a sort of natural symmetry of its own.

"'A queer business,' he said, shaking his head. 'How can it be possible?'—'It isn't possible,' I said, 'but it has happened.'

"At this moment cries were heard apparently coming from upstairs, and the same thought struck us: 'The children?' John Graham jumped out of bed and ran barefoot towards a door, the door of *his* half. He opened it, and I could hear cries, the sound of coughing, and then the Englishman's powerful voice mingling oaths with words of comfort. I made haste to rise, and looked in the mirror. My face looked just as usual. I then noticed that my night-dress was décolleté and looked around for my kimono; but I remembered having hung it in the half of the room which had stayed behind. Standing there in front of the mirror, I heard a pitiable voice behind me.

"The cries in the nursery were redoubled, weeping and appeals mingling with them.

"'Come and help me,' he said in a beseeching tone.

"'Of course I will . . . but have you got your wife's dressing-gown, and slippers?'

"'Oh, yes, of course. . . .'

"Handing me his own dressing-gown he showed me the way to the nursery. The children were splendid. I managed to soothe them. It was the youngest, a lovely fair baby, who seemed to be suffering most. I comforted him as best I could, and took his hand; he accepted my presence.

"In this way we spent a couple of hours in that room, both in a state of mental anguish, he thinking of his wife, and I of my husband.

"I asked if we could not telephone to the police. He tried, and found that his telephone had been cut off; his wireless aerial had also been cut; the house must have been looking extremely odd. When dawn appeared, Mr. Graham went out. The children had fallen asleep. In a few minutes he returned for me, saying that really the front of the house was well worth looking at. And it was! The unknown contriver of this miracle had evidently wanted to pick two houses of the same height divided in the same way, and he had succeeded; but the styles were so different that the combined effect took one's breath away. Our house at Neuilly was of brick, very plain, its tall windows framed with stone; the English house was a small black and white cottage, with wide bow-windows. The juxtaposition of these two utterly different halves formed a most ludicrous ensemble—like a Harlequin of Picasso's.

"I urged Mr. Graham to put on his clothes and send off a telegram to France, to find out what had happened to his wife. He told me that the telegraph office did not open till eight o'clock. He was a stolid creature, apparently incapable of conceiving that in such peculiar circumstances, one could infringe regulations and knock up the telegraph-clerk. I shook him energetically, but in vain. All I could get out of him was: 'It only opens at eight.' In the end, about seven o'clock, just when he was going out, we saw a policeman arriving. He was gazing at the house in amazement, and had brought a telegram from the head of the Paris police, asking if I was there and announcing that Mrs. John Graham was safe and sound at Neuilly."

It is not worth while continuing the quotation of this narrative *in extenso*. Suffice it to say that Mrs. Graham tended Mme. Martin's children as devotedly as the latter did the little English ones, that both couples declared themselves charmed by the amiability of their companions in adventure, and that both households remained close friends to their dying days. Mme. Martin was still alive ten years ago, in her family home at Chambourcy (Seine-et-Oise).

. . . .

The space allotted to this chapter in the general plan of this volume does not allow us to recount the analogous adventures which astonished mankind throughout that month of August, 1954.

The series of "sliced houses" was even longer than that of the "transportations." Over one hundred couples were interchanged in this way, and the changes became a favorite theme with novelists and film-writers. They continued an element of whimsical sensuality which was much to the public's taste. Besides, it was diverting to see (as it really happened) a queen waking up in a policeman's bed, and a ballet-girl in that of the President of the United States. Then the series stopped dead, and gave place to another. It looked as if the mysterious beings who amused themselves by disturbing the lives of humans were capricious, and quick to tire of their games.

The Caging.

Early in September, the hand whose power was by now known to all the world fell upon some of the finest minds on its surface. A dozen men, nearly all chemists or physicists, men of the highest achievement, were simultaneously abstracted from different points amongst the civilized countries and transported to a clearing in the Forest of Fontainebleau.

A group of lads who had come there in the early hours of the morning to climb the rocks, noticed some old men wandering forlornly amongst the trees. Seeing that they were in difficulties, the young men tried to approach them to offer help, but were taken aback to find themselves suddenly checked by some transparent but insurmountable resistance. They tried to find a way round the obstacle, but after making a complete circle round the clearing they realized that it was completely ringed by an invisible rampart. One of the scientists was recognized by a few of the youths as their professor, and they called him by name. He did not seem to hear them. Sound could not penetrate the barrier. The celebrated personages were there like caged beasts.

Before very long they seemed to accept the situation. They were observed to be lying down in the sunlight; and then, drawing pieces of paper from their pockets they began scribbling mathematical formulae and arguing quite cheerfully. One of the young onlookers went off to inform the authorities, and by noon many curious spectators were beginning to come on the scene. By noon the scientists were showing signs of anxiety; they were all of advanced years, and they dragged themselves rather wearily to the edge of the ring, where, seeing that their voices were not reaching anyone, they made signs that they should be supplied with food.

A few officers were present, and one of them had what appeared to be the capital notion of supplying the unfortunate men with supplies by airplane. A couple of hours later the drone of a motor was heard, and the pilot, passing skilfully over the circular clearing, dropped some packages of food exactly over the center. But unfortunately, about sixty feet above the ground the packages were seen to stop in their fall, bounce back and then were left suspended in mid-air. The cage had a roof composed of the same invisible radiations.

Towards nightfall the old men became desperate, signaling that they were dying of hunger and dreaded the night chills. The anguished onlookers could do nothing for them. Were they going to witness the perishing of this remarkable assemblage of great intellects?

In the pale light of the dawn it was at first thought that the situation had not changed, but closer examination showed that quite a new setting had appeared in the center of the "cage." The invisible hand had staged things so that the packages dropped by the airplane were now suspended at the end of rope about fifteen feet above the ground, whilst alongside this rope hung another which actually reached the ground. To any young man it would have been an easy matter to swing himself up and reach the packages that held the hopes of safety. But unhappily there was little likelihood that any of these venerable men of learning could undertake this difficult gymnastic feat. They were seen walking round the ropes and gauging their strength, but none of them ventured farther.

A whole day went by in this way. Night fell. Gradually the curious throng melted away. About midnight one young student took it into his head to ascertain whether the barrier of radiations still held. To his great surprise he found nothing barring his way, walked straight on, and uttered a cry of triumph. The cruel powers which had made men their toys for two whole days were consenting to spare their victims. The scientists were fed and warmed, and none of them succumbed.

．　　．　　．　　．　　．　　．　　．　　．　　．　　．

Such are the chief facts which distinguished this period, at the time inexplicable, but which we now know to have corresponded to a period of experiments on the planet Uranus. We shall now give a few extracts, in our opinion the most interesting, from the book of the famous A.E. 17.

The reader will understand that we have been obliged to find terrestrial equivalents for the Uranian words, and the translation is only approximate. Uranian time consists of years very much longer than ours, and wherever possible we have made a transposition into terrestrial time. Furthermore, to designate ourselves the Uranians use a word which signifies, roughly, "apterous bipeds"; but this is needlessly complicated and we have in most places substituted the words "men" or "Earth Dwellers." Similarly we have translated the queer word by which they designated our cities by the word "manheaps," which gives in our view a fair suggestion of the associations of analogous ideas. Finally, the reader should not overlook the fact that the Uranian, although endowed like ourselves with the sense of sight, is ignorant of sound. Uranians communicate with each other by means of a special organ consisting of a series of small colored lamps which flash on and off. Observing that men were without this organ, and being unable to imagine speech, the Uranian naturally supposed that we were incapable of communicating our ideas to each other.

Here we can offer only a few brief excerpts from the book by A.E. 17 on *Man and His Life*. But we strongly advise the student to read the book in its entirety; there is an excellent school edition published with appendix and notes by Professor Fischer of Pekin.

．　　．　　．　　．　　．　　．　　．　　．　　．　　．

MAN AND HIS LIFE

By

A.E. 17.

When the surface of the small planets, particularly that of the Earth, is examined through an ordinary telescope, large stains may be noticed, more streaky in texture than those formed by a lake or ocean. If these stains are observed over a long enough period, they are seen to expand throughout several terrestrial centuries, pass through a period of maximum size, and then diminish, or even in some cases disappear. Many observers have thought that they were related to some unhealthy condition of the soil. And indeed nothing could be more like the development and reabsorption of a tumor in an organism. But with the invention of the ultratelemicroscope it has been possible to detect that we are here confronted by an accumulation of living matter. The imperfections of the first apparatus did not allow us to see more than a confused swarming, a sort of throbbing jelly, and excellent observers, such as A.33, then maintained that these terrestrial colonies were composed of animals joined to each other and living a common existence. With our present apparatus it is at once obvious that things are quite otherwise. The individual creatures can be clearly distinguished, and their movements can be followed. The stains observed by A.33 are in point of fact huge nests which can almost be compared to Uranian cities and are known to us as "manheaps."

The minute animals inhabiting these towns, Men, are apterous biped mammals, with an indifferent electrical system, and generally provided with an artificial epidermis. It was long believed that they secreted this supplementary skin themselves. But my researches enable me to declare that this is not so: they are impelled by a powerful instinct to collect certain animal or vegetable fibers and assemble them in such a way as to form a protection against cold.

I use the word "instinct" and from the outset of this work I must lay stress on a clear indication of my feelings regarding a question which ought never to have been raised and has, especially during recent years, been treated with incredible levity. A curious mode of thought has become habitual amongst our younger naturalists, in attributing to these terrestrial vegetations an intelligence of the same nature as that of the Uranian. Let us leave to others the task of pointing out the distressing nature of such doctrine from the religious point of view. In this book I shall show its absurdity from only the scientific point of view. No doubt the beauty of the spectacle rouses a quite excusable enthusiasm, when one views for the first time under the microscope one of the these particles of jelly, and suddenly sees the unfolding of countless lively and interesting scenes—the long streets along which Men pass to and fro, sometimes stopping and apparently exchanging speech; or the small individual nest in which a couple keep watch over a brood of young; or armies on the march; or builders at their work. . . . But for a profitable study of the psychic faculties of these animals it is not enough to profit by the circumstances that chance affords the observer. It is essential to know how to procure the most favorable conditions of observation, and to vary these as much as possible. It is necessary, in a word, to experiment, and thus to build up science on the solid base of fact.

This is what we have sought to do in the course of the long series of experiments reported here. Before embarking on their description I must ask the reader to imagine and to gauge the immense difficulties which such a project was bound to present. Long-distance experiment, no doubt, has become relatively easy since we had at our disposal the W-rays, which enable us to grasp, handle, and even transport bodies through interstellar space. But in dealing with creatures so small and fragile as Men, the W-rays are very clumsy and brutal instruments. In our first tests it turned out only too often that we killed the animals we desired to observe. Transmitting appliances of extraordinary sensitiveness were required to enable us to reach exactly the point aimed at, and to treat the sensitive matter with the necessary delicacy. In particular, when first carrying out the transference of Men from one point to another on terrestrial territory, we omitted to take full account of these animals' respiratory difficulties. We made them move too rapidly across a thin layer of air which envelopes the Earth, and they died of asphyxiation. We had to construct a real box of rays, inside which the swiftness of transportation produced no effect. Similarly, when we first attempted the bisection and transference of nests, we did not make sufficient allowance for the constructional processes used by the Earth Dwellers. Experience taught us to prop up the nests after their division, by the passage of certain massive currents of rays.

The reader will find here a sketch-map of that portion of the terrestrial surface on which our main experiments were carried out. We would ask them particularly to note the two great manheaps on which we made our first tests, and to which we gave the names, later adopted by the astro-sociologists, of "Mad Manheap" and "Rigid Manheap."

These names we chose on account of the singularly differing plans of these manheaps, one of which at once impresses the observer by its almost geometrical star-patterns of roadways, whilst the other is a complex maze of rather tortuous streets. Between "Mad Manheap" and "Rigid Manheap" stretches a gleaming line which is believed to be sea. The greatest manheap on the Earth is "Geometrical Manheap," which is even more regular then "Rigid Manheap," but is far distant from the other two, and separated from them by a wider gleaming surface.

First Attempts.

At what point of the Earth was it best to direct our first efforts? How must we interfere with the lives of these animals in such a way as to obtain instructive reactions from them? I must confess to real emotion when I prepared for the first time to operate on the Earth, armed with an apparatus of adequate range.

I had around me four of my young pupils, who were also deeply moved, and in turn we gazed at the charming miniature landscapes in the ultratelemicroscope. Aiming the apparatus at the "Mad Manheap," we sought a fairly open locality so as to see the consequences of our action more clearly. Tiny trees gleamed in the spring sunshine, and multitudes of small motionless insects could be seen forming irregular circles; in the middle of each of these stood an isolated insect. For a moment we speculated on the meaning of this game, but failing to find one, we decided to try an application of the rays. The effect was staggering. A hole was scooped in the ground; some of the insects were buried under the debris; and instantly an astounding activity was loosed. It really looked as if these creatures were intelligently organized. Some went to the rescue of their overwhelmed companions, others went off to get help. We then tried applying the rays on several points of the Earth, but this time we chose uninhabited areas, so as not to endanger our subjects at the very beginning of our researches. We thus learned how to reduce the power of our rays and to operate more skilfully. Being now sure of our means of action, we decided to start the first series of our experiments.

It was my plan to take individuals in a certain manheap, mark them with a touch of a brush, transport them to different points, and then observe whether the transported individual would find his way back to the original manheap. At first, as I have said, we encountered great difficulties, first because the animal died during transference, and then because we had neglected to take into account the artificial epidermis with which these creatures provide themselves. They doff these coverings with the utmost ease, and so once we had set them down again in the midst of a manheap, we lost sight of them. For the subsequent transportations we tried to mark them directly on the body, tearing off the supplementary skin; but in these cases the animal made itself a new skin as soon as it arrived in the manheap.

With a little practice my assistants were at last able to follow one particular animal with the ultratelemicroscope and keep it constantly in sight. They found that in ninety-nine cases out of a hundred, the man returns to his starting-point. I attempted the transference of two males from the same manheap—the "Mad Manheap"—with the extremely

remote one which we termed the "Geometrical Manheap."
After ten (terrestrial) days my esteemed pupil E.X.33, who
had followed them night and day with incomparable devotion, showed me them returning to the "Rigid Manheap."
They had come back, notwithstanding the fact of their
unfamiliarity with the places to which I had transported
them; they were individuals of stay-at-home habit (we had
kept them under long observation), who were obviously
seeing for the first time the country where we had deposited
them. How did they find the way back? Their transference
had been so rapid that observation was out of the question.
What was their guide? Certainly not memory, but a special
faculty which we must confine ourselves to noting without
claiming to explain it, so remote is it from anything in our
own psychology.

These transferences raised another problem. Would the
returning individual be recognized by the others? Apparently he is. Generally speaking, great excitement is to be
seen in the nest when the absent one reappears. The others
place their arms round him and sometimes even place their
lips on his. In certain cases, however, the feelings manifested
appeared to be those of rage or displeasure.

. . . .

These first experiments showed that some instinct enables
Men to recognize their own manheaps. The second problem
to which we turned was to find out whether, amongst these
creatures, there existed sentiments akin to those of Uranians, and whether, for instance, conjugal or maternal love
could exist on the Earth. Such an hypothesis struck me as
absurd; it attributed to the Earth Dweller refinements of
feeling which the Uranian has attained only through millions of years of civilization. But the duty of the experimen-
tal scientist is to approach his subject with an open mind,
and to make all his experiments without any prejudice
regarding their outcome.

At night the male Earth Dweller generally rests beside
his female. I asked my pupils to bisect some nests in such a
way as to separate the male from the female without in-
juring either, and then to join up one half of Nest A with

the half of Nest B, observing whether the little animals took notice of the change. For the experiment to be carried out under normal conditions, it was essential that the selected nests should closely resemble each other; and for this reason I instructed my collaborators to select two nests containing cells of the same size and broods with the same number of young. E.X. 33 showed me, not without pride, two almost identical nests in the "Mad Manheap" and the "Rigid Manheap," each of them containing a couple with four little ones. The bisection of the houses, and their transportation, were carried out with admirable skill by E.X. 33, and the results were conclusive. In both cases the couples thus artificially put together by us showed slight surprise at the moment of waking, adequately accounted for by the movement and shock. Then, in both cases, they remained together with no attempt at flight, and in apparently normal attitudes. An almost incredible fact was that, from the very first moment, each of the two females tended the other's brood with no sign of horror or distaste. They were plainly incapable of realizing that they were not dealing with their own offspring.

This experiment was repeated on numerous occasions. In 93 per cent of cases, the nests and offspring were tended by both couples. The female retains a stubborn sense of her proper functions, without having any idea of the individuals towards which she performs this duty. Whether the children are hens or not, she toils with equal fervor. It might be thought that this confusion is caused by a close resemblance between the two nests, but at different stages we chose nests of quite different appearances, joining up, for instance, the half of a shabby nest with the half of a rich nest of a different species. The results were more or less the same; Man does not distinguish between his own cell and another.

Having thus shown that in the matter of sentiment the Earth Dweller is an animal occupying a very low place in the scale of creation, we sought an appropriate means of gauging his intellectual faculties. The simplest way, it seemed to us, was to isolate a few individuals in a ray-cage and to put at their disposal food which could only be reached by means of more and more complex actions. I took particular pains to choose for this experiment certain Earth Dwellers for whom my colleague X. 38 claimed signs of scientific intelligence. In Appendix A will be found the details of this experiment. It showed beyond any possible doubt that the space of time within which Man lives is extremely limited in the past and future, that he immediately forgets, and that he is incapable of imagining the simplest method of self-preservation as soon as he is confronted by problems slightly different from those which he has, by heredity, become used to solving.

After a long period of experimenting on individual Earth Dwellings, my pupils and I became familiar enough with the movements of these animals to be able to observe them in their ordinary life without intervention on our part. It is of the utmost interest to follow, as I have done, the history of a manheap through several terrestrial years.

The origin of these human societies is unknown. Why and how did these animals abandon their freedom to become slaves of the manheap? We cannot tell. It may be that in this grouping process they found a support in warfare against other creatures and against natural forces; but it is a support for which they pay highly. No animal species is so ignorant as this one of leisure and the joy of living. In the great manheaps, and particularly the "Geometrical Manheap," activity begins at dawn and is prolonged through part of the night. Were this activity necessary, it would be comprehensible; but Man is a creature of such limited nature, so much dominated by his instincts, that he produces hardly anything beyond his requirements. Over and over again have I seen objects accumulating in the reserve stores of a manheap in such numbers that they seemed to be a source of embarrassment; and yet, only a short distance away, another group would continue to manufacture the very same objects.

Little is also known of the division of Mankind into castes. It is established that certain of these animals till the soil and produce nearly all the foodstuffs, whilst others make the supplementary skins or build nests, and others seem to do nothing but move swiftly to and fro over the planet's surface, eating and coupling. Why do the first two classes consent to clothe and feed the third? That remains obscure to me. E.X. 33 has written a notable thesis seeking to prove that this tolerance has a sexual origin. He has shown that at night, when the individuals of the superior caste foregather, the workers collect round the entrances to these festivities in order to see the half-nude females. According to him, the compensation of the sacrificed classes consists of the aesthetic pleasure provided by the spectacle of these easy existences. The theory strikes me as ingenious, but not so firmly based as to convince me of its truth.

For my own part, I would rather seek an explanation in Man's amazing stupidity. It is a supreme folly to be forever seeking to explain the actions of Men by Uranian reasonings. That is wrong, profoundly wrong. Man is not guided by a free intelligence. Man obeys a fatal and unconscious incitement; he cannot choose what he shall do; he slides along haphazard, following an irresistible predetermined slope which will bring him to his goal. I amused myself by following the individual existences of certain men in whom the functions of love seemed to be the essentials of their existence. I saw how the conquest of one female to start with brought upon his shoulders all the burdens of nests and young; but not content with that first load, my male would go off in search of a second mate, for whom he set up a new nest. These simultaneous love affairs led the wretched animal into endless battles of which I was the spectator. It mattered nothing to him; his successive woes seemed to hold no lessons for him, and he went on putting his head into his wretched adventures without seeming to be one whit the wiser after the third than after the first.

One of the strangest proofs of this inability to keep contact with the past and imagine the future, was afforded me by the frightful struggles which I witnessed between individuals of one and the same species. On Uranus it would seem a grotesque idea that one group of Uranians could attack another group, hurling on it projectiles meant to injure it, and trying to asphyxiate it with poisonous gases. That is what happened on the Earth. Within a few terrestrial years my observation showed me compact masses of men thus confronting each other, now in one corner of that planet, now in another. Sometimes they fought in the open; sometimes they crouched in earthworks and strove to demolish the adjoining earthworks by showering heavy lumps of metal on them. Note that they themselves were at the same time peppered in the same way. It is a hideous and ridiculous sight. The scenes of horror which one witnesses at these times are such that if these creatures had the slightest faculty for remembering, they would avoid their recurrence for at least several generations. But in the course of even their brief lifetimes, the same men will be seen plunging madly into the same murderous escapades.

Another striking example of this blind subservience of Man to instinct is to be seen in his habit of tirelessly rebuilding manheaps at certain points of the planet where they are fated to destruction. Thus, for instance, I have attentively watched a very populous island where, within eight years, all the nests were destroyed three times by tremors of the outer coating of the Earth. To any sensible observer it is plain that the animals living in these parts ought to migrate. They do nothing of the sort, but pick up once more, with a positively ritual action, the same pieces of wood or iron, and zealously rebuild a manheap which will once more be destroyed in the following year. But, say my critics, however absurd the goal of this activity, it remains true that the activity is regulated, and proves the existence of a directing power, a spirit. Again, a mistaken idea! The swarming of Men disturbed by an earthquake, as I have shown, resembles the movement of gaseous molecules. If the latter be observed individually, they are seen to describe irregular and complicated trajectories, but in combination their great number produces effects of decided simplicity. Similarly, if we demolish a manheap, thousands of insects collide with each other, hamper each other's movements, and show every sign of disorganized excitement; and yet, after a certain time, the manheap is discovered to be built up again.

Such is the strange intellect in which it is now fashionable to see a replica of Uranian reason! But fashion passes, facts remain; and the facts are bringing us back to the good old beliefs regarding the Uranian soul and its privileged destiny. For my own part, I shall be happy if my few experiments, modestly and prudently carried out, have helped towards the downfall of pernicious teachings, and restored these animals to their proper place in the scale of creatures. Curious and worthy of study they certainly are; but the very naïveté and incoherence of Man's behavior must force us to bear in mind how great is the gulf fixed by the Creator between bestial instinct and the Uranian soul.

Death of A.E. 17.

Happily, A.E. 17 died before he could witness the first interplanetary war, the establishment of relations between Uranus and the Earth, and the ruin of all his work. His great renown endured to his last days. He was a simple, kindly Uranian, who showed vexation only when contradicted. To ourselves it is an interesting fact that the monument erected to his memory on Uranus bears on its plinth a bas-relief designed from a telephotographic picture showing a swarming mass of men and women. Its background is strongly reminiscent of Fifth Avenue.

THE ROLE OF MYRRHINE

THE better writers of our generation had, for the most part, great admiration for Christian Menetrier. He had many enemies, for success always creates them, and furthermore this success came late, at a moment when his confrères and critics had become accustomed to considering him a sort of poet in an ivory tower, worthy of respect but incapable of pleasing, and this made admiration of his work an honorable and harmless sentiment. His wife, Claire Menetrier, an ardent and ambitious person, had "launched" him around 1927 by getting the musician Jean-François Montel to make a lyrical drama of his *Merlin and Viviane*. But it was the actor Léon Laurent to whom we owe the metamorphosis of Christian from poet to author of dramas both playable and played. This story is little known and to me it seems worth remembering, for it illuminates certain little-studied aspects of the creative imagination.

Léon Laurent, who played such a big part in the French theater renaissance between the two wars, seemed on first acquaintance as little of a "bad actor" as a man can be. Never impressed with himself, always ready to stand aside objectively at the service of his art, he practiced the religion of the theater to the letter. His culture was astonishing. Not only that, what he liked was good; he also knew and understood the most difficult and the most rare. As soon as he directed his own troupe he had the courage to put on Aeschylus' *Prometheus Bound*, *The Bacchae* of Euripides, and Shakespeare's *Tempest*. His Prospero, and the Ariel of Hélène Messiere, remain among our finest memories. He revived Molière, Musset, and Marivaux, as much by his interpretations as by the productions themselves, and did it at the time the sleeping Comédie Française was still waiting for Edouard Bourdet to awaken it. Furthermore, he knew how to find, among contemporary writers, those worthy of continuing the fine tradition of the poetic theater. French dramatic literature owes him a school, and a staff. I said that at first acquaintance one would not have taken him for an actor. That was true. His tone, his manner, his vocabulary, reminded one more of a young professor or perhaps of a physician. But that impression was brief. It took only five minutes of seeing him act to recognize in him a great comedian of unbelievable range, a comedian just as capable of portraying the dignified Auguste of *Cinna* as the pleasant abbé of *Il ne faut jurer de rien,* or the tragic buffoon Bazile of the *Barber of Seville.*

Christian Menetrier admired him, going to see him in each of his rôles but probably never entering into direct contact with him, for both of them were shy and would have remained so if Claire Menetrier had not got mixed up in it. Claire joined in her husband's enthusiasm for the actor Laurent; she wanted Christian to get into the theater; she thought, with reason, that only a truly cultivated actor would be able to influence him to do so. Therefore she deliberately undertook to know Léon Laurent, and she succeeded.

Claire, with her pale skin and her keen dark-blue eyes, was extremely beautiful, and feminine beauty had always affected Léon Laurent. Besides, after the two men got to know each other, they found constant pleasure in "talking theater." Christian had many ideas on the subject and most of them coincided with those of the actor-director.

"The great error of the realists," said Christian, "is to want to imitate our day-to-day language on the stage. That's exactly what the spectator is *not* looking for in the theater. It must never be forgotten that drama, at its origin, was a ceremony, and that the retinues, the entrances, the choirs, occupied an important place in it. And even in comedy. . . . We are told that Molière listened to the language of the street porters at the Pont au Change. It's possible, it's even certain, but he listened in order to stylize what he heard."

"I agree," replied Léon Laurent. "I agree absolutely. And that's the reason I would like *you,* Menetrier, to work in the theater. Your lyrical couplets, your rare images . . . All that, in depicting character, is, for an actor, excellent material. Fashion us statues; we will love them." Laurent's sentences were short, but his beautiful voice made the echoes long.

"But I *am* in the theater," said Christian.

"No, my friend, no. You write poems in dialogue. You write for the theater but you do it from an armchair. You never address the public."

"Because no one produces my plays."

"Say rather that you've never tried to have them produced. Until now you've never taken into account the demands of the theater. For *they* make the theater. Write a piece for me. Yes, my dear friend, for me, such as I am. You will see then what the lessons are. It will be like going to school. You see, there still remains in you, and in my opinion it's your one fault, something of the affectation of the symbolist. As soon as your dialogues are spoken, you yourself will hear the discords. A scene on the stage is for the playwright what a record of his own voice is for the orator. In it he can see his faults and correct them."

"That's what I tell Christian from morning till night," said Claire. "He is made for the theater."

"I don't know," said Christian.

"Try it at least once. I repeat, write a play for me."

"But on what subject?"

"You have scores of them," said Léon Laurent.

"What are they?"

"Well, every time I spend an hour with you, you outline a first act, and it's almost always excellent. A subject! All you have to do is sit down at your table and write everything that you've already told me. The rest is simple. I will try to play what you write."

For an instant Christian seemed to be dreaming. "Yes, I may have an idea," he said at last. "You know how much I am upset by the imminence of war, how I have tried in vain to draw the attention of Frenchmen to the obvious designs of those fools in the German government. . . ."

"I read your articles in *Figaro*," said Léon Laurent. "I think they were good, and to the point. Only for the theater, too journalistic, you know. . . ."

"Oh, I'm not suggesting a play about current events. No,

what I'm thinking of would be a kind of transposition. You remember the Athenians' attitude at the time that Philip of Macedon demanded 'living space' and occupied the little cities of Greece one after another? 'Watch!' Demosthenes told them. 'Watch! If you don't go to the help of Czechoslovakia, you will be devoured in your turn!' But the Athenians were confident and frivolous, and Philip had a fifth column. Demosthenes failed. Then one day the Athenians' turn came. . . . That will be the second act."

"Fine!" Laurent exclaimed enthusiastically. "Very good! There's our subject. Get to work. Right away!"

"Hold on," said Christian. "I'll have to do a little reading first. But I can see you as an admirable Demosthenes. For you will play Demosthenes, won't you?"

"Naturally!"

Claire, delighted, listened to them discussing the play until five o'clock in the morning. When they separated, the main scenes were in order. Christian had even found the perfect last line. After many a denouement, the death of Philip suddenly saves Athens, as if by miracle. But Demosthenes did not believe in lasting miracles, nor that Athens could be saved otherwise than by the will, courage and loyalty of the Athenians. "Yes," he said, "I hear. Philip is dead. But what is the name of Philip's son?" And someone replied: "Alexander. . . ."

"Perfect!" cried Léon Laurent. "Perfect! I already know how I am going to say that. . . . Menetrier, if you haven't written this play within a month, you aren't worthy of the theater."

A month later, the work was finished. We know today that it justified all the hopes both of Claire and Laurent. However, when the latter, after a triumphant reading, went to see Menetrier to discuss various production matters, he seemed thoughtful and reticent. Christian, very sensitive as are all artists when it's a question of their own work, had the uneasy impression that the actor was not entirely satisfied.

"No," he said to Claire after Laurent's departure, "No, he wasn't pleased. Why? He didn't tell me. In fact, he said nothing to me. It isn't that he doesn't like the piece. He discussed his rôle and the scene before the Assembly with unmistakable enthusiasm. But I had the feeling he had some thought in the back of his mind. What is it? I don't know."

Claire smiled. "Christian," she said, "you are a man of genius and I admire you with all my heart. But you remain deliciously naïve when it's a question of elementary relationships between human beings. I, without even having seen Laurent, assure you that I know very well what the trouble is."

"And what is it?"

"You should say, What *isn't* it? What's missing? What your play lacks, my dear, is a rôle for Hélène Messiere. Remember now that I warned you."

Christian said impatiently, "And how could there be a rôle for Messiere? She is a charming comedienne, perfect in Musset or in Marivaux, but what place is there for her in a political tragedy?"

"Oh, my love, how you can think up all the wrong questions! It's not at all a matter of knowing what Hélène would do in a political tragedy, but much simpler, of knowing how Léon Laurent will be able to live in peace with his mistress."

"Hélène Messiere is the mistress of Léon Laurent?"

"Where have you been, my dear? They've been living together for four years."

"How would I have known that? And what's it got to do with my play? You think that Laurent would like . . ."

"I don't *think* so, Christian. I am *certain* that Laurent desires, and if necessary will demand, a rôle for Messiere, and I might add that to me it doesn't seem very difficult to give him that satisfaction. If you added a character who . . ."

"Never! If I did, that would destroy the whole balance of my drama."

"Very well, Christian. But we'll be talking about this later."

Indeed they talked about it soon after, for Laurent became more and more reserved and sober, raising this and that difficulty, arguing over this and that interpretation, inventing previous engagements and creating unexpected impasses. Christian, with his play written, was burning with the desire to see it produced, and in his turn became anxious and irritable.

"Listen, dear," Claire said to him. "Will you let me talk to Laurent alone? To me he'll try to explain what torments him and I promise you I'll fix things up. On the condition, of course, that you will write the rôle."

"But how? I can't transform a play which attempts to be a work of art just because . . ."

"Oh, Christian! It's so easy and you have so much imagination. For example, in the second act where you show the Macedonians organizing a fifth column in Athens. Why wouldn't they make use for that purpose of an intelligent courtesan, beloved by powerful Athenians, bankers and politicians. . . . There is your character, and it would be entirely plausible."

"Yes, perhaps. . . . It might even be. . . . Yes, you are right, it would be interesting to show those secret propaganda methods which are as old as human society. . . ."

Claire knew very well that the seed she sowed in Christian's mind would germinate. She took Laurent in hand and the conversation was a big success.

"Ah, what an excellent idea!" he said with relief. "You know, I didn't dare speak of it with your husband, who is uncompromising where his own work is concerned, but a play without women is very difficult to get across to the public. Shakespeare himself, in *Julius Caesar* . . . Corneille added the character of Sabine to the drama of *Horace,* and Racine added *Aricie* to the legendary myth of *Phédre.* And then, madame, I'll tell you the whole truth: I wouldn't like to act in a play in which Hélène had no part. She is very young. She has some affection for me, but she loves to dance and she has a horror of being alone. If I abandoned her every evening, she would go out with other men, and I promise you that would bother me. But if your husband can write a rôle for her, that would change everything. The play will run eight days longer."

Thus was born the character of Myrrhine. Christian, when he created her, had thought both of certain cynical and witty women in Aristophanes, and of those loves of Marivaux whom Hélène Messiere had triumphed in portraying. The product of this paradoxical mixture was, to the great surprise of the author, an original and alluring character. "A priceless rôle!" said Laurent. Claire invited Hélène Messiere to dinner, so that Menetrier could read her the new version. She was a ravishing person, with long, frequently lowered lashes, a tiny person who, with the cautious skill of a kitten, spoke very little but never said anything stupid. She pleased Christian.

"Yes," he said, "that very ingénue ingénue is going to make a dangerous and plausible fifth column."

"She doesn't please you *too* much, does she, Christian?"

"Oh, no! And besides, doesn't she love Laurent? He is not only her lover, but her creator. He has modeled her as a sculptor models an image. She wouldn't be anything without him."

"Do you suppose, Christian, that knowledge of that debt inspires much tenderness? I am a misogynist, but I notice a sort of unconscious spite. . . . But what difference does it make to us? Messiere loves the part. All goes well."

As a matter of fact all went well for eight days. Then Laurent became taciturn all over again.

"Now what's the matter?" Christian demanded.

"This time, I don't know," said Claire. "But I'll find out."

Laurent actually didn't have to be begged to explain. "This is it," he said. "The rôle is charming and Hélène is an angel in it. Only . . . You see, we live together and to come to the theater we take the same taxi. Anything else would be silly. But if Hélène doesn't appear before the second act, what will she do in the loge for that first hour? Well, she will get bored, which she can't stand for long, or else she'll receive visitors, and then I know . . . My part will suffer. . . . Without considering my heart . . . But my heart doesn't interest Menetrier, as much as my part. . . ."

"In short," interrupted Claire, "you would like Myrrhine to appear in the play during the first act?"

"One can hide nothing from you, madame."

When she carried this unusual request to her husband, he objected loudly. "Never has a writer had to work in such a manner!" But Claire knew her spouse's intellectual mechanism; first of all, he had to reassure his conscience.

"But, Christian, *all* playwrights work like this. You know very well that Shakespeare considered the physical appearance of his actors, and that Racine wrote for Champmesle. Madame de Sévigné mentions it."

"She detested Racine."

"She knew him very well."

Myrrhine appeared in the first act. It's hardly necessary to add that the taxi problem, important for the arrival of the couple at the theater, was no less important than it was a matter of returning home, and that Myrrhine, in the final version, had also to be put into the third act. There again Claire had to intervene.

"And why, Christian, couldn't Myrrhine became virtuous and patriotic after her nation's defeat? Make her a guerrilla. Make her the mistress of Demosthenes."

"Honestly, Claire, if I listened to you, I'd fall for all the sentimentalities in Hollywood. No, I've had enough of this. I won't add another line."

"Why do you consider it so banal and unreal that a woman of easy virtue could also be patriotic? That's happened often in life. La Castiglione won Napoleon III over to the idea of unity with Italy. All you must do is convert Myrrhine in a subtle and unexpected manner. You can do that better than anyone else. . . . Naturally, the idea of making her the mistress of Demosthenes was a joke. . . ."

"Why a joke? Look at certain men in the French revolution. . . ."

Completely reassured about her husband, Claire also succeeded in pacifying Laurent, and the rôle of Myrrhine, expanded and enriched, became one of the most important in the play.

Opening night was a triumph. All Paris saw Messiere with the eyes of Laurent. Those people who felt, without expressing it, some of the political anguish of Menetrier, and who wished, without knowing it, for a national theater of the kind that had brought about the *Persians* of Aeschylus, gave the author an ovation. Technicians praised the skill with which a classic subject had been transformed into a modern one without once falling into parody. Fabert himself, always quite hard on his confrères, had a kind word for Claire.

"You must have had your hand in this Myrrhine, you beautiful shadow!" he said with his habitual surliness. "There's no denying it. It's a woman, a real woman, and your austere spouse, left to himself, would never have conceived of her. Be frank, he doesn't know a lot about women, your Christian."

"I am happy that you like the character," said Claire. "But I had nothing to do with it."

The next day Robert Kemp, in his review, spoke only of Myrrhine. "From now on," he wrote, "we will speak of Myrrhine as we speak of Agnes or Celimene. . . ." Claire, who was reading with infinite happiness over her husband's shoulder, couldn't keep from murmuring:

"And to think that without that problem of the taxi Myrrhine would never have existed."

The rest of the story belongs to literary history. *Philip* has been translated into all languages and has served as a model for an entirely new national theater. What the public doesn't know is that last year, when Hélène Messiere left Léon Laurent to marry a Hollywood stage-manager, Laurent suggested to Claire that the rôle of Myrrhine be eliminated.

"After all," he said, "we know, you and I, that it isn't essential to the play. It didn't even appear in the first version—why not take it out? That would give the rôle of Demosthenes an ascetic severity which, to me, would be more pleasing. And that would make it unnecessary to search for another Myrrhine. . . ."

But Claire, with sweet obstinacy, held firm. "Look, Laurent, you will create a new Myrrhine without any difficulty. You know so well how to do it. As for me, I will not permit anyone to alter my husband's play. There's no need to tear apart something Christian has put together."

So Myrrhine, daughter of genius and necessity, continued her triumphant existence.

THE SCHOOLBOY'S RETURN

LITTLE Alain was very gay, rolling toward the station in the carriage. He had never left home, and the idea of entering a mountain school did not displease him. Some comrades had told him that there was less studying there than at the lycée. Alain had seen the director, M. Benzod, when the latter was in Paris, and he had found him young and encouraging.

"You know, Papa, he said that in winter, afternoon classes are stopped, and the students skate or ski."

"I hope you will also study Latin a little," sighed M. Schmitt. "You need it."

On the platform, before a train with bright new carriages, Alain began to sing. He was proud of his beige suit, his leather valise, his chestnut-colored gloves, proud above all of leaving on a trip alone with his father.

"What are we going to read on the train, Papa?"

"I've brought some work for myself, my child. . . . You? . . . If you like, I will buy you some illustrated papers. . . . Haven't you anything to read?"

"No, Papa, but it doesn't matter. . . . I'll take a walk down the corridor. . . . I'll watch the tracks."

He disappeared and returned, two minutes later, all excited:

"Papa! I've found a friend. . . . Jean-Louis Dujarrique. . . . He's three compartments off with his mother."

"Is he going to school too?"

"Yes, but not to the same school as I go to: his is called The Priory."

"It's too bad he isn't going to M. Benzod's. . . . Well, if The Priory isn't too far from Gastaad, you'll be able to see each other now and then all the same. In the meantime go back and play with him during the trip."

Bertrand Schmitt loved children, but could not hide his

impatience when his work was interrupted by them. Alain, who recognized his father's absent air, hastened to disappear. The train rolled on. When he raised his unheeding eyes, M. Schmitt saw two twelve-year-old boys passing and returning in the corridor, on a background of posts, rivers and hills. An hour later Alain returned, very upset.

"Papa, do you know what Jean-Louis has told me? That he is very unhappy in his school. . . . That the big boys are cruel. . . . They take everything from him, his books, his candy, and if he resists they hit him or crush him against a wall until he smothers."

"And why doesn't he defend himself?"

"But, Papa, he is the only freshman in the school. . . . He has begged his mother not to send him back to The Priory, to keep him at home in Paris, but she doesn't want to. She has just married again, a Russian with whom she is in love, a Colonel Kiriline, and Jean-Louis annoys him."

"Who told you this story?"

"Jean-Louis."

"Jean-Louis is wrong to speak of his parents in such a manner."

"In what manner, Papa? He told me he loves his mother very much, and she used to love him too . . . after the death of his father she used to busy herself with him a lot . . . but now that she's in love. . . ."

"Don't use words you don't understand. . . . What does she look like, this Mme. Dujarrique?"

"But, Papa, she is no longer called Mme. Dujarrique; her name is Mme. Kiriline. . . . She is very pretty. . . . Do you want me to take you to her compartment? It's right by."

"Presently, my son."

"Papa, do you think if there are big boys at M. Benzod's that they will beat me?"

"I should hope that you would return their blows. Besides M. Benzod seems to me to be an energetic man, who knows how to keep discipline in his school. . . . Now go join your friend."

At Dijon M. Schmitt got out on the platform to walk

about, and found the two boys. Jean-Louis was a handsome little boy, with deep sad eyes.

"Papa, I present Jean-Louis."

Bertrand Schmitt tried to give some advice:

"If the big boys persecute you, you must go to them, make friends. . . . I don't think that they are wicked at heart. Doubtless they don't understand that they make you suffer. . . . Explain that the jokes they think are inoffensive. . . ."

"Those fellows?" said Jean-Louis. . . . "They would have a good laugh at me. . . . If you don't talk just like they do they put you in quarantine. . . ."

On departing Alain got back into his father's compartment.

"Do you know what Jean-Louis was saying when you joined us, Papa?. . . . He was saying: 'I am so unhappy at returning to that hole that I would like to throw myself under the wheels; only I don't dare. . . . Push me, Alain, you will do me a service and I will leave you my whole fortune.' . . . Because, you know, since he has lost his papa, he has a fortune. . . . But I didn't want to."

"I should hope not. . . . He's a little crazy, your friend."

"No, he isn't crazy. . . . You know, Papa, he says that if his mother could picture to herself his life out there, the fights with the older boys, and at night in bed, when he cries, she would not have the courage to send him back there."

"Take me to this lady."

Mme. Kiriline was surprisingly beautiful. She made delicate and melancholy remarks on childhood in a sweet voice. Bertrand sat down, and left the compartment no more. When the maître d'hôtel appeared, M. Schmitt took four tickets and the travelers lunched together. The silent children listened to their parents who were exchanging titles of books, and names of musicians with animation. They felt themselves forgotten. From time to time Jean-Louis looked at Alain, and his eyes seemed to say: "You see that's how she is. . . ." On leaving the table, Bertrand, without thinking, went into Mme. Kirline's compartment, and the two boys went out to play in the passage.

"Our sons play well together," she said. "I hope they'll be able to see each other a little out there."

He hesitated a moment.

"Excuse me," he said, "for speaking to you of a subject which concerns me so little, but the accident of a confidence has made it almost a duty. . . . You certainly are not aware of your son's state of mind. . . . Do you know what he said to mine?"

Mme. Kiriline seemed distracted. Through the window one could see hills becoming mountains, fir trees succeeding the oaks, chalets the houses, torrents the rivers.

"Good heavens!" she said. . . . "But this is frightful. . . . Poor little fellow. . . . I well knew that he did not like that school; I put it down to laziness . . . and above all to jealousy . . for he detests my husband, and he is wrong, for what could I do without a man in the house? Even for my son he will soon be a precious support."

"Of course," said Bertrand, "but your son is a child, he doesn't reason."

Her eyes were filled with tears.

"What shall I do," she said. . . . "Do you think I ought to take him back to Paris and give up the idea? My husband will be so angry. . . . He says I spoil Jean-Louis and that I will thrust him into life badly prepared. . . . I think he's right. . . . Jean-Louis is a little boy with too much imagination. . . . Since this marriage he thinks he's a victim. . . . It isn't true, not at all, but when a child has an idea in his head. . . ."

Mme. Kiriline and her son left the train before Bertrand. When they had gone Alain remained quiet for some time.

"Papa," he said finally, "if the big boys are too mean, I will telegraph you and you will come to get me, won't you?"

CHELSEA WAY: PROUST IN ENGLAND *

(Translated by Hamish Miles)

IT WAS during a dinner at the Pré Catelan that I learned from M. de Norpois how the government of the Republic had decided to recall him to the active list, and send him to London at the head of the French delegation to the Conference on Air Armaments. In congratulating the ex-ambassador, I made a point of mentioning that I had long been anxious to see London, and that his presence in England might well induce me at last to undertake the journey. He replied, I think, that the work of the Conference would unfortunately leave him scanty leisure, but I was hardly listening, as my attention had for a moment been engaged in observing the solo violinist, who, boldly cutting loose from the orchestra and wandering out among the tables like some venturesome and resonant outpost, still with amazing precision, remained in unison with the rhythm and movement of his colleagues, all as if some invisible headquarters-staff, by veiled and exact instructions, had maintained liaison between this mobile patrol and the main body of the melodious forces. With the closing bars of each piece, the violinist bowed in the direction of the blonde American ladies whose brightly colored gowns enframed the glazed wooden platform, lowering his bow as if saluting with a sword, and then turned back to his comrades, who were waiting with calm curiosity for him to bring back a report about the enemy whose pink camp-fires they could discern beneath the far-off bushes, and so enable them to launch a new offensive of harmony. With his head thrown back and

* Marcel Proust himself, in his *pastiches* of Flaubert, Saint-Simon and others, showed that these exercises can help a writer to understand a style different from his own—and one that he admires.—A.M.

eyes dim with happiness, he turned the caresses of his responsive bow on to the great air from *Pagliacci* or from *Samson,* and one felt that under cover of these long, sustained, insistent notes, he was inwardly and securely violating the hearts of those haughty damsels, like some Julien Sorel, schooled in the Conservatoire, reading a doubtful love-tale to the proud Mathilde de la Môle. But as ten o'clock drew near, there loomed up behind the musicians several large Negroes in dinner-jackets, whom the fiddler watched with a look of anguish so affecting that, when one white-eyed giant of these blacks placed a saxophone beside the violoncello and a drum beside the viola, it seemed to me as if a really despairing and quite beautiful grief were lending its nobility to the waltz he played, which was a very antiquated pre-War favorite; for there is no music that is absolutely bad; through even the flimsiest, an impassioned player can say all that there is to say, and we ourselves are that player when, deeply stirred by some grave personal misfortune, we transfer our own distress, and thereby a genuine and affecting beauty, to the jingle of a hurdy-gurdy or the raw symphony of a wayside fair.

Precisely on the first stroke of ten o'clock, one of the Negroes, who, erect and resplendent, had been dominating this picture like the black slave standing in the foreground of Lorenzo the Magnificent's procession in the fresco of Benozzo Gozzoli, laid hold of the drumsticks, bent forward, and proclaimed with a loud, long-drawn rattle of the drum that the days of easy languid life and artlessly voluptuous phrases were over, that the fierce, streaked, mechanical hour of swift rhythms, of skyscrapers and streamline cars, had struck at last. Across the tables that throbbing rolled as the drums of mobilization had rolled over France fourteen years earlier; even in the most secluded bushy corners, its sustained, muffled energy tightened the muscles of bodies limp in the softening languors of peace, and made warrior Amazons of those pale madonnas of the luminous gloom.

"I do not disguise from myself," said M. de Norpois, "how complex are the duties of a French emissary in England. Nevertheless, he can, I think, steer his barque safely through somewhat menacing reefs provided he keep two guiding

principles in sight—the first, that he is representing France,
the second, that he is representing her in England, which
amounts to remembering, on the one hand, that he is charged
with the acceptance of our government's views by a friendly
but dissimilar nation, on the other, that he must interpret
to the former the frequently peculiar (and to a Frenchman,
most surprising) ideas of the Foreign Office. And pray note
that I say, in speaking of France, 'our government,' and in
speaking of England, 'the Foreign Office,' and not 'the
Cabinet'—no, nor even '10 Downing Street'; and I draw
this distinction of set purpose, for the permanent officials of
the Foreign Office have their own policy, one which is often
successfully opposed to that of the Cabinet."

But I was no longer listening to the ambassador, my whole
attention being absorbed by the fascinating and manifold
spectacle which the orchestra was by now presenting to
me. As soon as that prolonged kettle-drumming rattled out,
as if to give warning of the Last Judgment or the perils of
the triple somersault, the solo violinist was apparently
seized by some mortal, animal fear, rather as the flies which
a cruel, heartless keeper thrusts into the metal cage to be
devoured by the chameleon, and which, at sight of the
monster, cling vainly to the farthest corners of the walls.
Thus my violinist (who was not unlike Morel, but could
not be Morel, who would not have been playing in a restaurant), ever since observing the entrance of the Negroes, had
borne his languishing melodies away amongst the farthest
tables, even away beneath the firs of the Bois, as if hoping
that in colonies so remote from the metropolis, barely even
linked to it by far-traveling maîtres d'hôtel, he could perhaps maintain a tenderly Pucciniesque regime for yet awhile
after the wild tambourining revolution of the Pré Catelan.
But the Negroid rattling had drowned his phrases as
Santerre's drums did the voice of the dying King Louis, and
the extremity of his alarm reminded me suddenly of all
the heroes of story and legend tortured by the dawn of some
tremendous day of reckoning, of Faust or of Peter Schlemihl
at the hour when their souls are claimed by an infernal and
ruthless creditor, or of Cinderella on the night of the ball
when the twelve strokes of midnight ring out.

He stopped short and hastened over to the band, and I
imagined, seeing him lean over to the Benozzo Gozzoli Negro, that he had managed to extract a promise from his
black conquerors to let him triumph just once again, as he
came forward, blissful and triumphant, and began with an
all-too-tender stroke of his bow on *Plaisir d'amour ne dure
qu'un moment.* . . . But his pleasure was briefer even than
that of love, which is not so very short (being not, as is
supposed, the pleasure of making love, but that of experiencing it), because suddenly a little fury-faced monster
with a napkin in his hand, conjured up by the first tearful
notes, sprang upon the musician and held out his watch
with a gesture of domineering brutality. Pursued by this
monster, who was the manager, the fiddler and *Plaisir
d'amour* backed away towards a yawning doorway (that
of Hell, no doubt) which engulfed the musician, whilst the
infernal gnome, with an imperious flick of his napkin, un-
leashed the Negroes, who were joined, as I noticed with
feelings of scorn, by a traitor to white music in the person
of the violoncellist, who now became the diminutive prop
of a gigantic silver instrument from which he drew certain
discordant sounds.

"The mission with which I have been honored," said M.
de Norpois, "will be made a trifle easier for me by the
fact that France and England no longer possess either
divergent interests or common and disputed zones of influence. No French statesman nowadays has any serious
thought of reviving our claims to Egypt, still less to Canada.
As for an attack on India, that is for the moment placed in
the sphere, if not of impossibilities, at least of improbabili-
ties, both by reason of the inadequate radius of flight possessed by the machines in actual use, and by the temporary
impracticability of maintaining subsequent supplies. . . ."

But the voice of the jazz-band swamped that of the ambassador in my ears, just as for the fair Americans it had
swamped that last plaint of the violinist, and powerless to
hear anything else, I observed the strange exactness with
which it evoked the rhythm and movements of love. Admittedly, this was no fresh observation, and I recall how,
being at a concert one evening with Saint-Loup, I had

analyzed a Beethoven symphony and discovered how it moved forward through phases of repose, resumption, and torment, towards the crowning deliverance of perfect accord, as a pair of lovers toward that brief shock which will mark the simultaneous term of their pleasure and their pain, but comparing the songs of my doomed violinist with the syncopated twitchings of the Negroes, these two musics seemed to correspond with two conceptions of love, the one romantic and factitious, seeking to believe in a perfection of understanding between bodies and souls, in the unbroken classic progression of sentiments, a conception expressed in the melodic simplicity of Puccini, of Gounod, and even of Schubert, the other cynical and realist, accepting fitfulness as a law of love which it seeks amid the wailing dissonance of a unique and elsewhere undiscoverable rhythm, a doctrine transposed with stern clarity into a language of sound by the short, panting, spiteful confession of saxophone and drum.

Meanwhile, there began to roam among the tables certain dark and restless animals, their eyes seeking a prey in the darkness. They emerged thus every evening, at the hour of the violinist's withdrawal, just as the darting of bats succeeds that of the swallows, or as the tiger goes questing at nightfall. These prowling, famished beasts were the professional dancers. And I noticed that, like all carnivora they preferred their prey plump. They did not go over to those delicious, parti-colored nests of pink and green and blue girls twittering round the lake-side tables, but kept peering into the gloom of the jungle to find some quadragenarian bovine, tethered to the base of a striped parasol by a halter of large pearls. Our table was on the boundary-line between the hunting-grounds of two of their number, and when they passed close to each other I could observe a strange glance of hatred and complicity. For a long time I wondered why both their bodies seemed to incline in one direction, as if in fear of reprisal from some harsh and invisible master, a master whose hiding-place seemed to be hinted at by their deflected glances, just as the warped apples-trees on the plateau of Méséglise, all leaning towards the same quarter, serve, even in calm weather, to point the

direction of the prevalent winds, or again, just as street-
walkers, hurrying alongside the passers-by in the yellow
shadows of nocturnal streets, will reveal, by the unconscious
orientation of their anxiety, the lurking-place of the pimp
who is keeping his eye on them. And at last, by gauging the
exact angle of fear of these dancers, whom every check made
thinner and more avid, I espied, half-hidden behind a tree,
the diabolic little manager, his flapping napkin giving them
reminders of the pains of Hell and the wretchedness of
their lot, like those cruel winged spirits who mingle sometimes on the canvases of Breughel with the throng of the
living.

So deeply interested had I been by this spectacle that I
did not notice that M. de Norpois, contrary to his general
habit, had for some time been sitting silent, apparently in
expectation of a reply from me. Not knowing what he had
said to me, I asked whether he would be seeing Desmond
Farnham, the novelist, in London, and whether he had read
his books, of which I myself was fonder than of any author's
then living.

"I know Farnham's name very well," he said. "He is a
brother of Lord Shalford, and I have heard mention of him
in Rome, Vienna, Tokio, and Paris as well, for he belonged
at one time to the service and has been stationed in all these
capitals. He is, I believe, a gifted fellow, but I have not
read his novels myself, although excellent judges assure me
that they are remarkable. For my own part, I must admit, I
remain loyal to Walter Scott and Dickens, and especially to
Thackeray, who to my mind represents the essence of
the English spirit (but no doubt I ought to say 'British' for
the author of *Waverley* was a Scotsman, and you know
the strong attachment of the two races to nationalist dis-
tinctions, which nevertheless are no bar to close understanding, for the United Kingdom could not be described as a
house divided against itself, although up in Scotland in the
days when I had the honor of being invited to Balmoral by
King Edward the Seventh, I have frequently heard natives
of the Northern Kingdom, when they were going to England
speak of 'going out of the country' . . .)."

But seeing that the ambassador was again well under

way, and in no danger of stopping for a considerable time,
I passed the remainder of the evening in watching my
violinist, whom I had descried sitting gloomily behind the
jazz-leaders, like a captive king fettered in the train of a
conquering barbarian's triumph.

Although M. de Norpois had scored a great diplomatic
success in contriving to bring that evening at the Pré Catelan to a close without having invited me to pay him a visit
in London, I nevertheless made the crossing a few days
later. The name of a train on the lips of Bloch (a frequent
visitor to London, where his plays were performed with
much success) had abruptly decided me to undertake a
journey both distant and formidable in my eyes. This train
was called the "Golden Arrow," a name which evoked that
symbolic and delicious arrow of gold to which Sainte-Beuve
longed to fasten his equivocal friendships, and that Zeno,
"cruel Zeno, Zeno of Elea," whose swift, motionless arrow I
could fancy linking with its quivering, gilded streak the
sandy dunes of Calais and the white cliffs of Dover. Unable,
alas, to bring Albertine, I had persuaded Andrée to vouch-
safe me her company, and we started together from the
Gare du Nord by that splendid midday train, which, by the
central, culminating and majestic hour of its departure, set
there in the middle of the day like a royal box in the middle
of the sweep of a balcony, acquires a glamour over and
above that of the winged emblems on its long blue coaches.

There could be no doubt that this crowd on the platform
was already an English crowd, and for a long time Andrée
and I kept wondering what gave it this undeniable British
character, for men nowadays are dressed exactly alike in
every country in the world, and Englishwomen wear clothes
bought in the Rue de la Paix or the Champs-Elysées, and
yet, now in the train as later on the deck of the boat, as we
sat beside our suit-cases in the midst of a huge encampment
where squatting families watched over the tribal baggage,
whilst our tongues could feel the salt tang of the sea on our
lips, our minds, little by little absorbing these unknown
faces, were quite unmistakably tasting the flavor of England, a flavor which came partly from the types around us,
for the males of the Continent can never show those bright

pink complexions on which a white moustache stands out
pure and snowy, as the brittle, lunar peak of a lofty mountain will stand sometimes against a rosy sunset sky, and
partly too from the clothes, for although a "foreigner" can
attire himself in tweedy clothing, yet, on him, its very
informality has a touch of affectation and deliberateness,
whilst it is only on the English that this carelessness is
really unstudied, and therefore elegant. Near us on the deck
was an old lady, wearing a grey dust-coat and crowned
with an incredible hat of green tulle, who looked so lamentable a figure that Andrée, convinced that she must be on the
first-class deck by mistake, was commiseratingly awaiting
the arrival of the boat's ticket-inspector and his doubtless
gruff expulsion of the poor old beggarwoman to the steerage.
I reassured Andrée, and advised her to go over and read the
name painted in white letters on the old lady's luggage
surrounding her where she sat. A moment later Andrée
returned, slightly confused, and told me that the bags belonged to the Duchess of Surrey, who was, of course, a
cousin of the King's, and that the old lady must be a maid.
But I told her that I thought that this was the Duchess in
person, and actually it will be seen that I proved to be right
when I met her during a week-end at Lord Shalford's.

Behind us the French coast became paler and more faint,
in the same degree as the English coast ahead of us grew
sharper and more distinct, so that I seemed to be watching
some mysterious transfusion of strength, such as one can see
taking place in some of those cruel and fantastic films in
which the scientist, with his long alchemist's beard and
surgeon's overall, makes use of a living woman to animate a
statue, and one sees the beautiful body outstretched on the
table becoming limp and collapsed whilst the artificial
creature opens its eyes, comes to life, and smiles all round.
Thus it seemed as if that romantic castle, rising clearer
every instant in the white Dover cliffs, were fashioned of
the flesh and blood of the Calais watch-tower and the lighthouse of Cape Gris-Nez.

This crowd on the boat differed also from a Continental
crowd in two rather subtler characteristics, one being its
relative good-humor, not marked by any positive action,

yet apparently permeating all the social relationships of this mobile gathering. A smile came into spontaneous being on every face one met. The Pullman official, for instance, moving to and fro along the deck in his blue frock-coat, entering up the seat-reservations for the English train, did not show that combination of obsequiousness and officiousness which a like functionary on the Continent would doubtless have assumed, but was self-respecting, kindly, and yet inexorable, in his efforts to satisfy our wishes without going beyond his rights, and accepted a half-crown tip with the startled dignity of an admiral and the pleased gratitude of a poor man, and with an air which made it clear that the service in question had been rendered before any question of the half-crown had arisen, and consequently that it would have been rendered even if you had not been a gentleman and had forgotten the tip.

Thanks to him, Andrée and I were able to find ourselves in opposite seats in the train from Dover to London, with tea laid before us in blue-and-white china on which Chinese dragons were battling with Dutch windmills. And whilst we were enjoying all those details in the carriage, the clothing of the attendants, and the manner of serving tea, which struck us as different from France (for in traveling we find something acceptable in anything out of the ordinary, because, in our fundamental awareness of the vanity of these transplantations and the trifling sum of real pleasure which they bring us, we act like those shady men of business who inflate a balance-sheet by crediting worn stock and worthless plant at full value, and we place to the credit side of our journey the most minute variations of manners, be they quite insignificant in themselves—the actual debit side being so burdened with the weight of our headaches, our fatigue, our ravaged stomachs, our uprooted intestines, and with the sense of having lost a whole day, that every single item must be entered to make a balance), the train was sweeping us through stations to which we felt grateful for their being English, and for having the outward appearance thereof, for being called "Folkestone Junction" and not "Embranchement de Louviers," and for proclaiming "Mazawattee Tea" rather than "Quin-

quina Dubonnet." We were passing through small towns made up of strings of identical glazed-brick cottages, each protruding its two bow-windows which bulged into infinite distance like the lines of beautiful, athletic, and full-breasted maidens on the friezes of the Panathenæa. It was pleasing to observe that the sheep in the fields did not look like the Norman sheep, but were smaller and woollier than ours, their legs being hardly visible, which made them look like the ill-carved toys of a Swiss wood-worker, and that the trees, though of the same stuff and substance as the trees of Tansonville or Méséglise, were nevertheless planted in an English style, not in the straight lines that we know, but isolated in the midst of wide grassy fields, and were also lower and more bushy (this coming no doubt, as Andrée pointed out to me, from the nature of the soil, which does not allow the roots to plunge deep and forces the tree to expand in girth rather than height), which makes an oak, even when standing alone, look like a landscape of Gainsborough or Constable, whereas it could not possibly be an oak of Corot or Daubigny, and further, that the grass appeared to be of a closer texture than French grass, which in point of fact is quite true, as I found later when I lay on English lawns and discovered how closely this green tissue is fitted to the ground, veiling the tiniest patch of its original soil with its clipped, curving blades, rather as the vigorous, close-trimmed hair of a young soldier spreads its dark, air-tight coating over the pinkness of his scalp.

Andrée, who was an even greater enthusiast in this game of differences than myself, pointed out to me the beauty of English graveyards, sullied by no fearful erections of iron and glass, but ranging their lines of flowery graves on a carpet of mossy grass only broken, here and there, by the decorative triangular shape of an arbor vitæ or a cypress, or by the drooping tresses of a weeping-willow, a beauty which is one of the countless and touching products of that English craving to veil the seamier side of life, which is a key to the melancholy humor of Dickens and Charles Lamb, to the cheerfulness of English soldiers during the War, to the graciousness of their hospitals, and which results in there being no more instant evocation of the happiness of being alive than a nursery of lovely fair-haired children, reared on porridge and rhymes, in some great house in Belgrave Square, or than the flowery, smiling serenity of the cemetery at Folkestone.

At last it grew dark. On the outskirts of the small towns through which the train was passing, the white tennis-players grew pale like those phantasms of which Madame de Sévigné speaks in the "moonlight" letter, and beside me my English traveling companions, with dignified and disdainful deliberation, were beginning to bestir themselves. Hats coming down from racks, venerable and initialed leather suit-cases emerging from the depths of the carriage, and the bustling of the admiral of the Pullman—all told me that we were entering London. When I stepped out of the train, I saw that alongside us, on the other side of the platform, a long rank of taxis was waiting, and the fact of these vehicles, attributes of the city, being actually *inside* a station, left me as much surprised as I might have been by the entry of a motor-omnibus into a cathedral. The mixture of two elements took me aback; I felt that the French method of penning up railway-trains in the stations behind closed barriers allowed these monsters to preserve a glamour essential to our enjoyment, and retained in travel that element of mystery and the nether world which is doubtless its sole charm, and then, linking this trait with others in the British character, I discovered a fascinating symmetry in the intellectual edifice which I was raising, for railway-trains, amongst this maritime race, came in like ships alongside a quay, and it was quite natural that access to terra firma should be unrestrained; those bare-headed young men in dinner-jackets, accompanied by those girls with their fair-skinned pallor who were drawing the mauve feathery collars of evening-cloaks closer to their throats, coming to meet the ruddy-faced old general, must surely have emerged from some neighboring casino, and in my eyes Victoria Station came alive with the faintly swinging masts and all the kindly twinkling of a harbor. But when once our wits have found an explanation that strikes us as ingenious, we derive so keen a pleasure from it that we seek to carry it always a stage further, and as I crossed the narrow platform alongside which the coaches were moored, and was gliding still on the rails of the taxi, I reflected that this people is one loving in all things imperceptible transitions and open barriers. Just as the tides of the railroads pour freely into the heart of the city through those great docks that are called Victoria, Charing Cross, or Paddington, so the English aristocracy likes to plunge sometimes into the commonalty, not only mingling with the latter in its games, but also returning to it through its sons (for a great-grandson of the King himself might be plain "Mr. Windsor"), and welcoming the better plebeians without any water-tight barrier surveyed by a functionary in a peaked cap, or so, again, in English history, the monarchy assumed the form of democracy not by a bloody revolution, but without its being possible to point to any single year as that of the change, with the result that Lord So-and-So, an all-powerful nobleman, holding rights of territorial jurisdiction, having the gift of seats in the Commons in his hand, and being proprietor of four towns, is at the present day bereft of all real power, may see his own son a defeated candidate for those same seats, and yet is not left humiliated or with any feeling that a change has taken place, so, seated beside Andrée in a taxi of old-fashioned build, I found myself wafted all unawares from the peaceful shelter of the Pullman into the lurid turmoil of Buckingham Palace Road.

On arrival at the hotel, I inquired for the room I had engaged, and the porter, a small mischievous-faced fellow who looked like that old man with his nose blossoming in a huge pimple who is teaching a child his letters in one of the rooms of the Louvre, answered me with a particularly agreeable smile, but in French, which at once pleased and vexed me, for although knowing that I spoke English with a foreign accent, I was incapable of detecting that accent. Listening to Andrée, I was instantly struck by the odd turn of her English phrases, by the over-stressing and over-sibilance of her "the's," but I myself, speaking worse than she, kept thinking with every new phrase I uttered that I would suddenly, by some phonetic miracle, catch the exact sound, for we match the sounds we produce, not at all with the real sounds which an Englishman would give to the words (and which we can no longer remember), but with a sound preserved by our memory, one that is already inexact, for if it were exact, we should know English like an Englishman, which is not the case.

Next morning, after a deft and silent chamber-maid had pulled up the black paper blinds which had cut me off from the light, and brought me that sleepy morning cup of tea with which the English wash the night's burden of digestion from their tongues and cleanse their brains of the last lingering images of dream, I lost no time in calling Andrée and hurrying to the window. How delightful! From our rooms on the sixth floor we overlooked Hyde Park. As far as I could see stretched the green billows of trees, their greenery becoming more and more blue as they receded into the distance. Of London itself one saw only the misty outlines of houses on the farther bank of the Park, like those vague white towns in pictures by Turner (whom I then knew only through Ruskin, but to whom I was soon to be indebted for enjoyment as keen as those to which Swann had quickened me before Vermeer or Mantegna), which shelter the loves of Dido or Armida. When we came out into the street after breakfast we tried for a long time to find just what it was that gave this dreamlike aspect to a city which we had imagined to be entirely mercantile and maritime. Was it those red motor-buses revolving in long files round the Marble Arch, seemingly in antlike obedience to some obscure law which bade them forever follow as close as possible on each other's heels, or was it those dark policemen who seemed at one moment like Fates, their diligent fingers spinning the thread of British destinies on some invisible distaff, and at another like Spanish dancers, the outstretched left arm holding a transparent, impalpable guitar and the right twanging its single string whilst the traffic speeded before them? But no, it was neither the omnibuses nor the policemen; on the contrary, these all shared an equal appearance of solidity, metallic or carnal. Faced by this impression, I felt now, as formerly I had felt before the three trees at Tansonville, the duty of explaining it. And at last, as I came up Whitehall, I was struck by the fact that I was walking, not through a town, but through the drawing of a town, or more precisely a wash-drawing, or perhaps one of those frenzied romantic drawings in which Victor Hugo loved to heap up black and white cathedrals, in a sort of mediaeval Babel, high above walls and battlements. And this idea of a pen-and-ink drawing suddenly threw light into a whole dark tract of my consciousness. As London is a city whose air is laden with dust and fog and coal-smoke, each one of the grey houses along the street we followed was streaked with strange shadows, with gleaming white shapes which, being quite unrelated to those of the building, distorted the latter and deprived it of the aspect of a construction planned by human hands, so that these blacks and whites seemed to have been placed there by those unwitting artists of genius, chance and smoke, who had given the city this air of fantastic yet moving unreality which is only possessed by the comedies of Musset, certain dialogues of Shakespeare, and the hall of the Gare Saint-Lazare.

Towards noon I went downstairs to the apartments which the French delegation occupied in the same hotel, and had my name sent in to M. de Norpois. He received me almost immediately. "I am all the more pleased to see you," he said, "because circumstances enable me to do you a service (I say 'circumstances' and not 'my intention,' for I discovered, long before being summoned to represent France in the country where the phrase has been made proverbial, that honesty is the best policy). For I must tell you that last night I happened (a curious coincidence, on the eve of your arrival) to be dining at Lord Shalford's, and there made the acquaintance of his brother, the Desmond Farnham of whom you spoke to me and whom you are anxious to meet. I told him of your admiration for his works, and if you wish it, I can easily give you a line of introduction to him. As a matter of fact," went on M. de Norpois, "I cannot say that I care much for his novels; I have made an attempt to read them, as well as those of the other English writers you mentioned during that pleasant dinner, but I shall remain faithful, if you don't mind, to my old friends of the Victorian age, whose humor, and whose narrow, but praiseworthy, conception of life conformed in my opinion much more closely to the authentic British temperament than these new works which have been subjected to the dangerous morality (or, as I ought to say, immorality) of the Russian novelists. Since here, I have discovered the existence of a young England which would cause me much alarm on our friends' behalf, did I not feel it to be numerically weak, and powerless against the compact and vigorous bulk of traditional England. But this does not alter the fact that your friend Farnham, or, as everybody calls him here, 'Desmond,' is a delightful and courteous person."

M. de Norpois wrote a few words on a card and rose, to let me understand that he had more weighty functions to fulfil than his reception of myself; an English manservant, who looked like that admiral with a purplish complexion portrayed by Reynolds in the National Gallery, showed me out with a slightly more pronounced degree of politeness, as appropriate to someone whom the head of the delegation had received without causing him to wait. I rejoined Andrée, and found her with a lady's maid whom she had engaged by telephone during the morning, a dark little person dressed entirely in black, about forty years old, who reminded one of an engraving intended to represent in human form the ant of the fable in some illustrated volume of the Romantic period, and who doggedly answered Andrée's inquiries as to her name with the words: "Tuttle, ma'am."

"Tuttle?" said Andrée.

"Yes, ma'am—Tuttle," repeated the maid.

"Tuttle?" said Andrée.

"Tuttle," said the maid.

"I am glad to see you back again," Andrée said to me. "You know, I thought my English was fairly correct—at least my governesses kept telling me so, and you remember how when I was translating George Eliot with you I was only very seldom obliged to look up a word in the dictionary, but this woman doesn't seem to understand what I say, and answers me with a word I simply don't know."

I then explained to Andrée that in England a master and mistress invariably address a lady's maid (and likewise a butler) by her surname, a usage which strikes me as more reasonable than the French one, the relation of master to servant being of a social order, like that of captain to soldier, or judge to prisoner, and in no way of a sentimental order, as that of husband to wife or lover to mistress. And so Andrée's English maid was perfectly right in answering "Tuttle" to my friend's questioning, Tuttle being her surname.

I must say a word about this Tuttle, who was with us throughout our visit to England. During the first half-hour of life in common, Andrée and I thought her stupid, because she answered any orders given with "Yes, ma'am," replying with such extraordinary rapidity, even, as it seemed, before she could have had time to transpose the sounds of our voices into thought, but we were not long in discovering that we were mistaken, and were convinced within a few days that Tuttle was a person of admirable intelligence, gifted with a sense of organization bordering on the marvelous; for if Andrée had said to her at six in the morning, "We are leaving at noon for Constantinople, Bagdad and Calcutta. Pack the bags, take tickets, and see to the passports"— Tuttle would have answered, "Yes, ma'am," Andrée and I could have gone to sit in the lounge and read *Punch* (the subtlety and intelligence of whose comedy, for all its simplicity, delighted us both), and about half-past eleven we should have seen Tuttle appear, and Andrée would quite casually have asked her, "Is everything ready, Tuttle?" and she would have answered, "Yes, ma'am," which would be quite true, and if I had added, "Will you please order a taxi, Tuttle," she would have given me a slightly surprised and much offended look and said, turning not towards myself but to Andrée, "The taxi is at the door, ma'am," thus making it perfectly clear not only that one general order sufficed and that detailed arrangements ought to be left to her own initiative (like a good chief-of-staff, pained if the new general wants to meddle with transport lines, and giving him respectfully to understand that he knows his job), but also that she was in Andrée's service, that she was a lady's maid, and that if the gentleman saw fit to travel without a valet, he did not thereby acquire any right to turn a lady's maid into a courier. On these two points, during the whole time of her being with us, Tuttle remained as obdurate as the Duc de Saint-Simon on the question of his wife's stool, or as the Duchess de Guermantes in her resolve not to receive Madame de Cambremer. She did not refuse to perform services for me, and was admirable in the art of running the iron down a pair of trousers or in folding waistcoats in a suitcase, but she declined to take the order to carry out these functions, although in themselves they were a pleasure to her, from myself. If I did ask her for such favors, she went to see Andrée in the adjoining room, consulted her, and then, having received confirmation of an order which, as it was signed by a personage without due authority, she had been unable to take at its face value, she made ready to execute it.

I sent M. de Norpois's card to Desmond Farnham, adding quite a long letter to it, and whilst awaiting a reply, Andrée and I began our visits to the museums of London. At the Tate Gallery we spent long hours in front of the Turners. Spiraling in long whorls, the trails of white, golden and vaporous cloud floated across skies far different from those, with their rotund cloud-shapes, of Constable or Gainsborough. Strange cities, where Grecian temples mingled anachronistically with feudal keeps, seemed to soar upward into a pale mist from green unfathomed ocean-beds. Placed within the field of this wavy and distorting vision, every landscape suffered an engulfing sea-change, every city became an Atlantis peopled with swirling phantoms. Following the life of the painter along the walls by means of the dates of his pictures, I could trace his growing obsession with images of the sea and the idea of dissolution. As a young man he observed sunken boats and shipwrecked vessels, and loved to fondle the deep-green white-flecked hollows of towering waves. Then the whole universe became for him one billowy ocean. The saffron and pale-rose hollows of the valley of Orvieto softly unfurled themselves, the walls and trees took on that strange rich air of the deep-sea forests of Shakespeare, and his palace of Calypso seemed to be awaiting the bleached bones of the drowned mariners of *The Tempest*. Standing with Andrée near the entrance of that long room, I pointed out to her that, viewed from a distance, each picture seemed like a breaking wave of color, on the crest of which floated an ocean pine, one fragment of uprooted flotsam, toppling upon floods of red coral and amber. We went over to *Childe Harold's Pilgrimage;* the trees of the Italian landscape drooped on to the rocks like seaweed; a sandy beige, gripped in Rembrandtesque fashion by a yellowish light, formed a neutral background for the enamel tints, and then, in Turner's old age, the sea itself was dissolved, and the *Morning After the Deluge* became, in the eye of a floating God, no more than a whirlpool of light drawing down to itself the pale bodies of sirens.

I tried to show Andrée that landscape painters could be grouped under two heads, which, in a quite personal and in no way pedantic classification, I called the "glossy" and the "distorters," the former being the men of objective habit, whose main care is for accuracy, who concentrate on rendering the wonderful simplicity of all natural transitions, and are in painting what the Tolstoy of *War and Peace* is in literature; the "distorters," on the other hand, being the subjective minds, more concerned with a manner of seeing than with the thing seen, and, like a Renoir or a Monticelli, transmuting the visible world as a Giraudoux or a Virginia Woolf does the world of sentiment.

"Look at the Corots of the Roman Campagna," I said to Andrée "those in the Moreau Collection at the Louvre, or, if you like, at that little view of Avignon here in London, or amongst the English school, at that man I am so fond of, Richard Parkes Bonington. These are pure 'glossy' painters. Now come and see these Gainsborough landscapes, with trees like ostrich plumes; there you can just catch a beginning of the 'distorting' genius."

"Of which Turner would be the climax," said Andrée.

"You are most intelligent, Andrée dear. Yes, Turner, and also of course some of our own Impressionists. Rembrandt bequeathed them his light, as I showed you in Turner, and as I could also show you in certain Constables. But Constable is particularly interesting because he was skilled in both schools of painting. You remember the other day how we admired that small landscape in which he depicted so well the 'painted wood' aspect, the 'quilted sofa' aspect, of certain grassy downs in the limestone districts of England—just like the Italian Corots. Now, on the other hand, look at this farmyard; it has all the strange gleam, all the 'sheet silver,' of Turner. And that twofold aptitude makes me prefer Constable to Turner, just as I prefer Boudin to Monet. We must go and see the Boudins at the Tate; they are excellent, and they'll show you that Boudin, like Constable, does not harp on one string. He is 'glossy' in the manner of his painting, in the exactness of the vivid colors, so few and so well detached on the sandy uniformity of the backgrounds, but in his drawing, with its sparse, black, enchanting lines, he is a 'distort.' "

Passing without stopping (for Andrée did not like them, but I knew I should have found some pleasure, perhaps artificial, in them) through the Pre-Raphaelite rooms ("And yet, Andrée," I said, "you declare that Millais is very bad, and I certainly grant you that almost always he *is* bad, but look at that tiny picture in which a woman in a pale yellow gown is seated under a blue umbrella beside some tiny red flowers which look like Luca Signorelli's—how good that is! Now come, you are often unjust in your judgments, and even you and I, who believe we are open-minded, will be victims of a fashionable opinion."), we went over to the portrait-painters, amongst whom I was especially glad to find Reynolds again, and his Robinetta, so triangular, voluptuous, cruel, and frank.

Three days after my arrival, the hotel porter (who, although I was a guest of no importance, was very friendly towards me, because he spoke French with a very pure accent, so that I gave him an opportunity of displaying a talent, and this is a much more potent cause of good feeling than a tip) handed me a letter, the typewritten address of which presented the most astonishing appearance, its lines heaving up and down like a stormy sea, some characters being blue and others red, quite meaninglessly, and yet this untidiness and incoherence, far from offending the eye, succeeded, on the contrary, by an astonishing victory of man over keyboard, in giving that cold mechanical writing the air of intimate and privy courtesy in a handwritten address. When I opened the letter, I was stirred when I found it signed "Desmond Farnham," and read that he was inviting me to lunch that same day, at half-past one o'clock.

I did not note, when I was recounting my conversation with M. de Norpois, how greatly surprised I had been to learn that my favorite novelist was the brother of Lord Shalford. Certainly I had never cherished that prejudice, foolish enough, but widely spread amongst intelligent men, which consists in regarding talent or genius as reservations of the commoner classes, and refusing to recognize them if they appear in a man of high birth, or even in one who merely mixes in the best society (which, in the seventeenth century, would have meant denying genius to the author of the *Maximes,* and in the eighteenth to Saint-Simon), but Farnham's name, and the nature of his novels, had always led me to imagine a gentle, shrinking, solitary man, traits of character which I could not readily associate with the name of the Shalfords, famed and gallant Cavaliers in Stuart days, who for three centuries have been giving England a numerous band of ministers, generals, admirals and viceroys. Andrée, who made "Debrett" her favorite companion in the hotel reading-room, informed me that after the name of Lord Shalford, G.C.B., G.C.M.G., G.C.V.O., 9th Viscount and 15th Baron, there occurred this entry: "Brother living: Honble. Desmond Farnham . . . educated at Winchester . . . secretary of Embassy . . . Colonel . . . War, 1914-1918. . . . D.S.O." So not only was the frail and delicate author of *Tiziano Sorelli* the son of a lord temporal, but he was also a diplomat and a colonel; and yet (although Debrett, with strange shamefacedness, did not add that he was one of the great writers of our time) there could be no doubt about his identity, a revelation which forced me to a total refashioning of the image I had formed of him, just as I had to do, even more curiously, a few days later in the House of Commons, where I had asked to be taken, when a Labor member rose to question Sir Austen Chamberlain on certain points of foreign policy, and I pleasantly pictured to myself this man of the people patiently training himself in the moments he snatched from his manual toil, and poring over the map of Europe and its

history when he came up from the mine or out of the workshop. I asked my guide the name of this socialist, and he
told me without further comment that it was Arthur Ponsonby, which I accepted as quite satisfactory. Well, it happened a few days later that M. de Norpois was speaking of
King Edward VII in my presence, and saying, "It was not
easy for him to forgive Arthur Ponsonby his opposition, for
after all, as he said, Ponsonby was born in the purple." I
asked what this phrase might mean, and M. de Norpois,
looking at me with some surprise, replied, "What could it
mean, except that Arthur Ponsonby was born in Windsor
Castle?"—which gave me yet one more proof that we do not
perceive reality, but perceive what we believe to be reality,
for I had in all good faith been admiring the hereditary
features of a great aristocrat as the toil-worn face of a
worker. And when I became more familiar with them, I
took great pleasure in those complicated names of English
families, and just as Françoise at home loved repeating to
herself that the son of the Duc de Guermantes was the
Prince de Laumes, and the sons of the Duc de la Roche-
foucauld were the Duc de Liancourt and the Prince de Mar-
sillac, so I was delighted to discover that the charming Eric
Phipps, who was at the British Embassy in Paris, was descended from the Marquesses of Normanby, that the eldest
son of the Marquis of Headfort is that Earl of Bective whose
pleasure it is to do electrician's jobs (so that in many
London houses the maid will come in and announce, "Lord
Bective, ma'am, has come about the bells"), his second son
being called Lord William Taylour, and even such blended
historical and topographical information as that the Duke
of Westminster's family name is Grosvenor, and the Duke
of Bedford's, Russell.

It had been my hope to lunch alone with Desmond Farnham, but when the butler who opened the door of the small
Chelsea house to me, with tortoise-shell spectacles planted
on his very youthful features, and having at once the air of
a student of an eminent family and that of an overgrown
child (an aspect which all British butlers have in my eyes,
on account of their striped trousers, which, in conjunction
with their silk-lined coats, brings back to my mind that

costume known as "Eton," so much so that even today, after encountering him a score of times, I cannot set eyes on the venerable and almost centenarian butler of the Duchess of Surrey without thinking of a senior schoolboy), took my overcoat, I saw that other coats were already lying on the seat where he placed mine, and I gathered from his haste that I was the last arrival. For I had not yet learned that in punctuality the English are the second people in the world, the first being the Swedes, who, if they are invited for seven o'clock, arrive in a body two seconds before seven and only press the button of the door-bell at the precise moment when the hour strikes so as to enter then in a steady stream while the seven strokes are sounding, like those figures in the Strasbourg cathedral clock who emerge at noon from their gilded abode, while the English, with more indulgence, grant, if absolutely necessary, a respite of two minutes (but yet some of them do not grant that, for Lady Oxford said to me one day: "I don't wait for anybody, except the King"). I had barely time to observe as I entered the drawing room that the decoration was French, and Second Empire, for Farnham came up to me at once with a very kindly smile, whilst I murmured a few words, to which, however, he did not listen, for he was engaged in presenting me to Lady Shalford, his sister-in-law, to Lady Patricia Crawley, to Lord Shalford, his brother, who was like Sargent's portrait of Lord Ribblesdale, and to Osbert Sitwell, who looked like Sacha Guitry in his youth, a brief formality after which the conversation was resumed as if I did not exist, a conversation which it was difficult for me to follow, primarily because it was in English and extremely fast, but more especially because its theme was the life of certain mysterious beings whom I did not know, and who in any case, being mentioned only by their Christian names and even, frequently, by their nicknames, were impossible for a foreigner to identify. Lady Patricia, who had just returned from Italy, brought news from Florence:

"Aldous and his wife are flourishing; Aldous is working on a long novel. Sybil is with the Berensons. Diana is at the Lido, Tiny at Danieli's. Your father was away, Osbert. Gladys is at Siena with Mr. Wilkins, who's getting more and more like Queen Victoria; I went to their place and Mr. Wilkins met me at the station himself in his Packard."

It was plain that the very names of Mr. Wilkins and Gladys contained an inherent comicality, invisible, as it seemed, to me, but no doubt luminous to the initiate, for whenever they appeared in any sentence, everybody laughed except myself, who literally did not know what to say. I had rehearsed a few amiable remarks, quite genuine though certainly awkward, on Farnham's books and the influence they had had on my life, but I now felt that it would be not only ludicrous, but shocking and inept, to utter them, and so I could only try to ask in a whisper who Gladys might be, at which he laughed without replying, and asked Lady Patricia to explain Gladys to me.

"It's a long saga," said Lady Patricia (and I set myself the problem of deciding whether the word had been restored to fashion by Galsworthy and his Forsytes, or whether, the other way round, Galsworthy had used it because it had remained current). "How is one to begin, Desmond? Ten years ago Gladys was Gladys Weston. In those days she was a young American who, shortly before the War, took London by storm in a single night because she turned up at quite a serious party dressed in a man's jacket and with white satin trousers. Her husband was Douglas Weston, who had a good voice."

"And for whom, you remember," interrupted Lady Shalford, "she extracted some lessons from old Van Dyck, who no longer gave any to anybody, by just going and sitting on his doorstep until he agreed to receive her."

"Do you remember the little studio, Desmond?" said Lady Patricia to Farnham. "Gladys and her husband" (she went on, addressing myself) "had rented a small studio down here in Chelsea where the greatest musicians in the world used to come. You heard Cortot, Pablo Casals, Artur Rubinstein, Chaliapin. About four in the morning the music stopped, and everyone went to bed, just anyhow, on the divans covered with cushions which went right round the studio. Most of the musicians were going back by the morning boat-train, and they used to leave there straight for the station. Sometimes one would go with them. It was charming. And then the War came, and the studio was closed, and that was the end of Gladys Weston in London."

At that moment we went into lunch, and while the young Etonian with his tortoise-shell glasses passed round the caviar with such a perfect air of it being a matter of course that I really took him for a butler, Lady Patricia went on:

"In New York, apparently, the Westons went on having an amusing time. Gladys went quite mad, but really charmingly so. She used to steal the firemen's axes in Broadway theaters, and leave them in taxi-cabs, and then she would put an advertisement in the *New York Times* saying: 'Left in a taxi, fireman's axe stolen from Theater Guild. Please return to Mrs. Gladys Weston. Reward.' A fortnight afterwards she had a letter from the taximan: 'Madam—I beg pardon for not having returned the axe sooner, but I have had cramp in the stomach. If you still need it, it is at your disposal.' "

And so the saga of Gladys Weston was unfolded throughout luncheon, Lady Patricia alternating with Lady Shalford like the two parts of a Greek chorus. I was told how Weston was dead, and how Gladys had married a very rich banker, who was mentioned only by his Christian name, Edward, and how, when traveling with Edward in New Mexico, she had caught sight, through the door of the railway carriage, of an Indian who looked just like Queen Victoria, and had said to Edward, "I'm sorry, darling, but I love that Indian and I'll have to leave you." (A phrase which enabled me to suppose, though it was not said, that the Indian was Mr. Wilkins). These stories were told in a very agreeable vein of humor, and I should have found them most amusing had I not arrived at Farnham's with the absurd but persistent idea that it was my duty there to make exposition of my soul, and likewise to garner exact and fresh ideas regarding the younger English writers, with the result that I was gradually overcome by despair when I saw that an hour which I had so much looked forward to was being frittered away in chatter which, though possibly charming, was certainly pointless. For a moment the presence of Lord Shalford, who was a member of the Cabinet, led me to hope that my taste for the serious might be satisfied, and that we should at least have some talk of English politics, but he gave a long description of the state of health of two of his friends, Stanley and Austen, so that I ceased listening until, surprised at the interest Farnham showed in these medical remarks, I asked him who these two gentlemen were, and received the reply "Stanley Baldwin and Austen Chamberlain, the Prime Minister and Foreign Secretary."

But now, as I was on the very point of yielding to my despair, it turned out to be just this conversation on Sir Austen Chamberlain's illness that saved me, for Lady Shalford said:

"At last, I'm glad to say, they've managed to convince him that he must take some rest, and he's going to take a sea-voyage. I went to Hatchard's this morning to find some books for him."

"I hope, Alice," said Farnham, "that you remember my Americans?"

"Of course," she said. "I sent him *The Bridge*, the 'Willa Cather,' and *The Great American Band Wagon*."

In this way books were introduced, and for a quarter of an hour they remained on the stage, which at last enabled me, as I so eagerly wished, to hear Desmond Farnham talking of literary matters. In point of fact, he and his friends talked of them in a way quite different from that in which a French gathering of the same intellectual standing would have done. Here again, authors were referred to only by their Christian names, so that it took me some time to realize that Arnold was Arnold Bennett; Virginia, Virginia Woolf; Harold, Harold Nicolson; and Maurice, Maurice Baring; moreover, pedantry was so scrupulously avoided that one sometimes had the impression of an affectation of nonchalance and frivolity in passing judgment. Lord Shalford, in particular, a most cultivated man, tried to make one believe that he read nothing but detective stories and only went to see "mystery" plays, and when his brother recommended Gerhardi's *Futility* to him—"It will amuse you, Howard: you know such a lot about Russia"—he asked with feigned apprehensiveness, "But isn't it rather Virginia Woolfish?" Whereupon his wife said to him, "Really, you're intolerable, Howard. . . . You pretend you don't understand *Mrs. Dalloway* and you simply can't put the book down."

"Not at all, Alice! The truth is that I *try* to understand because I'm jealous of your high-brow friends. . . . It's perfectly true, Patricia, Alice is terribly high-brow, you know. . . . She is quite ashamed of me in front of you, Sitwell, or in front of M. Jean Cocteau when he comes to see us at Antibes."

"Oh, Howard. . . . How *can* you say I'm high-brow? Why, I'm simply terrified when I do happen to find myself amongst a Bloomsbury set!"

During my stay in England I was very often to hear the two expressions which had just taken me by surprise (I mean "high-brow" and "Bloomsbury"), and although their meanings were outwardly very different, the former indicating a physiognomical trait and the latter a district in London, yet in point of fact they were both applied to one particular group whose aesthetic and literary judgments were regarded as important, consummate, not to say extreme, by the very people who spoke of them ironically, for, like those saints whose virtues touched the hidden hearts of the agnostic patricians who sent them to the torture, the aloof and subtle critics of Bloomsbury perturbed these English spirits who were the most hostile to their tastes, leading them to voice their glorying incomprehension with a vigor the very excess of which was an immediate pointer to its weakness. The timidity of the all-powerful Lord Shalford, a secretary of State, in the face of this group was not feigned, for a few weeks later I saw him reduced to speechless uneasiness when confronted by an old lady living in a thatched cottage near Cambridge, who had written a book on John Donne which had been praised by Bloomsbury, so that really it is a great mistake to say, as people will, that the intellectuals in England have not the same status as they have in France. True, they have not, and would not wish for, the same position in society, but by the very fact of this detachment they maintain the unimpaired luster and the consecrated character which are the only fitting attributes of intellectuals.

Greatly pleased by Lord Shalford's ingenuousness, whether feigned or actual, I maneuvered myself into closer proximity to him, and asked him whether, as he was the Air Minister, he had had occasion to meet M. de Norpois in the course of the recent negotiations.

"Yes," he replied. "And I feel a certain admiration for M. de Norpois as one who, unlike so many European statesmen, is no slave to formulas. It is to America, and in a more general way, to the popular Press, that we owe the dangerous habit of the 'slogan,' the telling phrase, on which a minister imagines he can construct both a program and a platform, and of which he merely becomes the servant. Your friend Norpois certainly has a taste for formulas, but he likes them multiple and contradictory, and this leaves them for the most part innocuous. If he is not altogether my diplomatic ideal, that is only because he is too perfect a diplomat, a quality which inspires a certain distrust in one who has to deal with him. I have always felt that the best negotiators are men like Mr. Balfour, who will pursue a conversation with unwavering precision, but will always keep an air of being lost in some erudite reverie or of making a mental translation of a Greek poet, or else, in a different but equally effective style, men like Lord Derby, whose joviality and, as you call it in France, *'l'air bon enfant,'* preclude any lurking Machiavellism."

Now, obviously, nothing could have been more likely to interest me than these observations of Lord Shalford's, and I should have enjoyed them keenly had I not received the impression whilst we were talking, that he was inexorably eyeing the light-colored uppers of my boots, uppers for which I was not really responsible, as my bootmaker had persuaded me before I left that these kid uppers were fashionable in England, and I now noticed, not only that I was alone in advertising my lower extremities with this startling conspicuousness, but even that everybody else's were extremely old, and Lord Shalford's indeed almost in holes. Now this indifference to elegance, this loyalty to things old, struck me as admirable virtues, contrasted with which the insolent newness of my almost white uppers struck me as ostentatious and damnable. I was conscious that nothing accorded less with my character than a desire to attract attention by such means, that, on the contrary, I had ordered these hateful boots through a craving for conformity and simply because of my bootmaker's remarks, but of this Farnham and his friends knew nothing, and, thinking that they would doubtless judge me by this detail and by a few awkward words which had not (my English being only middling) exactly conveyed my thoughts, I felt desperate. But just when I was painfully and clumsily taking leave, convinced that I must have left a very bad impression on these Englishmen and that they would not invite me again, Farnham suddenly asked me, with a great deal of kindly concern, what I proposed to do in England. I told him it was my intention to remain for a few weeks so as to see the English countryside.

"A good idea," said Lord Shalford. "You ought to come and stay somewhere near me, in Surrey. . . . Look, there is a beautiful house that has just been turned into an hotel by an old friend of mine, Major Low. . . . You know Ashby Hall, Desmond?"

"A capital idea," said Farnham. "That's it—he must go to Ashby Hall, and as we're all going to Bosworth, my brother's place, next week, we can be neighbors"—turning towards myself with these last words.

And with the sudden discovery of this extreme kindness, this determination to be pleasant to me, amongst people whom I thought I had shocked, not to say disgusted, I felt such a surge of inward happiness that I now saw them as the most interesting and charming group of people I had ever before known, and when I returned to the hotel I sang their praises to Andrée with fondness and vehemence.

"You know," I said to her, "I think they're right. We ought to go and stay near them. I should greatly like to see one of these great English houses, and it will be very pleasant to have the Shalfords as neighbors. I shall try to get an invitation for you too, and in any case we shall be able to take lots of walks together, for Ashby Hall is in splendid country. What we must do is to hire a car for the time of our stay, and we can send Tuttle by rail with the trunks. . . ."

Andrée called Tuttle, who was of course in the next room, for she never moved far away and when not working for Andrée remained reading *Home Chat*. Tuttle gave us a look of authority, self-effacement, and dignity, and a-waited Andrée's orders.

"Tuttle," I said (and for an instant she turned a surprised head in my direction, then fixed it again towards Andrée, judging, I suppose, that although she could not, alas, sup-press me, still the sounds emanating from me would then, by refraction from Andrée, reach her from a proper direction). "Tuttle, we are going to stay at Ashby Hall. It is a country hotel lying between Guildford and Dorking. I don't know which station is the nearer. . . . You are to go there with the luggage. We shall go by car, but we shall have to find a chauffeur. I know that this is all rather complicated. . . . If you fetch me a time-table, I shall tell you the time of your train. As for the car . . ."

Here Tuttle stopped me, gently and firmly.

"If you will just tell me, ma'am," she said in a tone of polite reproach, "what time you wish the car to be at the hotel, and what time I ought to meet you with the luggage at Ashby Hall . . .?"

And sure enough, at the appointed time, in front of the door of the Hyde Park Hotel, we found a car driven by a French chauffeur whom Tuttle had somehow or other dis-covered in London within an hour or two, and when we arrived at Guildford that evening, we likewise found Tuttle, there in Andrée's room, having already unpacked our trunks, and seemingly having spent all her life in this house, and yet being ready to leave it without any regrets at five minutes' notice.

The hotel Lord Shalford had told us about was an old red-brick manor-house, which Farnham had told me was beautiful and not unlike Ham House, where Lord Dysart lived, but for the first few days I could not succeed in grasping this beauty, which, for all I could see, was no more than that of any other brick house; for our aesthetic pleasures are built up of unconscious comparisons with examples we have already encountered and recorded, and just as during the first days of a sojourn amongst Negroes or Eskimos, all the women seem to our eyes ugly until the moment when a certain picture of the norm of the Negress or the female Eskimo enriches us with that seemingly eternal idea, in the light of which alone we are able to view objects, so for several days Andrée and I were always surprised to read in the guide-book, "Note at *Dunsfold* the Clock Hotel, one of the finest Georgian houses in England," and then to see a quite ordinary house, its porch, with a triangular pediment, resting on twin white pillars, while its red façade was relieved at the top by a narrow band of stone with only a trace of carving. Well, a week later we were both in love with this supremely simple architecture, delighting to draw each other's attention to the exactness of the proportions, to the perfect grace of this or that sash-window, to the fanlight surmounting a doorway, or to the color of a brick here and there, its half-vitrified red recalling the glowing warmth of some Egyptian jewel.

Round Ashby Hall spread a broad, mown lawn, its tightly stretched carpet seeming to be nailed down right against the walls of the house, and ornamented by four immemorial yews clipped in the form of gigantic bowls, the insides of which seemed as if they might have formed as it were a darkened rest-room, had not the eye distinguished the monstrous network of their thick twisting stems, the foul framework on which that luxurious, almost insubstantial, shell of bosky green was stretched. Beyond a white rail lay wide meadows with a stream flowing through them, and these, being as free and untamed as the lawn was trim and clipped, made a pleasing contrast with the latter. This wide stretch of land was doubtless marshy, for the grass covering it had the shaggy, wavelike, and almost aqueous appearance of water-plants, a sea of rushes and tall swordlike stems whose tide, when the wind stirred its yielding surface, beat against the strong, solid breakwater of the lawn. A few miles from Ashby Hall rose the high hills of Hindhead, covered with yellow furze and with heather, the dead colors of which I liked, the crackling rosy purple and dull green, that aspect of being at once dead wood and flowered beds which invested these heaths (as those in Scotland) with a subtle and mysterious charm. Farther on, the road ran

through a small town, old and flowery; a black clock-face
with gilt numerals jutted out, slightly askew, over the High
Street; the white inn with its black beams still bore the
same name as in the days when the Portsmouth coach came
cantering in beneath its archway with the postboy cracking
his whip. The little grey-stone houses, with their twin
bulging windows, had kept their lattice-panes cross-hatched
with lead. Andrée was surprised to notice how the old
house-fronts blended decorously with those standardized
shop-fronts which seem in England like the *leitmotiven* of
urban life, the red pediment, flat yet noisy, of Woolworth's,
the rounded, multiple and very unpharmaceutic window of
Boot's, and the glazed tile strip of W. H. Smith & Son's,
Booksellers, but I tried to show her that the peculiar genius
of England lies in her incorporation of a quite modern life
within an antique setting, and that a small town like Guild-.
ford is a very close image of the mind of a young Englishman as shaped by Oxford and Cambridge, for that mind, like
the charming houses of this steeply pitched High Street, will
be found to contain a timbered building of the sixteenth or
seventeenth century occupied by an intellectual Boot's or
Woolworth (say Freud, or Einstein, Ltd.), a character
which makes the English High Street very different from
the American Main Street, because in the latter neither the
intellectual nor commercial branch-shops have found a pre-
existing and picturesque framework waiting for them to
step into, and are left to provide their own background,
modern, still and monotonous.

To Andrée and myself, who had both been devoted to
English history and English literature, nothing was more
moving than to be here, suddenly, in the very places where
that history had been enacted, those books and poems written. At first I thought we should be disappointed, for I
have noted elsewhere that names, and especially place-
names, are fraught by ourselves before any actual contact
with certain images of great beauty which represent their
essential content, and that reality is often powerless to
surpass or even to match these. But we quickly realized that
this is not so with England, the beauty of whose poetry,
humanity, and woodland, remains tangled enough to shelter

the dreams of her poets. Looking at the map, I saw myself ringed in by names which I wreathed with wondrous, if perhaps deceptive, visions. Eton, which I pictured as girt by those fields on which Waterloo had been won and Shelley's boyhood lost; Winchester, which I would have sterner and still more aristocratic; Marlborough, which I mistakenly associated with the Duke and Queen Anne; Bath, whose Roman and Georgian renown evoked the fair Miss Linley, and the graver beauty of Mrs. Siddons; but what was true of the names of towns was still more true of proper names, for when, thanks to Lord Shalford (a telephone message on the day after my arrival at Ashby Hall invited me to take tea over at Bosworth), I was able to meet under his roof some of the bearers of those names so dear to me, I could not help painting in behind each of those faces a background which recalled the history of its family. The soft, dazzling beauty of Lady Diana Cooper, when I learned that she was the granddaughter of John Manners, stood out to my eyes against the glowing mirage of Belvoir Castle, in the fine features of Lord Lytton I pleased myself with the fancy that I was beholding the very author of *Pelham*, and in the face of Lord Shalford himself, the charming, tender, poetic traits of the friend of Charles I.

Because of a certain smoothness, amounting almost to softness, which infused their ease of manner, their courtesy, the surface calm of their faces, a smoothness that inevitably reminded me of their springy, well-trimmed turf, I had been tempted at first to regard these Englishmen as blissful and insensitive. But little by little, as I came to know them better, as much by my personal observations as by the stories of Desmond Farnham, with whom I had reached terms of intimacy, I discovered that the tranquil tone of their voices was capable of masking the same passions and sufferings that stir other men; thus, Lord Shalford really did feel shy before his wife's high-brow friends, and Desmond, telling me of the veiled loves of a friend of his, described how this man's jealousy reached such a pitch that when a clumsy hostess, at a river-party on the Thames, did not allot him a place in the same boat as the woman he was fond of, he jumped into the water in evening-dress to rejoin this lady (which confirmed Stendhal's theory, for no Frenchman, from sheer pride, would have done such a thing), the difference between the English and my Continental friends residing in the fact that these dramas, for all their violence, left no trace on their pink cheeks or in their blue eyes, but were enacted on a different plane, far removed from the observer and yet coinciding with the perfectly tranquil presence of the hero himself, rather like those secondary pictures which a cinematographer will sometimes throw upon the screen simultaneously with the principal picture, to evoke a memory or suggest a comparison.

One evening (we had been staying at Ashby Hall for about a fortnight) I was struck on my way back there by a curious and quite powerful sensation which I recognized as that of wonted habitude. For the first time since being in England I seemed to be "coming home," and on analyzing this impression I found that it arose from my memory having gradually recorded, exactly and infallibly, the pictures which made up the Ashby road and the park surrounding our house. I now knew, when I saw a certain white rail beside which stood a cottage of grey stone with its windows framed with lead strips, that a hundred yards farther would bring me to the beginning of a long alley of lime-trees, and sure enough, one minute later, the real alley of limes actually arrived and set itself with scrupulous accuracy over the one already outlined in my mind, this evoking in its turn a clump of three oaks, a dark curtain of yews, a rose-garden, and once again the three oaks, the somber yews and the vivid roses of nature came and played themselves in the concave matrix which, graven within me by an artist of marvelous accuracy, was awaiting them. Now the sentiment of "home" is nothing else than this coinciding of our expectancy with reality (an impression that is agreeable because in all of us, as a legacy from the long centuries of terror when the universe, a monster with unknowable reactions, made men afraid, there survives a taste for whatever is fixed and familiar), and it had needed only a fortnight for this impression to become as powerful to me in this foreign land as it might have been at Combray, or later at the Hotel at Balbec. And so, reflecting that what was true of places was true no less of persons, that now Desmond Farnham as once Bergotte, now Lord Shalford as once the Duc de Guermantes, were becoming in my eyes straightforward characters whose reactions, whose ideas, nay whose very answers, I could foresee, discovering also that, if I let myself go, Lady Patricia would soon inspire in me those sentiments which I had formerly owed (different though they were) to Gilberte, then to Albertine or the Duchesse de Guermantes, I realized yet once more that our sentiments are independent of the objects that give them birth, and that we carry with us to new places and even into new countries, certain possibilities of emotion which all, sooner or later, find in our environment their means of satisfaction, a reflection which might well have led me also to question the worth of national sentiments if, after seeking in my new life the sentimental equivalents of all the elements in my past life, and after finding, as I said just now, Ashby Hall for Combray, Farnham for Bergotte, and Shalford Abbey for the Guermantes mansion, I had not noted that after the experiment, at the very bottom of the retort, there remained a sort of indescribable residue, slight but irreducible, and such that not all my efforts could produce an English substance with which it had any affinity, a residue that seemed to me unsatisfied, almost plaintive, powerless to achieve a stable compound with anything in my present environment, and which, by its microscopic presence (just as some slight aberration in the orbit of a planet, constant, vexatious, and inexplicable by any mathematical error, is proof to the astronomer of the existence of some invisible heavenly body) made me continually aware of the presence, the distant, veiled, silent, and yet unmistakable presence, of France.

IF LOUIS XVI HAD HAD AN
ATOM OF FIRMNESS

(Translated by Hamish Miles)

THE illustrious Historian to whom, Gentlemen, we are today offering our last, mournful tribute, understood more fully than any of his predecessors the formation of contemporary France. In that great work of his, so justly crowned as a classic, *The Remoter Consequences of the Revolution,* he showed how modern Europe was entirely shaped by the men of 1789. "An accurate scholar no less than a philosopher. . . ."

But in the coffin, draped with its black pall, on which the undertaker's men had laid an Academician's sword and a cushion covered with decorations, there remained neither scholar nor philosopher to hearken to the ministerial panegyric. For two days past the soul of the aged Historian had been soaring through the empyrean toward the Paradise of Honest Men, and had just arrived, far, far from that muddy cemetery where the rain was drenching his colleagues, in the Historians' Heaven. For the paradise of scholars, as one could well foresee, is to carry their researches forward through all eternity, in a sphere where all documents are accessible, all sources reliable, all witnesses available.

Within the first few minutes the Historian had thrown new light on three problems which had vexed his conscience during his worldly existence, and the celestial blessings seemed more gracious even than the poets and psalmists had described them. He was wandering now through the infinite rooms of the Archives of Eternity. How delightful it was going to be, to fly down those long cloudy corridors, right

421

to the places where the infinitely complete records of the pre-Cretan civilizations, of primitive China, of Atlantis, were preserved by learned, if myopic, angels!

But just then, as the soul of the Historian was blissfully gliding amid the nebulous files, he suddenly found himself confronted by three tall pillars of cloud, forming as it were the peristyle of another Heaven. These columns upheld a pediment on which was inscribed, in letters of fire, "ARCHIVES OF UNREALIZED POSSIBILITIES." And before the door stood a youthful Archangel, leaning on a flaming sword.

"Excuse me," said the Historian, approaching. . . . "I am quite a newcomer here, and I dare say my question is absurd. But how can there possibly be Archives of 'unrealized' possibilities? Things that haven't happened can't leave traces, can they?"

"O human presumption!" said the Archangel. "Every thought that traverses the mind of God partakes *ipso facto* of a manner of existence no less real than that which you, mankind, ascertain through your five poor senses. . . . There is no privileged Past. . . . There is an infinitude of Pasts, all equally valid. . . . At each and every instant of Time, however brief you suppose it, the line of events forks like the stem of a tree putting forth twin branches. . . . One of these branches represents the sequence of facts as you, poor mortal, knew it; and the other represents what History would have become if one single detail had been other than it was. . . . These infinite branchings make up the Unrealized Possibilities, and I am here as their Curator.. . . Do you understand?"

"Not altogether," said the Historian shyly, for here in Heaven he remained the same scrupulous, ingenuous scholar that he had been on earth. . . . "Not altogether; for if all Possibilities have the same validity, why bestow the title of 'real' on the one which *I* have lived, and that of 'unrealized' on these others which, you say, are equally valid?"

"Because," said the Archangel, "this is *your* Heaven. . . . Paradise is individual."

"What! These endless palaces, those countless archives, this multitude of angels—have they truly been created only for myself?"

"O man of little faith," said the Archangel, "to the Lord God an infinity of infinite creations is not so much as an eddy in eternity. . . . Would it give you any pleasure to step inside?"

The Historian followed the Archangel. Rows of volumes, bound in a glassy and flexible substance, stretched away as far as the eye could see. All their titles began with the word *If.* . . . Swiftly the Archangel winged his way from room to room. At last he stopped.

"Here we are," he said, "in the *'If France. . . .'* library. . . . I think it might interest you."

Already the Historian was feverishly scanning the shelves. *If Dagobert . . . If the Battle of Châlons . . .* And unknown names took him by surprise. . . . *If Jacques, peasant of the Brie. . . . If Pierre, townsman of Darnétal near Rouen. . . .* But he hurried on, for he was seeking "his" period, that of the French Revolution, to which he had devoted that earthly life of his which now looked like the skimming of a dayfly, and yet had been so packed with toil, enthusiasms, and disappointments. . . . *If the Fronde had been victorious. . . . If Louix XIV had married Marie de Mancini. . . .* He was getting nearer. Suddenly he seized a volume: *"If Louis XVI had had an atom of firmness. . . ."* he murmured.

Gently the Archangel took the beautiful book from his hands, and carried it over to the outspread wings of an eagle in the center of the cloudy room.

"Reign of Louis XVI, 1774-1820. . . ." read the Historian. "1820?" he said with surprise.

"1820," replied the Archangel, decisively.

And soon the Historian was so completely absorbed by his reading that he forgot the celestial librarian who stood there beside him, turning the pages with the point of his sword.

.   .   .   .

REIGN OF LOUIS XVI, 1774-1820

The King and Queen

The youthful King who mounted the throne of France in May 1774 at first roused grave fears amongst thoughtful men. It was a dangerous epoch. An excessive trustfulness in human nature and a completely abstract philosophy had given birth to an infinity of hopes. Emerging from an unhappy reign, France viewed the change with high expectations. A sovereign, however excellent, was faced with the risk of causing disappointment or dislike. The inexperience of a man of twenty was all the more to be dreaded at a time when the state of affairs would demand a full measure of prudence and maturity. Now, Louis XVI was believed to be a man of but middling parts; it was feared that his character, like that of his father, the Dauphin, would prove to be weak and indecisive. But it was soon realized that he was of greater worth than that prince. True, his intelligence was not particularly lively, and he was incapable of sustained application to business. But he had qualities which, if not brilliant, were solid. In an age of the chimerical and the nebulous, he gave token of a slightly vulgar good sense, and a healthy distrust of mankind. A foe to ostentatiousness, and ever ready to cut down expense, he was remarkable for his early display of a firmness that touched the bounds of obstinacy. His life, more than any other sovereign's, gave proof that, in politics, character counts far more than intelligence; for this mediocre king, simply by dint of stubborn will, restored the monarchy to a rank and brilliance which it had not known even during the preceding century.

Queen Marie Antoinette was lovable, but ill suited to reign over France. She was only nineteen, and flaws were found in her which, though harmless enough in any pretty woman of that age who had not happened to be queen, certainly left a harmful impression when seen in a princess who lived under the scrutiny of a whole race. She was giddy, and a coquette, and, although good at heart, seemed to have thoughts only for pleasure. The truth was that, although she respected the King, she did not love him, and like many young women she sought to lose herself so as to forget the fact of her unhappiness. Dependent on her companions in pleasure, she gave them all her devotion. Had it not been for this coterie of Vaudreuils, Besenvals, and Adhémars, she would doubtless never have meddled in politics. But pushed forward by them she quickly sought to aid their friends and exclude their enemies, with no thought for the interests of a country that was not her own. There was good reason to fear that, with no evil intent and even with a manifest generosity, she might jeopardize the monarchy by the entirely capricious influence which she was capable of exerting over her husband, and by a horror of ceremonies which was blameworthy in a country where they had always been loved, and where they are always demanded of its governors.

State of France in 1774.

The youthfulness of the royal couple was the more disquieting as the plight of the kingdom was not without difficulties. The dangerous and the reassuring elements in that situation should here be indicated.

(a) Unfavorable factors. Faulty administration at the close of the preceding reign had left the finances in a state of embarrassment. Taxation, however, produced a trifling total when one bears in mind the population, and compares that total with the sums which were later raised in the nineteenth, and particularly in the twentieth, centuries. England during that same period, with a smaller population, supported a budget far higher than that of France. But the methods of tax collection in France were hateful. So great was the number of privileged persons (nobles, priests, and bourgeois in the towns), that the persons actually liable to pay taxes represented only a trifling section of the country, and that section the poorest. Many towns paid lump sums, which amounted really to very little. The *corvée,* or tax in kind for the upkeep of roads, diverted farmers from their work, and tribute was paid all the more unwillingly as the state expenditure seemed unproductive. In 1774 the total expenditure of the budget was two hundred and twenty

millions, sixty-two of which were for war, twenty-eight for the Navy, and thirty-three for the King's Household. The receipts, after deducting interests on debts, were only two hundred millions, the balance presenting therefore a deficit. The perfervid admirers of England, at that time numerous in France, observed that the Civil List in that country gave the King only twenty-three millions, and that he also still paid the administration of Foreign Affairs. The financial system thus seemed to be contrived to create the maximum of discontent for the minimum of result.

In many parts of the countryside, poverty was making itself felt. Towards the middle of the eighteenth century the peasantry had acquired the land because the nobility were falling into debt. It now seemed as if the exchequer would gradually despoil them of their property, whilst the *corvée* would prevent them from tilling it. So little did the soil yield, that even in this naturally rich country famine was endemic, and was made harder to fight because the transportation of grain was not free within the boundaries of the kingdom. Bread-riots broke out yearly at one point or another of the territory. Many enlightened landlords, such as the Marquis de Mirabeau, observed that these poor folk could not go on being starved with impunity. In an unhappy country, aware of being badly administered, and where at the same time minds were being stirred by thinkers of extreme freedom and extreme boldness, the spectacle of a gay and extravagant Court, of a young Queen as useless as she was capricious, might well bring grave developments in its train.

(*b*) *Favorable factors.* These fortunately were very numerous. The small importance of the deficit should first be noted. As we have seen, it amounted to twenty millions a year, that is to say, one franc per head of the population. It did not seem very hard for an able financial minister, ready to economize on some useless expenditure, to wipe it out. Still less hard when it is added that France in 1774 was a rich country. Poverty could be seen in rural districts and among the lower orders in the towns, but the middle class had become wealthy. Financiers and those who had lent money to the State had made vast fortunes at the expense of the public finances. The new buildings in Paris and the large towns bore witness to the wealth of a whole class. At no time have so many fine mansions been built. And even as regards the peasants, the distress of some among them should not lead one to a conclusion of universal misery. Trickery had often been efficacious against the tax collector. "The large amount of manufacture, the tone of fashion set in all parts of Europe, and the flood of money circulating within the kingdom, showed that France was still sturdy."

Abroad, the King of France, arbiter of the quarrels of Austria and Prussia, remained the most powerful of sovereigns. At home, the monarchy was still not only respected, but regarded as the only possible form of government. The King was law incarnate; none had thoughts of any possibility of dispensing with him. The people, when quickened into anger against the privileged, were always ready to have recourse to the King who had formerly established his power by his championship of the Third Estate against the Nobility and Clergy. As for the expenses with which the Court was blamed, these really resolved themselves into sums so trifling that their pruning seemed easy. Certain expenses of the Queen's which infuriated the Parisian pamphleteers were only matters of ten or twenty louis. Ill-timed talk did more harm than the gravity of the facts. Thus, grounds for despairing of the future seemed small, means for maintaining the monarchy seemed simple and ready to hand, and there was good reason to think that with a little firmness the young King would have no trouble in restoring his throne to the position it had enjoyed in the time of King Louis XIV.

The Maurepas Ministry. M. Turgot

The reign of Louis XVI opened with two decisions, one of them hotly criticized, the other praised to the skies, and both justified by the outcome of events. The first was the entrusting of the ministry to M. de Maurepas. This step was distasteful to public opinion, which was disappointed, at a moment when it desired bold and youthful policy, to see the return of a minister of seventy-three, reared in the traditions of the former Court, trained in the school of intrigue, expert in cabals, and whose mind was subtle rather than generous. It turned out that just such a sceptic was indispensable to guide through the snares of Versailles the first steps of a man of very different character, who proved to be the instrument of salvation.

M. Turgot's career had followed the line most apt in the formation of a minister, but one that is only too seldom followed by those who destine themselves for these responsibilities. They think to obtain them more speedily by the arts of flattery and ingratiation. M. Turgot had not sought high place, but had prepared himself for it most admirably by a provincial administration. Nothing enables a man better to study the general needs of a kingdom than a thorough knowledge of one of its parts. M. Turgot, appointed as *intendant* of the province of Limousin, voluntarily spent thirteen years in the post. There he had studied the bad system of tax collection, the causes of popular discontent, and there he had succeeded in lightening the burden of the *corvée,* constructing fine roads, and suppressing famine. He had thus earned amongst enlightened minds a high reputation for work and integrity.

It was a notable sign of good intention, in the young King and in his advisers, that such a man should have been summoned from Limousin to undertake, first, the Naval Ministry, and then the supreme control of Finances. No intrigue had been at work. A few men who knew and admired Turgot, in particular the Abbé de Véri, spoke of him to M. de Maurepas, who in his turn spoke of him to the King. Naturally enough, so young a prince was moved at having to start his new career by dismissing the Abbé Terray, who had hitherto been administering the exchequer. M. de Maurepas bluntly hustled the King.

"You always told me, Sire, that you wished to have an honest minister. Is yours honest? If he is not, change him."

"You are right," said the King. "But I did not dare. I still have only four months behind me, and they have accustomed me to feel afraid whenever I speak to a minister. But I clearly feel that I must show decision if I am to put the country in order. M. Turgot is to have the exchequer."

When the choice was known, the Abbé Terray's cabal

strove hard to intrigue round the King, but the only answer he vouchsafed to anyone who tried to mention the matter was: "M. Turgot is to have the exchequer"—and not a word would he add. The same evening the King received the new minister in audience, and gave him his word of honor to accept his views and support him in all the bold measures he would have to take.

.   .   .   .

"But this is almost true," said the Historian, raising his eyes to his companion.

"True?" said the Archangel. "What mean you by that word? One of the data in the problem, the character of the King, has been changed. . . . The moment approaches when hypothetical history branches off from human history. . . . Read the title of the next paragraph."

"*Refusal to summon the Parlements,*" read the Historian. "*Refusal* . . . But Louis XVI, alas, agreed to summon the Parlements."

"Exactly," said the Archangel. "Read on."

And the Historian bent lower over the luminous volume.

.   .   .   .

Refusal to summon the Parlements

The opportunity arrived for the King to keep his word, sooner perhaps than those who had given him M. Turgot would have wished. The Parlements, as we know, had been dispersed by Louis XV in 1771, one of the few reasonable measures of the last reign. These Parlements had all the authority of a popular chamber without being, like the latter, representative. By refusing to register an edict, they wielded a genuine right of veto which could only be raised by the vexatious ceremony of the Lit de Justice. The opposition of these bodies, their insolence and pretensions, made all government in France impossible. To summon them again would have been a fatal error for the monarchy.

Yet from several directions efforts were made to extract this decision from the King. M. de Maurepas himself, springing, like his wife, from an old parliamentary family, was anxious for it. The Choiseul party, that is to say the Queen, the Comte d'Artois, the Prince de Conti, and almost all the nobility, were intriguing in favor of the Parlements. Even the bourgeoisie and the populace of Paris, through some strange ignorance of their true interests, were willing to regard the Parlements as defenders of public liberties.

Turgot, and many of his philosopher friends along with him, had a better discernment of the true interests of France and the paths of liberty, which lay beneath deceptive appearances. M. de Maurepas, M. de Miromesnil, M. de Sartines, all had frequent consultations on this subject with the King, in the course of which M. Turgot uttered the famous phrase—"Sire, give me five years of despotism and France will be free." He showed that the return of the Parlements would make impossible all the legal reforms which he was then engaged in preparing, for these fellows held the selfsame opinions as in the fourteenth century, were puffed up with a pride that matched their ignorance, and were foes to all enlightenment. In these circumstances M. Turgot finally displayed all the obstinacy which was supposed to be in his character, and carried the day in spite of M. de Maurepas, the King taking upon himself the responsibility of the refusal. This was in September 1774.

The Parisian populace, stirred up, it is said, by emissaries of the Prince de Conti, attempted to give a triumphal escort to some of the former magistrates who had ventured, on the rumor of their recall, to return unbidden from their exile. This rising, which was dubbed "The Cat's Fur War," was suppressed with some difficulty, and ought to have given instant warning of the need for reforming the police of Paris; but graver happenings were needed before this was taken into consideration.

Turgot's Reforms. Successes and Difficulties

Now that his hands were freed from the Parlements it seemed to M. Turgot that his first objective should be a revolution in the system of taxation. He could see no means of quelling the universal discontent other than the abolition of privileges and the submission of Nobility and Clergy to taxation. As he said to the Council, "The expenditure of the Government being in the interests of everybody, everybody ought to contribute thereto." This, as may be imagined, was not accepted without a struggle. Miromesnil, Keeper of the Seals, sought to answer that, although this principle was admittedly just, a prejudice to the contrary existed and would be difficult to overcome. Turgot retorted that the notion of fiscal privileges was abandoned by all enlightened minds, even among the privileged orders themselves.

Supported this time by the King and by M. de Maurepas, he first of all suppressed the *corvée* (1776), and then, as will shortly be seen, all exemptions from taxation (1780). He had even prepared a project for the suppression of the tithe levied for the benefit of the Clergy, and sought to replace it by life pensions to the actual beneficiaries, and, subsequently, by the voluntary offerings of the individual citizen paying his own minister of religion. But this separation of Church and State came as a shock to the King and the party of the devout. On this point M. Turgot felt so strong an opposition that he did not press it. (This reform, of course, was only effected a hundred and twenty years later, under King Louis XXI, by the chancellor Aristide Briand.)

Turgot likewise had already had the utmost trouble in defending his other measures. His restoration of order into finance was displeasing to all who had previously been profiting from its confusion. Bankers who had grown accustomed to the issue of loans to the royal treasury at usurious rates of interest were furious when they saw M. de Vesnes, the chief clerk, finding loans at four per cent. The Dutch bankers, considering that France was now properly administrated, took confidence and, unasked, made an offer of money at three and a half per cent. The day could be seen approaching when, by enlarging the radius of taxation and by pruning expenditure in the Royal Household and the war services, the exchequer would be able to pay cash, and even to repay the funds.

The financiers were thus losing one of the safest sources of their revenues, and opened a veiled war against Turgot; not daring to attack him themselves, they sowed a crop of false rumors regarding him in the fertile credulity of the Parisian populace. From 1776 onwards the privileged classes, enraged at finding themselves taxed like the common herd, joined hands with the financiers in this enterprise. They found the credulity of the public increased by recent bad harvests and a scarcity of bread in several cities. From that it was but a step to lay the blame on the new edicts, and the opposition were quick to take it. A petty rising in Paris had to be suppressed. The King appeared there in person, and gave proof of considerable courage. To M. de Maurepas's compliments thereon, he merely replied, "Why should I be afraid of them?"

There was proof that the rioters had been suborned. Those were the days when the Duc d'Orléans could say: "You can have a rising for twenty-five louis." These events all pointed yet again to the need for a reorganization of the police, which was then in such a sorry state that a criminal found himself safe merely by putting a few leagues between himself and Paris. The chief of police and the Maréchal de Biron (both guilty of weakness in this "flour war") were dismissed, and one of the first uses made by Turgot of the economies which he effected was to set up the civil police of Paris which later rendered such great services.

Conspiracy of the Queen's party against Turgot

The financiers and the mob were not alone in pursuing Turgot with their hatred. A minister of finance who administers the State like a wise paterfamilias is seldom loved by his colleagues. M. de Saint-Germain, Minister of War, could not but view with aversion a colleague who had refused him three hundred and fifty thousand francs for his furnishings and several millions for his department. M. de Maurepas, hostile since the trouble about the Parlements, began to feel that Turgot's power over the King's mind was becoming too strong. But above all, the Queen's party had vowed that the minister must go. The Queen's dislike came less from her own feelings than from the hatred of a cabal, but, flippant in politics and loyal in friendship, she had come to a clash with the minister over the subject of M. de Guines, the ambassador at the Court of St. James's.

M. de Vergennes and Turgot had requested the recall of M. de Guines because his trafficking was compromising the interests of France. The Queen's project was that Turgot should be sent to the Bastille, on the day that the Comte de Guines would be made Duc. In the streets of Paris the hirelings of the Prince de Conti were singing:

"Monsieur Turgot cracks the pot,
    Monsieur de Maurepas mocks the lot."

During April 1776 there was very nearly a complete rupture between Court and minister. It was then that Turgot wrote the King that famous letter in which he said: "You lack experience, Sire. I am well aware that at the age of twenty-two, and in your position, you have not the resources which the habit of living amongst equals gives to private persons. . . . Reflect, Sire, that in the ordinary course of Nature you will have fifty years to reign, and think of the degree of confusion which disorder might reach, when we have seen what it has done in twenty! Oh, Sire, do not wait to attain so fatal an experience, and learn to profit from the experience of another. . . . Never forget, Sire, that it was weakness that laid the head of Charles I on the block; it was weakness that made Charles IX cruel; weakness that made Louis XIII, and today makes the King of Portugal, mere crowned slaves. It was that which brought about all the woes of the last reign. I cannot sufficiently reiterate to Your Majesty all that I foresee, all that everyone foresees, from a chain of weaknesses and misfortunes, if once the plans we have begun be dropped, and if the minister who has launched them succumbs to the efforts of those united in resisting him. . . . In all truth, Sire, I cannot comprehend you. You were vainly assured that I was a chimerical hothead; yet I cannot think that the words I now write you have any likeness to a madman's prating."

Doubtless there was a certain pleasantry of exaggeration (which M. de Maurepas did not fail to point out to the

King) in threatening with the block a sovereign beloved of all his people, and that too in a century of enlightenment and tenderness of sentiment. This letter might have caused the dropping of Turgot, but on the contrary it worked marvels. The King was stung. That evening, when the Queen informed him of her project regarding M. de Guines and M. Turgot, he answered her very dryly: "Those are your wishes, Madame. I know them, and that is enough. The taking of decisions is my part." Next day, when the cabal reproached the Queen for having failed to obtain her desires, she answered scornfully: "Well, what can you expect with a wooden dummy?"

But the Abbé de Vermond, secretary to the Queen, and several others intervened to make her realize what manner of man this was whom she wanted to throw overboard. She was light-headed, but quite capable of good sense when the interest of the kingdom was made clear to her. Not only did she desist, but she consented to receive M. Turgot. The Abbé de Véri has described this interview: "The Queen said to the King: 'I realize now that I was mistaken about M. Turgot, and I wish to say that I am very pleased with him.' The King was overcome with joy and ran to embrace her, clasping M. Turgot's hand in one of his own. The Queen, rising from her couch to respond to the King's caress, happened to drop her hair ornament, and M. Turgot as he bowed to kiss the King's hand was just within reach to restore it. All of which produced a blend of tenderness and merriment, and gave rise to a concerted feeling which to this day has not been broken. That same evening the King, pleased with the Queen, came to watch her playing her backgammon, and for several days gave the most manifest signs of his satisfaction. Observing this, the Queen expressed gratitude to the counsellors who had advised her, and from that day it was noticed not only that she no longer ventured to act directly against the King's ministers, but also that her husband's display of firmness seemed to heighten her love and esteem for him."

War of American Independence. Refusal to aid the Colonies
When the British colonies in America declared their

independence in July, 1776, they reckoned on the support of France. It had been promised them by M. de Choiseul, and Vergennes, on his arrival at the Foreign Ministry, had found carefully prepared schemes for expeditions. He himself was in favor of supporting them, but wanted this to be done at first in secret. Turgot was opposed to this policy, not through any lack of sympathy with men fighting in defense of their liberty, but from a fear that a war against England, inevitably a long one, would ruin France. He remembered the blows dealt to French credit by the Seven Years' War, and was of the opinion that, without discouraging the colonists, there should be indefinite temporizing. The discussion in council was violent. Turgot told the King that if England persisted in subjugating her colonies by force, she could only succeed by exhausting all her means. France would meanwhile have been able to restore her finances and increase her navy. If ever a struggle with England had to come, it would then be started with superior forces. If, on the other hand, Great Britain were defeated and forced to grant the Americans their independence, the results would have been secured without dealing a blow or loosening the purse strings.

The American cause, supported by the philosophers, was popular in France, and a loud outcry rose against Turgot, and even against the King, which became an uproar when Benjamin Franklin came to Paris to plead the cause of his compatriots. He was welcomed by everybody, even by Turgot, but, thanks to the obstinacy of the King, obtained nothing. M. de Vergennes was displeased, and resigned, being replaced at Foreign Affairs by M. de Saint-Priest, who there showed good sense.

The King's Exchequer

The policy followed in this affair was profoundly vexing to many Frenchmen who had cherished keen hostility to England since the Seven Years' War, and judged the occasion favorable for paying off old scores. But Turgot and Saint-Priest patiently put up with the pamphlets taunting them with cowardice. They consoled themselves for their unpopularity with the prosperity which the peace had enabled them to restore to the national finances. Since 1780 the measures they had taken had brought the budget of receipts from two hundred millions to two hundred and ninety millions, and that without burdening the humbler classes and even without asking very much of the two privileged orders, most of it being obtained by the reform of the lump payments by towns. As for expenditure, this had been reduced from two hundred and twenty to two hundred and ten millions, notwithstanding countless new naval constructions and the creation of a body of police.

It was from these surplus receipts that there sprang the accumulation of the famous King's Exchequer, which rose to three hundred and fifty millions, lent so much strength to France in the councils of Europe, and was only dissipated in 1843, at the time of the first European War.

The Revolution of the Talents, 1776-1785

Historians have given the name of the "Revolution of the Talents" to this period, and in truth it was a real, though bloodless revolution which transformed France during these five years. M. Turgot had asked for five years of despotism. He had them, and more, and profited thereby to build up a system of edicts which renewed the whole of French law. The first of these edicts aimed at freedom of trade, the suppression of guilds and corporations. Turgot was hostile to these associations, and used to declare that men of the same trade never met together, even on the pretext of drinking, without conspiring against the public and raising prices. Opinion has since changed on this matter, and it will be remembered that the corporations were re-established a century later under the name of syndicates, by the comptroller-general, Waldeck-Rousseau, under King Jean VI.

M. Turgot, with the powerful aid of M. de Malesherbes, also concerned himself with safeguarding liberty of thought. He settled the question of Protestant marriages, and favored the return of Protestants; he put an end to the oppression under which the Jesuits still labored, and wanted to abolish *lettres de cachet*. On this last point he failed, and it is curious to note that the most liberal minds at the time held them to be indispensable, whether to make sure of a guilty man who was still only under suspicion, or to prevent unruly young men from dishonoring their families. It was during this period also that there were set up the first French bank, the Caisse d'Escompte, the Committee of Public Hygiene (a body of medical men who rendered great services), and the Council of National Instruction, which was to unify the schools under one system and try to give all Frenchmen an education tending to national unity.

Such were the detailed reforms, but the glory of this ministry rests on having transformed the kingdom from a despotism, based on a few privileged persons, into a modern nation. The essence of the charter which today unites all Frenchmen to their dynasty is already to be found in Turgot's memoir to Louis XVI: "The cause of the evil, Sire, comes from your nation having no constitution. Instead of ruling, like God, by general laws, Your Majesty is obliged to decide everything on its own merits. Your especial orders are waited for to contribute to the public weal, to respect the rights of others, and sometimes even to make use of people's own rights. . . ." All of which was true. National representation was becoming indispensable if national needs were to be known and administration reformed.

Accordingly, in 1784, the King set up a whole hierarchy of assemblies: municipalities of the parish and the province, crowned by a national municipality, these assemblies being composed of delegates from all property owners, privileged and unprivileged. It was, all in all, a suffrage such as then existed in England, but fairer than that because it was not cumbered, as among the English, by countless traditional anomalies. The National Municipality was to be concerned in a consultative capacity with public works, charitable assistance, and taxation. The system, in truth, was far from good, but such as it was, it soothed hot passions, and allowed Frenchmen to have recourse to gentler means than rioting for the voicing of their grievances.

Despite the support of the King, ten years were needed to overcome the opposition set up against this constitution of the kingdom by all whose privileges were threatened. In 1784 Turgot's disgrace seemed certain. M. de Maurepas withdrew with the words, "Sire, your comptroller is too strong for me." The King seemed anxious. "The Turgot is crumbling . . ." wrote Madame du Deffand. But the edicts on the *corvée*, and the freedom of traffic in grain, had already begun to produce their favorable results. The Parisian populace, no longer short of bread, supported Turgot. A mob of people friendly to the minister came out singing verses all the way to Versailles, and the King on this occasion made one of those gestures of which he was capable in desperate emergencies. Taking M. Turgot by the arm, he led him out upon the balcony. Shouts became cheers. On the same day as the edict was proclaimed, Monsieur le Prince de Conti and Monsieur le Comte d'Artois were sent away from Versailles, and the first municipalities were summoned. Thus did France, with an ease that won the admiration of Europe, accomplish the transition from absolute to constitutional monarchy.

Agitation for the English System. M. de Mirabeau
The municipalities were only consultative. King Louis XVI, it is true, granted them the right of voting the budget in 1798, on the occasion of the war with Austria. . . .

. . . .

At this point the Historian raised astonished eyes to the Archangel.

"King Louis XVI?" he said. "In 1798! But he was dead!"

"He was dead in the space-time combination in which you lived your earthly life," said the Archangel, "but in the universe you have just entered King Louis XVI died from a congestion of the lungs in 1820."

"So there was no Terror?" asked the Historian.

"There was no Terror," said the Archangel.

"And what happened on July 14, 1789?"

With the point of his sword the Archangel turned over a few pages.

"On July 14, 1789?" he said. "Nothing important. The Queen played with her children. . . . M. de Fersen came from Paris to the Trianon gardens. He gave his coachman thirty-six livres. . . . The King was hunting. . . ."

"But Turgot was dead?"

"Yes, Turgot died in 1786, five years later than in your reality."

"And who succeeded him?"

"First M. de Vesnes and M. de Boncerf, his chief clerks, who became comptroller-general and naval minister respectively."

"And who were the ministers in 1793?"

"In 1793 . . .? M. de Saint-Priest, M. de Montmorin, M. de Mirabeau, and M. de Talleyrand."

"And M. de Necker?"

"M. de Necker. . . . He was a Genevese banker, and didn't take any part in French affairs."

"And there was no Jacobin conquest of Europe? No Directory? No Consulate . . .? And Napoleon . . .?"

"Napolean?" said the Archangel. "I don't think there is any Napoleon in the space-time in which we are at present. . . . But I can look up the general index. . . ."

At a sign of his sword, great luminous leaves passed swiftly over his head, gliding across the vaults of clouds. Milliards upon milliards of names were entered in them.

"L. . . . M. . . . N. . . ." said the Archangel, "NA. . . . NAP. . . . No, there is no Napoleon."

"Try Buonaparte," said the Historian.

And back flew the leaves with amazing rapidity.

"Ah, Buonaparte," said the Archangel, "yes, there are several. . . . Napoleon Buonaparte, young Corsican whose career was obscure, but of noble and eager character, died in the church porch of Bastia in the course of a local disturbance, September 3, 1796."

"What!" said the Historian. . . . "Not even the second-lieutenant of Brienne?"

"Do not forget," said the Archangel, "that our branch forked off in 1776."

"But there are other branches."

"There are infinite branches, as every moment of Time can be transformed by a will."

"Ah!" said the Historian, with passion in his tone, "I should like to know every one of them. . . . Which is this?"

"*If the King*," read the Archangel, "*in October* 1789 *had listened to the Comte de Saint-Priest* . .*"

"Wait a moment," said the Historian. . . . "That interests me. . . . Why, I remember that on October 5, when the National Guard was marching on Versailles, Saint-Priest advised the King to take the head of his troops, defend the bridges, and, in case of a check, retire on Rambouillet."

"It was the second advice that was followed here," said the Archangel, now running over the pages of the new volume. "Hardly was the King at Rambouillet, when the deputies of Dreux, Chartres, and Orléans arrived, begging him to seek refuge in their towns, and offering their lives and property for his defense. Within four days the King had raised his military strength to ten thousand men, by calling on the regiments stationed in the neighborhood, safe men, who had not yet been tampered with by the agitators of Paris. Within a fortnight, this was doubled. Moreover, he was not attacked, for the National Guard, knowing that the royal troops were in strength, had not dared to go beyond Versailles. Within the month, the army at Metz under orders of the Marquis de Bouillé had rejoined the King. Paris was invested. The city could not hold out long, for it drew its sustenance from regions actually in the hands of the royal army. On March 3, 1790, Louis XVI entered his capital. . . . The Revolution was ended."

"But the sequel?" said the Historian. "The sequel . . .? For here the deep causes of the Revolution are not suppressed as in the Turgot hypothesis. . . . Was it really possible for the absolute monarchy to continue? For privileges without corresponding duties to be maintained?"

"No," said the Archangel. "And they were not. . . . The celestial historian whose task it is to compare these possibilities, more numerous than the grains of sand on the riverbank, soon discovers that the history of human societies, viewed over a fairly long period, is always more or less the same. The facts change; on one hypothesis there is a little more suffering, on another a little more order, but, a hundred years sooner or a hundred years later, things reach the same point. . . . Without going outside *your* history, you may see an example of that if you compare the history of France with that of Germany or of England. . . . The events are very different, but the political and social state of the three countries is today very much the same. . . . Similarly with our hypothetical histories. . . . Without the Revolution, the French monarchy nevertheless transforms itself, first into a constitutional monarchy, then into a democratic monarchy resting on universal suffrage. That is done by successive stages, like the English electoral reforms. . . . If you continue your reading in the book we have opened together as far as the year 1930, you will find France under a king whose powers are a trifle less than those of President Doumergue, the comptroller-general Paul Reynaud. . . ."

"And the war of 1914-1918?"

"It does not exist, but there were others. . . . The planet is divided somewhat differently. The United States did not break away from England, but so vast have they grown that they now dominate the British Empire. . . . The Imperial Parliament sits in Kansas City. . . ."

"Why not Washington?" said the Historian.

"Washington?" said the Archangel. . . . "But there is no town called Washington here. . . . You must not confuse the 'Possibilities'. . . . Between the Anglo-Saxon world and the United States of Europe, the capital of which is Vienna, a terrible conflict is in preparation."

"In the hypothetical world?" said the Historian anxiously.

"Of course," said the Archangel with a smile.

"And what will be its issue?" said the Historian.

"Ah!" said the Archangel, "all our books stop at the present moment. To every living soul God leaves the power, and the responsibility, of shaping the next."

The Historian sighed. Across the last page of the open book, a new line was quietly taking shape. Far away, on planets revolving in the night, unforeseeable acts were shaping the future.

"And Napoleon?" said the Historian shyly. . . . "What

becomes of him in this new hypothesis? This time he surely got to Brienne, didn't he?"

"Napoleon?" murmured the Archangel with a touch of weariness. "Napoleon. . . . Oh, that's the Buonaparte you were talking of just now. . . . Yes, here he is. . . . Captain of artillery in 1791, he was killed in 1798, near Damascus, in the course of the Turkish campaign."

Musingly, the Historian gazed at the image of the flaming sword as it gleamed in the opaque glass of the binding wherein these figures flitted past, beautiful and bewildering. . . .

FRAGMENT FROM A UNIVERSAL HISTORY PUBLISHED IN 1992 BY THE UNIVERSITY OF * * *

(Translated by Hamish Miles)

MORALS—PURITANISM AND REPRESSIONS—FREUDISM AND ITS INFLUENCE—SUCCESS AND ABERRATIONS OF FREUDIANISM (1930-1940)—SYMPTOMS OF REACTION (1940-1950)—SCHMIDTISM—TRIUMPH OF SCHMIDTISM—REVERSAL OF VALUES

Sexual Morality in the early Twentieth Century.
BEFORE the World War of 1914, especially in the Anglo-Saxon countries, official morality had remained very much the same as during the preceding century. True, even in England there were writers like Wells, Arnold Bennett, George Moore, and Galsworthy, who had ventured to treat sexual questions rather more boldly than the novelists of the Victorian epoch. Actually, and in the capital cities especially, morals were distinctly lax, but this laxity did not extend to the middle classes, and even in aristocratic or artistic circles was not openly admitted. In America as in England, puritanism was still powerful enough for a sentimental scandal to ruin the career of a statesman. Vices existed, as they always have existed in every human society, but to be tolerated they had perforce to borrow the mask of hypocrisy and the language of virtue. . . .

Freudism and its Influence: 1910-1930.
The human animal, thus constricted by a rigid society, took strange and perilous revenges. "Repressed desires" (as

they were later to be termed) took refuge in the unconscious, where they provoked grave discontents. An old seer of the eighteenth century, William Blake, had already proclaimed that "he who desires but acts not, breeds pestilence." This pestilence took the form of nervous afflictions and mental disturbance, and above all roused a general sense of ennui, pessimism and anxiety, which was possibly one of the hidden causes of the War of 1914.

This is not the place to set forth the doctrine of Freud; but we know how this great Austrian doctor and psychologist showed that such repressions lay at the root of most nervous afflictions. This teaching met with no great success in the Latin countries, which, having always enjoyed a measure of sexual liberty, were unfamiliar with the malady and had no need of the remedy, but in the Teutonic, and particularly the Anglo-Saxon countries, it was a genuine emancipation. Under cover of a scientific vocabulary, it became possible, permissible, and even easy, at last to speak freely of subjects which for centuries had been banned. Psychoanalysis, becoming widespread, confronted a large number of puritans with their real minds, and made them more tolerant of the desires of others. A certain freedom and boldness in morals was encouraged by the doctors, who deemed it their duty to free their patients from repression that might bring them to insanity. From about 1928 writers like Joyce and D. H. Lawrence displayed a boldness which was to seem half-hearted to the readers of 1940, but which in its day was something new. Physical shame disappeared at the same time as intellectual and verbal shame. Women shed more and more of their clothing. About 1935 men and women in complete nudity could be seen on numerous American and European beaches. In Germany and the Scandinavian countries the "nudist" sects multiplied. Tolerance of sexual liberties and even sexual abnormalities, became general. . . .

Aberrations and Excesses.

Human morals swing like a pendulum, continually passing the middle position. In the beginning the Freudian influence was beneficial. It seemed to be true that excessive austerity was contrary to the moral and bodily health of such human beings as were neither saints nor impotent. It is a fact that from 1930 onwards the number of cases of insanity diminished, both in America and Europe.

But before long, on the ground of respecting the desires of everyone, a point was reached when all social contracts were broken. The ancient institution of marriage was completely destroyed by the coming of divorce by simple declaration, by companionate alliances, and by the refusal to bear children. Strictness of morals, under the rule of the older morality, had lent value and charm to harmless delights. In the nineteenth century, historians show, young men and girls had enjoyed being together for purposes of innocent games, sports, or studies. From 1935 onwards, most gatherings assumed the character of a debauch. Public feeling had changed so completely that in England, formerly so strict a country, anti-puritanism became a positive virtue. It was not imposed by law, but custom was sovereign and the social sanctions were merciless. In 1954 the Prime Minister, Mr. Shallow, found himself forced into retirement by public opinion and the Press because he was suspected of conjugal fidelity. It was he who had formerly passed the Act for Compulsory Psychoanalysis in Nursery Schools. He was accused of hypocrisy. More than one Continental newspaper opened a campaign to show that sexual liberty in England was a pretence, and that in actual fact, underneath all the extreme freedom of speech and literature, it cloaked a large number of chaste lives. It was an unfair accusation; but the fanaticism of the "emancipated" became ferocious. . . .

Symptoms of Reaction: 1940-1950.

About 1940 the graph of cases of insanity rose quite rapidly. To the unprejudiced observer it would have been obvious that this was symptomatic of a check to the new morality. But the "emancipated," in their blind intolerance, nevertheless made a bid for new audacities. Signs of reaction, however, began to show themselves. So far they were slight, but they were unmistakable. In 1942 there appeared anonymously that curious book, *Confessions of a Child of the New Century,* in which the inward confusion of the younger generation, and their craving for sentimental feelings, were set out with a naïve shamefacedness. Its success was enormous, even to the pitch of several writers, emboldened or jealous, trying to exploit the same vein, notwithstanding the danger of legal proceedings being taken against them. In 1943 Miss Brushwood's famous novel, *Conjugal Happiness,* was published, in which, with an audacity that then seemed incredible, she depicted the pleasures of fidelity, normal love, and indissoluble marriage.

The book was banned by the English censorship, but was immediately reprinted in France, and thousands of copies were surreptitiously imported. An international group of writers protested against the Home Office decision and claimed the right to freedom of virtue. The body of the "emancipated" were furious, in the name of morality. The campaign roused lively curiosity, and the circulation of the book, which was translated into every language of the world, reached immense figures. More than 1,300,000 copies were sold in the United States, 800,000 in Germany, 300,000 of the clandestine edition in England, 70,000 in France, and 20,000 in Holland. The young people of both sexes seemed to find a pleasure which the classic moralists styled "unhealthy" in reading these descriptions of forgotten sentiments and modes of living.

The influence of *Conjugal Happiness* and the new "chastitist" school soon became obvious. Small groups, still rather timidly but in increasing numbers, tried to live their lives according to the principles of Miss Brushwood. Aged Americans can still remember the New York and Boston fashion during the winter of 1943-1944 for giving "conjugal parties," secret of course, to which were invited only married couples who passed the whole evening together without separating. These "goings-on" caused scandal, but Europe followed suit. In Hyde Park the police were forced to prosecute married couples who came in broad daylight and sat reading verses together on the grass. In Paris the Prefect of Police had to establish a special body of police on motorbicycles to cleanse the Bois de Boulogne of women wearing the so-called "virtue" dresses, which, buttoned up to the

neck, were shocking respectable passers-by. In one ancient
European university a professor of philosophy was expelled
for impenitent asceticism. It was becoming manifest that
the morality of freedom, though still clung to by the masses,
was no longer being respected by the elect. . . .

Schmidtism.

In 1954 Dr. Schmidt, the Lausanne physician whose name
was to become so famous, published his book on the repressions of modesty. Nowadays his doctrines strike us as
self-evident, but at that time they came to innumerable
readers as a revelation. Dr. Schmidt maintained:

(a) That as man had been a member of organized
groups for more than fifteen thousand years, social
morality and the constraints imposed thereby had become an instinct in him, no less powerful than the
sexual instinct or that of self-preservation. (It was
the old theory of Trotter.)

(b) That in thwarting this instinct by an artificial
reversion to a completely animal life, repressions of
modesty were caused in men, just as painful and dangerous as those of desire had been.

(c) That a great many nervous maladies could be
cured by making the sufferer aware of this secret
modesty and by sanctioning his obedience to it.

In support of this theory, Dr. Schmidt produced numerous
psychoanalytic cases which disclosed the existence of repressed social elements.

His doctrine became known as Schmidtism and enjoyed
widespread success, especially in the Anglo-Saxon countries,
where its scientific vocabulary made permissible the confession of sentiments and scruples which had long been
taboo. From 1959 onwards there was an excellent course in
Schmidtism at Columbia University. In the following year
the Institute of Schmidtian Psychology was inaugurated at
Baltimore, and became the nucleus of a body of Schmidtian
doctors. In 1960 Dr. Schmidt came in person to America,
and was enthusiastically received by students and patients.

The happy effects of Schmidtism were soon manifest. Persons with conjugal, virtuous or normal inclinations no longer felt themselves regarded with hostility, and lost the uncouth manners and haggard appearance which had for some years become familiar to them. Their writings became less violent. The curve showing cases of sexual insanity, which once again had risen in a very alarming manner, began to drop. This period, to which Professor Gilrobin has given the name of "period of reversal of values," lasted approximately from 1960 to 1975.

At the moment of writing (1992), it is undeniable that the Schmidtian reaction has in its turn been excessive. A new puritanism, more aggressive than the old, threatens to dominate our activities and our thoughts. What Freud or Schmidt, as yet unknown, will rise to free us from this evil spirit?